Happy reading!

C.D. Breadner

Sin Eater

C.D. Breadner

THE FREAK CIRCLE PRESS

CreateSpace, a DBA of On-Demand Publishing, LLC

Prologue

The Sin Eater let his boot hit the puddles of the road, water splashing on to the hem of his trousers. He didn't worry that the water was probably more shit than rain. He'd been around humans so long their barbaric and primitive practices no longer shocked him. He accepted it. That's why whenever he was in London his trousers were only worn once and discarded; left for a chamber maid or concierge to wear if they wished. After all, the fabric was fine and expensive, and if they could sell them it was as good as a tip.

He just didn't want to wear pants with shit on them.

The hovel in his sights was a pathetic structure, listing to one side, lucky to be propped up between two stone structures with much stronger foundations. It looked as though a squatter had put a front door on someone's garden and then stretched a thatched roof overhead. It just didn't fit. And neither did the dying man inside.

The Sin Eater could smell the man's fear from across the street. It never ceased to amaze him how people could suddenly find their God and faith at the exact moment they got a whiff of the fact that they were not much longer for this world. For all their disgusting behaviors and rough manners, humans were delightfully hypocritical, hence his wealth and purpose in this life.

Or was this all just a slow, meandering death? It was hard to tell. His employer, after all, took delight in not always sharing the whys and ways of the immortality He bestowed on souls. The contingencies were always an uncomfortable surprise.

When the Sin Eater reached the door of the shanty he knocked for outward appearances' sake, then let himself in as though invited.

The room stank not only of death but also of sin; the mingling smell of moldy onion and rotten meat. Not everyone could smell it that way, but the Sin Eater could. He could sense many things strictly by smell. Anger, fear, sorrow, frustration, deceit ... even evil. And over the smell of death, it was the smell of evil that brought him to this house.

A small man was wasting away on a straw mattress, mumbling "The Lord is my shepherd, I shall not want ..."

The Sin Eater shook his head, pulling a wooden stool across the floor loudly and sitting at the man's bedside. That's when the man noticed he was there, and as though sensing the load the Sin Eater carried, he shrunk away from him.

"Who ... who art thou?"

"Worry yourself not about who I am. Worry about the why of what I am."

The man clearly wasn't up for riddles, and frowned, his hands forming feeble claws and pulling at the thin, filthy blanket covering him. "I have no wealth, no money, no gold. Take what you want, but I am dying and know that it is a sin to steal."

The Sin Eater barked a laugh at that. "Believe me, old man. I can tell you what is sin and what is not."

The man looked back to the ceiling. "He maketh me to lie down in green pastures ..."

The Sin Eater shrugged, not caring if the man needed to know why he was here or not. It wasn't necessary for his job. And no amount of praying could change what he was about to do anyway.

He closed his eyes, made a steeple of his fingers and rested his forefingers on his forehead. It wasn't necessary, but he always did it for some reason. The ... ritual of it made him feel one with these human animals.

With his mind he reached out to the man's brain, his stream of consciousness touching at the man's thoughts like phantom fingers. The man seemed to sense it and tried to physically pull back from it, but once the Sin Eater was in your head it was already too late.

He rifled through the useless blue sky and white clouds and golden gates drivel the man was concentrating on and reached deeper, through years of memories and back to the past; his terrible, terrible past.

Back when the man had been young, strong, and handsome. Before disease had weakened him and addled his mind. Syphilis, the Sin Eater recognized it immediately. There was always syphilis these days. Obviously, it was due to the whores.

But this man had done more than lay with them, and that was the other stench the Sin Eater could recognize; the stench of garbage and sulfur. The smell of evil.

He found the episodes the man was trying to hide from him, now that he wanted God as his savior and master and desired to arrive at St. Peter's gate as innocent as the day he was born. But he wasn't ... he was just as drenched in as much filth as the Sin Eater. That's what had brought the Sin Eater to his door, wasn't it?

The Sin Eater found the sins as sure as he'd put them there himself. He immersed in them up to his optic nerves, dipping his very being into the squalid depths of this man's past depravity.

As far as sinners went, this man was pretty standard. Not the worst by a long shot.

The memories came back as fully-encompassing revelations, taking over the Sin Eater's senses and putting him in the moment as though he had been in the man's body. But of course he had no control over what that body was doing, because humans all had free will and this had all been in the past.

The man had paid whores to lay with him, and the whores hadn't minded the looks of him, even though he never presented himself as wealthy. He had been strapping and comely, they had been pleased to service someone that wasn't old, ugly, drunk or malodorous.

But when the man had them alone in an alley or back walkway he had slaughtered them. He kept a blade hidden in his sleeve, and it wasn't very sharp either. It was startling how the man had been able to carve these women into macabre art exhibits of hatred without anyone noticing. It had taken time to skin their heads, shred their faces, and then fuck their dead bodies.

In all, he found thirteen slayings. It was hard to be completely sure if that was all of them, since the man had lost his mind and the Sin Eater also picked up visions of the women as demons who wanted to consume his soul. The Sin Eater may have used the man's point of view, but he could still recognize delusion over reality. The insanity sat like an uncomfortable coat, it brought distaste to the Sin Eater's mouth. He hated the insanity. It was disorienting, like stumbling into someone else's nightmare.

The man was weeping. That was another side effect of the Sin Eater's ability. No matter how the man fought to keep the memory at bay, he saw exactly what the Sin Eater saw and realized that because of it, he was damned.

The Sin Eater laid his hand on the man's chest, his own skin crawling at contact with that filthy flesh. But this was the important part; this is what his employer paid him for.

The man drew a deep breath, and the Sin Eater sent him a warm, cleansing sensation that took the sin and replaced it with ... nothing. The events were erased.

The man calmed, he stopped scrabbling his hands against the blanket and his chest, and his face went slack ... almost peaceful. Then he fell into a deep sleep. Judging by how his various diseases had progressed, this would likely be his last rest. The Sin Eater had arrived just in time.

When sins were admitted and divinely forgiven they vanished. Washed away by faith and purity. But when the Sin Eater worked, the sins were not gone. They were still here. They didn't stay with the Sin Eater; they just stayed on the human plane to find another ... host? Carrier? The more down here that was dark and evil, the more ground the good guys lost. Plus, it sure pissed off the guy upstairs when someone else was running around, removing sins; encroaching on His territory, so to speak.

These souls that the Sin Eater sought out were never admitted to heaven anyway. With or without their sins present, evil was evil and could not abide. It was the potential, not the deeds. Damned souls were damned. The sin was either wiped clear by the hand of ultimate power, or, after the Sin Eater's visit, left to fester elsewhere.

As it was, a sinner would never reach everlasting life without forgiveness from righteousness. And that didn't mean a priest, either. Any faith, even those with no faith, could earn redemption for what they had done once they passed. It was a simple bequest once a soul passed over. Only true menace could not be "let in." So the Sin Eater's true purpose was just to make sure the potential evil was not only realized, but enhanced over time. He broke the chain of command from sinner, real evil, to absolution. But again, these sinners were not stealing bread to feed their families, and they weren't eating meat on Friday. These sinners sought out to harm and inflict pain on others of their own kind. And what's more ... they enjoyed it.

When he'd been sent to the human world to become a Sin Eater, he'd been annoyed by his human form. As immortal as he may be, the constant maintenance and unreasonable reactions to stimuli were so bothersome. But once he grew to understand how their very make-up inevitably led to their sins, the whole ridiculous system seemed invariably ... perfect. Genius, even.

The Sin Eater witnessed the man slip into deep unconsciousness, well on his way to passing into the hereafter. He found the deaths comforting, like his hard work finally coming full circle.

The last breath passed the man's lips, and as the divine silence fell over his form, the Sin Eater rose and returned the stool to its home at the small wooden table littered with bottles and old bread. He never knew the man's name. It didn't really matter. There was inevitably another one just like him right around the bend.

Chapter One

"So, what are the big plans for the weekend?" Jasper did a piss-poor job of hiding the fact that he was trying to steal a glance at some coy but breathtaking cleavage while his co-worker logged off her computer. When she pulled her purse from a bottom drawer in her desk, he had to give a sigh of defeat. The blouse stayed stubbornly put.

Iola Day rolled her eyes at his question but laughed anyway. "Yeah, Jasper, you know me. I've got big plans. Huge. You wouldn't even believe me if I told you what I had in my social itinerary."

He laughed too, then sat on the stool that had been abandoned in the corner of the bullpen, looking down at his hands. God, why was he nervous? At his age, asking someone out? "Come on. If you have no plans, why not let me take you out for dinner. Or just a drink."

She shook her head. "Jasper, I appreciate that. And it's flattering. But ... you know that's a bad idea. We work together."

"Yeah. And we're always here, working the same shifts, including nights and weekends when no one else is around." He shrugged. "Who else could we possibly date?"

"It's just ... a bad idea. I'm sorry. But you have to stop asking me this."

He shrugged. "I'm not going to stop trying. Until you call HR anyway. Get me fired." That was weird levity. Make a joke about sexual harassment in the work place. Better move quick to cover up that moronic statement. "What are you working this weekend?" Even though he knew already. She was a DJ, she had set shifts. Since he was in news, his shifts were all over the place like a toddler with pudding.

"I work late Saturday and Sunday, off Monday and Tuesday. How about you?"

"I actually got the weekend off. I'm not sure what to do with myself. There's nothing on TV during the weekends." That just sounded sad. Why was he such a retard around this woman?

Because she was kind, that's why. And to prove it, she helped him out of this awkwardness with a suggestion. "What about playoffs? All hockey all the time."

He shrugged. "Even that's only in the evenings. The days are confusing to me. Since we usually work nights."

Iola stood, and he did too, ever the gentleman. If he'd had a tail, he'd be wagging it and hoping she'd pet him behind the ears for his troubles.

She smiled, wished him a good weekend, then made for the hallway out of the bullpen that led to the back door of the radio station. He followed as expected, then watched her from the window as she made her way to the subway platform. He always watched to make sure no one messed with her on her way to catch her train.

Funny, when he was in a room with her he was ever the gentleman, sitting on his hands and trying to impress her, all hearts and flowers. Like a total sap. He was the younger brother doing everything big brother wanted, all in the hopes that eventually his big brother would pass him the keys and let him take his car for a spin. Not that Jasper would compare Iola to a car.

He was a goddamn lap dog around her. But as he watched her through the window, he was clocking her ass and liking how it moved in the jeans she was wearing. Better than a car, that's for sure.

When she'd first started at KLCD two years ago he couldn't say he noticed her right off. They ended up working together a lot, and as time had passed he ... liked her. A lot. It wasn't that she was knock 'em over gorgeous. If she came into a room conversation didn't grind to a stunned halt. But when he heard her voice on air for the first time ... man. He was a goner. And now he'd moved on to notice other things about her.

Her clothing was modest over a body he always imagined was perfect. That was nice, a woman that didn't need to advertise the goods. It was getting rare. And her eyes ... they were the oddest color. A very pale but bright green, like the flesh of a lime. And those eyes were smart, too. He looked into them and became the pathetic goober he'd just been moments before; unable to say or even take action towards what he wanted.

He behaved like the pal. And of course, he wanted so much more.

Iola Day used her transit pass to get on her train, and took a seat facing the center aisle. In her experience, creepy people liked to trap you in the benches that faced forward, so if you had to take one of those seats, sit on the outside edge and don't let anyone pen you in.

She held her bag tight to her side without looking like she was worried about anyone grabbing it. It's not like she carried anything of real value, but replacing all the things she needed to carry would be such a pain in the ass. Plus, her ID had her address. The very thought that she was on the radio and people could find out where she lived made her skin crawl. So of course she was unlisted, on the advice of Jasper.

She had to smile at the thought of Jasper. He was so funny around her. The thought he was attracted to her made her not uncomfortable, just ... sorry because she didn't see him that way, really. And dating a co-worker was a terrible idea. No matter how nice the guy seemed. So she really, really wanted to keep it "just friends."

But to herself, she admitted that she liked the flirtation.

Iola studied the other subway patrons around her. It was a pretty dead time of the night, before the drunks and after the five o'clock work crowd, so her scrutiny didn't take too long. A teenage boy in jeans, a hoodie and an iPod was off in his own world, tapping his toe in time with the music only he could hear. He was sitting right across from her, ignoring her since she was over the age of thirty and not interesting in the least.

Another man was slumped down on the bench to her left, as far from the iPod kid as he could get. He had a hand to his forehead, with his elbow propped up on the window ledge. He looked like he had a terrible headache. But he was handsome nonetheless. The man sitting to her right on the first of the forward-facing benches was reading his paper. Both men were dressed nicely in suits. That wasn't incredibly strange for 3am, but it was a bit rare to see two suits out this late. She would have sworn that these three people were right out of central casting for "subway extras." But another guy ... he really stood out.

He was at the back, standing even though there were plenty of available seats. He was ... twitchy. He kept scratching at one eye. His clothes were dirty, his face had many scabs, and his pale eyes ... well, Iola had the sense that he really had seen bad things. And had maybe caused most of them.

Iola resolved to keep one eye on him for a little while anyway, since the sense of malice coming from him was almost like a taste in her mouth. God, he stunk. No one else seemed to notice, or they were all being polite like she was. After all, it couldn't be an accident that they were all bunched up at the front of the car, as far away from him as they could get.

The movement of the train jolted each person in unison, and the motion was unfortunately soothing. It always made her drop her guard. So when she got off the train, she only noticed that the man with the headache rose to his feet as she did, and he let her go ahead of him out the front door of the car. She didn't notice that the oddball at the back of the train used the other door to jump out to the platform as well.

She took the stairs to the street. Her apartment was a block down, on the third floor above a bakery. She always associated the smell of bread and cinnamon buns with coming home. And in four years she had not once eaten anything from that bakery.

She picked up the pace as the wind blew. Even though it was spring, the air felt damp and it was sharp against her legs through her jeans. She got her keys ready, holding them weapon-like in her hand. There were scuffling footsteps behind her, and she didn't look back, she just kept walking. Once she got to the pool of light at the foot of a lamp post she stopped and wheeled around quickly to face whoever was behind her.

The scruffy guy stopped, clearly startled by her sudden movement. He froze in his tracks, eyes wide.

"Can I help you?" She asked in a confident, authoritative voice.

He mumbled a few noises, shaking his head.

"You better turn around and walk the other way," Iola suggested.

Then he looked angry. He took a step to her.

She wanted to cower and back up, but she held her ground. He seemed confused by that, too. He scratched his head, looking down at his feet. But he didn't back off.

Iola looked around, but the corner was deserted. Just her and Scratchy ...

Who didn't smell any better out in the open air. She wrinkled her nose. He was positively rank. How long could it have been since he'd had a shower?

Iola's hands tightened around her keys. The biggest key she had, the one to the dead bolt on her door, was sticking out the inside of her fist. She was ready to swing it at him if he grabbed her. If he grabbed her bag, she'd let him take it. Having a plan minimizes the panic.

"What are you waiting for? Get the hell out of here before I call the police." A big bluff. Her cell phone was dead, in her bag, waiting to be charged once she got home. If she got home.

He seemed to get agitated when she mentioned the police, and she took a step backwards. Just a small one, hoping she didn't appear to be giving up any ground. Please, please just turn around and fuck off, she thought, willing herself not to wince at the thought. She wanted to appear stronger than him, make him think twice about his choice of ... victim? Okay, she wasn't sure if he meant her harm, but who in their right mind follows a woman walking alone at night?

When he brought his eyes up to hers, she froze. She didn't even blink. If eyes were the windows to the soul, then ... he didn't have one. They were blank, cold ... if he hadn't blinked she would have thought him an evil, malevolent mannequin.

Iola's heart started to beat faster, and a sickly feeling spread through her chest. It was that feeling you got when you saw a two-year old with grape juice walking on a white rug. Impending doom.

Scratchy took a step towards her, and as she backed away her mind fired off two words that echoed in her head like she'd screamed them: *No! Stop!*

He froze right where he was. He continued to stare at her in the same vacant way then after a screaming moment he turned and walked away.

When he was half a block down she finally exhaled, her breath punching out of her in one short jab. The unease in her chest dissolved and her knees almost gave out. The stink of him still lingered, however. She was still breathing in and out like she'd just run in an 80-yard touchdown, but she was calming down ... gradually.

What the hell? She'd been scared before, even had a drunk grab her once. But that ... that man felt like the essence of danger. He definitely had bad intentions towards her.

She got her keys sorted out again in one hand while keeping her head up, and then made her way to the door of the stairwell that led upwards. She checked over both shoulders before opening the door and then basically sprinted up the stairwell to the safety of her apartment.

The Sin Eater had followed her, caught her scent in the subway, and had stayed in the shadows. Correction. He followed the homicidal nut job that was following her out of the subway and up to the street. He had a boatload of sin strapped to his shoulders, and the Sin Eater felt completely compelled to follow.

Bullshit, he would have followed her anyway. She smelled ... pure of heart, as lame as that might have sounded. She was beautiful. If he didn't know any better, he'd say she was a brand new soul. He almost chuckled. She still had that "new soul" smell.

But this human following her had the stink of evil all over him, and the Sin Eater could all but taste his psychotic rage and violent lust for her. He'd never interjected to stop humans from doing what they wanted. After all, he was there to lap up their messes. But as the man's frenzy of bloodlust was piqued and the Sin Eater found himself actually wanting to get involved and help a human female, something amazing happened.

This woman, this gorgeous creature, who looked as delicate as an orchid, pushed this scumbag. With her ... *mind*? She may as well have reached out and shoved him. No one had made any movement, but suddenly the man had reeled back, turned on his heel and stalked away like it was his idea.

The Sin Eater froze in his tracks. He'd felt it, the force of her will emanating outward like a fist. He felt the man retract the intentions he'd had, just pulled them back and tucked them away.

The Sin Eater had stopped breathing. How the hell had she done it? He could do that. He could reach into people's minds and change their very personalities if he wanted. There was nothing he couldn't do to someone when he had complete control of their mind.

But she wasn't like him otherwise he would have recognized it when she sat down across from him on the subway. She was human but she was a complete puzzle.

He watched her enter a door next to a closed bakery, and he imagined she was going up the stairs to an apartment above. Sure enough, after a moment, a light came on in the front of the building. He watched her approach the window, pouring water out of one of those stainless steel bottles into a sad pile of green next to the window. Some kind of house plant, who knew what it was supposed to be. You didn't have to be a Sin Eater to know it wasn't much longer for this world.

Her mouth was moving, and as he watched, she seemed to be talking to someone. Husband, boyfriend, he assumed. Then she bopped her head twice to one side, and kept talking, pausing only to bop her head again. She's singing, he realized, and he smiled ... but lost it almost as quickly as it appeared. Normally he could touch a person's mind and find out their entire history with one glance.

But this one ... she was a blank page. He read nothing from her ... except the smell of jasmine and vanilla. So. Damn. Pure.

Chapter Two

"So," Iola breathed. "What's everyone up to tonight? It's Saturday, after all. Tell me you're with someone you care about, please. And if not, at least pretend. Here's a song to get you a bit closer. Let me give you a word of advice, fellas. Whatever you do, however badly you want to, do not kiss her. Touch her softly, hold her lightly, and sway to the music but do not kiss her." Iola started the next song, using the intro under her continuing narrative. "Let her do the work. Trust me on this."

Iola used the slider to bring up the level of the music and cut her mic. Dylan's voice came through the speakers and she leaned back, contemplating how odd it was to be the only person in a workplace at night. Like an informal guest, but she was definitely supposed to be there.

She was lonesome ... well, maybe. Perhaps she was lonesome. After all, she worked the weirdest shift a person could. Eight pm to two am, on air the whole time. The news room shifted once during her stay, some roving reporter coming and going, chasing fire trucks and ambulances. But she sat there in her dim control room the whole time, helping people set the mood. Get romantic. Get some loving.

What a sad fraud that was. She didn't even really have friends anymore. She was going to work when they were cleaning up the supper dishes. She was going to bed when they were running to the bathroom because they'd been woken up by a full bladder. And they were getting up just after she finally was able to fall asleep. Yeah, that sounded pretty lonesome when she thought about it more.

At least she was popular with listeners. She had more fan mail than any other disc jockey at the station. She had women writing letters saying they found her music comforting and soothing, very contemplative. Not that she picked all the songs, she just maybe had a bit more say than the morning and five o'clock drive guys, the peak hours. But she liked that people were listening and appreciated listening to her. She also got marriage proposals, indecent photographs, and the odd male caller that just wanted to ... chat with her. Usually not in a PG manner, but still ... she had a wide variety of listeners. And she appreciated all of them, even the perverts. It meant she got a check, after all.

One love in her life: a poetic songwriter. Beyond vocal abilities, a song's performance should always ring authentic and true. If there was one artist that had the most entries on her "mood music" playlist, it was Mr. Dylan.

It would be great to find a guy that was as into mood music as she was. She loved the atmosphere of a song more than anything else. One of her private fantasies was to be made love to while listening to all the perfect love songs the world had known. Why weren't men into that kind of thing? Why was it all about spontaneity and visual appeal and ... well, just the sex?

Well, she wasn't going to unlock all the mysteries of men with one little brain work out; that was for sure.

She rubbed her forehead, looking ahead to the next song on her play list. Ah yes, a jazz trio. Another good one. This was a day where she just loved her job.

As the trailing guitar tune wound down, she brought her mic back up and let the music fade out. "Okay, now if you've got her kissing you after that, good job. And if not, don't worry about it. It's still early, and I'm here until two. I'll get you through this. So now we'll switch to jazz, and before you start whining at me, just shut up and listen. This is soulful, and if you just feel it and listen to it and ... love it, you will get it. Eventually. You're listening to KLCD Late Night with Iola Day."

She brought the music up just as the velvet of the female's singer's voice was rolling out. Iola sighed and took a look at the next few songs. The next one was going to pick up the pace quite a bit. So she got up to go get a cup of coffee because she still had two and a half minutes before this song ended.

Iola grabbed her mug and hot-footed to the coffee room, grabbed a cup of the coffee she'd started before she'd gone on the air, then bolted back to her booth with time to spare. She set the coffee on the table behind the chair she sat in, well away from the board and computer. The city lights were visible through the control room window and over the partitions in the newsroom bullpen.

Iola shivered, remembering the previous night and the psycho that had followed her off the subway. Tonight she'd brought pepper spray, and she made sure her cell phone was charged before she even left her apartment. Still, the thought of riding the subway home tonight, or *tomorrow*, was making her nervous.

The phone rang, and she snatched it up quickly. "KLCD Late Night."

"Iola? I just called to say I'm the president of your fan club."

She smiled into the receiver and leaned back in her chair. "Jasper ... what are you doing?"

"I'm bored. I'm sitting at home, listening to the radio, and this chick keeps playing the most boring songs I've ever heard."

"Jasper, just one minute. I've got to switch it over."

She put him on hold and then brought up her mic again as the song faded. "Well, I've just had a caller requesting something with a bit more energy. So, in honor of getting close, here's a tune that means you can maybe squeeze her a little bit tighter." She hit the slider just as the vocals started.

Then she picked up the phone again, just in time to hear Jasper laughing. "Okay Jasper, is that better?"

"Man, I love this song."

"Well, good." She was surprised. She didn't know he liked anything other than the current Top 40. "Is there anything else you'd like me to play?"

"Nah. This is a good one. I just ... I just thought I'd call."

"Man, you must be bored. It's your night off. You should really be out doing something."

"Well, I keep asking this girl out and she keeps shooting me down. It's pretty bad for my self-esteem."

Iola laughed, but he didn't. She stopped, and the music was the only sound for a moment. "Jasper, I told you - "

"Yeah, I know. Co-workers shouldn't date. But the thing is ... there's no one else I want to date. Even casually. You ... you're it for me, Iola."

Her breath caught and her panic mode set in. She absently wondered if he had been drinking. "Jasper, maybe you should sleep on it before you say anything else."

"When I'm around you, I can't say what I want. For some reason I just become this schmuck ... but maybe that's how you want me to be. Maybe I'd make you uncomfortable otherwise. I don't know. I don't what the fuck I'm saying. I've had ... some beers."

Bingo. "Jasper, I have to go. We can ... we can talk about this another time."

"Really?"

"Sure. But ... I'm working here, right? So I'll say good bye now and we'll talk another time." Then she waited.

"All right. It's a date."

"Jasper - "

"I know, I know. Co-workers. See you, Iola." A click sounded as he hung up.

She felt terrible. She knew how much he liked her, and the flirting was nice, it really was. But ... it had been a long time since she'd dated. She wasn't even sure she liked Jasper in that way, at all. How would she even know? Well, she wouldn't know unless she tried it.

There was the rub. If it doesn't work out, there goes one of the few people she might actually count as a friend.

She flicked her mic on at the end of the song. "You're listening to KLCD Late Night and I'm Iola Day. I've got a very kind email here from Larry, and Larry's written that he enjoys the late night programming here on KLCD because he says it puts his girlfriend in the mood. Well, you're welcome Larry, and let's hope right now you are with your girlfriend. Here's a good one to help you out, because Larry, I'm your wingman."

As the piano riff began she closed her eyes. God, she did not want to see Jasper again next Wednesday.

Jasper looked down at the coffee table in front of him, counting seven dead beer cans that he'd gotten the better of. The phone was in his hand, and he stared at it next, wondering if he'd really just called Iola drunk off his ass and revealed he was insanely into her.

Yep. It appeared that way.

Well done, fantastic work. Next you can put your balls in a blender. The night can only get better than this.

He put the phone on the table, knocking over an empty can. He'd always been a lightweight when it came to drinking, but this much beer on an empty stomach was a disaster looking for a place to party.

He groaned and flopped back on to the sofa, listening to the song on the radio. The singer was talking about being stripped naked and vulnerable.

Well he was sure as shit naked now. When would he see her next? Wednesday? And it was only Saturday now. Maybe she'd forget it by then.

That was another drunk delusion right there. Holy shit. The way her voice had sounded; like he'd creeped her right out. What a frickin' idiot.

Maybe he should just go out and get laid. Maybe that's what he needed, someone completely the opposite of Iola; someone fake and primped to the point of being ridiculous. Maybe she smacked her gum with her mouth open and asked the most retarded questions he'd ever heard. And he'd answer just to get her into bed. But he'd been there before, too. And he didn't want to go back to that. Plus he was already a slobbering mess that even the skankiest blow doll wouldn't come near.

This is when he needed a pal. An honest-to-God male friend to kick him in the nuts and call him a moron. Just to teach him a lesson, because he still knew he hadn't learned anything from this.

The beer was churning his stomach and the ceiling above him tilted like he was on a carnival ride. He closed his eyes again, commanding himself to breathe easy.

Iola was cool, he rationalized. She wouldn't make a big deal of this, and she wouldn't try to make him feel like a complete loser, it just wasn't her way.

And man, if that wouldn't make him feel like a bigger ass, what would?

The Sin Eater was at a restaurant, sitting at a patio table. The late night traffic was heavy, since this was the first truly warm night of spring and a Saturday besides. Show offs cruised the streets with car stereos pumping loudly. Groups of loudly giggling girls were looking to be looked at, trolling for bars and people to notice how short their skirts were and how long their list of "dos" was compared to their "do nots."

He was in an expensive suit again, a dark brown Ford this time minus the tie, pretending to read a paper while watching the human horde coming and going past him. No one was evil, but everyone was horny. It was amazing how the warmer weather brought it out in them.

Women smelled of chocolate when they saw a man or woman they desired. Men gave off an aroma of cinnamon or cloves or some other dark, exotic spice. Every time a pair got together around him it made him incredibly hungry.

No evil, though. Just everyone walking around smelling like a bakery.

He took a sip of the espresso he had at his elbow, and in doing so, caught a glimpse of a woman walking past, having obviously worked late. She gave off a metallic pang of annoyance, since everyone was in her way, drunk, and keeping her from getting home as quickly as possible. She was harried and exasperated. She'd had a long day. The stress was apparent even without his keen olfactory.

She dressed in a conservative skirt suit, the blazer locking and loading her upper assets in a professional way; a look he'd always liked. And the skirt was of an office-appropriate length. As she passed him she didn't look over, just continued on her way. And that's when he saw her ass, and it made his hand freeze with the espresso halfway to his lips.

Her ass was perfect. In his long life he'd gone through all the male obsessions with the female anatomy, and his present fixation was on the ass. Again. The skirt she wore was snug enough to show its roundness and its firmness. Her coat short enough to courteously allow a full view. As she passed he saw it from behind, her hips curving to her outer thighs in a perfect arc. It was so perfect it pained him ... and then he realized his pain was from a throbbing erection punching forward against his fly. This ridiculous human body. Shouldn't a person have more control over the damn thing?

He put the cup down without looking away from her. He could just imagine running his hand up over the arc of her hip, then dipping it back down to caress just under that muscle that was flexing as she walked. She came to a stop at a cross walk.

Well, he was a Sin Eater, capable of accessing someone's mind and central nervous system on a whim. He found her neuropaths easily, and just by imagining his hand running down her lower back to caress one cheek, he sent the sensation right into her cerebral cortex.

She straightened her back where she stood, squaring her shoulders. Keeping her composure, she turned, trying to see it someone was behind her, grabbing her ... but he knew she liked the sensation. He read it from her mind. Hell, she was even letting a small smile show as she tried to figure out where it came from. But she had the angle wrong, because in his mind he had her bent over in front of him, and now he imagined his hand sweeping up over her lower back, and pulling her against his hips as he bent to kiss her between the shoulder blades.

He watched the woman catch her breath, closing her eyes and weaving slightly on her feet. When she opened her eyes again she was blinking rapidly, a delicious flush to her cheeks. And she was looking right at him. She smiled.

Gotcha.

Chapter Three

"Iola!"

The voice shouted at her as she was just about to cross the street to the subway platform. It was a female voice, but that didn't matter. She palmed the pepper spray anyway, turning to see who was yelling at her. Then she smiled.

"What, you want to throw down with that? Trust me, I'm packing." Claudia Bauer was standing next to her car, arms crossed over her chest. She was grinning, too. One long leg was out to the side, her hip jutting out, and she looked like she was ready to rumble if Iola got serious with the pepper spray.

Iola laughed, putting the can back in her purse. With Claudia she was more than safe. Claudia was as good as a bodyguard. "What are you up to tonight, Sergeant?" she said with a bit of a jibe.

Claudia might have had the face of a runway model, but one mention of it and she'd likely remove your gallbladder without the aid of surgical tools. She was a cop, on the SWAT team, and she was also in the Armed Forces reserves. A weekend warrior. She was the toughest person Iola had ever met. Most men were scared of her.

They had good reason to be. Claudia had a terrible past where many indignities and humiliations had been inflicted on her by men. So as a result, she had no use for them. Absolutely no use. What so ever.

They'd met when Iola moved into her apartment just over two years ago. Claudia lived across the hall, and had been off duty as Iola was moving in. She'd helped her move in a few boxes and some furniture. Claudia had been very talkative, and it was only about a year of friendship later that she admitted she'd been checking Iola out the entire time.

Talk about dense. Iola had no idea. And Claudia said that's how she could tell Iola was straight. But they got along great, and they both had wonky work schedules. Sometimes it would be weeks before they'd actually see each other.

"Are you off tonight?" Iola asked, approaching her friend.

"I am. And I think we should go get something to eat. I'm starved."

"Where should we go?" Iola circled the car to the passenger side.

"Let's try that new place on 19th."

A diner that took the greasy-spoon genre very seriously. They'd been talking about it last week. Iola nodded. "Sounds good."

Claudia drove her black Challenger like it was a Formula One car, so it took only about ten minutes to get to the heart of downtown where the bars were closing and the drunks were spilling out into the street. She parked outside what looked like a diner from an old film noir. Shift workers like cops and paramedics were in the know about the best places to get a varied menu at a good price. This spot had only been open a month, but rumor already had it rated at "delicious."

They occupied a booth by the window, looked over the menu that was sitting on the table, and were ready to order when their waiter arrived. That was how these late night places worked. He wasn't going to push the special on you or suggest an appetizer. Just be ready to order.

Their waiter was about twenty-two, cute as a button, and at the sight of Claudia he was a bumbling mess. He dropped his pen, spilled the water he poured for them, and had a hell of a time saying, "Are you ready to order?"

Iola hid her smile out of embarrassment for him, but Claudia was ... well, a bit dense and not as kind. She looked at him like he was having a seizure, and she wasn't sympathetic.

"Are you alright, son?" She asked, sounding like a drill sergeant.

He balked, looking down at his notepad, then back at her. He wiped the palm of one hand on his pants and then nodded, stammering, "Y-yes. What ... what can I get you ladies?"

"I'll get the fish and chips," Iola spoke up, saving him from Claudia's withering glare.

"Steak sandwich. No gravy, thanks."

He all but ran back to the kitchen, and that's when Iola let herself laugh. "Claudia ... you can be so cruel."

"What do you mean?" Claudia asked, putting the menus back in their holder behind the ketchup bottle.

"That guy was totally twitter-pated by the very sight of you, and you just ... decimated him."

Claudia shrugged. "Wasted effort, right? So, what's up with you? Haven't seen you in about a week."

Iola shrugged. "Not much. I think I almost got mugged last night, but I scared the guy off. I think. I'm not sure how it happened but ... he changed his mind and walked away."

Claudia's shoulders tightened under the snug T-shirt she wore, and it made the muscles in her arms stand out. "Where?"

"After I got off the subway, right on the corner by our building. The guy was on the train and he followed me. I'm not sure how I didn't notice right when I got off, but ... there he was."

"So that explains the pepper spray. Would you recognize the guy if you saw him again?"

"Probably. He was dirty, his clothes were filthy. He was always scratching and twitching. And he stunk. If nothing else I could identify him by his stench."

"Meth," Claudia surmised, taking a drink of water. "I'll tell patrol to case the subway platforms. Better to prevent than investigate, right?"

"I always thought that was the point of a strengthened police presence. So thanks."

"I wish you'd get a car. Drive yourself places."

"No parking spots, remember? You park a block and a half away from the building. I walk less than that to and from the subway platforms I use. So who's smarter? I have no idea."

"Good point. At least let me show you how to defend yourself."

"I had my keys ready, just like you showed me."

"Good. But there's a few other things I can teach you."

Iola let her voice get low and sexy. "I already told you, I'm not interested in wrestling."

"Let a girl dream, Day." She raised her hand and waved the waiter over. "I'm thirsty, you thirsty?"

"Be nice," came Iola's warning. "Bad enough you're a cop. I'm already perpetually worried that people will spit in our food. Or worse."

Claudia made a face at her, and then the waiter was back, all nerves and sweaty palms again. "Yes? Did you need something?"

"How about a beverage order?"

"Oh, I'm sorry, what can I get you?"

Claudia leaned forward on the table, smiling up at him brilliantly. "I am just dying for a glass of iced tea. I'm absolutely parched," she explained, chin on her hand, pinky finger right at the corner of her mouth. "I am in desperate need of refreshment." Then she licked the tip of her pinky and widened the smile further. "Can you help me with that, Tyler?"

He was transfixed, but he smiled. "Yeah. Yeah, I think I can do that." Then he started to leave.

"Oh, Tyler?"

He turned back to her, all goopy smiles and breathless again. "You forgot my friend. Iola, sweetie, what would you like, honey?"

Iola smiled at Tyler too, shaking her head. "I would just like a beer. Whatever you got, it will be fine."

"Okay, no problem." He turned back to fetch their drinks, and Claudia dropped her arm and the act.

She turned an expectant look on Iola. "Nice enough for you?"

"You're terrible."

"They're so fucking ridiculous."

"Who?"

"Men."

"Oh, speaking of that - "

"Don't tell me you got laid? I know it's been a while and I'm pretty sure I would have heard something. The walls are pretty thin."

"No, I didn't get laid, Claudia. And you're right, you'd be the first to know. No, it's ... Jasper again."

"Oh Christ. What did he do? Did he touch you? You don't have to put up with that."

"No, no, that's not it." Iola found it weird that Claudia got so protective when it came to Jasper. But whatever, she was a friend, right? "He drunk dialed me tonight while I was at work."

"What?"

"Yeah. He has the weekend off and he called me. He said ... well, he wants to date me and I know that. But ... like I've told him. I'm not interested in dating a co-worker. It's too awkward, and especially when you start dating, you need space, right?"

"And you should only need to tell a guy 'no' once."

"I feel sad for him sometimes. He's a wreck."

"Wow, sounds like a personal ad. You should totally hit that." Her tone was dry and sarcastic.

Iola laughed. "He's going to be so embarrassed the next time I see him."

"Serves him right ... the dumb ass."

The Sin Eater enjoyed the view as the woman opened her door in front of him, leaning over just a bit, before she pushed it open, stepped through and stood to the side so he could enter her condo. He nodded his head in appreciation, surveying the view from the living room window. The city was stretched out in front of him, all lights and traffic and telecommunication towers. He knew this made it a valuable property, so whatever this Ellen did for a living was apparently pretty high-profile.

Before he could reach into her brain and find out what her occupation was, she was on him, pressing herself against his body tightly, hands on his shoulders, pushing her tongue into his mouth and moaning hotly.

All right then. Apparently he'd really done a number on her, and she'd liked the look of him even more. When she approached him, he was pleased to note the scent of cocoa wafting ahead of her. She'd simply said, "I'm Ellen," then just stared at him.

The Sin Eater used her mind to look at himself, gazing up at her. He let his eyes trail down, feeling her tingle as she sensed it, zinging up her spine.

"Ellen," he said in his low, growling voice. "Would you care to join me for an espresso?"

"I have an espresso machine in my condo," she said, and then blushed deeper. She couldn't believe she'd just basically invited him to her place. She didn't even know his name ...

He offered his hand. "I'm John." Nice and ambiguous. And his real name didn't transfer well in the English language.

"John. I'm not usually this forward but ..." she didn't let go of his hand. "Would you care to walk me to my building?"

"I'd be delighted."

He stood and buttoned his suit coat, hiding that ridiculous bulge in his pants. Not that she would have noticed. She was staring at his face, his eyes, his mouth, and she kept licking her lips. It was a terrible distraction to him.

He offered his arm, and she looped hers through it, falling into step beside him and staring at him with the same rapture she'd first shown.

Now, as she pushed his jacket off his shoulders and her fingers pulled at the buttons of his shirt in the dark, she had none of that false shyness. She wanted him, and the smell of chocolate was nearly overwhelming.

At first when he'd come to this world he'd found it easy to just seduce with the use of his mind. Nothing like he'd done to this woman on the street, much more blatant. He'd gone into bedrooms, pushed his way into their minds, inserted himself into their dreams and fucked their bodies and when they woke, they were already sure they'd given consent. Then he'd started planting orgasms in their psyche, just to make himself feel better about how easy it was to take advantage of them. He could do that; make men and women experience something they hadn't really done. Like earth-shattering, write-a-letter-to-your-best-friend, did-you-catch-the-number-on-that-train orgasms.

When that got tiresome and he started to feel like a real bastard, he decided maybe he should just learn how to do it the good old fashioned way. If he could sense what people enjoyed, how hard could it be to just listen to a woman's thoughts and give her body what she wanted?

It wasn't complicated after all, and really, all women kind of liked the same thing. Once you figured out if she was in soft and gentle mode, friendly playful mode, or leave the shoes on and just fuck me raw mode, it was all basically ... the same. Pay attention to when she was climaxing, and don't change anything.

He could also get on whatever train of sensation they were experiencing; that was the really messed up part of it. He could assume their point of view, and feel their emotions and sensations. He could feel their orgasm as they went through it. And that ... that was what he became addicted to. Men's orgasms were great, intense and quick. But for a woman ... he couldn't believe the difference. And the seduction, the build-up, it was all necessary for that explosion to be perfect.

He pulled Ellen's blouse off her shoulders, pressing his lips to her light brown flesh, inhaling the cocoa scent deep into his nostrils. His mouth tasted that skin along her collarbone, and her head fell back in a divine sigh, her body still, back under his control. And it was the lips on the flesh, nothing to do with his mind.

He relieved her of her bra, let his shirt fall to the floor since she'd freed all the buttons, and held her up to his skin, the warmth from her body penetrating deep into his. She was no longer crawling all over him like some kind of jungle cat, she was satisfied that he was going to take her to bed good and proper, she didn't need further convincing. She also had a death grip on the chain around his neck, but that was fine. It would hold.

His lips came to hers again, and she responded with passion and not fury. Her tongue was delicious in his mouth, still aggressive. Oh, he liked this one very much. No apologies for having a libido. It was refreshing.

He gathered her up in his arms easily, already knowing where the bedroom was. These places all invariably had the same layout. He left the lights off as he took her to her bed, laying her down. He did turn on a small, shaded bedside lamp. He had to see them, the women he laid with. He loved to watch their faces.

She reached to turn it back off but he caught her hand, pressing her palm to his mouth. "Please, leave it on," he whispered against her skin.

She shuddered. Reached out to him, coaxed him down on top of her. As her kisses became more and more urgent, he removed the rest of their clothing, lying naked next to her, stroking the secret places of her body that her mind was begging him to touch. This seemed to calm her, and yet she was burning under his hands.

He teased each nipple with his mouth, and she gripped his hair to hold him in place. She let him trail downward, out of her reach, to the juncture of her legs. He dove in without much more preamble, rewarded by the sound of her guttural moan and the arching of her back. One leg came over his shoulder, the heel digging into his back so she could work against his mouth. He risked a glance upwards, and she was totally lost to what she was feeling. Her eyes were closed, her head was tossed to the side, her mouth drew breath through her parted lips, and she was softly tracing circles around her own nipple. Unembarrassed, totally willing to pleasure herself while he paid witness to it. This must be what she was like privately, on her own. Oh, she was definitely a rare breed. So lovely.

Her orgasm arrived quickly, so quickly he didn't have a chance to piggyback on it. That was okay. He decided she was going to have a few more anyway.

As he parted her thighs to make room for himself her eyes fluttered open suddenly and she whispered, "I have condoms."

He smiled down at her, running a finger along the curve of her top lip. He carried no human disease and could not transmit one, and since he was not technically a living thing he could not impregnate her. But he didn't want to break the spell he had over her that had very little to do with imposing his will on her. "Where?" He asked gently.

She looked to her bedside table, made up of three legs and a circular top. On the stand next to the lamp was a carved wooden box. Inside, under a travel pack of tissue, he found the prophylactic and made quick work of getting it in place. She watched while he did, and her respect for her own body was another turn-on for him.

"Ellen, are you ready?"

She just nodded, mouth dropping open further. She swallowed nervously, and he kissed her roughly. She held him tight, and as he lifted her slight weight, gripping her by that ass that had first captured his attention he drove home the male appendage that could not be ignored. Her inner muscles grabbed hold of him tight but slick, and he found himself bellowing into the pillow right next to her head. He had to concentrate, wanted to get into her mind, but if he lost it now ...

Gritting his teeth, he went back to kissing her, which helped. Her mind was throwing off pleasure and want and desire like mad, and he locked on to all that information until he was sensing everything her body did. He could feel her physical invasion; what his body was doing to hers. He moaned, and she answered as well. When he found that spot inside, behind her belly button, she cried out. He had to calm himself again, he'd felt that first contact as well. It nearly sent him over the brink.

He concentrated on that spot, his pace not intensifying, just stroking at it, letting the heat build. She clawed his back, dug her nails into his ass, trying to get him to speed up but he refused. Her legs were locked around him, her ankles crossed behind his thighs, and the closer they came to the inevitable the less he had to rear back and plunge in again. She felt it, she was sending all that pleasure to him, and as it crested and flowed through her the Sin Eater bellowed as she called out, "John!" Whoever the hell that was.

That was him, he realized groggily. That was what he told her his name was. He turned his head to kiss her neck tenderly. "So lovely," he whispered.

She stroked the back of his head, her body still shuddering through what he'd done to her. "Oh ... wow," she muttered, eyes closed.

These damn humans. Sex was one thing that other species could envy; the fact they could actually take pleasure in the act of "creation." It's one of the few things they had going for them. And they would choose to look on it as a sin and punish themselves for wanting it.

The Sin Eater looked down to the woman who had willingly brought him home. He would take her again, he could already feel the want stirring him. Then the Sin Eater got a clear reading on her past lovers. As she caught her breath and steadied her pulse she was remembering her other experiences.

She'd had plenty of externally-induced orgasms, and most of those she'd done herself, of course. She'd never had the kind of explosive release she'd just experienced. He wasn't stroking his own ego: he lifted it right from her brain. Thirty-three and she'd never had the "G-Spot" orgasm. Now that ... that was a real sin.

Chapter Four

Iola giggled as she ducked to get in Claudia's car. It seemed so low ... She almost fell, but didn't hit her head. She was all-out laughing by the time Claudia got behind the wheel.

Claudia shook her head, then reached over to fasten her seatbelt. "Holy shit, Day. You are such a light weight."

"Who knew it would take three beers to get our food?" Iola asked, trying her best not to laugh, which of course sent her into a fresh round of giggles.

Claudia was laughing too as she buckled up herself. "You are so fucking drunk."

"No, I'm not that drunk. I feel very happy, and everything is just very funny."

Claudia turned the key in the ignition, still shaking her head. "We've got to get you hammered more often. You're hilarious."

"I'm not funny. No one ever says that I'm funny."

"I say you're funny. After three beers anyway."

She tried to stay calm, concentrating on appearing "normal" as Claudia drove back to her parking arcade with the same speed and maneuvering she'd demonstrated before. It did not agree with Iola's stomach and she closed her eyes until the speed slowed and they were pulling up a ramp to Claudia's parking spot.

"Thanks for coming to get me. We haven't done this in a long time."

"Yeah, it was fun."

Claudia parked her car in her spot, and helped Iola make her way down the ramp to the street. "Shit, I guess I could have dropped you off at the building."

Iola shook her head. "Nah. It's okay. We can walk."

"Just don't make me pick you up off the ground. I hate messy drunks."

The street was silent. After all, it was four-thirty in the morning. They crossed against the light and started down the main thoroughfare to their building with not another soul in sight.

Iola stuck her arm around Claudia's shoulders. "You're a good friend. You're the only one I have, come to think of it."

"Yeah, I know." Claudia paused so Iola could concentrate on stepping up on to the curb.

Just as they got going again, Iola stopped, blinking and turning back around, looking to the mouth of an alley across the street.

"What is it?" Claudia asked, starting to sound annoyed with her now.

"Someone's over there. They're watching us."

Claudia's entire body tensed, even her jaw, ready for a fight. Iola had an abstract moment of thinking it was actually pretty sexy.

Three beers and now she's a lesbian.

"Where? I don't see anyone." Claudia's face was straining in the bright glare of a street light. They wouldn't see shit in the shadows with all this overhead illumination.

"That alley. They're just around the corner. In the shadows."

"How can you see them?"

"I can't. I can just ... feel him."

Claudia looked at her with concern. "They might have slipped you something in one of those beers."

"Claudia - "

"I don't think there's anything there. But if there is I'd rather be locked in my apartment than out here propping up my delightfully intoxicated friend. So let's get the lead out."

She hurried Iola along, unlocking the door, only relaxing once they were in the stairwell.

"Are you going to be okay on the stairs or should I try to fireman-carry you up them?"

Iola waved her hand. "Please. It's just stairs."

"You go first. I'll catch you."

She did it slowly but got up to the second floor without incident. She futzed with her keys until Claudia took them from her and unlocked her door for her.

Claudia flicked on the inside light for her as well then steered her to the sofa. "Sit down. You need to drink some water."

"Bring some for my plant, too, please." She leaned back and willed the walls to stop moving.

"All right."

Claudia came back with two glasses, handed one to Iola and took the other to the window. "Babe, these are almost dead."

"I know. They get plenty of sun there, and I water them every day. They just ... keep dying on me."

Claudia turned a wary eye to Iola. "You're over-watering then. Just water them when the dirt starts to get dry."

"What?"

Iola got up, set her glass down and stalked over to the window. Claudia laughed, not exactly at her, just the situation. "Oh, Iola. Just look how floppy it is."

Iola looked at her sheepishly. "I can't believe I'm drowning my damn plant."

They locked eyes. Claudia's were so deep and brown, almond-shaped, the kind of eyes that women applied make-up to achieve. Hers were all natural with a few flecks of gold in them. Her eyebrows were ridiculously perfect, high and arched. A small beauty mark was next to her left temple. Skin was flawless, olive-colored. Good God, she was so pretty.

Claudia put a hand to Iola's cheek softly. Iola jumped at the contact, but Claudia didn't mind. She touched her hair, her other cheek, then leaned in very carefully, slowly, not rushing.

Iola leaned in the rest of the way, meeting her somewhere in the middle. It surprised her, but Claudia's lips met hers softly and gently, moving ever so slightly as she angled her head sideways. Iola found herself following Claudia's lead, totally out of her element. But really ... this wasn't so different from kissing a guy.

Until Claudia urged her lips apart with her tongue, very gently, achingly tender. Okay, that was ... different. She didn't feel consumed. She didn't feel overwhelmed. She was feeling treasured. Like a rare territory first being explored.

Then Claudia backed up, wiping her lip and turning away. "Fuck," she muttered. "Fuck, Iola, I'm sorry. I don't know what ... fuck."

Iola put a hand on her shoulder. "Claudia, don't worry. I kissed you, technically. I don't know why. But ... I'm sorry."

"It's not your fault. You're not in your normal state of mind, and I shouldn't have encouraged it. That was wrong."

"Please don't - "

"No one should ever be taken advantage of. I can't believe I did that. I'm sorry, Iola. I'll ... just take care. Drink plenty of water, take a couple Aspirin. You'll thank me ... well, you'll appreciate it." And then she was gone with the speed of a couple of quick strides across the small living room and the shutting of the door.

Iola stood where she was, feeling awful. It didn't take a genius to realize that Claudia's reaction was due to her tumultuous past. She'd been raped while passed out drunk in college, and that wasn't the start of her horrible history. Iola felt like she'd brought up a whole lot of ugly, and she couldn't make it better.

So she did as told, got a couple Aspirin from the kitchen, washed them down with the water Claudia had brought her, then quickly downed the water that her plant apparently didn't need. Her eyes wandered back down to the street, to the mouth of the alley they'd passed. The hair on the back of her neck stood up.

The figure of a man was standing on the sidewalk, now a shadow himself, thrown by the street light behind him. It was hard to be sure, but he appeared to be looking at her window. She stared a few more minutes, then shook her head like there was a fly buzzing close to her ear or something. When she looked back, he was gone.

Iola turned off the lights and went to bed, suddenly totally sober.

The Sin Eater continued down the alley. He was cursing himself for letting himself be seen, but on the other hand ... he didn't mind her knowing he was there.

This woman still wasn't giving him anything. He could read nothing from her. When he saw her and her ... friend coming down the block he'd instantly noticed she was intoxicated, thought maybe that would help. But there was nothing.

And then when the tall woman had looked at her with such care ... he couldn't help himself, he pushed his way into her brain. And he convinced himself that he didn't make the woman do anything she didn't want to do anyway. He took over her body, and made her kiss the object of his new obsession. But the tall, dark-haired woman was strong, and she stayed mostly in control of her mind. He was really just the navigator, telling her to do it. And when she did, he felt it.

He wiped his mouth, still feeling the petal-soft lips against his like they were the ones that had actually kissed her. And as he pulled his hand away, he could still smell the woman from earlier that night, Ellen. Dammit, he hadn't wiped himself from her memory, like he should have. That was his ego. He wanted her to remember him.

A familiar smell wafted to him over his pondering, and he stopped, turning back to the mouth of the alley. Sulfur. Very strong, since the source of it was nowhere to be seen, and yet still the scent lingered.

He frowned and paced back to where he'd first caught its trace. There was a huge metal trash receptacle to one side, and behind it ... that's where the stink was coming from. Someone had lingered here, hiding from ... the street. It had to be.

He closed his eyes, scanning the area for mental activity. There was no one around, he was alone. So who the hell had stood here so long ...

The man from the night before. It had to be. The scent the Sin Eater had picked up on was quite potent, but once the woman had gotten rid of him on the street all on her own, his attention had shifted completely from the man to her. And where had that smelly little toad gone?

The Sin Eater had let him wander off, unseen. Hadn't even tried to find him afterwards. He'd been caught up in her.

That's why he needed to focus, dammit. The man reeked of evil deeds done in the past and more to come. And he'd let him get away.

Fuck. No more women; that was the new resolution. And if he had been put in a less humanly body that would actually be possible, wouldn't it? Some human instincts he could stop, others he was totally at the mercy of his own physical weaknesses.

He had to find the source of this malice. If the man had decided this woman was the subject of his next nefarious act, the Sin Eater knew he could find him tomorrow night, right here, behind the dumpster. He was sure the man would come back. The man was a source of evil waiting to be released back into the natural order of things.

And wasn't it just awful that he would have to come back and possibly see her again?

Claudia had changed into her pajamas, washed her face, tied her hair back and made herself a cup of tea, but none of it had calmed her nerves. She was shaking, she was appalled. She couldn't believe that after two years of platonic friendship she'd made a move on her only real friend while the poor thing was intoxicated. If she wasn't an eleven-years-sober alcoholic she would have had a stiff drink.

She had a real issue with unequal partnerships, and that's what that had been. They were not both in their right mind, so it was wrong. Simple as that.

She flashed back to her dorm room, waking up on top of the covers of her bed, her shirt pushed up, her bra around her neck, and her jeans and underwear on the floor. There was also a condom package on the ground, the condom itself nowhere to be seen. And she was sore. Claudia had a lot to drink at a kegger the night before, since even before that she had been unable to control her drinking. Which led to a lot of casual sex. Which may or may not have been what happened before she woke up that day.

No one could tell her who had been in her room that night, no one noticed if anyone had come in or gone out. But they all noticed how tanked she'd been. So who would believe her? Would she even believe it if it happened to anyone else?

As time had gone on, she thought she could remember flashes. She remembered pushing at someone in the dark of her room, but he overpowered her easily. Her limbs were not moving the way they should have. She was falling in and out of consciousness, but she remembered the pain of the act itself. That came back to her quite clearly. She'd never forget that feeling ... she'd known it before then.

Claudia shook herself back to the here and now. She wasn't the same as she'd been then, she was stronger now, sober, and she would never be a victim again.

No, now she was on her way to being the offender. Okay, it hadn't gone that far, but she had scared herself.

She put her tea cup in the sink to wash the next day, and continued pacing. If all else failed, she could wear a track in her floor, agonizing over what she did that was wrong and what was right.

Then came the fear that she'd overreacted and totally freaked Iola out. Or even worse, made her feel bad. Made her look at her differently. Her only friend ...

Warm bath. That's what she needed. A nice warm bath, a glass of milk. Then she could sleep. But before she undressed and got in the tub, she checked all the cubbies and empty rooms of the apartment, and under her bed. She always did that, just in case.

Charles couldn't remember how he got to the roof of the office building across from the bakery. But he knew why he was there, and she was now sleeping in bed. She'd come home with the woman from the night before, who maybe was the one he wanted. But it was so hard to be sure, and he got confused so easily.

But the one with the long dark hair and the long legs and arms was what he wanted now. She was perfect. She'd be a challenge to break. And all these degenerate bitches had to be broken.

He watched her window as the light turned off in her bedroom. He'd have to be careful getting in. She looked tough, and he thought she would fight to the death. But there wouldn't have to be a death. Just as long as she was ... hurting.

He cracked his knuckles and his focus returned. Yep ... she was the next one. He knew for sure once she kissed that woman, right in front of the window for everyone to see. It was disgusting.

She'd be sorry for that ... and while he had her, maybe he could show her the natural order of things. Sometimes the master let him have them first, before he completely broke them. This one ... he would like very much to take her before she died.

And he knew which subway train her friend took on a regular basis, so he wouldn't have to remember this place. Just the trains. He even knew which stop she got on, it was right next door to his little apartment.

This was going to be perfect. He just had to surprise her.

Chapter Five

Iola was worried about herself now. She woke from a restless night with only a headache, made herself some coffee and toast, and tried to figure out what the night before had meant. Not the kiss - that she could explain quite easily. Claudia had always found her attractive, and in her drunken state Iola was feeling experimental. She sure wasn't the first woman ever to get buzzed and kiss someone she didn't intend to.

No, what worried her were the sweaty, erotic dreams she'd had between her constant awakenings. She'd woken up completely breathless, blushing, and as turned on as hell. And who had the dreams been about? Claudia.

It didn't mean anything. Just ... dreams. Plural. *More than one.* To the point where she couldn't get rid of that constant, heightened arousal. Eventually she'd just had to ... well, take care of it herself. But when she fleetingly thought of Claudia's hand possibly doing what her own hand was doing ... she climaxed immediately.

Was she thinking she wanted to ... give the same-sex thing a try with Claudia?

No. No. Well, maybe ... No. Oh, who the hell knew? People got confused from time to time, and that gave her confidence that she was just having a crisis of sexual preference. Due to a long, dry spell in her love life. Right?

The toast and coffee were tasteless. She was jumpy as hell.

She showered slowly and lazily, not having anything to do that day other than go to work. And that wasn't until six o'clock. That's a lot of time to sit around worrying about one topic. This is how anxiety screwed with you.

Iola could go for groceries since there were a few items she needed. Yeah, that seemed like something she would do anyway. She should do that.

And go by the hospital. She hadn't been there in a while. She liked to visit the terminal wards. Most people thought it was depressing and odd, but for her ... it made her feel like she was helping people when they're at their most terrified. And most lonely.

That might be a good use of her afternoon. She'd head there first.

A plan of action took her mind off everything. She dried her hair, dressed, and then headed for the subway platform quickly, not wanting to run into Claudia in the hallway.

The subway ride to City General was about twenty minutes, and she had brought a magazine along for company. At the stop she tucked it into her bag absently, and when she started for the stairs she heard something flutter to the concrete behind her. She was stopping and turning just as a male voice said, "Excuse me, Miss?"

The man stooping to pick up her magazine was also smiling up at her. His accent was very strange, she couldn't place it. It was guttural and hard, but lovely to listen to at the same time, even if it was for three simple words. When he extended the magazine to her, she took it from a large, powerful hand. And when he straightened to his full height, she was gazing up at him, since he must have been six-three or six-four easily. Broad shoulders. Long arms. All cased in a gorgeous navy pinstripe suit.

He was definitely attractive in that foreign, tall dark and handsome way. His face had a few lines, but on men that was hardly considered a negative. His lips were full, his mouth wide. His brows were dark and heavy to match the hair that fell to just above the collar of his shirt. It was slicked back, but not greasily. It seemed to sit that way on its own. And his eyes ... she couldn't even be sure of the color. They were likely blue, but at the moment they seemed almost ... lavender? She found herself smiling at him. "Thank you," she said, aware she was blinking too much. That was her nervous twitch.

He put one hand to the left side of his chest. "My pleasure," he said with great dramatic flair, and when she laughed he granted her a smile.

Her heart stopped. Her breath caught. His smile ... what the hell was it doing to her?

She flushed, dropped her gaze and mumbled her thanks again. Then she high tailed it for the stairs back up to street level.

Iola moved with the intensity and concentration of a competitive speed walker. Her chest was heaving like she'd just done a 4K jaunt. Her face felt hot, and it was spreading down her neck and into her chest. And holy fuck ... she was so incredibly turned on she was wondering if it wasn't another one of her insanely intense dreams from the night before. When he'd smiled, it was like ... the sound of the subway went away. She was aware of it, but it sounded like it was coming down a long, echoing hallway. The people moving past them were walking in slow motion. And she had a hell of a time disengaging her attention from his face. Especially when all she wanted to do was kiss it.

She actually fanned herself with her magazine, nearly walking out into traffic to cross against a red light. A woman grabbed her arm to stop her from killing herself, and Iola jumped about three feet at the contact. The woman apologized, looking disconcerted by the expression on Iola's face. And she probably did look completely insane.

Waiting for the light to turn, Iola steadied her breathing, and slowly felt her body's core temperature returning to normal. By the time the walking man flashed on, she was ... better. Not back to normal, but *much* much calmer.

Calm enough to wonder ... What the hell was that guy?

The Sin Eater watched her as she sprinted away through the public transit crowd, heading up the stairs at top speed. The scent of jasmine, vanilla and chocolate was the only wake she left in the shifting crowd.

He avoided the urge to close his eyes while inhaling deeply. His human heart pounded, and below the belt of his designer suit his body was demanding that he find a means to take her, right where they were.

Her voice had pierced him, through and through, right down the center of his chest, with just those two short words. It wasn't percussion; she was too soft of tone. But the sound of her voice was like the audible definition of beauty.

Better yet, he could feel the trail her pale green eyes had left on him. It was like a trickle of hot water, seeping under his clothes and warming his skin. But had she known what he was? Had she sensed he was something other than human?

Through the glow of having seen and talked to her, he felt the prickle of disconcertion. No human had ever sensed what he was, unless they were dying and looking to repent. And she had bolted from him. But not before ...

He breathed deep again as he followed the scent of her. The smell of chocolate pleased him. She'd had the same reaction to him that he had to her; want, desire, and apprehension caused by her confusion of what he was.

There was no walking away now. There was no leaving her for the hands of fate and distancing himself from what he didn't understand.

What the hell was she?

"Mister Horn, so good to see you again." Iola congratulated herself. Her voice sounded normal, and she was pretty sure her smile was natural. It felt natural.

"Iola?" The elderly, withering form in the bed blinked to make sure he wasn't imagining her. "It's been a while."

"I know, I'm sorry. How have you been?" She settled next to him in the guest chair, and he turned his head to smile at her.

"Not good," he admitted, the sadness in his voice hurting her.

"Has your son been by?"

"He came by ... I think it was about three weeks ago. Haven't seen him since." His voice just got sadder. Then he perked up. "He brought the grandson along. He's getting so big!" Then he settled into a short burst of wheezing coughs, brought on by a chuckle. "Kept pushing the buttons on the bed, moving it up and down."

Iola smiled.

"Your smile ... reminds me so much of my Lily," he admitted. Iola knew that Missus Horn had passed away about thirteen years before. "She was so beautiful, just like you."

"Oh, Mister Horn, watch that flirting. Next thing you know I'm marrying you."

"I can't even take you dancing. Don't marry some sick old fart like me." Then came that wheezing cough again. Iola hadn't heard it this bad before. He was dying of lung cancer, started smoking while he'd served in the RCAF in World War Two, and all things considered, he was pretty lucky he'd made it this far. The nurses told her the nasty ones always lasted the longest.

"Want a cigarette?" She joked. They'd started that running gag the first time she'd come to see him. That first day she stopped by to say hi he had a hacking fit, then yelled at the nurse to bring him cigarettes. If he was dying what difference would it possibly make?

She knew he was rude to the nurses, yelled at them, even pushed one once. But to her ... he was kind. He liked her, and the nurses said he was calmer and he slept better after she'd visited. So they were usually happy to see her, too. She reminded him of his late wife, apparently.

"Why are you coming here anyway?" He asked dismissively when his coughing was exhausted. "Hang around us old folks, dying all over. You should be out having fun. Living it up. Dating some nice guy."

Iola shrugged. "I like coming here. I feel like I learn a lot from you sick old farts."

"Watch it, missy. It's only funny when I say it," he sounded stern but the twinkle in his eye told otherwise.

The pictures on the wall were from his wedding, he and his wife in their early twenties. He was home fresh from Europe, wearing his dress blues, wedge cap at an angle. She could still see that handsome young man in his face, especially when his eyes twinkled like they were doing right now.

"But I mean it," he said, bringing her back around. "It stinks in here."

"What do you mean?" She frowned, thinking she was in for another joke.

"It smells like dying. You can't smell that?"

She breathed in deeply through her nose. "It smells like hospital to me. What does it smell like to you?"

He shook his head. "I don't know. It just smells bad. Maybe it's me. I need a shower."

"Well, I'll let the nurses know. But I don't smell anything."

He actually looked embarrassed. "Maybe you should go. I shouldn't have company when I stink like this."

"Mister Horn, I don't smell anything. Honestly."

"I appreciate you stopping in, Iola. Come and see me again soon."

She got to her feet, smiling down at him. "You are such a gentleman. I will definitely be coming to see you again."

He smiled back at her in relief, more from the fact that she was leaving than the fact that she would be coming back.

She touched his shoulder, and he closed his eyes at the connection. She found it odd, but she still offered him a smile as she left.

"Take care of yourself, Mister Horn."

"You too, dear."

She made her way down the hall to stop in on Missus Dean. She hoped she was wrong about this bad feeling she had. She was pretty sure she'd just said her final good-bye to Mister Horn.

Douglas Horn breathed in relief as Iola left the doorway. He closed his eyes, trying to calm his racing pulse. When he felt better, he opened his eyes again, then blinked a few times.

"Who the hell are you?" He snapped at a large man dressed in a blue suit.

The man sat where Iola had sat, leaning in. His cold bluish-purple eyes made Douglas want to shrink back in fear, but he'd be damned if he was going to give into this dandy.

"Don't worry with who I am. The worry is why I am here. And Douglas, I'm here because you've been ... very bad."

"How do you know my name? Get out of this room. I'm calling a nurse."

Then his hand froze on the call button. He wanted to push it one moment, and then he just decided it was unnecessary. But he was still plenty pissed off.

"Well, what do you want?" He stubbornly crossed his arms, his IV tube flapping around him, ticking against the rails of the bed.

The man closed his eyes, rested his elbows on the arms of the chair, steepled his fingers in front of him and sighed. Douglas was about to ask him to take his damn meditation elsewhere, when he was jolted back against the pillows of his bed. He could see his room, could see the man sitting next to him in his periphery, but it all became background to a hazy, translucent image, a memory, fading into focus in front of him. A woman. On her back. Hands wrapped around her neck. She was scratching at arms, fighting to breathe. Her body was jerking up and down as it was invaded, violated against her will. He watched the life fade out of her eyes, and then he'd kept squeezing. And doing other things, too.

Tears poured down his face, and he was saying, "Damn you," over and over, low and almost to himself.

"You were drunk," the stranger relented. "You didn't necessarily have control of yourself. And it was ... a troubling time."

Damn straight it was troubling. He'd jumped from a Dakota over Normandy just seconds before it exploded, and every man from his boot camp days had died immediately. He was the first and only one out of that plane on D-Day. And he used to drink so much ...

He hated that he was crying in front of this guy, but the images kept replaying over and over. It was a videotape on a loop in front of him.

"Just imagine how troubling those times were for her," the bastard kept talking. "They'd all been so glad to see the Allies coming. Her town had been pillaged by the Germans, how could you Canadians be worse than the Germans? Well, the Germans did what you did to her as well. But they left her alive after. And they gave her that baby as well, surely you remember the child? Crying, bundled up in a drawer at the foot of her bed? The unwanted child she was selling herself just to feed?"

The tears were fast and hot down his cheeks. He felt sick, and his stomach was slowing turning over. He hadn't thought about this in years ...

"But you were drunk. So maybe this one's questionable."

"Who are - "

"I told you not to worry about that. Where you're headed, I'll be the furthest thing from your mind."

Rather than getting upset, that just pissed him off more. "I'm a good man. I had a family and I fought for this country - "

"Yes, you did. You're very decent and brave. So explain to me this: when you had sex with your wife, why would you always think of this woman?"

He wanted to jump out of the bed and pound this fucker into the ground. The guy sensed it, and had the gall to chuckle. "I am immortal, sir. You could not harm me with your fists in the prime of your life any more than you could do harm to the Hoover Dam with brass knuckles." The he gazed, off, thoughtful. "Where was she? Was this in Holland?"

"Fuck you."

"I thought so. So, you were drunk and troubled, having just witnessed great tragedy. Understandable. But ... what about this one?"

The image flicked by quickly, this time a dark-haired woman, up against a wall. His forearm was across her throat, and she was hitting at him, but she was too intoxicated to properly defend herself. She was a whore, in London, where he'd been billeted. This was before the first woman he saw. This was before D-Day. Oh shit ... he'd blocked this one out completely.

"You weren't even drunk. But she refused you service because you didn't have enough cash, remember it now, old man?"

Douglas was seething now, his teeth gritted with air sucking through them.

"That's it," the man was encouraging with a smart-ass smile. "I can see it. The anger. It's right there. In three years you killed five women, Douglas. You would have killed more if there'd been women in the service. Deployment takes you away from all that hatred, doesn't it? You didn't want to kill Germans as much as you wanted to kill these women. I couldn't see this potential before. Thought I maybe had the wrong room."

"Our Father, who art in Heaven, hallowed be Thy name ..."

"It's pointless. I am here to interrupt the forgiveness you're seeking."

" ... Thy kingdom come, Thy will be done on earth as it is in Heaven."

The stranger sighed, shaking his head and rubbing his temples.

"... Give us this day our daily bread and forgive us ..." he blinked back more tears. "Forgive us our trespasses as we forgive those who trespass against us."

"Almost done?"

"... and lead us not into temptation, but deliver us from evil. For Thine is the kingdom, the power and the glory, for ever and ever. Amen."

"Amen. Lovely. Now just ... be still."

Douglas didn't want to do anything this asshole asked him. But he found himself obeying anyway, even closing his eyes and doing his damnedest to calm down.

The women's faces all flew by, he remembered the smells around him, the feeling of their life choking away between his hands, the sensations overlapping from each individual woman, his body pounding into them, the pace getting more frantic as they died, even though he'd not been able to release into them. Then ... peace.

Nothing. The memories were gone. It was like ... like they were the work of someone else. The calm flowed over him like a warm bath, and he sighed, turning his head to the stranger. He had no illusions that this man was an angel, or that he'd saved him from eternal damnation. This man ... he had to be evil.

The stranger stood, straightened his jacket, and nodded. But as he got to the door, Douglas coughed to clear his throat. The visitor turned back to him.

"Stay away from her," Douglas warned, unable to focus his eyes.

"I beg pardon?"

"Iola. Stay the hell away from her. She's good. She's pure. And you ... you are not."

"No shit," the stranger replied, then walked out the door as the monitors and alarms started beeping.

Chapter Six

Iola was leaving Missus Dean's room as hospital staff was racing down the hall. She watched them with dread, and sure enough, they all headed for Mister Horn's room.

She winced and then stopped, staying out of the way in the hall opposite his door. There was a glass window behind her that faced out on to a courtyard, and the sun was shining in brightly. She stood not enjoying it, but staring into the room as nurses pulled his hospital gown down, put his bed flat, and yelled odd words at each other.

A doctor ran down the hall next, and the nurse started up the crash cart as he was entering, throwing more numbers and instructions into the mix of chaos.

All Iola could see was Douglas Horn's face, looking towards her. He had tears on his cheeks, and his eyes were brimming with regret. When he saw her he offered a small, apologetic smile. Then they jolted him with high wattage electricity, and his body jerked. But he kept his eyes on her face, his expression serene.

Iola covered her mouth, choking on a cry. But she stayed, keeping her eyes on his. It seemed important that he not feel alone as he died, but she couldn't say why. The doctor went from defibrillator to chest compressions to clock-watching to announcing the time of death. She only looked away when she knew he wasn't seeing her anymore.

At some point her back slid down the glass and she was crouching against the wall, one arm wrapped around her knees, the other still covering her mouth so no one would notice how loudly she was sobbing.

The doctor came to the door, looking weary and messy, his hair standing upright from shoving his hands through it. She'd watched him trying to save Mister Horn, she knew it bothered him to see someone die even though he was old, sick and a miserable bastard by all accounts. He was about to head down the hall one way when he saw her, and she was embarrassed to be noticed right then and there, but she was also very upset. She wiped away her tears angrily as he started to walk over to her. Oh God, don't stop and talk to me right now. I'm a mess.

To her complete surprise he leaned against the window then sunk down to the ground next to her, bending his legs at the knees.

Crap, she thought. He's young. And cute. Dammit to hell.

"Did you ... did you know Doug?"

Iola shrugged. "I visited a few times. Over the past five or so months. His family doesn't come here very often."

The doctor nodded, which she only caught in her periphery. She'd stopped crying out of politeness, but she still couldn't look at him.

"He was pretty tough. I'm surprised he lasted this long with his lungs the way they were. It was just a matter of time." Iola nodded, sniffling. He made it worse by taking a plastic-wrapped package of tissue of his pocket. "Here," he offered, holding it to her.

She took the package, stole a tissue, then handed it back. "Thanks." She wiped at her eyes, then did her best to blow her nose in a dainty way.

"I'm sorry, and I swear this isn't a line, but ... do I know you?"

She frowned, then had to look at him. "No, no ... I don't think so."

She certainly hadn't met him before. She'd remember meeting a cutie-pie doctor with the biggest brown eyes she'd ever seen. And freckles. And curly dark brown hair. And a set of lines on the side of his mouth that told her he smiled big, and often. Yeah, she'd remember him.

Well look who just lost her lesbian tendencies. Then she chastised herself. She was in a hospital and had just seen someone die in front of her. How about a little perspective?

He held out his hand. "Veneratio Aubericus."

Iola must have balked as she took his hand, which made him smile as though he's heard all the jokes before. "Yeah, I know. My parents were Latin freaks. They had their name legally changed from Awbrey to Aubericus when they got married. And as for my first name ... well, people just call me Vinnie to make it easier."

Iola smiled then. "Iola Day."

He blinked, then cracked a huge smile. "You are, aren't you?"

"Sorry?"

"I mean, we listen to you in the doctor's lounge when we work nights. I ... I mean," he actually blushed right to the roots of his hair, "we love your show."

Now it was her turn to get a little red in the face.

"The nurses say you sometimes come by to visit patients that are lonely. But I haven't seen you before." He paused, and she stole a glance over at him. He caught her eye, and she just smiled innocently. "You have probably one of the prettiest names I've ever heard. Is that a real name or an on-air name?"

"It's my real name," she admitted. "My parents wanted my name to be musical. It's Welsh, I'm assuming. I never looked into it. But my grandparents moved to Canada from Wales after the war. Our last name is from that region, too. I think it was used to identify dairy farmers or something." Miss Chatty all of a sudden.

"Day? Yep, that's where it came from. And your first name means *Valued by the Lord*."

"How ... what?" Now her mouth fell open as she frowned at him.

He laughed then, showing white teeth and dimples. "Sorry, languages and names are just kind of a ... hobby for me. Probably because of the insane handle my parents bestowed on me."

"Doctor Aubericus?"

They both looked up at the nurse standing in front of them.

"Yes?"

"The body is ready to take to the morgue. You'll need to sign the death certificate."

His face fell again, and he stood up as though he'd been doing something inappropriate. "Of course, I'm on my way."

Iola stood too, and Vinnie held out his hand to help her. "I have to go," he said to her, now ignoring the nurse. "But ... would you like to ... I don't know. Grab dinner sometime or ... just have coffee?"

"Ummm ..." she was uncomfortable again, but not because she didn't like this guy. She wasn't sure what was making her that way. But damn her if he wasn't incredibly adorable. "Sure," she said before she had concretely made up her mind.

"Great. I'm off shift tomorrow night ... can I take you to Ricardo's for supper?"

"Sure." She was repeating herself too much. How about something different? "That sounds great."

"What's your phone number?"

She rattled off the seven digits without hesitation, and he just stared at her while she did it. When she asked if he was going to write it down he just smiled sheepishly.

"Sorry, I have an overactive memory." Then he repeated the numbers back to her, and she nodded, almost laughing.

"That is quite a skill."

"That's another reason I like languages. They're a challenge for me. But ... I'll make a reservation, give you a call, and pick you up around ... seven?"

"Perfect," she nearly gushed. Then he smiled, nodded farewell and continued down the hall. Just in time to snap her back to reality and bring her guilt to the forefront, the stretcher rolled by with Mister Horn's body on it, covered with a sheet, following Doctor Aubericus.

Iola jumped when she realized the nurse was still there. It was a nurse she'd seen a few times, and she'd always been nice to her. Now she was looking Iola up and down with disdain. Like something that stunk, stuck to the bottom of her shoe.

Well, that's uncalled for, Iola thought. I've always been nice to her.

Then the nurse caught her looking and shook her head, all smiles again. "Sorry, Iola. I know he liked you. You were probably the only person in the world he liked, but ... well, I'm sorry."

When she realized they were discussing Mr. Horn, Iola smiled her appreciation. "Thanks, Irene. I know he made you guys crazy but ... I don't know why he liked me. He thought I looked like his wife, sort of."

Irene looked thoughtful. "Yeah, I can see it, especially their wedding picture in there. I think you guys sort of smile the same."

Iola didn't wonder if the nurse's change in attitude towards her was genuine or not, but she didn't dwell on it, either. All the weirdness and sadness of her day had taken her to a most unusual place, somewhere she hadn't been in a long time. She ... had a date?

The Sin Eater stayed around the corner of the nurse's station as Iola walked past to the bank of elevators, and she got in one without seeing him. Her expression was hard to read. She was clearly still upset, but she looked moments away from smiling. She must have been excited.

Iola ... *Iola* ... of course he knew the name. It was an old name and he had spent many years in the United Kingdom throughout the ages. *Valued by the Lord,* in Welsh.

How ... appropriate.

He had closed his eyes while she wept openly in the hallway. He could almost taste her sorrow ... like lemongrass. It was pungent. She was hurting his chest, he felt like crying with her, and yet still, he read nothing from her mind.

Then he'd listened in when the human man was talking to her. Veneratio. What a fucking hero. The name meant honor for Christ's sake. Of course she would catch the eye of an adult Boy Scout.

At least the human wasn't emitting cloves or nutmeg or a bakery load of spices. Just ... the scent of a meadow, which was almost as bad. He was completely smitten in a real, authentic and chaste way. Hell, he was almost as pure a soul as she was. Maybe he could get into Vinnie's mind and make the guy shit his scrubs in front of her.

The Sin Eater had a strong desire to punch something, and it was an emotion he'd never felt before. He had the need to grab Iola, make love to her, somehow show she was taken. Not available. He wanted her for his own. It was irrational and yet so powerful he actually saw red for a moment.

Jealousy. That had to be it. He'd never been jealous of anyone before ... what the hell was happening to him? If he didn't know any better he'd swear he was turning into a goddamn human. To prove to himself he wasn't, he locked onto the mental signatures of the nurse at the station next to him. She was flipping through a folder, head down while she stood at the high desk.

He reached into her brain, finding the necessary triggers, making her orgasm while she stood there. No arousal, just ... *bam*.

She twitched, her cheeks flushed and she gave a little squeak, then covered her mouth. She appeared horrified with herself, and looked around to see if anyone had noticed. There was only him, and while she stared to see if he had any inkling what had just happened, he nodded his head and walked past to the elevators.

"Bless you," he said as though she had sneezed.

Charles stared down at his clothes, wondering where the hell the blood had come from. He'd been clean when he went to bed, and now ... God, this wasn't his blood. Where did it come from?

He rolled off the sofa he slept on, struggling to his feet. The sun was at a low angle coming through his window, so it was late afternoon. He'd slept all day ... but when had he gone to bed? He couldn't remember.

He shuffled into his tiny, filthy bathroom, and pulled the shower curtain back. Before he could turn the taps on, he shrieked like a woman and backed up against the far wall, hitting his elbow on the open door.

A body was lying in the shower, slumped up against the inside corners, her blonde hair matted with dried blood. Her short skirt was pushed up so he could see her one butt cheek, and her shirt was ripped down the front. He could see bite marks on her shoulder, her arm, her breast ...

Fuck. He'd done this to her. He had to look away.

He saw his own face crumple in the mirror over the sink. Why couldn't he remember this? How did he even get her here? Where'd he find her?

He took his panic out into the living/kitchen/bedroom, pacing around the few items of furniture he had. Shit, oh shit. He was in so much trouble. And that's when he noticed the huge pool of blood on the floor.

Relax.

He stopped, hands still shaking, but closing his eyes to concentrate on that voice that could always chill him right out.

Remember? You needed her, I let you have her.

He closed his eyes and jammed his thumbs into the inside corners, pushing until it hurt. It took attention away from the throbbing at his temples.

No, no ... he couldn't have done that. Who was she? He didn't even know her.

Just some woman. She was coming out of a bar, remember? She had a broken heel on her shoe, and she bent over to take them both off so she could walk better. You wanted her immediately.

He hadn't wanted her dead, surely?

You tried to kiss her. She shrunk away. She was scared of you.

Well that wouldn't be weird. Women never liked him.

It made you angry. She laughed at you.

Then the memories jolted back to him like a nightmare of lightning. Her face as she took him in upon seeing him at first. Him clumsily trying to kiss her. She jerked back, and it made him jump. When she saw she'd startled him, she actually laughed.

Yeah, he remembered that. Her sneer. That's when he noticed she had lipstick on her teeth, which were sort of yellow. And her skin was bad. But her hair was nice. He had punched her right then. Her nose has given way under his fist, and her head snapped back. She wobbled back into the alley behind her, stumbling on bare feet as blood gushed down her chin. She had been totally startled. He would have laughed, but the sight of the blood infuriated him first. It was her own fucking fault, the whole thing.

A few more shots to the face and she was out like a light. He carried her up to his apartment without anyone seeing them, using alleys and the fire escape of his building. Well, hopefully no one saw him. Actually, it would be a miracle no one saw him.

She came around while he was hefting her through the window. She hit the floor of the living room, and that's when she came to, crying. Since her nose was crushed breathing was proving to be difficult for her. She sputtered and was gasping as she wept.

But at least she was awake. It gave him strength when she fought him. He held a hand over her mouth to cover the screams, although in this building screaming of many different kinds were par for the course. As long as she was squirming he was aroused, and the longer she fought the more he liked it. She fought until she was exhausted, and that's when he fucked her, on the floor, half unconscious. Likely from blood loss, or maybe she was concussed. He'd beat her head against the floor a few times, so who knew what had knocked her out.

As usual, there was no orgasm for him. His erection withered, unfulfilled, and he was furious at his own impotence. So he strangled her with his belt, then dragged her to the shower. She was still slowly leaking blood from her head as he moved her, he remembered that, too.

You wanted her, I let you have her. It's not my fault you're a fucking pussy.

Shut up, he wanted to scream. Then he set about finding a plan to get rid of her corpse.

Chapter Seven

"I thought I'd bring you back a latte," said the new girl sunnily, putting a cup on the table behind her in the control room.

Iola smiled, tilting her head. "Aww, that's so nice. You didn't have to do that."

The new girl shrugged. "You're kind of trapped in one place at night, it's no trouble. Like I said, I was stopping there anyway."

Now what the hell is your name? Iola wondered, offering a nod of thanks. "Well, I definitely appreciate it."

The girl just waved as she left the booth, taking her own sleeved cup with her out to the hall.

Iola took a sip of the new girl's offering, happy to see it was still piping hot. She knew the new girl had just been at the scene of an apartment fire, and the fact she'd stopped anywhere on the way back to file her report was probably not a good thing. But ... as long as she brought caffeinated gifts Iola was so not going to tattle on her. And really, it was one o'clock in the morning. Who listening at this hour expected up to the minute news coverage?

"All right folks, you're still with Iola Day on KLCD Late Night. It's about time to start mellowing out for the evening, so pull someone you care about close and enjoy a little Miss Joan Baez with me."

As she brought up Joan Baez a few notches she took another sip of coffee. Man, that was hitting the spot. New Girl was becoming her favorite reporter for sure. She'd have to listen to the one-thirty news report to get her name.

Iola went back to her previous train of thought before New Girl had brought the coffee in and felt morose once again. She'd never seen anyone die before. That was ... an awful experience, no matter how serene Mister Horn had seemed at the end. She couldn't shake the sludgy, thick and incredibly sad feeling she had. She was mourning him and had barely known him.

Hit by inspiration, she got on the computer and did a search of the digital music library. She went back to the music they saved just for November 11th, and scanned through the titles, looking for one particular song. Sure it was a German song, written during the First World War, but it was perfect.

As Joan Baez trailed out, she flicked her mic to life and began the music at a low volume. "This is a bit different, but I wanted to play something for a friend of mine, a World War Two veteran of the Royal Canadian Air Force, a survivor of D-Day. He passed away today, and this song is just for him. Here's Vera Lynn."

And then she brought her head down to her arms and cried.

The Sin Eater turned his head to the top floor windows of the KLCD building, where a few lights were on, illuminating a hallway where a tiny woman was carrying a take-out cup of coffee from one door to another.

The car interior was lit by the dashboard, and he breathed out the flavored cigar smoke he'd been holding in. It smelled like chocolate, so his body's natural Pavlovian response to that was ... well, venture a guess.

Her voice was completely captivating. It was lower than the majority of female voices, and when she used it over the airwaves she dropped it even lower, almost to a femme fatale level, which was not authentic for her in actuality but it still did what it was supposed to do.

The playlist seemed strange, jumping genres and eras and tempos, all the while remaining decidedly mellow, but as long as she was in between the songs, tying it all together, it worked. He was sure half the city was probably in love with her, all based on that voice. And again, the very thought of anyone out there desiring her, lusting after her – even on the basis of her voice alone - made him furious.

He had to get a grip. And he certainly shouldn't be out here, sitting in a "borrowed" car like some kind of news-story stalker. He should be doing his goddamn job.

He put the car in gear and slowly started away from the curb, but left the radio tuned to where it was. He knew where to find the sinners in this city, and it wasn't hard to make his quota at all. Not that he had quotas, necessarily, but he liked to see how many sins he could let loose on the world in one day, always trying to better the day before.

It was the only way to job satisfaction for an employee who never had to attend staff meetings or fill out a performance report. His job type fell into that No News Is Good News category. If the Boss never asked to see you in His office, you were doing just fine.

And this Sin Eater had never seen the inside of his boss's office.

He headed for a bar in the heart of downtown, where drug deals were made and women were traded for cash by private contractors that all paid a percentage of their profit to the business owner. It was seedy, dirty, dark, and hardly resembled an actual licensed establishment.

He parked well away from the curb directly in front of the place, and noticed the scum of the earth that were huddled in the shadows eyeing up the Jag and seeing it as however many kilos of whatever substance they craved to their very core. And yet there was no trace of real evil in any of them. They were just weak, sad, and pathetic.

He turned back to them in the middle of the street, and pushed into their minds all at once like a public address system. Make sure no one steals the car, I'll pay you.

He felt their agreement, and continued into the bar with no worries about anything happening to that ride.

Inside the crowds parted to let him pass. But a flash suit and lack of BO tended to do that in places like this. He felt the women looking him over like a meal ticket, hungry in many different ways. The men were suspect, like he was a narc ... or maybe even a big dealer that no one had seen before. Their unease was a tool he could use nicely, without exhausting any of his persuasive energies. Some humans were just too easy to control.

He reached the polished wood bar as the bartender came forward eagerly, his face conveying how badly he needed good tips to pay off his child support and light heroin habit.

A light heroin habit. The Sin Eater was absolutely delighted by oxymorons.

"What can I get you?"

"Your best Scotch please. A double." He laid a fifty on the bar, and the man's eyes went wide. "In a clean glass, if you would."

The man nodded, then reached under the bar for a reserve of glasses separate from the ones behind him. The Sin Eater had been here often enough to know that no dishwashers were employed during the night.

The amber liquid put before him was bottom-shelf at best, barely above "bath tub" grade, but that was hardly the barkeep's fault. He pushed the fifty towards him, told him to "Keep it," and then carried his glass to a table in a far corner, sitting alone behind the beer bottles some other party had left behind that no one had bothered to clean up.

The Scotch was harsher than he would have liked, but he sipped it slowly and surveyed the room. There was plenty of sinning going on in the biblical sense, har dee har har, but he could find none of what he was really looking for. He could pick up a man ODing in the men's room, slumping to the floor next to the urinal, his eyes fluttering closed as his breathing became ragged.

There was a whore up against the opposite side of the wall behind him, fucking a guy while her mind was focused solely on her next hit. The man doing her had no thoughts in his head; he was close to coming and his mind hit a blissful empty state as he did so. Dumb fuck wasn't even wearing a condom.

Come out, come out, wherever you are, he thought. It was only a matter of time before he spotted someone that deserved his special attentions. The other people in this place were just making him depressed.

A half hour passed before his senses tingled, and he was brought upright in his chair. Across the room, moving amongst the people "dancing" on a square of hardwood, a woman moved along the fringe of the crowd, skulking in the shadows. She carried such a strong sense of menace he was stunned no one in the room could tell. Then again, people rarely suspect women of evil.

He downed the Scotch, set it on the table, and rose to follow her as she ducked to a back room beside a door that read "Manager."

He heard raised voices beyond the fake-wood veneer, but his mind did a much better job understanding what was going on. This woman was a complete fucking mess. Her brain was addled with drugs, and she'd gone days without sleep. Hard to sleep when you're basically trafficking children.

His blood boiled. The longer he was among humans the more he had sympathy for certain groups of people. And children were ... well, they were the original innocents, weren't they?

And maybe he was starting to blur the lines of what his actual job was. He wasn't supposed to interfere ... but fuck that. She was hurting kids.

He cut through her sad biography, abuse at the hands of a babysitter, turning to drugs, running away from home, living on the streets, turning tricks to make money, falling in with a boyfriend that had a strange appetite for young girls, helping him lure them and degrade them just so he'd tell her he loved her ...

A Sin Eater could have no pity for a sinner, and he didn't. The old man in the hospital was a light weight compared to this human trash. She was begging for a few more days to come up with some cash, she was going to come into some green soon and she'd be able to pay them back then. And in her mind, she saw the young girl she had locked in her apartment, tied to the drain under the bathroom sink. Not touched yet, ready for the highest bidder.

Shit. Now he had the urge to save someone, and that wasn't part of his job. He was not supposed to interfere –

He'd lost track of what was going on in the room behind that shut door. That is until he sensed heightened alarm, adrenaline, and fear.

A shot rang out just after he ducked, and it ripped through the flimsy wall right where he'd been standing. Using someone else's eyes came in handy when there was a wall between you and them. He saw the woman's point of view as the gun was drawn on her, and as she made to run the shot sounded.

He heard panic in the barroom, bodies scurrying, sending off their fear to a degree that he could no longer concentrate with the aid of others. He had to use his own instincts.

Another shot rang out, and a weight hit the door. The door sprang open, the woman falling out into the hall at his feet. Blood just started to drain out of her chest, and was now also trailing from the corner of her mouth. She was definitely shot in the lungs. And knowing how long it took emergency services to arrive in neighborhoods like this, she was going to die on this dirty floor. And he wasn't going to stop that, but he was going to take back what he came for.

He put a hand to her forehead, the contact helping all the distractions around him fade to background. He quickly located her sins, including the killing of a john that hadn't paid her the agreed price. That one actually surprised him; he'd assumed she was too weak to do something so bold. He lifted it out of her, setting it loose to find a new host.

It was hardest for him to allow the filth of a pedophile to linger. But whores didn't love the men they slept with, either. It was just part of what he had to do.

The office had emptied behind him, and he reached out mentally to ascertain that the man who'd shot this woman escaped through a door leading out the back of the building to his car. And though he'd just shot someone, he was still a business man, and the evil in him wasn't as rank as it was with this sad sack lying next to him.

"Your address," he demanded of the woman, patting her cheek to bring her around.

"What?"

"Your address."

"What for?" Her voice was thin.

He leaned closer, and she widened her eyes in fear of him. "I am going to get that girl out of your apartment. Before she is ruined. Now give me your address."

She knew he meant to save the girl and not rape her. The tears rose in her eyes, and she rattled off some numbers for a location he recognized. It wasn't far from here.

He left her where she lay, heading out the doors calmly now that the crowd had scattered, and just like he suspected, his car was right where he left it, untouched.

He pulled out his money clip, handed over fifty dollar bills to the crowd of ten street people that surrounded him immediately, and with the powers of his mind he sent them the sensation they craved, the loosening of the drugs' hold over them, a high that they would do anything to achieve. It was like a collective group sigh around him, and as he climbed in his car he hoped they might use the cash to buy themselves a meal or two.

Wasn't he just turning into humanitarian of the year?

"Dispatch to Car 67."

Claudia picked up the radio. "Go ahead, Dispatch."

"Anonymous tip was just called in, someone reporting a young girl being held at a downtown address. Think it might be your girl?"

Claudia felt the hope flair up in her heart, but knew better than to get too carried away. "Could be. What's the address?"

"17598, 24th Avenue North. Two patrol cars are en route now, and child services are on their way. Thought you might want the chance to be there, too."

Claudia smiled. "Thanks, Holly. That's why you're my favorite dispatcher."

A male voice came over the airwaves right then. "Thought she was your favorite dispatcher because she's got the prettiest eyes, Car 67."

Claudia laughed, then replied, "This radio is for police business, asshole."

"Roger that."

She put the mic down on its cradle, then pulled a U-turn, heading towards the north end of town, the bad part of town. It would take ten minutes to get there, but she just had to know.

Rebecca Jane Simon had disappeared yesterday, walking home from school. It was a nicer neighborhood, a good thirty-minute drive from the part of town Claudia was now headed to. A few people had seen a suspicious car around at the time, but no one caught a plate number or actually saw anything go down.

Claudia had been at the house as the parents had reported their daughter missing, and even though it had been less than 24 hours since her disappearance, Rebecca was just eight years old so they were on the lookout for her immediately. So Claudia really hoped that this was their girl, even though there were still dozens of missing kids out there that had never been found. Kids that all came from households that were still waiting for them to return.

The odds were better with this one because it was so soon ... but as for her coming back totally okay, those were odds that Claudia wasn't going to consider.

The building she was headed to stood out like a sore thumb. The street was dark, the lamp lights being broken who knows how long ago, and she couldn't blame a city crew that wasn't jumping at the chance to come down here and change a bulb. But this three-floor tenement was lit up like Christmas by red and blue lights.

She parked across the driveway behind another patrol car. She recognized the Constable that approached her. Trevor Vance was a good guy with a pregnant wife, and he never gave two shits whether she liked men or women. He was always business and never razzed anyone about anything.

"It's her," he said, skipping the small talk and greeting. "It's Rebecca, we got her."

Claudia closed her eyes, putting her hand to her forehead. "Thank God. Is she ... is she okay?"

"They're letting a psychologist talk to her before they take her out of the apartment. The lights and all these people might scare her. Do you ... do you want to be in the room?"

Claudia nodded immediately, and he led the way for her into the building. The psychologist was talking to Rebecca on the sofa in the filthy living room, and other patrol officers were taking pictures of the bathroom where she'd apparently been handcuffed to the sink drain. Claudia felt like screaming. She had to find out whoever had taken this girl and locked her up like this and make mulch out of their balls.

Rebecca was quite thin, just starting to grow taller than the boys in her class. Her long hair was a dark auburn-brown, and her brown eyes were wide with fear. But there was also ... relief. She was glad to see the police, she was glad to be going home.

Claudia exhaled one long breath. She knew what that meant. She'd seen it before. Rebecca hadn't been ... messed with. She was going to be fine.

Claudia wanted to slump to the floor and cry. Her rage melted, and she just wanted to weep with joy. She couldn't imagine how much better the girl's parents would feel to find out that very fact.

The psychologist must have said something funny, because the girl even gave a little laugh. Then she looked over at Claudia, and smiled.

Claudia gave a little wave, then came over. "Hi, Rebecca." She said, nodding to the psychologist. The shrink gave her a look that said Don't push her, but Claudia could have told her to go fly a kite. This is one place where she always felt she knew what she was doing.

"Hi," Rebecca said, her leg swinging against the side of the sofa. "I know you. I saw you on TV. You were with my parents."

Claudia smiled. "I was. We've been looking for you."

"I know. That's why I was never really scared. I knew the police would find me."

Claudia felt tears sting the corners of her eyes. Truth was they wouldn't have found her without the anonymous tip. She smiled, even laughed. "Well, we sure wanted to find you, honey."

"Don't cry," Rebecca said, touching her arm. "I'm not sad at all. They gave me McDonald's and let me stay up late to watch TV."

Chapter Eight

A knock on the door brought the Sin Eater out of the bathroom of his hotel suite in a robe, and he opened the door completely confident that the person on the other side wouldn't care that he wasn't dressed. And he was right.

At the sight of him, the human woman inhaled so deeply her nostrils flared. She radiated the cayenne pepper smell of her anger, but it dissipated immediately. Her eyes trailed over his chest, the bare skin that wasn't covered by the terry cloth. Cayenne pepper became hot chocolate.

"Portia," he greeted her, shutting the door behind her as she stalked past him. Well, if she was going to play angry that was her prerogative.

"You took my fucking car," she snapped, weight on one foot as she crossed her arms and glared at him, doing a terrible job of faking annoyance.

"I needed it. You said if I ever needed anything ..."

"And where the hell have you been? I haven't heard from you in days and when you do show up it's at my house when you know very damn well I'm at work and you take my fucking car."

"Let me get you a drink." He knew it pissed her off how he stayed so calm, because he genuinely didn't give a shit if he pissed her off or not. And no matter how mad she was right then eventually she was still going to end up underneath him.

"I don't want a fucking drink. I want an explanation."

"I don't have to explain anything to you," he said, pouring cognac into a highball glass for her. It pained him, but otherwise he would have had to call the front desk for a proper brandy glass. "You said whenever I need a favor, just to help myself."

She took the glass angrily. "I never said 'help yourself,' I said 'just ask.' Asshole." Then she downed the two fingers in her glass in one swig.

He smiled fondly at her. "My mistake. The keys are right there. On the dresser."

She handed her glass to him, demanding more. "Is that ... is it L'Art?"

"I couldn't find any Jessen Arcana, so Martell will have to do."

"Paid for with my money, no doubt?"

Like it mattered. The money she made couldn't be spent faster than she acquired it. He was so glad he'd found her. She was a benefactor of sorts, but of course she had no idea what she was sponsoring. Just a ridiculously extravagant lifestyle for a man whose real name she didn't even know.

"I'm sharing, aren't I?" He took a sip from his own glass then lowered himself down on to the sofa. He avoided her gaze, but he knew her eyes were trolling over him. Without a single effort from him he knew he had total control of her due completely to her physical attraction to him. The control was what he liked most in this arrangement, maybe even more than the money. "Besides, isn't it your birthday next week? Thought you might like something special when you stopped by."

She softened, and he could have grinned like Alice's Cheshire Cat. But he didn't, he locked his eyes to her and took another sip, holding her spellbound.

She worked with nothing but men, men in flashy suits who ran big corporations just like her. She dressed manly to fit in, smoked cigars with them and drank cognac like a pro. And yet she was never getting the key to the boys' club, and on the other hand, women didn't trust her either. At least here, with him, she knew what her role was. She was a woman with him. The fact that he was the only one who knew her this way was another part of the attraction. In fact, it was making him hard as he thought about it.

She put down her drink and took off her blazer with angry, jerky movements, but he knew this was still just for show. She was braless under the jacket, and he knew that she felt because her breasts were very small a bra was over kill. The sheen of her blouse showed that her nipples were hard. She grabbed the glass again, taking another swig, but not sitting down. She paced instead. He admired her long legs as they worked her across the floor under her trousers, her dark, short-cut hair shining under the hotel's dimmed lights. She was long, lean, very thin, with a small high butt as well. He liked the butt view the best.

Anyone else would have felt like a real bastard for taking advantage of her like this ... but the difference was this bastard knew she liked it. She didn't want a husband, didn't want to be married with kids and a house in the suburbs and all the rest that came with it. Her drive was to be successful, and she achieved it. She was not going to be sharing that with anyone, she did it on her own. Plus, having a man under her thumb pleased her to no end.

She was still a woman, though, and she still liked sex.

Portia was never up-front about it, never asked or begged for it, never made the first move, but the Sin Eater knew when she was ready and when she wasn't.

She was ready.

He set his glass down, stalking over to her slowly. He took the glass from her hand, and she snarled at him, "I'm not done with that."

He handed it back with a rueful smile. She downed the rest of the liquid, then gave him her glass, which he set loudly on the coffee table. She started to unbutton her blouse, and he let his smile widen. "I thought you were angry."

"Shut up." She let her shirt hang open and pulled the tie from his robe, then pushed it off his shoulders to the floor. She took a deep breath as she took him in, her nails cutting down his collar bone and across his chest.

"Tell me what to do," he mumbled low. It made her shudder.

"You know what to do."

"Nuh uh. You tell me. Say it."

"Kiss me." He had her pulled against him in an instant, hands under her blouse, across her thin back, the front halves parting to let her breasts press into his chest. As her skin made contact to the metal pendant around his throat, she gasped a bit, and he figured it was cold. Her nipples further confirmed it.

He let one hand fall to her butt, and she rolled her hips upward to give him a better grip, in doing so rubbing right against his erection. Yep, that was about enough foreplay.

He pushed her on to the bed, and as she crawled up to grab the top of the comforter he grabbed her by the hips, holding her down at the foot of the bed with him. He reached around front to undo her pants, then pulled them off her legs, along with her panties. She struggled to get out of his grasp, but it was feeble at best. And she was so much stronger than that attempt.

With her knees on the mattress he yanked her hips upwards, getting her up on all fours before plunging into her without any more preparation. She was wet, warm, and she cried out as he did it. He ran his hands along her hips and ass, loving the way each part curved into the next, even though she was so thin and angular. It didn't matter, like this she was soft and rounded and female.

But the thing he liked most? He didn't have to pull any of his mind tricks to get her like this. It was all pretty standard, human, sexual power-play bullshit. And she was totally willing to be a part of it. For once, the man was the whore.

"I'm sorry I took your car," he growled, pulling out and pausing.

She choked on a whimper. "Keep it," she gasped, then he drove his arousal home again as a reward. She was panting as she repeated, "Oh God, just keep it."

Iola slept until noon, got up and began a ridiculous flurry of activity that would likely rival most brides on their wedding day. She took a nice long bath, deep conditioned her hair and shaved her legs. After a moment's hesitation she also did a bikini home-wax.

Well, who knew?

She put her hair in rollers while it was still damp, and then as she ate she read the newspaper. Turns out a little girl that was missing for an entire day was found safe and sound and returned to her family overnight. It made Iola think of Claudia, and how happy she must be.

That done, she painted her finger and toenails a bright red. She had a black wrap-around dress she intended to wear, then began to stress that maybe that was too formal for Ricardo's.

She'd never been there. Actually, she had no idea where Ricardo's even was.

And who the hell could she even ask?

She darted across the hall in shorts and a T-shirt, knocking on Claudia's door. She hadn't seen her neighbor since that weird kissing moment, but she was sure their friendship was strong enough to not make this weird.

Fingers crossed.

When Iola was about to knock a second time, the door opened inward and Claudia stood before her, in flannel pants and braless under a tank top.

Iola forced herself to not notice that Claudia's breasts were absolutely perfect. Flawless. Guaranteed winner in any wet T-shirt contest.

"Iola? What's up?" She covered her mouth as she yawned. "Come in." She left the door open and went back inside, flopping down on her couch. Iola closed the door behind her.

"Were you still sleeping?"

"Late night."

"Oh, I'm sorry Claudia. I'll come back."

"Just come sit. I'm up. What's doing?" Claudia patted the sofa, but Iola stayed by the door.

"Do you know a restaurant called Ricardo's? Is it a really nice place?"

Claudia frowned. "Ricardo's? You're going to Ricardo's?"

"Claudia, is it a formal place?"

She shrugged. "Yeah, it's pretty fancy. You're going to Ricardo's? Like, tonight?"

Iola sat next to her, one leg drawn up underneath her. "I have a date tonight."

Claudia raised her eyebrows. "When did that happen?"

"I met this guy yesterday, and he asked me out."

"For tonight? That's quick. Never mind that it's Monday."

"Well, he's a doctor and he wasn't shifted to work tonight. So he asked."

Claudia threw her head back and laughed. "Oh hell, Iola. A doctor?"

"Shut up!"

"Oh my God, tell me about him. Is he cute?"

Iola smiled shyly. "Oh Claudia, he's adorable. He's got curly hair and brown eyes and ... he's so cute. And he seems really nice."

"What's his name?"

"Veneratio Aubericus." She hoped she was remembering how to say it all correctly.

"What the hell kind of name is that?"

"Latin. And he's smart, you know how you can just tell when they're smart or not?"

Claudia nodded slowly, her tongue in her cheek as she was grading Iola's reaction to the very thought of this doctor. "Well check you out. You're excited."

Iola blushed and looked down at her foot on the sofa. "I am. The more I think about it, the more excited I get."

"I admit, I'll be checking him out through the peephole when he comes to get you. I'll do a background check on him, too."

"Claudia, that's not necessary, it's just dinner."

"Mmm hmm. And you've got your hair up in rollers, nails all painted, legs all shaved up just to go out for dinner."

Iola had to giggle. "Okay, I did all that ... but it's just, you know, in case."

"So's a background check. But you better write that name down for me. That's far too many letters."

They both giggled over that, then Claudia stopped, pushing her hair over her shoulder and assuming the look of someone wanting to start a Serious Conversation. "Look, Iola, about the other night - "

"I don't want you to apologize." Claudia looked up at her, surprised. "I mean it. Or, I'm not sure if that's what you were about to do or not. But I don't want you to. It's fine. I don't feel taken advantage of. And Claudia, I really did kiss you, right? And you stopped it all. So ... what's there to apologize about?"

Claudia bit her lip. "I know. And I just ... I care about you, you're my only real friend - "

"I feel the same. So let's not make it weird and wreck our friendship just because I can't hold my beer."

Claudia made a sudden face of almost comical alarm. "Maybe you better not have anything to drink tonight. I'm just saying."

"Already thought of that. And yes, Mom, I'm taking cab fare with me."

Claudia was serious again. "Thanks, Iola. Just ... for everything. I just think you're awesome. And I value our friendship."

Iola gave her a hug of appropriate length, then got up. "Wanna see what I'm going to wear? I want your honest opinion."

"Sure. Let's go."

"I want to know if I look hot in it or just ... skanky."

"Trust me, that I will tell you, and I'm pretty accurate about this kind of thing."

The Sin Eater wanted to be at the apartment when Doctor Love showed up to pick up Iola. Luckily, Portia usually had no interest in staying past their exchange of goods and services so she was already gone when he'd gotten out of the shower the night before. She'd left him a note saying, "I changed my mind, I'm taking the car back."

He'd laughed when he read that. Like he needed her car. He could just buy one with her cash anyway. Which, of course, he did.

Now, the next day, as he stood on the sidewalk outside the building, he paced. Dammit, he was too early. That schmuck wouldn't be here for another hour and a half. What was with all this urgency?

He hoped to see her, of course. Just her, on her own, not gazing up at someone else with girlish adoration. He couldn't take that.

And yes, hypocrisy was something he excelled at.

By some miracle of miracles, the front door of the building opened and she stepped out into the dying sunlight of the evening, her hair arranged in gorgeous waves that fell just past her shoulders, looking a bit much for the jeans and T-shirt she wore. A tall, attractive woman was with her, and he recognized her as the woman that was in the apartment the other night, the one he used to kiss Iola, just to see what it was like.

They headed towards him, crossing the street at an angle, and he turned into the shadows to avoid being seen, ducking behind the alley's dumpster. They were talking quickly as they passed.

"I never usually wear mascara, Claudia."

"I know, but let's get sexy, all right? Ricardo's is very romantic, you should look like you fit in there."

The drug store, he'd spotted it on his way over. It was right on the corner.

"And while we're there, pick up a few rubbers."

"Absolutely not!"

"Better safe than sorry."

"No! And what if I'm just tempted to use them then?"

They were in the drugstore, and he punched the brick wall, feeling the bones in the back of his hand snap as they made impact. He swallowed a curse, jammed a few of the broken bones in place where they'd knit back together properly, then flexed his hand. As he watched, all was restored.

Chapter Nine

"This one's really good. And here's a great blush color for you."

Who knew a lesbian friend would be helpful picking out makeup?

Iola took everything Claudia handed to her. Blush, eye liner, mascara, lip stick, eye shadow. She was wondering if asking Claudia to help would be awkward, now she found it overwhelming.

"And I'm serious. Get some condoms."

"What makes you think I don't have any already? You know, kept around for spontaneous situations?"

Claudia looked skeptical. "Do you?"

Iola shrugged. "No."

"Come with me."

It wasn't embarrassing picking out condoms; it was embarrassing to buy them, especially since the drug store had shifted an 18-year-old stoner to work the cash register that day. He scanned the box last, looking up at her and nodding. "Excellent choice," he said quietly, leaning forward ever so slightly.

"Thanks," she said wryly, handing him her debit card.

Everything was stashed in a bag, and they made their way to the door and out on to the street again. She was turning to ask Claudia a question when she ran headlong into a man on the street, on his way into the store.

Hands caught her by the arms, steadying her.

"I'm so sorry," she was saying, and she looked up and up ... into pale lavender eyes.

The man from the subway.

She must have looked surprised, and he looked just as shocked as she was. "I'm ... I'm sorry," he insisted, tucking his tie into place under his jacket. "I keep meeting you by accident."

That strange yet incredibly sexy accent suited him so perfectly. Iola had to blink to get herself to respond. "Yeah, I'm ... a klutz."

Claudia was standing to the side, looking back and forth between them. It wouldn't be surprising if she was getting a tan from the heat Iola was throwing off instantly, just at the very sight of him.

"You rushed off so quickly in the subway yesterday, I didn't get a chance to introduce myself. I am Damien, Damien Talon." He took her shaking hand, kissing the back of it. The touch of his lips made her heart flutter in a totally ridiculous manner. His large hand was so warm. She didn't want him to let go of her. But of course he did.

"Iola," she returned. "Iola Day. You remember me from yesterday?"

His chuckle rumbled in his chest, and she felt it vibrate through her entire body. Especially the parts that were already extra sensitive. "I do," he admitted. "I thought I might have scared you."

She couldn't tear her attention from his eyes. "No, no. You didn't scare me. I was ... I was running late. I had to go."

"I see. And your stunning friend is ..?" He held a hand out to Claudia, and to Iola's shock Claudia took his hand. At his touch, Claudia's lips parted, and she look a breath so her voice sounded too whispery to really be coming from Claudia.

"Claudia Bauer," her friend said.

Well, holy shit. Apparently the reaction wasn't just happening to her.

"So nice you meet you both. I don't want to keep you." He looked down at the bag she held, and Iola wished the plastic wasn't so see-through, because Damien raised his eyebrows then gave her a brilliant smile. "I unfortunately seem to run into you when you're in a hurry."

"Iola's getting ready for a date," Claudia offered.

He smiled at Claudia, then turned it back to Iola. "What a lucky man. I'll let you ladies continue on your way."

"Right." Iola said, lost on the way his lips were moving.

He stepped around them and went into the drugstore. A sleek black Beamer sat at the curb, and Claudia let out a low whistle. "Holy shit, the X6-M. That would be fun to drive."

Iola looked at her friend, confused. After the reaction Claudia had to that stranger, now … let's discuss the car?

"Did you see that guy?"

Claudia looked to her, frowning. "Yeah, I saw how he was looking at you and how you were looking at him." Then her tone went teasing. "Didn't take long for you to forget the good doctor, did it?"

Iola was totally confused. Had Claudia totally forgotten how she'd been staring at him like a chocolate soufflé? Apparently she had a case of amnesia.

"Let's go back. I have to finish getting ready."

"Okay."

They crossed the street once a van drove by, and headed back up to Iola's apartment. Claudia had assured her that the dress was perfect, and she was lending her a long, chunky gold chain to wear with it. And she'd volunteered to do Iola's makeup.

Iola was glad Claudia was taking this all so well, and that the kiss the other night was no longer bothering her. She was really helping her relax … and after seeing that stranger, Damien, again … she needed the help relaxing.

"You know what?" She decided as they entered her apartment and she tossed the grocery bag onto the counter of the kitchen.

"What?"

"I think I'd like a glass of wine."

"You sure you want to do that?"

"I've had lunch. I should be fine."

"Well," Claudia said, cracking the fridge open, "let's get to it then."

Charles was jittery, more jittery than usual. He'd changed his clothes, but he still felt like everyone was staring at him because he was covered in blood.

He couldn't go back to his apartment; he had no idea where the hell he was going to go now. Maybe if he went back after dark he could find a way to get rid of her … as long as no one got in there before then. But he wanted to distance himself from it during the daytime.

He was pacing up and down a street in the downtown core, people giving him a wide berth, and hopefully that was just because of his twitching. He kept checking his fingernails to make sure he'd gotten all the blood out from under them.

Maybe he should cut her up and throw her out in the trash. Wouldn't draw so much attention to himself. He's just taking out the garbage.

But could he do that? Cut her up in smaller pieces?

Probably not. He wasn't that tough in most instances. The only time his stomach manned up was when the other voice took over.

He was well and truly fucked.

Before long his mindless meandering took him to the block where that lesbian woman lived; next to the woman that first caught his attention on the subway. That's right ... he meant to come here before, but got distracted. That woman was supposed to be the next one he did in. Well, he still had time, right?

He stood, looking down at his reflection in the glossy paint of a sharp black sports car. He looked crazy, even to his own muddled eyes. He needed to pull it together or someone was going to call the cops on him, just for looking so damn wild.

A male throat was cleared behind him, and he spun around quickly, ready to be hit. The man was well-dressed and was just saying "May I help you?" when he froze. And Charles froze, too.

He felt ... immediate and irrational fear. Dread. He wanted to crawl into a hole and hide. And yet he had a connection with the man, like he was staring at the inevitable.

This man in the nice suit was totally evil. He was a danger to Charles, how Charles knew this, he had no idea. But he knew it.

He swallowed, and shook his head, backing away. He most certainly did not need help from this man. He had no idea what the man meant to do with him, but he didn't want to hang around and find out. And when he felt the pressure on his mind, pressing on it, trying to dig into it, pull something from it, his instinct was to turn and run. He yanked his mind back to himself, and took off at a dead sprint, cutting through the crowd of people that were just starting to mill about, finding somewhere to eat supper.

And he never looked back to see if he was being chased.

The Sin Eater was rooted in one spot, not sure he'd seen what he thought he might have. The man had recognized him, maybe not necessarily for what he was, but more from a sense that he was a threat to him. And the Sin Eater sure recognized him from the subway.

When the Sin Eater had reached out to take a taste of what this evil vessel possessed, the man had felt it. And he hid it all from him.

Plus, the man had a touch of mental illness. The Sin Eater hated pulling the sins from the mentally ill, it was unpredictable. Trying to use the sinner's point of view to find the memories was paramount, but when that person wasn't sure what was real and what wasn't, it all got muddled and confused. The few times he'd done it before had left him almost ill, probably what humans felt when they had a severe flu. And he was weak, unable to use the abilities he depended on daily. He felt ridiculously vulnerable the entire time. He tried to avoid the trouble whenever possible. Even now as he'd just touched the surface, he felt a slight wave of nausea. He had to close his eyes to let it roll past.

That's why he let the man run away and didn't give chase. He'd try to protect Iola if he could from the man, because obviously she had caught his eye. But he was not going to attempt to consume his sins. Not yet, anyway. He had to be sharp, especially if this guy really had it in for the object of the Sin Eater's current obsession.

But why did he have to save her if she needed him? That wasn't in his nature. The only thing he should ever want from humans was to devour their foul tendencies and have sex with them. Well, he wasn't sure if the drive for sex was par for the course, but that's pretty much the only other thing he had to amuse himself with.

Although, from what he could remember from when there were many more just like him wandering around, every single one of them had the same obsession with sex that he had. They'd nail anything that had a pulse.

Maybe the reason was obvious. On their Other Side , there was no sexual function necessary. There was no creation. So ... no sex. And when they were assigned to this world with a functioning human body, with no consequences for their actions, and add in the fact that most humans were inexplicably attracted to them ... well, just guess what might happen.

But that didn't explain why he had this protective instinct towards a human female. Looking down at his hand, he frowned at a reddish spot that marred the inside of his palm. He couldn't remember burning himself, but ... as he watched, it cleared away, leaving him unblemished as before.

That was odd. And the crazy person aside, he had to get Iola alone and figure out what there was to her that held him in check like this.

Blackness ... utter blackness. He tried to blink it away, like trying to clear motor oil from his eyes. But it wouldn't budge for all his efforts. What the hell?

He'd dozed off on his sofa, and even though he knew his eyes were open, he still couldn't see. He was vaguely aware of the slant of the sun coming through the patio doors off the living room. But he still couldn't see.

He stumbled to his feet, irritation making him quite pissy. He stubbed his toe on the coffee table, swore loudly, his anger and frustration building in his head, pushing down his neck. Fuck, he wanted to kill something. But first, he had to get this shit out of his eyes.

He leaned over the bathroom sink, managing to get down the hall and to the bathroom door without hurting himself further. He cranked both taps on, scooping the water up into his face, rubbing his eyes furiously. They burned like crazy, and he might be blinding himself, but what was the difference? He was blind now.

Through his watery blinking, the black was diluting, and he could make out the sink, the water, and his hands.

Oh, thank God, he breathed, wanting to weep in relief. Then he looked at his hands.

They were coated in a deep, inky almost black residue. Well, not quite black. It was the deepest red he'd ever seen. It was washing off, but it had the consistency of sap. He used the soap from the pump bottle on the counter, and it came off with that. Then he looked up into the mirror.

His eyes were rimmed with the stuff. It was now running down his face, mingling with the water. As he blinked, more of it got pushed out of the way. He kept washing his eyes out with the water, until all the crap was gone. Then he looked to see if he was actually bleeding from somewhere.

As his panic subsided he noticed the smell. It was like ... garbage. Rotting meat and vegetation. Rotten eggs. All at once.

He made a face, then took off his clothes and turned on the shower. Immediately as his underwear hit the floor, he felt pain shoot through his penis, and he looked down in shock. It was rock-hard, even though he wasn't sure what had happened to make it that way. It hurt, his balls hurt, and he had to wince at the movement of it as he climbed into the shower over the edge of the tub. The world's worst case of blue balls ever.

He washed his hair, ran soap all over himself, and knew the stink was going away. He felt better, himself again. But what the hell was doing down below?

It wasn't going away on its own, so he palmed himself and went to work relieving his arousal. It didn't take long, and when he came he nearly cracked his neck, jolting his head back violently. He stopped breathing for a good fifteen seconds.

Holy shit, he was actually seeing stars. Christ, had it ever felt that good before?

His body relaxed, he released his hand and raised it to the spray to wash it off, his erection subsiding and falling back downward almost like it was sighing. But when he looked down at his hands, under the spray of the water, his heart stopped.

He tried to rear back from his own hand, but of course the thing came with him. He fell over the edge of the tub, ripping the shower curtain off its rings in a series of popping pings. He hit the ground hard, knocking the wind out of himself. He was lucky he didn't crack his head on the edge of the toilet or the countertop or both.

He was still staring down at his hand, at what he'd just come all over himself with. He wanted to scream, shout; he felt like he might actually be dying.

Red? Why the fuck was it red?

Chapter Ten

When the knock sounded at her door, Iola felt her heart race just a bit. She knew it was time for Vinnie to pick her up, but part of her was worried it might be that other source of excitement in her life. She had a wild notion of Damien following them upstairs, waiting for Claudia to leave her alone, then coming to her door, sweeping her off her feet and carrying her to her bed.

Ridiculous. Completely ridiculous, and yet it made her feel warm all over.

She opened the door, and at the sight of her Veneratio Aubericus smiled widely, the corners of his eyes crinkling. "Iola," he said, his voice cracking on her name. "You look … gorgeous."

She ducked her head down as though she was wondering what he could possibly be talking about. "Oh … thank you."

Then she checked him out. He was freshly shaven and wearing a dark gray suit with a light blue tie that made him look almost devastatingly handsome. "You look great."

He shrugged, then handed her a paper cone taped at one end. She popped the tape off and looked inside, smiling. Purple tulips.

"You didn't have to do that." She backed away from the door. "Come in, I'll put these in some water."

He followed her into her little kitchen, and she found an old-fashioned milk bottle under the sink. She trimmed the stems and filled the vase with water, watching him check out her small but clean apartment.

"This is nice," he said, sounding surprised.

She laughed. "I know this isn't a great part of town, but this block is nicer than most. And we all recognize each other, so it's kind of like a downtown scary-block Neighborhood Watch."

He laughed, too as she put the flowers in the vase. "I didn't mean this area was seedy. But I was surprised to find out where you live, and that you live alone."

She shrugged then put the flowers in the middle of her two-person dining table. "I have a good friend across the hall, she's a cop. I feel pretty safe."

He offered her his arm. "Shall we?"

She hooked her arm through his with a shy smile and they made for the door. As she opened it, getting her key ready to throw the dead bolt behind them, Claudia's door opened and she stepped into the hall too, ready for work in her uniform.

Iola made introductions, and was pleased that Vinnie didn't seem totally bowled over by how gorgeous Claudia was. It had happened to her once before. As they started down the stairs Claudia went back into her apartment, claiming she'd forgotten something. Iola knew she wanted to let them leave on their own.

On the street he opened the passenger-side car door for her, instant gold star there. She settled into the leather seats of his Audi without wanting to look too impressed. The car was somewhat compact, and she had to tilt her legs to the side. They were tilted in his direction; she'd done that without realizing it.

He got behind the wheel, turning the engine over. As he did so he smiled over at her, and his eyes also dropped down to take in the V-neck of her dress and her legs folded up in front of her.

The fact that he was such a gentleman helped the look not feel like a leer at all. The fact that he found her that attractive was ... more than flattering. He was just appreciating the view, and he gave her another sweet smile as he put on his seatbelt.

"I hope you like Italian," he said as he pulled away from the curb. "Have you been to Ricardo's before?"

"No, never." She didn't want to add on that it was a bit above her pay scale.

After a moment she realized his car radio was on KLCD. She glanced over at him nervously, hoping that her scrutiny was casual enough. He didn't seem like a stalker. He wasn't throwing off any creepy vibes whatsoever. But the radio station made her put up a bit of a guard, no more than what was prudent.

Then she watched his hands as they gripped the wheel, the right hand dropping down to shift from time to time. His hands were gorgeous. He could model watches, she realized. The skin was unmarked, not a mole or freckle to be seen, the palms wide but long, his veins popping up on the backs. And his fingers were elegant, beautiful. The hands of a piano player or a sculptor. She couldn't stop looking at them.

He caught her looking. She blushed when she realized he'd noticed, and she turned her attentions out the window, pretending she hadn't seen how he smiled, pleased. Yep, they were definitely taking note of each other physically.

At Ricardo's they pulled up to a valet station, and her door was opened by a uniformed attendant. She took his gloved hand as she climbed out, then stood to the side while Vinnie handed another attendant the keys. The Audi was whisked away, and Vinnie took her arm again and led the way into the darkened dining room.

"Doctor Vinnie!" A large man greeted them almost immediately, coming forward and kissing Vinnie on both cheeks. Her date seemed mildly embarrassed by the display, but returned the greeting.

"Ricardo ... how are you feeling?"

The man was an Italian caricature, made up of circles with a bald head and white Chef Boyardee moustache. He wore a nice suit, and on the whole he kind of looked like a super-friendly gangster. Like, if Sesame Street wanted to teach kids about the mob, they would cast this guy as a character. But she was sure it helped the reputation of the restaurant having him greet people like this.

"You know, the stomach, she still bothers me. But nothing like before. I'm getting better."

"I'm glad to hear it."

Ricardo turned his attention to her, putting a hand to his heart. "Bella," he greeted her, taking her hand and bowing low to kiss the back. "It's so nice to see the doctor with a beautiful woman. We were starting to worry about him, always working. But come, come. I've got your table ready."

He motioned for them to follow, and Iola had to smile at Vinnie as he shrugged in apology. "We operated on him once, not a topic for dinner, but ever since then he's been my best pal," Vinnie explained, putting a hand to her lower back and leading her through the room.

Their table was next to a natural gas fireplace, set for two with a bottle of champagne already waiting in an ice bucket on a stand. Iola was trying not to be impressed, but of course she noted that the champagne was Perrier-Jouët. Not only was he brilliant, he was so beyond her tax bracket it was making her nervous as hell.

The waiter popped the cork and poured their first glass, presenting them with their menus and then left them to decide on what they were going to eat.

Iola had wanted to pay for her own meal, even more so now. The price of everything was making her feel obligated to put out. Looking at Vinnie, she knew that was ridiculous but that's how she was feeling. As she took in the menu she felt like passing out. Jesus, a hundred dollars for filet mignon?

The salads weren't much better, but that was about as high as she could go. And didn't girls order salad on dates? Wasn't that the girly thing to do?

Vinnie had put his menu down and was just beaming across the table at her. She decided on some odd salad that included artichokes and salmon, then put her menu down as well, flushing under the attention he was showering on her. He held up his champagne flute, so she did the same.

"Iola," he said slowly, as though he loved the sound of her name and didn't want to rush it. "I am so glad I met you. Thanks for having dinner with me."

Iola smiled, turning a deeper red, no doubt. "Thank you for trying to save Mister Horn. Thank you for showing me that you were concerned for him, too. And thanks for asking me out."

As he took a sip from his glass his Adam's apple bobbed, and she caught sight of the corded muscles in his neck. That's when she decided that even a meal at McDonald's could have had put her at risk of putting out at the end of the night.

Claudia turned away from the mangled body in front of her, walking away from the dumpster and covering her mouth. Someone had attempted to dismember the blonde woman, and maybe they'd been interrupted or lost their nerve. They had, however, managed to kill a person and leave them out like garbage, hanging half-in, half out of a trash receptacle.

She'd been out in the sun on a very warm day, too.

Claudia's blood was hot and her hands kept clenching into fists without any directions from her. The woman had also been raped, that much was obvious, but the autopsy would outline everything else.

While they waited for homicide, the other officers were standing at the mouth of the alley, blocking traffic, telling curious passers-by to keep on walking, and discussing the NHL play-offs. Claudia was not part of that discussion; she couldn't be in this situation. They seemed to know that, and respected it. All she could think about was the blood.

She wanted the guy that had done this in front of her, right at this moment. And she wanted him unarmed. All she wanted in her hands was her baton. That would be all she needed, judging by her fury.

Across the street a crowd was gathering anyway, it was just human nature. They were discussing, whispering, pontificating on what could be happening in that alley. She scanned the faces, looking for someone that was more than curious. Someone that might actually get off on seeing the havoc he'd created. Or checking to see if the police had a lead on what had happened.

Bingo. On the far edge. A guy in ill-fitting clothes, thin as a rail, his face pock-marked with scabs. He kept looking around him, scratching at his head, his eyes, the side of his nose. Twitchy as all get-out. Maybe mentally ill, but definitely feeling the pressure of guilt and paranoia.

Claudia motioned another uniform over. "Check the guy in the black sweater, gray pants. A little warm for a sweater today."

Constable Dawson made a show of looking behind himself into the alley. "Far left side?" he asked for confirmation. "Itching like he's got fleas? I just clocked him when you motioned me over."

"Wanna head over?"

They crossed the street together, trying to be all casual, but they were definitely headed in the direction of this suspicious character. As he noticed them, he turned and started walking, too fast to be casually deciding to move on.

"Excuse me, sir?" Claudia called out, and that's when he bolted.

Claudia hit fifth gear right off the bat, adrenaline kicking her into high speed. She heard Dawson pounding the pavement behind her, calling for more assistance. But Claudia could run faster than both of these men.

The little worm ahead of her kept checking for her over his shoulder, and she was praying he was dumb enough to keep checking until he tripped and hurled head-first into a brick wall. And he did.

He took one corner into another through-and-through alleyway, and as he did so he looked to see where she was, stepped on the only unbroken beer bottle in the entire alley and sprawled backwards, his feet up above him as he landed hard on his back. It was like she had the help of the Three Stooges or something.

She planted herself on him, knees on his chest as he fought to regain the breath he'd knocked out of himself. Her efforts didn't help and he groaned in protest. She grabbed an arm, reaching to the back of her belt for handcuffs. "What's your name?" She asked, breathing heavy. "You got warrants or something? Why'd you run?"

The scrawny fucker totally shocked her by socking her in the jaw. Where he got the strength she had no idea, and it stunned her enough that he pushed her off of him and got to his feet again.

He kicked her in the jaw, and that's when she saw stars. She was completely disoriented, knowing she had to get up and stop him, because he was going to kill her. She didn't know how she knew that, but now he was kicking her again, in the ribs this time, and she had to get moving.

There was blood in her mouth. That scared her into action.

"Fucking bitch," he was snarling. "Who the fuck do you think you are, cunt?"

Very original, she thought wryly as she rolled to her side and pushed herself to her feet. Her head stayed focused with her, so that was good. As she convinced herself she wasn't that hurt she felt a bit better. When he swung another fist at her she blocked it, driving a good left into his kidney. He grunted, but it also made him angry.

Just as he pushed off of her and made to punch her again, a form was suddenly flying at him, tackling him from the side. The both of them hit the ground in front of her. Dawson she thought absently, unhooking the cuffs from her belt successfully this time and falling to her knees next to the two struggling figures. She grabbed one of the man's wrists, snapped a cuff on it, then wrenched the other arm behind him as well, eliciting a loud cry. Like she gave a shit if his arm came right off. She'd use it to beat him into the ground.

"Bauer? You okay?"

She looked up in confusion; Dawson was in the mouth of the alley, huffing like he hadn't had any exercise in decades.

She looked to see who had helped her, just as a tall man in an awfully nice but now dirtied suit got to his feet. He dusted himself off then offered her his hand, helping her stand as she took it. "Nice to see you again, Claudia."

She fish-mouthed a bit, not sure what to make of him. "Nice to see you, Damien, was it?"

The man from the drug store bowed his head in acknowledgement, releasing her hand and turned to Dawson. "I happened to see them run in here, and when it appeared this piece of shit had the upper hand I'm sorry, but I had to at least assist. Although, Sergeant Bauer seems more than capable of handling herself." And his voice showed how impressed he was.

Dawson was still suspicious, but he nodded. "She's pretty tough, but again, thanks for your assistance Mister ..."

"Talon." Damien shook his hand. "As long as you've got the guy."

Claudia was trying to concentrate on everything being said, but Damien's voice was like a warm breeze on bare skin. What kind of accent was that? It was thick and masculine, not Russian but sort of like that. More guttural, like German. But not that either.

The man on the ground started cursing at her again, so she yanked him to his feet and handed him off to Dawson like a load of laundry.

"Shut up," Dawson advised him. "Don't start spilling until we've got you in an interrogation room."

The other officers also arrived, and the man was herded to a patrol car that had been dispatched to the alley. As they all left,

Constable Vance from the other night looked at Claudia, shaking his head. "Go home, Sergeant," he advised.

"Note that you addressed me as Sergeant, Constable."

"It's not an order. You've been assaulted, you're bleeding, that's cause enough to end your shift early. File a report and then go home."

Then Vance turned his authoritative attentions to Damien. "Sir, I hate to bother you since you have done us a good turn by helping out our Sergeant, but we'd like you to issue a statement if you wouldn't mind. Just to show he was resisting arrest."

"It wouldn't be a problem at all."

Claudia couldn't stop staring at him, and she knew it had gone on too long when Vance cleared his throat. "Claudia? You okay?"

She shook her head, rubbing her temple. "Yeah, I'm fine, really. I don't need to go home."

"The hell you don't," Vance muttered, his eyes flickering from her and then back to her rescuer. Who was totally not her type. In the least. Right?

"Are you all right?" Damien asked, putting a hand to her elbow.

She jerked it away from him. "Fine." He seemed startled by her movement. How could she tell him that it wasn't because she found it offensive or unwelcome? How could she tell him that it was because she liked it?

"After you," he held an arm out, and she exited the alleyway ahead of him. Her boot kicked the beer bottle the suspect has slipped on, and it hit the wall, shattering instantly.

The Sin Eater followed Iola's friend out of the alley, assuring the other Constable that he would trail them to the station to file his statement. They let him drive himself in his car, of course, because that's what he wanted them to do. And he wanted to keep an eye on the Claudia woman.

The way she'd been able to defend herself had been impressive. But he wasn't surprised anymore at the strength of the female sex. God knew he'd been around long enough to see plenty of evidence that women were just as tough, strong and resilient as men. It took the mind to make someone truly weak, moldable. Whether a penis was involved or not, if the mind was strong and the intellect sharp, strength wasn't even a question. He'd seen muscle-bound schmucks unable to act to save their families from one human danger, and diminutive women who could move armies by simply raising an eyebrow. Physicality had nothing to do with it.

This Claudia woman seemed to have the benefit of many types of strength. She was smart, physically strong, and very intuitive. Now that he'd been "inside," so to speak, he saw that her frailty came from what others had done to her. Her strength was also armor. He knew her better already than some married couples knew each other. So he'd use this gained knowledge to keep himself in her mind.

She was a connection to his Iola, after all. He'd been in her body, taken it over in order to know what a kiss from Iola would be like. And while he'd been in there, that's when he'd gained such private knowledge.

He could never make a human do what they weren't already wanting to do, even on the smallest level, without completely taking over their physical form – which was exhausting. He was a helpful nudge at most. More like the influence of alcohol than the absence of free will. They were less inhibited, but their boundaries were basically the same. So he knew this woman desired Iola. That explained the kinship he felt with her.

So she preferred women. That had never mattered to him before. After seeing the glimpses of the past she kept buried, he understood how homosexuality in women could be a choice. Raped by a friend's older brother when she was fourteen, then raped again in college. What had happened to her then was fully in her mind, but her own defense mechanism on that was to let the alcohol be the excuse to not remember. She didn't even know she was protecting herself that way. And he could see that she had never been with a man sober or willingly. She could be a challenge ...

He couldn't think like that. She was an "in" to Iola, a connection he could use. "Damien" had to be on his very best behavior to earn her trust.

Chapter Eleven

Iola fiddled with her keys, standing awkwardly in front of her apartment door, not sure what she was supposed to do next. Dinner had been wonderful, Vinnie had not allowed her to pay for her meal, and had brought her right home after a nice, long, leisurely visit in Ricardo's lounge. She wasn't intoxicated, but she was under the influence of something.

Every part of her was ready to jump him, but Vinnie was agonizingly gentlemanly. He stood before her, smiling unassumingly, gazing down at her like he'd be happy to just look at her all day.

"Thank you, so much," she finally said, wondering why her voice sounded so loud in the hallway. "I had a lovely time."

"So did I," he said agreeably, then stepped forward.

Now we're getting to it, she thought, feeling an anxiety in her chest. It'd been a while since she'd been kissed. Had they changed it in some way? What if she messed it up? What if she was so sexed up she scared him away?

He put his hand on her waist lightly, just above her hip, and put his other hand to her cheek, his hand barely brushing against her. She took a deep breath at the contact. His hands were so warm ...

He dropped his eye lids, then pressed his lips to hers very softly.

She wanted to sigh, but that would have meant breathing, and she had just apparently decided to quit that. The heat of his lips was there, the softness of the touch making her want him to press those kisses all over her ... and then he backed up.

Her eyes flew open, and he was disengaging himself, still smiling. "Thank you," he said. "Can I call you again?"

She just nodded, then he made his way back to the stairwell.

She opened her door, closed it behind her and leaned on it. She touched her lips, as though looking for proof the kiss had actually happened. It had been nice and sweet but ...

"Well that was disappointing," she muttered under her breath.

There was a knock on the door and she jumped, then pulled it open without checking to see who was there.

"I can do better than that," Vinnie was saying as he wound one hand around the nape of her neck, circling her back with his other arm and pulling her close forcefully, his lips on hers still respectful, but definitely more passionate.

She moaned, and he kept her upright as though he thought her knees might have buckled. He didn't push her back into her place, he kept her in neutral territory in the hallway. She fell back against the doorway, not hurting herself in the least. One of her hands was grasping his lapel of his jacket, the other was looped around his neck.

She slid her tongue into his mouth, and he met it eagerly, stroking it with his own, his lips mashing against hers roughly. She was flushed, breathing heavily, and when the hand on the small of her back slipped down to caress her butt, she moaned louder without breaking contact with that mouth ...

"Iola," he said, stopping for air and to add in a whisper, "oh my God."

"I'm sorry," she said, totally shocked by her own reaction.

"Don't be sorry," he laughed, taking his hand off her ass and caressing her more northerly cheek. "Never be sorry. Kissing you is like ... I don't even know. It's amazing."

She smiled at him, letting her eyes fall closed. "You're very good at it."

"After that, I feel like I've never really kissed anyone before."

"After that kiss I'd have to say you were lying."

He gave her another peck, and when she tried to follow him as he raised his head again he laughed. "Iola, don't tempt me, please."

She stopped, backing up. "Oh shit, I'm sorry."

"Please, don't be sorry. I want ... I want to see you again. Can I?"

She nodded eagerly, and he held her face by the chin as he gave her another controlled kiss before backing up, breaking contact with her body. "Goodnight, Iola."

Iola gave a small wave, still leaning on the door jamb. "Good night, Veneratio."

He seemed pleased that she used his proper first name, then headed back down the stairs. She took a moment to calm her pulse before returning to her apartment.

Mmm hmm, she agreed. *Much better.*

Claudia ducked back around the corner of the building, moving quickly so she didn't run into Doctor Latin what's-his-name Romeo. He was exiting the stairwell then striding on long legs to his car. When she heard it pull away in the opposite direction she finally circled back to the door and silently made her way up to her apartment.

Once inside she threw all the locks, pulled off her belt, dropped it on the sofa and went to the bathroom while dropping clothing in her wake.

She was sore, bruised, and now her heart was aching too.

She hadn't meant to see Iola and the Doc kissing in the hallway, she thought she might have missed them coming back. But there they were; spot lit by a pot light in the hall, wrapped around each other and clearly enjoying the experience.

Iola had looked so beautiful, her face a mask of pleasure, her small body fitting against the doctor's physique like it was meant to be. And the way he was kissing her, holding her and working his hand down her back convinced Claudia he'd know how to make love good and proper. Just how Iola would like it. She'd left when his hand had cupped Iola's butt and she'd made that gloriously erotic sound.

Claudia stood under the showerhead, telling herself she was not in love with her best friend. There was no way, no how. It was a disastrous concept.

But her chest was aching, and it was nowhere near where that little freak had kicked her. She looked down at her side, and a bruise was forming on her rib cage. Luckily nothing got broken. Her jaw was going to be tender for a while, though. And bruised. And swollen.

Charles Goodwin had been his name. They had an address on him, and when patrol had stopped by his apartment they found one hell of a huge bloodstain on the living room floor, blood all over the bathroom, and a handsaw in the sink. He'd apparently lost his nerve chopping her up, because there was also vomit on the bathroom tiles. Case pretty much closed.

Claudia was more troubled at the fact that a civilian had come to her rescue. Maybe "irked" was a better way to put it.

Was it the fact he'd helped her, or ... the reaction she'd had to him.

It was nothing. Just push it away. You're sexually frustrated right now, attracted to someone you can't have, and now this.

But his voice and his eyes and his hand on the bare skin of her elbow ... Her heart fluttered. She felt like she might be blushing. Claudia felt her body warm everywhere, and it wasn't the shower. It was that Damien. Who the hell was that guy?

What did it matter? At the thought of him her body was in overdrive, almost like when she thought too long and hard and inappropriately about Iola.

A man had aroused her. How had she let that happen?

He was everything she'd never been attracted to. Tall. Wide shoulders. Heavily muscled. Dark in every way: thick dark hair. Olive skin. Lips that didn't just ask you to kiss them: they wanted you to chew on them. Be rough with them. And those purple eyes were a real trip: otherworldly, almost. The crinkles around his eyes meant he smiled a lot, too. And that smile tickled parts of her she couldn't think about without feeling all warm.

"Although, Sergeant Bauer seems more than capable of handling herself." Her eyes closed at the memory of his voice, deep, rumbling, so male. Damn straight she did.

She hesitantly moved her hand down her stomach, pausing like her intention was ridiculous. But the memory of him smiling at her ... she slid her hand between her legs, not at all surprised to find herself already halfway to heaven. His smile seemed to imply he knew what she would be doing later on anyway. Why disappoint?

She closed her eyes, leaning her other hand on the shower wall. As the orgasm rolled out and through her, she cried out very softly, biting her lip. She steadied her breathing and then shook her head as though gathering herself. She shampooed her hair, did a careful body wash, mindful of the bruises, and then got out of the shower wrapping herself in a giant, fluffy towel. She decided she wanted to go out tonight. She was going out alone, and hopefully not coming home that way.

The Sin Eater watched the Good Boy leave the apartment. He almost felt a protective growl build up in the back of his throat, but that wasn't fair.

The doctor looked happy, maybe a bit sexed up. All in all he was honest, authentic sweetness. The Sin Eater couldn't get a reading on the doc's thoughts, which was worrisome, but he knew what the skip in his step meant. His smile told him everything else he needed to know.

Damn it. The guy was perfect. What Iola likely deserved.

The Sin Eater watched the police woman, also known as Iola's friend and neighbor, enter the building. She was clearly avoiding having to see that doctor. He could smell her sadness, and it closely resembled his own, only with a lot more true love and caring. It smelled like rain. She was heartbroken as she climbed the stairs.

The Sin Eater felt bad; he could relate. He too desired what he couldn't have. This Claudia had slightly more pure intentions than he did, true. But he was also disarmed in that way that people in love experience. After all, if he couldn't reach into Iola's mind, could he understand her? Please her? He wasn't so sure. He'd never gone in "blind," so to speak. How the hell did humans do it?

He could pick up the friend's brain signature inside her apartment, and he felt her heartache. Poor thing. The frailty came out when she was alone.

He put the car in gear, but suddenly froze with his hand on the shifter.

She was ... thinking about him. With heat.

He closed his eyes, locking down all his senses to concentrate on hers. And he smiled.

He was such a bastard, but he couldn't help that the majority of women were drawn to him. There was some evil, cosmic trick in his genetic make-up, for lack of a better term. Men he could charm easily, but women were always going to desire him physically.

When Claudia touched herself, he found his body responding in kind. He even felt his breathing speed up, he could feel the warm water of her shower washing across him like he was there. He could feel the pull building in her belly, the tension itself so incredibly delectable. She made herself hold off, reveling in that anticipation until she was imagining him inside her body, frantically and roughly thrusting away until she gave the softest of cries, at odds with the violence of what she imagined he would do to her. He withheld his own orgasm of course. He couldn't be caught playing with himself in a parked car. But he felt hers twitch down the back of his neck. He even smiled as she did.

The Sin Eater could feel her thoughts and intentions. Claudia wanted to go out looking for trouble. Because he had put her in the mood for bad decision-making.

Looks like he already had a foot in the door ...

He sat in the waiting room at the clinic, chewing his nail. If the wait was much longer he was going to lose it. And his apparent impatience was making the poor nurse at the desk very nervous. But he couldn't stop twitching.

He had to find out what the hell was happening to him. Right. Now.

When they finally called his name he burst out of the waiting room, following the other nurse down a short hall to the exam room. She told him to change into the paper gown on the table, and then left him alone.

He got ready quickly, but this was just in preparation for more waiting. He paced this room, since no one was there to unnerve.

He hadn't used his real name, pulled one from ... who knows where. The nurses hadn't even asked him for ID, almost like his willing them to believe him had made it so.

So now he just had to get the doc to take his blood or something, just to explain what it might be. Because he sure hadn't found anything online.

When the doctor came in, he wanted to curse. It was a woman, and she was attractive. At least she looked professional, so he figured he could tell her everything that happened.

"So, Mr. Chang. What seems to be wrong?" She wasn't suspicious that he didn't look Asian in the least. So that was in his favor already.

"I ah, I woke up this afternoon after taking a nap, but I had stuff gunking up my eyes. It was ... it was dark, dark red. And really thick. I washed it off, but it really stunk, too. Then I ... I uh ... I ejaculated, and it was red, too."

"Did either event hurt? Your eyes or the ejaculation?"

Yeah, she was professional. The question came out like she was asking if he drank eight glasses of water a day. She was also moving closer while pulling a penlight out of her white pocket.

"The eyes stung. The other part ... felt the same. Maybe just a bit ... better than usual."

"Well then, what's the problem?"

He looked at her in surprised, then realized she was making a joke. That's wasn't right. He didn't like that too much. But he laughed dryly anyway.

She shone her little light in his eyes, her brow furrowed. "Your eyes appear normal. I don't suppose you kept a sample of this gunk?"

He shook his head. "No, I had to wash it off. Like I said, it smelled terrible."

"I can take a blood sample. And would you mind leaving us a semen sample as well?"

He nodded, offering out his arm. She rolled her wheeled stool to a metal cabinet in the corner, pulling out a few supplies, a packaged needle, a vial, and then a blood pressure cuff from the top of the cabinet. She rolled back to him with all of it. "Okay, just relax and this will be done soon."

She applied the arm cuff, squeezing the rubber ball to apply pressure to his arm. He looked down to see his vein pop up, and he drew in his breath in a hiss.

His veins looked black.

The doctor frowned, and suddenly she couldn't wait to get that needle in his arm and take a closer look at his biology. He felt how excited and fascinated she was. It felt wrong. A danger to him.

He panicked. He didn't know why, he really wanted to know what the hell was happening to him, but when that needle got close to his arm, he let out a roar and backhanded the doctor across the mouth. She didn't even have time to react. She flew back across the room, slammed into the door, hit her head hard against the wall and slumped to the floor.

He sat frozen where he was, on the little exam table, his paper gown crinkling against the paper that was unrolled across the vinyl. It was so quiet. Except for the sound of that paper ... and his own deep breathing.

He looked from her to his hand and back to her. How the hell had he done that? There's no way he had the strength to send someone flying across the room from an open-handed slap.

And it had been noisy, too. Not the slap. The tray she'd upended was metal and it clanged like a son of a bitch, knocking against the thick wood door and then the floor. The other tools on it had tinkled like bells as they'd rained down around her. Good God, it couldn't get any louder than that. Which meant someone would be coming to investigate.

He threw his clothes back on, vaguely aware that his T-shirt was backwards, but at least his fly was done up. He beat a land-speed record down the hallway and out the front door. He heard voices yelling after him, but he sure wasn't stopping to gum-flap.

He hit the street, ran for his car like a madman, and gunned it. Maybe tomorrow he'd be better. Maybe ... maybe tomorrow he'd realize this had all been a bad dream.

But first ... he really needed a drink.

Chapter Twelve

This club played the kind of music that Claudia hated, but at least she was surrounded by people just as sad and desperate as she was. The bass was thumping loudly, and that was all you could hear.

When she'd first walked in, a young guy with a tight tank top and well-worn jeans had wrapped an arm around her waist and asked her where she'd been all his life. Since he was only about 21 she assured him she'd been driving vehicles and smoking cigarettes for all of his life. Bit of an exaggeration. But he hadn't understood so she calmly removed his arm and continued on to the bar for her soda.

She was dressed the same as the other women, but she felt she must stick out like a sore thumb. Men were gawking at her. Was it because she was older? Maybe they thought she was as attractive as Mr. Romeo had, but she tried to give off the vibe that she wasn't interested in them. So no one talked to her.

She took her diet cola to a dark booth, sitting down and feeling ridiculous. She was at least five years older than the oldest demographic here. She felt more like a chaperone. What had she been thinking?

Her eyes were on the women. And it was quickly becoming apparent this place was a heterosexual hangout. The best she was getting here was a three-way.

She felt even more alone. What a great damn plan.

Claudia felt her phone vibrate and ring, and she pulled it out of her pocket, checking the number. It was work.

She got up from the booth and made it to the hallway that led to the washrooms, where the music wasn't as loud. She'd missed the call, but she dialed back immediately. Constable Vance answered right away. "Bauer?"

"That's me."

"I got bad news."

"What?"

"Charles Goodwin. He got away."

She felt her heart collapse. "What?"

"They were taking him to a cell, and he went totally ape shit. He knocked out two officers, made a run for it, got on the subway, and then at the next stop they got to, he was ... gone."

Claudia covered her face, shaking her head. "How ... I mean, Vance, what the fuck?"

"I don't know. It makes no sense. I just wanted to let you know. He is ... at large. We're getting his picture to all the TV and radio stations in town, and an APB has been put out."

"Thanks for letting me know."

"Where are you?"

"Out. I'll see you tomorrow."

"Are you feeling all right?"

"A little sore. It'll take more than that to slow me down."

"Okay. See you tomorrow. Take it easy."

She hung up the phone, then went back her table to find that her place had been taken by a group of university students and her half-full, eight dollar Diet Coke had been cleared away.

Yeah, this was a stupid idea.

Claudia felt like she could legitimately burst into tears. Suddenly the music seemed even worse than she'd originally thought, there were too many conflicting male colognes in the air, and she just wanted out of there.

She started through the writhing mass of dancers to the door, and as she looked up to avoid plowing into some hottie blonde with amazing, if fake, breasts, the crowd ebbed away from her and she ... saw him.

She breathed in immediately, stopping in her tracks. The people surrounding her seemed to move in slow motion. The lights went to mostly blue, bathing everything in a surreal ultra-violet glow. Except him. His tie was gone. The suit seemed extremely black, and the severe white of his shirt made his skin look even darker. His hair was down. Loose. Thick. He was holding a drink in one large hand, and his head was lowered, his eyes on her over the rim of the glass as he drank. She couldn't read his expression, but he looked like a predator.

Shit.

She wanted to leave, right? No, she wanted to stay right where she was. Just so she could feel him looking at her. The sensation of her touching herself in the shower came back to her, and she must have blushed. She felt her cheeks warm.

He put his drink on the bar without turning around, and walked towards her, shoulders back, shaking his long hair out of his face. He had one hand to the buttons of his jacket as he walked, just so his suit jacket stayed in perfect position. His shoulders rolled with the strut, and he was so ... masculine. She should have hated him. Usually she'd want to face-plant a guy like that. But him ... she wanted him under her.

He stood immediately in front of her, looking down at her. She didn't step back, just tilted her head upwards. She caught the scent of him. Some kind of soap. The slight musk of woodsy cologne. He seemed old and ancient then. And wise. From somewhere else.

Claudia swallowed with great difficulty, and he smiled. "Nice to see you again, Claudia."

His accent made her name sound so exotic and wonderful, as though he enjoyed the taste of it. She closed her eyes as she weaved on her feet, and he put a hand around her waist to rest on her lower back. His hand was immediately warm through her clothes. She was about to step away when he took her hand in his other hand, holding it down at her side, then he took a step forward and back.

Oh. They were dancing. *Try and keep up*, she scolded herself.

She was crushed against him, and he felt firm and rock-hard against her stomach and chest. She put her free hand across the back of his shoulders, and he smiled then. She was going to pass out, she was sure of it. She did manage to smile back, however.

She kept her focus up on his face, and she couldn't have told anyone what song was playing or whether or not they were the only two on the floor. They were just swaying, mashed against each other, but the effect it was having made her imagine they were grinding to beat the band. It likely looked a lot like sex. It sure was starting to feel like it.

His eyes kept hers in check. And every moment he was staring at her was making her wetter. When he dropped his gaze to trace her lips she wondered if he could smell it on her. When his arm yanked her in tighter she felt the swollen bulge in his pants, and instead of reacting with fear and revulsion, she raised her head up and kissed him.

In public. In the middle of a dance floor. That was just something she did not do.

His lips were thick, full, and heavy. As he responded it felt as though there was more of him than her. His mouth was completely covering hers, his tongue was completely in control of her. Claudia was overwhelmed and for once the thought didn't panic her. She reveled in it.

When he pulled back he slid one hand to the side of her face, fingers pushed all the way back into her hair. His forehead rested against hers, his thumb going to her upper lip and touching it with agonizing tenderness.

"Oh, dear, dear Claudia."

She closed her eyes as he said her name. "I want you," she admitted, her voice hoarse and uneven. She caught his thumb between her teeth, then sucked it in her mouth completely.

"What a happy coincidence," he returned throatily, his voice catching only slightly. "What do we do about it?" He freed his thumb, rubbing the wetness she left on to her bottom lip.

"Come to my place," she suggested, wishing it didn't sound like she was begging. But she was.

"I would love to." He freed her from his spell long enough for her to lead him off the dance floor by his lapel.

Charles stood back behind the dumpster across from that bitch's apartment. He couldn't believe it when he saw her coming at him on the street that afternoon. He didn't know she was a fucking cop. That didn't bode well.

And she'd recognized him as suspicious?

He knew he could still get her. He'd almost had the upper hand in their little brawl, until that fucker with the creepy eyes had stepped in, playing hero. Fucker acted like he'd never seen him before, too.

The lights in the apartment next to the bitch's place were on. That meant he'd have to be quiet getting in there, and knock her out right away. Much better to kill someone in their own place, not leaving a big fucking mess in an apartment that had his name on the damn lease.

Idiot.

He crossed the street, making quick work of the flimsy locking mechanism on the main door. He checked the names on the buzzers. Bauer, that's what the other cop had called her. And there she was, Bauer, C. Number 202.

He stepped lightly up the stairs which spanned right across the whole side of the building. As he made his way down the hall moving past 205 and 203 on the right and 206 and 204 on the left, he could hear television sets behind the closed doors. Some of them were really loud. No one was hearing him with that racket for cover.

Number 202 was the farthest from the stairs on the left, and from the outside he could see she had two deadbolts as well as a locking door knob. But nothing fancy.

He used his lock pick set, frowning when the door still didn't open. What the hell ... ah yes, the old trick of leaving one or two locks open so that the lock picker was actually engaging the locks instead of releasing them.

Didn't stop him at all. He was opening the door in under a minute, shutting it behind himself and reengaging the top and bottom dead bolts, just how she'd left it.

He left the lights off so he could see what she did when she first came in. There was a wonderful spot around the corner leading to the kitchen. Assuming she headed the opposite way to her bedroom or the washroom, he could sneak right up on her.

He tried the hallway. No squeaky floorboards. Things were looking up.

He returned to his hiding spot, crouching down to his haunches and leaning against the wall. He wanted to be comfortable, but ready to move at any moment.

There was a knock at the apartment door, and he froze. Then a voice.

"Claudia?" Pause. Wait. "Claudia, it's Iola. You in there?"

Pause. Wait.

The handle was jiggled, but nothing happened. She didn't have a key. He exhaled. Then he hoped this woman, whoever she was, didn't railroad his prey when she got home. Maybe that Claudia bitch would be out past her nosy neighbor's bedtime.

Her neighbor. The one from the train, likely. Right. She was the one that brought him here in the first place. He wouldn't hurt her unless he had to. After all, she showed him this bitch. He owed her some loyalty just for that, right?

He slumped back against the wall, waiting.

Iola stepped away from Claudia's door, confused. She could have sworn she heard Claudia come home, but there was no answer and no light shining out from under the door. She must have heard someone further down the hallway.

She went back to her apartment. After her date she'd changed into a T-shirt and flannel pajama pants, and she'd scrubbed the makeup off her face. Now she just felt listless. It was too early for her to go to bed. She usually worked until 2am and she didn't want to throw off her sleep patterns too much.

She sank back on to the sofa, flicking through the channels for a good thirty seconds before settling on a romantic comedy. She assumed it was a romantic comedy; it had Kate Hudson in it.

But almost immediately a news flash broke in, and she was about to change the channel when the anchorwoman broke in saying police were on the lookout for a man wanted in connection with the murder of a local woman.

Well, she had to know what that guy looked like. She would avoid him on the subway if she were to see him –

She almost dropped the remote. It *was* the guy from the subway. Holy shit.

She picked up her cordless phone, not sure who she was going to call. Claudia, but she's not home, remember?

She dialed Claudia's work number as the anchorwoman prattled on about the suspect. Charles Goodwin. Five-foot-ten, two hundred pounds, sandy-colored hair, grey eyes ...

She just stared at the mug shot. It was him.

"Hey, you've reached Sergeant Bauer. I'm away from the phone right now –"

She hung up. She was frustrated, but what was she going to do? Calling the police and telling them that he had scared her on the street three nights ago wasn't going to help them find him. And was it even a crime? He hadn't done anything to her.

"... police had Goodwin in custody after he fled police from the site where the body had been found. Following a brief foot chase Goodwin then assaulted a female sergeant before being subdued. No details are being released as to how he was able to escape police custody. Police are asking the public to exercise great caution and to not approach him. If you see this man please contact the police department immediately at ..."

Iola got up to get a ... drink. A glass of wine. That would be great.

Seeing that picture rekindled that same fear and uneasy jumpiness from the subway. Likely more than he had on the street that night. Now, knowing he might be a killer ... Iola shivered, remembering his empty eyes, the way they had stared at her before he just decided to walk away ... god, she could have been dead. It was worse than she'd thought.

She didn't bother with a wine glass. She poured the wine into a large water glass and carried it back to the living room after double-checking the locks on her doors. The movie was back on, and she turned on a few extra lights, too.

Iola hoped Claudia got home soon. She always felt safer knowing her friend was just across the hallway.

What in the hell are you doing? Claudia knew that voice very well. It was her conscience. She always listened to it, ever since she'd cleaned up and gotten sober. And now, here she was, leading a man she didn't know up the stairwell to her apartment. She was playing with the keys nervously, and yet no part of her wanted to tell him she'd changed her mind.

On the drive over he'd been utterly silent. She had barely noticed his gorgeous car. She'd been content staring at his profile in the street light that came through the windows. In a flash they were at her apartment building. He parked in one of the unofficial guest spots on the street. He even opened her door for her. He'd offered her hand to help her out of the car, and she hadn't let go of it, except to open the security door. She still had him by the hand; he was a step below her. She hoped her ass looked good.

Damien was thankfully quiet, leaving her to wrestle with her inner voices.

She unlocked the door, flicking on the light over the entryway.

"Would you ... like a drink?" she asked absently over her shoulder as her guest shut the door, locking it, even throwing the chain.

"Sure," he replied easily, turning back to her and holding her in his gaze.

A drink, she reminded herself, then moved to the kitchen. "I think I have a beer from when I had a friend over a while ago -"

The fist came at her out of nowhere. It caught her not quite square in the nose, but close enough that she felt her nose start to bleed instantly, and her eyes teared up as she ducked. She ducked because she sensed the man in front of her was rushing at her. While dropping to her side she kicked one leg out, catching him on the inside of the knee. He hollered and went down.

Her nose was hurting but she was on him, pushing him over to his stomach by tightening the neck of his shirt and twisting it, her hand pinning the back of his neck downward. He was squirming, so she gave him a good elbow to the kidneys for good measure.

The man was snarling at her like a wounded animal. The kitchen light was flicked on, and she looked up to see Damien with his hand on the switch. The man's left arm thrust outward, and that's when she saw the blade that he had dropped when he fell. Before he could reach it, Damien lowered a foot down cruelly, right on the back of the man's hand. The snarling turned to squealing.

"Shut up," Claudia muttered, repositioning herself so her knees were holding his arms at his sides. It must have made his left arm very uncomfortable since it was bent up under a very nice leather Prada loafer. "My cuffs are in the bedroom, dresser's just to the right of the door. Could you get them for me?"

He didn't ask if she was sure she could handle the guy, he just removed the heel of his shoe and strolled down the hall like he'd asked to use the washroom.

"How have you been, Charlie?" She muttered, pulling his head up a bit by his hair.

"Charles," he corrected, spitting all over the floor he was so pissed off.

"Bad time to start beating up on girls, isn't it? What with the vote, being allowed to drive cars and own property, we're also learning to kick a little ass now, hey?"

"Shut up," he spat.

"This is my kitchen floor," she shouted, mashing his face against the linoleum, wishing for the first time it was dirtier. "This is my house, how dare you come in here and tell me what to do."

"Fucking dyke."

She lowered her mouth right next to his ear. "I'm worse than a dyke, Charlie. I choose to be this way."

He reared his head back, catching her in the nose again. She let go of his hair to cover that same pounding, gushing fountain as white sparks setting off a light show in her head. He managed to pull his arms out from under her knees, rolling her to the side. Her head hit the cupboards, pain intensifying the white flares in front of her very eyes. She was a bit stunned, but then he was on top of her, his hands clamped around her neck and squeezing so hard it felt like her throat might pop like a grape.

She was kicking her feet to try and throw him off, she even managed to give him a jab right to his nose, but he was in such a rage nothing was working. He was lost in bloodlust, and he was going to kill her.

Then he was lifted up and away, his feet kicking and his mouth falling open in surprise. Damien turned him to face him, gave him a good right-hook and the guy went down.

Claudia sat up, her hand to her throat, feeling the air rushing in as refreshing as natural spring water. She heard dripping, looked down, and realized she was bleeding all over her floor.

She put a hand below her nose, looked up at her gentleman caller and said in a muffled voice, "Call Constable Vance for me." Then she rattled off the number.

Damien dialed the number swiftly on the phone hanging in the kitchen, and the number connected him directly to Vance's cell phone.

Claudia realized her skirt was up over her hips. Her shirt was askew. She straightened up her clothes, then stared at her blood on the floor. He'd gotten into her apartment ... he'd known where she lived. The adrenalin was abating and it was leaving behind way too much anxiety.

"Constable Vance? I'm calling on behalf of Claudia Bauer. We have your suspect here at her apartment. He broke in." Pause. "No, he's quite unconscious. But you might want to send an ambulance for Sergeant Bauer."

She shook her head no, but he pointedly ignored her.

"No, she'll be fine. But he did assault her again." Pause. "Thank you, Constable." Then he hung up. "Help is on the way." Then he handed her the cuffs. "I trust you'd prefer to do the honors?"

Chapter Thirteen

When Iola heard the commotion in the hall, she hung back for a moment. The news had her very hesitant to unlock anything that separated her from the outside world. But when police radios got thrown into the mix, she went to her door in alarm, pulling it open. Claudia's door was propped open by a large man in a police uniform, and as she stepped into the hall another uniformed police officer walked out. He stopped mid-step and held up a hand. "Please go back to your apartment, miss. We have everything under control."

"Is Claudia okay?" She found herself asking in a tiny voice.

He stopped, then tilted his head. "You know Claudia?"

"She's my friend. We've lived here for years now."

She didn't know how to interpret his look, but after a moment he caught himself. "Yeah, she's fine. You can go on in and see her."

Iola then became aware she was in her pajamas and all these men were looking at her with piqued interest. Then she remembered that they all knew Claudia's sexual preference. And now here she came to check in on her friend.

Well, fuck 'em.

She stepped into the apartment carefully, looking around. One officer was cleaning blood off of Claudia's floor, and he looked a little pale. Another officer was pushing a man out the door –

Iola froze as the man's eyes fell on her. It was the guy from the subway, the one the cops had been looking for. He was bleeding from his nose and a cut above his eyebrow. When he looked to her she braced herself for that look of hatred and malice ... but got nothing. He was blank. He looked over her like she was a house plant.

That's when she realized he'd been here ... looking for Claudia?"

Oh god, where was Claudia? She turned for the living room, then stopped dead.

Damien was in the entryway, already looking at her. She frowned, wrapping her arms across her chest. What in the hell was going on?

He smiled easily when he saw her, and then she found herself not wondering what was going on anymore. Her heart went triple-time. Oh holy hell, that smile was something else. The room noise seemed to momentarily fade into mumbled echoes, then he spoke and it came rushing back to normal.

"Iola. Claudia's in here, she's fine."

Iola stepped past him to the living room, doing her best to ignore the blast of heat that went through her when she was near him. Then she saw Claudia.

"Oh my god!" She covered her mouth. Not the best reaction, but it was honest.

Her friend was most definitely not fine. Her nose was swollen, one eye was closing up, and was that another bruise on her chin?

She rushed to Claudia, sitting next to her and hugging her without hesitation.

"Iola," Claudia began but didn't get much further.

"What happened? Oh my god." She was repeating herself way too much. The she saw Claudia's hands, the knuckles were scraped raw. She'd given as good as she'd gotten at least.

"That was our murder suspect. He ran from us today, got a couple licks on me then. He escaped tonight. I don't know how he found out where I live but when I got home he was in here, waiting for me."

Iola covered her mouth. "I heard someone in the hall. I even came to the door, I thought you'd come home."

Claudia's face paled. "Oh Christ, Iola. He could have killed you."

"It was him," she whispered. "That's the guy that was on the street the other night, the one that I thought was going to mug me."

Claudia frowned. "Are you sure?"

"Completely. I'd recognize those eyes anywhere."

There was a burst of laughter across the room, and they both turned to see three uniformed cops looking on them with great interest.

"Do they think we're dating?" Iola asked under her breath.

"Ugh. In their dreams. Ignore them. I'm just so glad you didn't come in, and I'm glad he didn't answer the door."

Damien Talon was still next to the entryway, feigning great interest in Claudia's bookshelf. Iola leaned closer to her friend.

"What's he doing here?"

It might have been her imagination, but Claudia's face colored under all the bruises she was cultivating. Iola took in her friend's clothing then; Claudia'd been out herself earlier that night, not at work after all.

The cop that had let Iola in stepped into the hallway outside the living room, clapping his hands together.

"All right, folks. Show's over. Let's let Sergeant Bauer get some rest."

At that the three cops started laughing all over again, that raunchy, masculine kind of laugh that made Iola incredibly uncomfortable. But they left, taking the other boys in blue with them.

The nice constable that had shooed them all away came forward and put a hand on Claudia's shoulder. "You need anything, just call, okay? I'm calling in a sick day for you tomorrow."

"I'm fine - "

"Shut the fuck up and get some rest." But it was said with care and concern and a smile. Then he too left and the apartment got a lot quieter.

Just the ... three of them.

Iola looked from Claudia to Damien and then back to Claudia. Man, in this equation she never thought she'd feel like the third wheel.

"Well, I'll let you rest, too," Iola said carefully, getting to her feet. She checked over on Damien, and he caught her gaze.

"Yes, I too shall be going."

"Wait."

They both stopped at the doorway, turning back to Claudia. She was fidgeting, and Iola had never seen her neighbor so damn jumpy.

"Would you ... could you stay?"

Iola and Damien looked at each other.

"Damien," Claudia clarified. "Would you mind ... staying out here. On the couch? I'm not ... I'm not comfortable being here alone."

Iola's head was reeling. Maybe she was sleeping, maybe this was all made up.

"If you would like me to, I can do that."

His voice brought warmth to Iola's lower body that made her wonder if she *wasn't* dreaming. She just shrugged. "Well, I guess we'll talk tomorrow." She made no attempt to hide the fact that it was an order not a question.

Claudia nodded. "Of course. Lock up your place tight, Iola."

She nodded. "Yeah ... you, too."

The smell of jasmine and vanilla lingered as Iola left the small apartment, shutting the door reluctantly behind her. Across the way, Claudia was no longer emitting heat and arousal. She was ... devastated.

The Sin Eater wasn't such a bastard he would try to get her worked up again. But when she asked him to stay ... he couldn't believe his luck. A friend to both these women? Bringing him closer and giving him a chance to understand what made Iola so ... different?

Man, let's buy lottery tickets. Right. Now.

Claudia got him pillows and a blanket for the sofa. He waited respectfully, knowing she was in charge of this place and he wasn't about to suggest she needed any help from him. He didn't need to mind-read to pick up on that vibe.

She wished him a good night and flicked off the overhead lights on her way to her bedroom, leaving a table lamp on next to his "bed" for the night. He sat back for a moment, letting his mind toss around all the weird and wonderful ways things sometimes just worked out without him having to impose his wants on anyone. Much more of this and he wouldn't have to influence anyone for anything ever again.

The clock was ticking on the bookshelf. Four hours until the sun came up.

Getting himself invited here had been a lot easier than he would have thought. But Claudia was kind of a major assist on the whole thing. He didn't have to play any mind tricks at all. She was attracted to him like all humans were, plus she was very lonely and sad. Like taking candy from a baby. And here he was, spending the night.

Not how he intended, true enough. But if there was one thing he had it was time.

Dancing with Claudia had been a hell of an appetizer. She was lean but curvy, voluptuous even. And having those gorgeous breasts pressed against him ... his cock twitched just remembering it. He wasn't going to be able to settle down unless he thought of something else for a while.

As a Sin Eater, he didn't need to sleep. It was unnecessary. From time to time he may fall into a meditative trance-like state, and it was almost as though that charged his psychic batteries. He felt rested and refreshed, but usually that only happened once every couple of months.

He kicked off his shoes, tossed his blazer on the back of an armchair, undid his shirt and put that on the armchair as well. If he was going to be "sleeping" it may as well look like he was sleeping. So when he pulled the comforter over himself and settled into the pillows he was only wearing boxer shorts. The blankets smelled like Claudia. Earthy, like patchouli and ginger. The effect was very pleasant.

He stared at the ceiling for about two hours, willing the meditation to come, but it wouldn't. He was surrounded by the sleeping patterns of all the humans in the building around him. They were chaotic, and latching on to one to follow it was hardly worth his time. True, he could plant a few nightmares if he wanted, or send a zinger of a wet dream to the guy down the hall that had his girlfriend sleeping over for the first time. But he didn't ... he decided to just behave and not eavesdrop.

Well now, until then. His senses perked up, and he caught a dream ... and it was coming right though the wall behind him, Claudia's bedroom. Now his interest was piqued.

She was touching someone's pale and velvety skin, trailing kisses along soft, feminine flesh. A belly button, a soft stomach.

She was hot. He knew how this dream was arousing her. It was making his breathing a bit ragged, too.

It was Iola. She was dreaming about ... oh god.

He almost moaned he was so caught up in it. She dreamed of dipping her head between Iola's legs and pleasuring her with her tongue and lips. And she could hear Iola's reaction in her dream as well. It was encouraging to say the least.

Jesus Christ, his mind burped when he realized he'd gotten hard in his boxers. *Maybe I should be taking notes on this.*

Then it ... stopped. Claudia jolted herself awake, but he could smell the arousal still lingering around her.

He closed his eyes, holding on to the feeling of his lips on that sacred skin ...

The bedroom door opened. She was coming down the hallway carefully, not wanting to wake him. She needed a drink of water.

No shit.

He waited until he heard the water pour, leaving her to her thoughts. Then he got up and made his way to the kitchen.

Fuck him, but he couldn't help it. His erection needed somewhere warm to land.

She jumped when she saw him, but then he felt her ... well, not calm. She liked the sight of him, and it appeared that his was a male form she didn't mind at all. He only let that feeling intensify.

See? Free will. Nothing to do with him.

"Claudia?" He said in a low voice. "Are you all right?" She shook her head. "How's the nose?"

"I probably look like a UFC fighter right now."

"You're beautiful."

The only light was coming from the open refrigerator door, but he didn't need light to feel her need intensify when he said it. She put the glass down on the counter, shut the door, walked right for him, and kissed him, rising up on her toes. Her lips and tongue were cool from the water. It did not have the same effect as a cold shower.

He held her around her lower back tightly, a groan escaping him that he hadn't expected. But ... he was a little extra worked up at the moment. Her stomach was taut but still very feminine against his arousal.

"Take me to my bedroom," she whispered, pulling back,

He scooped her up in his arms as though she weighed nothing, and while her lips were firmly attached to his he carried her through the darkened apartment, down the hall to her room. He laid her out on her bed, crawling in alongside her.

He had to be careful; he could easily lose her due to her experiences with human men. He made sure she didn't contact his erection, keeping it against the mattress. He didn't put his weight right on her at all, instead propping himself up next to her on one arm, leaving one hand free to go wherever she liked.

She needed no warming up whatsoever. Her tongue was working his mouth like a pro, and he almost found it overwhelming. Almost. Without hesitation she took his free hand, pushing it down and under the nightshirt she'd gone to bed in. The only thought he had from her mind was somewhere along the lines of *Touch me. Now.*

His hand found its way under her panties easily, seeking the wet skin she presented by moving her far leg over to its side. As he touched the spot she wanted him to she moaned but didn't stop kissing him. He wet his finger on her and found a rhythm that she seemed to enjoy very much. Her kissing was ferocious, and he didn't care in the least that he wasn't the one that had brought it all on.

She didn't want to consider what she was doing at all. She wasn't in a thinking mood.

He freed his mouth by kissing her neck and whispering her name against her skin. It took only a split-second before she came, crying out loudly, her entire body completely tensing and then jolting. He let that orgasm work its way through her, then pushed her underwear to her knees, wiggled down the mattress and raised her legs up, bending them at the knee and parting them.

"Stop me when you want," he said softly, kissing her inner thigh. She responded by rolling her hips upward then down, and he caught the way her abdominal muscles flexed in the street light coming though her curtained window.

The smell of her was totally intoxicating. He was drowning in chocolate. So he struck quickly and hard with his tongue, and she dug her nails into his hands where they rested on her hips. She was trying to be quiet now, and he was wondering how thin the walls were in this place.

He closed his eyes to pick up on her brain waves. She liked this, and she was surprised by that. She was also somewhat worried he might want to mount her and penetrate her, and that thought had her tensing slightly ... because she was worried she might like that, too.

He sent her a message he hoped would ease her, and it seemed to. He made noises of his own, happy ones, hoping to reassure her he was happy with just this.

She sighed, her legs relaxed, and again she climaxed while biting her lip to keep from calling out. He was smiling as he began to move his tongue again, and her whimper had his eyes rolling back in his head.

He didn't want to push her too far and too fast, but his dick didn't have to be the part of him that entered her, right?

He lowered his chin, letting his tongue ease inside, and she arched her back. Yeah, she was totally okay with that. Better than "okay."

After a moment he eased one hand out from her grip, and let two fingers test the waters. She pushed her hips downward on to them further.

He let them slide as far as they could, and he found that secret location after a moment. When he did, her mind plowed into his and he almost came all over himself at the sudden explosion. Her hand gripped him by the hair, holding him in place while she moved against his tongue. He matched the motion with his hand.

At that moment, and for the first time in a while, he had that fleeting notion that he could totally fall in love with this girl.

Chapter Fourteen

Claudia was totally in uncharted waters, but Damien was so in tune with her it was like she was with ... a woman. If it wasn't for the stubble on his jaw, chin and upper lip that is. But to her surprise... she really liked that, too.

She was brutally using him for her own means, and he totally didn't care. He was doing everything he could to keep up with her. And his hands ... oh good god, no one had ever touched her there. How did he know how to do that? How did he know what to do?

She was only vaguely wondering these things, because there was a fire building behind her belly button that she couldn't ignore. The pressure had her gasping and clawing at his arm, but she didn't want to do anything to impede him. There was an odd mewing sound in the room, becoming more and more urgent, speeding up, and she realized it was her. Every sound she made Damien was echoing, and the sound of his voice was vibrating through her.

And then ... it stopped. The pressure was just gone. And she was about to cry out in absolute frustration when it hit her like a baseball bat right through the back of her head and into her central nervous system. Her legs and arms twitched out of her control, and she knew she was hollering, but hopefully it was graceful hollering. And hopefully it wasn't too loud. And hopefully she wasn't waking up Iola.

Damien continued to lap at her gently while the sensations rolled away, very gently, until all that remained for noise in the room was her own ragged breathing. When he stopped she realized she was absolutely exhausted, but in a wonderfully fantastic way, of course.

"Oh, my dear Claudia," he whispered, pressing kisses to her stomach as he pulled his hand away.

"Holy shit," she replied, totally inelegant.

He laughed, and the low rumble of it carried through his chest and against her, reminding her of the effect his voice had on her pleasure receptors. It made her shudder again.

Now comes the part you might not like as much, her conscience reminded her as he stretched out beside her, but he was being careful not to crowd her. Here's the part where you return the favor.

"I have to apologize," he said, kissing along her neck, nipping at her ear.

"Oh?"

"I uh ... I seem to have made a mess of your sheets."

She frowned, looking over at him in the dim light. "What ... oh. Oh, you ..."

"I'm afraid so. Would it be all right if I ... used your shower?"

"Oh, of course. I ... I'm sorry." That sounded out of place, it didn't even make sense.

"Sorry? My dear, never be sorry. You are resplendent."

Any other time she might have known what the hell that word meant. But even mentally at that time she was completely relaxed. Blissful, even. Whatever it meant, it sounded good.

"Towels are in the hall closet," she said, then returned the peck on the lips he lowered to her before making his way down the hall, still walking with all the confidence of a man wearing more than just boxers.

She shoved her nightshirt back down over her hips, sighing. That was weird. She didn't sigh. She'd never sighed. But then again, she'd never been this ... satisfied before. Her blood felt like sunshine. It was incredible.

Before she knew it, she'd let her eyes slide closed, and immediately drifted off to sleep.

The Sin Eater was soaping up his business center with a ridiculous smile on his face. His jaw and neck were killing him but he could care less. Claudia's climax had been so satisfying, he didn't even push her for more. That was ... perfect. Totally perfect.

He couldn't say he wasn't a bit proud of himself. He hadn't needed to read Claudia's mind at all to get instruction. And he hadn't needed to influence her to enjoy herself. That had been all instinct. All he'd used his mind for was to make sure he wasn't pushing her somewhere she didn't want to go.

He was getting ridiculously good at this. He couldn't explain the tenderness he always felt for these human women after they coupled, but ... well, maybe getting chicked out every time was helping him get the job done in the long run. Maybe it was all just practice for when he finally got Iola right where he wanted her.

"It's because you're feeling their orgasms."

He jumped, flattening himself against the shower wall, then immediately shielded his mind by throwing up images of beaches and seagulls and many different boring things because he did not want this guy in his head.

Edo Edi Essum, or just Essum, was in the shower with him, standing calmly behind him, the water not touching him or his clothing. It moved right through him, because he was, after all, an apparition. A Sin Eater of the past. His old friend.

"That's why you're such a girl after sex. You're still joined, so to speak. You're still in their heads. You're feeling their afterglow. But that other one, across the hall? You'll never have her. Not even like this one just now."

"Essum. You fucking prick," he was still too startled to catch what the guy was saying.

"Lesbian, hey? Nice. But part of the game is picking up another woman. She's hot, too. Fuck is she hot. I like those tough ones ..."

"Stop watching me. It's creepy."

Essum stepped through the shower curtain, and he knew the guy was just waiting on the other side for him. He rinsed off quickly, turned the water off and left the exhaust fan running. It would camo his voice.

He threw the curtain back, and his peer was sitting on the counter, stroking his chin.

"What are you doing here?"

"Just letting you know what's doing with the woman you can't get a reading on."

He frowned. "What?"

"Yeah, I know about her."

"Well, that doesn't surprise me. You always seem to know everything."

Essum smiled. He didn't like the look of it. "You know, I couldn't read Daphne, either."

"*Daphne* Daphne?"

"Yeah. She was ... a wall. But she was feeling me the whole time we were together. But in that time ... we were never *together* together, know what I mean?"

His frown deepened. "You two never ..."

"Nope."

"But Essum ... you dropped your guard for her. It killed you."

"I know, Voro. But really ... she killed me, didn't she? And then I got sent back to Hell."

"Well, that I knew. But ... what happened?"

"I was ... unable to be with her, if you read my meaning."

He smirked. "Well, I'm told that happens sometimes."

"I was physically able, but ... the closeness made my skin burn. I thought I was going to die. I really did."

He sat down on the closed toilet lid. "You never told me this before. Why now?"

"Because, I've since found out what Daphne was."

"The love of your mortal life?"

"She was my *frustro*, the trick that was my evil end."

"Are you drunk?"

"Fuck you. I can't drink. You know that. I can't do anything that's so fun about this place. I miss the drinking. And the fucking. God, I really miss the fucking."

"Well, what happened then? What's with the *frustro* thing?"

Essum sighed, leaning back against the mirror. "When the man upstairs is trying to weed us out, he sends us a *frustro*, a human we will be drawn to. We're unable to read their minds or affect their actions. No ability to influence them at all. And because of that, we swarm around them like bees on honey. But you won't be able to fuck her."

"Watch how you talk about her," he growled in a warning tone.

Essum smiled, his back straightening. "Look at you. You're nearing the end of your road as we speak. It's only a matter of time."

"I don't see how Iola can bring about my demise."

"Oh, it's not the *frustro*. Each *frustro* is paired with a *decipio*. And they are the ones that will end your mortal life. They are just as powerful as you are."

"If the guy in white is sending me a *frustro*, who's sending the *decipio*?"

Essum shook his head. "Oh, Voro. Voro, Voro, Voro. They come from the same place."

He couldn't track all this. "But the *decipio* would be ... evil, no? How could His Holiness send us something that dark? Impure?"

Essum gave him an indulgent look. "You mean ... like a fallen angel? No, never. The old man in the clouds has never stooped to the Dark Prince's level to get rid of a few of us."

Voro's shoulders slumped forward. "So ... Iola's got a *decipio* circling around her somewhere, and his goal is to end my mortal life?"

"It's as easy as lopping off your head, my friend. Or a massive brain trauma. But don't worry. It doesn't really hurt."

"What's the point of the *frustro*? If the *decipio* is as powerful as I am, why can't he or she just kill me outright?"

"It's the oldest trick in the book, old friend. You can't spring a trap without bait."

Voro ran his hand through his hair. "Fuck. Me."

"Indeed. And you want to know the beautiful part?"

"What?"

"The Boss has started up the old rotation system."

Well that made him hopeful. In the old days when one of the Sin Eaters met an untimely end, the next one in line was put to work. The one that just returned home went to the back of the queue, and the progression continued. Usually it took about fifteen years for one of them to be returned to the world of mortals.

Except for him. He'd been roaming the planet for ... about six hundred years. Good god ... has anyone else been around that long?

"Nope," Essum answering, annoying the fuck out of him and reading his mind. Voro had let his seascape screen saver slip. "You're the longest serving Sin Eater around. And The Boss thinks it's time you took a break, too." Then he scratched his jawline. "That woman ... the one with the kid locked up in her apartment? With the big bad boyfriend coming back to do all kinds of nasty to the kid?"

Shit. Busted. "What about it?"

"Well, with her last dying breath that woman saved the life of an innocent, so she's ... she's saved, too. And it's only because you called in that tip, turned the kid over to the cops. So ... you're responsible for that piece of shit's salvation. And that was the last straw for The Boss."

"What does that mean?"

"He helped set up your *decipio*. And this one ... well, this one makes mine look like a Sunday school teacher."

"What?"

Essum smiled wider. "You're being set up on both sides. The good guys captured one of ours to get the blood of evil for the *decipio*. They don't know yet that it was planted for them."

Voro felt anger rolling in his chest. "Well, who is it? You have to help me out, Essum."

His pal laughed. "Fuck no."

Now he was totally taken aback. "You asshole. Tell me who it is, what he looks like."

"Absolutely not."

The way Essum was swinging his legs back and forth with mirth gave Voro pause. Then he saw it, plain as day. "You're next in the rotation, aren't you?"

Essum giggled like a hyena. "And I can't wait. I told you, I told you, I miss the fucking. And I'll have to remember this building. They keep good-looking women stored here, don't they?"

"You bastard."

"Worse than a bastard. I'm next in line for a promotion, and I can't fucking wait."

"And there's no way to get around this?"

Essum shrugged. "Technically, the *frustro* could slay the *decipio*. But then ... then your *frustro* takes on your curse. And you ... you are rendered mortal. As long as you live your natural life span, she will have to carry your burden and release the sins of mankind."

Of course. The fine print just keeps getting worse the further into it you get.

"If she takes on my curse ... does she become one of us for eternity?"

"Nah, she's an intern at best. She'll live a mortal lifetime, too, and then be called home. Upwards, not down. Because those are the powers that put her here. But ... can you see the darling Iola killing anyone?"

Voro shook his head. "Of course not. She is ... she's too pure."

"That's another part of the draw. But the worst part is ... you can't just avoid her. She's drawn to you as much as you are to her. You can't even distance yourself, she will seek you out. And for some reason we can't sleep with them."

That made him take a different train of thought. "Really? What happens?"

He held his hands out as if to say *Hello?* "Your dick falls off. Then you die, retard."

"Really?"

Essum broke into giggles again. "No. I'm just messing with you. We just can't. No matter how you try, something always happens to stop it, get in the way. Ruin the mood. And we can't even touch them. It burns. Like their skin is trying to purify that very contact. Blisters, acid burn. It hurts."

He thought back to kissing Iola's hand. His lips hadn't blistered. But he'd had that burn on his hand. Yes, it had healed quickly. But it was the lightest of touches ...

Essum was still talking. "Don't forget, they come from a pure place, and we don't. They can't have us sullying their little fluffy-tailed spies." Then Essum became thoughtful. "They're different from other humans. They can influence their own kind, slightly. They can ward off danger to themselves. They can hold others at a distance when they're uncomfortable. And ... they are absolutely delicious. They are the ultimate temptation."

"This sucks."

"And don't think you can save her in any way. Because after the trap is complete and you are gone ... the *decipio* will kill her."

Iola woke to a strange sound, and she couldn't possibly be hearing what she thought she was. But ... what else could that be?

Her room and Claudia's room shared a common wall, since they were at the end of a corridor and their apartments wrapped around the front of the building. So ... common wall. The bedroom. Awkward.

Claudia wasn't kidding when she said she'd be the first to know if Iola got laid. The reverse was also true. Iola was staring at the ceiling as the sounds started off soft, but they were definitely ... cries. Claudia was trying to be quiet but ... she was failing on a grand scale.

There was a pause, and Iola rolled over to her side, closing her eyes and trying to go back to sleep. Then the sounds started again, more intense and desperate. And louder.

Holy shit. Either Claudia was really worried about Damien's self-esteem, which was highly unlikely, or she was really getting the ride of her life. By a guy.

Well, if Iola could have a moment of considering switching teams, Claudia could definitely be forgiven a moment of weakness against the walking sex that was Damien Talon.

Iola flopped over on to her back again, sighing. How long could that go for?

When a male voice joined in for a couple of the cries of ecstasy, Iola bit her lip and closed her eyes. Damien ... she'd know the voice anywhere. Even though he was with her friend at that moment, the sounds he was making ... she wanted him making those sounds while he made her cry out like that.

She felt guilty about the fact that she'd been out that evening with Vinnie, and here she was, eavesdropping on the world's best sex ever ... but the presence of Damien's voice just the width of a wall away ... she felt like shit for it, but she touched herself anyway. She was only human, after all.

Chapter Fifteen

He couldn't believe this. He'd headed to a cocktail lounge after hitting that doctor into a wall, and no one had even followed him. Then he'd ordered a drink, realized he had no cash, but they never asked him for money.

Talk about luck.

Then as he'd watched a woman at the bar get annoyed for being ignored by the men in the room, he thought to himself that she wasn't half-bad, he sure wouldn't kick her out of bed.

As he'd had the very thought, she'd turned on her bar stool, her long legs crossed in front of her, and she leveled her gray eyes right at him.

That was fifteen minutes ago. Now, here he was, balls deep in the men's room as she was moaning and hollering random words and sounds. He knew how she wanted it, he knew what he was doing ... and he was good at it.

He'd never really been that good at it before.

He'd begun to think she was faking, so as he concentrated on her, he became ... aware of her. Her emotions, the effect his body was having on hers. And as he was just getting into his rhythm, he could have sworn she said, *"To the left ... hard."* But she couldn't have said it because she was sucking his tongue out of his mouth at the time.

He shifted his stance to angle himself to her left, and he increased the pace and ... then he just held on. She came fast and hard. He thought she could probably break his dick in half. But then it had passed, and she was still good to go.

When he came it was with her third or fourth orgasm. As his body was calming and he was reluctant for her to get into the whole awkward, "Here's my number" conversation, she stepped down off of him, smoothing her hair and leaving the stall with just a "Thanks."

He braced himself against the wall with one hand, trying to catch his breath, then he pulled off the condom in exhaustion. Of course he noticed that he was cumming fucking maple syrup again. But that had felt even better than the last one.

Whatever had happened to him ... he had to believe it was for the better. People were doing what he wanted, and apparently he was now a rock star when it came to sex.

He was starting to think he might be okay with all this, however it had happened.

He left the club, walking down the street with a bit more backbone then he'd ever experienced before. Of course he was likely grinning like a complete moron, but who gave a shit.

There was someone behind him. He could almost hear them going through his pockets, wondering if he was a VISA man or had a MasterCard hidden in a wallet somewhere.

Good luck, he thought. *I'm broke as fuck. Have fun robbing me.*

Hands grabbed his shoulders, pushing him into a recessed doorway. He hit the wall hard, but instead of it hurting, he got pissed. He spun on the guy behind him ... check that, two guys. One of them was pulling a switchblade. The other had his hands in the front pocket of a heavy metal band's tour hoodie.

Oh shit.

"Wallet," Switchblade barked. "Now."

His rage was bubbling, and in a voice that even surprised him he said, "No. Go fuck yourself."

Switchblade was taken aback, stepped forward and raised his weapon. Did Switchblade think his eyesight was failing?

"I see it," he spat. "Very nice. Vending machine at the mall?"

"Listen fucker, I want your wallet and no lip."

He reared one arm back shoulder level, and his fist shot out so quick he barely saw it. It was flying past him and then embedded in Switchblade's face.

Like, in the guy's face. His nose gave way, totally inward, and he dropped. All his menace, all his stench and loathsome essence just ... stopped.

Like he was dead.

He looked down at the ground, then up at the metal fan, who was now looking at him like he was insane. He took a step towards the guy, who mirrored with a step backwards. His hands came up, empty.

"What the fuck ... what's with your eyes man?"

That made him pause, then metal head decided to turn and run. That pissed him off too. He just ... shot a death wish at the guy's back. The kid's legs stopped working, and he stumbled clumsily to the ground.

It's like he could track what was happening in the guy's cerebral cortex. His legs didn't follow commands, his heart was shutting down, and his lungs were refusing to draw air. The guy's own body was killing itself. His mind was whipping around in a frenzy, recalling pointless shit like field trips to a dairy farm. The birth of his little sister. The first time he'd gotten laid. The first time he'd stabbed a guy in juvie.

Wait. How the hell could he see this?

He rubbed his eyes, but the images stayed there, even when his eyes closed. Then, like someone had yanked the cord on a movie projector, it all faded to black.

He opened his eyes slowly, and the kid in the hoodie was lifeless on the sidewalk, open eyes straining upward, seeing nothing.

Had he seen what the guy was seeing? Had he actually done that to him?

His hands started to shake. He began to hyperventilate.

He'd wanted the guy dead, and here he was, definitely dead. He'd wanted that woman to take him to the bathroom with her, and she did it. He'd wanted the medical clinic staff to accept that his name was Mr. Chang without seeing any ID, and they had.

Holy crap. People were definitely obeying his unspoken commands.

His hands stopped shaking. His nerves smoothed right the fuck out. And he grinned.

This was going to be so fucking fun.

At ten o'clock the next morning Iola gave up trying to sleep in, threw back her covers and made herself a pot of strong coffee. She started getting eggs ready to scramble when there was a knock on her door.

She checked the peep hole before opening her door, and it was a man in a cheerful yellow and blue golf shirt and matching hat, holding something wrapped in colorful cellophane.

She opened the door, returning his pleasant smile.

"I have a delivery for Iola Day."

"That's me."

He handed her the purple package, then tipped his hat and left.

"Bye," she said weakly, then shut the door and reengaged the locks. She put the package on the kitchen table, opening the top. Inside was a potted African Violet.

She frowned. That's a weird plant to give someone.

There was a small card inside, so she reached inside to pluck it from the leaves. She popped the card out, smiling as she read it.

Iola, it turns out your name is also Greek for 'violet-colored dawn.' Good morning. I'll be thinking of you. Vinnie.

She smiled widely, feeling her heart swell. She ripped the plastic away from the pot, and carried it over to the window while reading the plant care instructions carefully.

Out of the corner of her eye she saw a form on the street below suddenly duck into the alley right across from their building. She couldn't see anything remarkable about them ... but she felt them. No, that was ridiculous. She was aware they were there, and she really thought they were up to no good. She could tell by how the pounding of her pulse got louder in her ears, and how a cold breeze seemed to graze her neck, raising gooseflesh on her arms.

But that was silly. She was just freaked out because of what happened to Claudia, right? Seeing bad guys where there weren't any. The police had carted that guy off with them last night. Her instincts were just terribly overactive.

Iola put her new plant next to the one she'd nearly killed a few days ago, smiling to herself again. The thought of Vinnie made her all aflutter, and she couldn't wait to see him again.

Aww shucks, she thought as she skipped back to the kitchen. *I've got a boyfriend.*

When he'd seen her gorgeous face and bright green eyes come to the window he had to beat feet to get back in hiding. But just at the sight of her, his heart swelled.

And so did his cock.

Fuck, okay, that usually stirred at the sight of her, but he couldn't just walk around rockin' an erection like this. It was like his libido was in complete overdrive.

The night before, after he'd killed the two would-be muggers, he'd gone home just as the hot broad across the hall from him was coming home from a rough night. When she'd seen him in the hall, her eyes had widened and she almost breathed in deeper just to get a whiff of him. He was in complete shock and disbelief. This chick had never even said "good morning" in the hall to him, and here she was, planting her back against the wall, tilting her head, licking her lips and eyeing him up like a diamond necklace.

He had sex with her three times, and it was just as good as with the chick in the bathroom. Better, even. She couldn't get enough of him. He'd had to kick her out of his place when she started nodding off while riding him like a pogo stick.

And he'd still woken up at full-mast. And it hurt, it was throbbing like hell. If he didn't know any better he'd think it was blue balls. But that so couldn't be the problem. In the shower he'd done a little manual relieving, glad when the swelling went down and he could be on his way.

But the sight of her, up in that window ... Christ, he could almost smell her. It was like vanilla cake with an exotic icing. And his jaw was aching for a bite.

He shoved his hands through his hair. Strange that this would be so stressful: every female he saw he wanted. And they all knew it and they were all willing. This was going to kill him.

Oh, but what a hell of a way to die.

He looked back up at her window, but she was no longer in sight. That thing that had a mind of its own stayed put in his pants, behaving itself. Maybe he should just head home for a while. As long as he didn't run into anyone else, he'd likely be fine.

Next to him, her mouth parted as she breathed through a sleep that was starting to loosen its grip on her, Claudia was in a weak dream that included a trip to the beach when she was little. He could almost smell the sun on her skin. He knew that smell.

She was happy. She was content.

Voro put a hand behind his neck, liking the feel of her leg wound across his left knee, trapping him against her. She was incredibly warm. He couldn't remember the last time he'd spent the night with someone, but she'd been scared last night when she thought he was leaving. He'd woken her when he left the washroom after his shower and she called him back to bed with her.

He'd been there ever since, watching her.

Claudia was classically beautiful, with the eyes and full lips that about 80% of the world's population would say was attractive. Her hair was long and glossy. Her body was thin but so incredibly strong. He'd really liked the feeling of those leg muscles under his hands, and especially pressing against his shoulders. Or the way her abdominal muscles had sprung into sight as her hips rolled under him. Her skin had been so soft in comparison to that muscle.

Her nightshirt was still on, but he could feel the swell of her breast against his arm. They were very full, almost like they didn't fit her lithe frame, but who the hell had ever complained about breasts being too big? They were soft as pillows. They were gloriously real.

He thought about what Essum had said. That he was such a girl because he tapped into them when they were at the peak of pleasure, and the tie didn't sever completely. That it was their afterglow he was feeling.

That made sense, actually. He felt like even though he always took off and never saw them again, theoretically wiping him from their very memories, it still felt like it meant something.

Claudia's head tucked tighter into her pillow and she closed her mouth to swallow. She was beginning to ease out of sleep. The warm smell of sunshine on skin was very strong now, and he had to smile to himself. This was definitely all ego trip for him.

But who cared? He was a self-serving asshole. It was in his nature.

Her head moved forward towards him, her chin and lips contacting his bare shoulder. That surprised her, and she stirred slightly, her eyes squeezing tight, then opening very slowly. As he watched her wake the memory of the previous evening flooded back to her. The smell of her contentment faded slightly. Her hand went to her black eye and swollen cheekbone, and she groaned.

He took her hand away from her face and offered her his most consoling smile. "Good morning."

His voice stilled her, and she smiled over at him. "Good morning. How bad is the damage?"

"I don't know. My neck's still sore but I'll get over it." His joke made her blush bright red, even under her bruising. "Oh, you mean you?" She covered her face and he took her hand away again. It made him chuckle. "You're fine. You look bad ass."

She rolled away from him on to her back but he caught her by the shoulder and turned her back to him, hand to her cheek to keep her place as he kissed her slowly, lazily, as though it was for no expected outcome. But of course he knew there would be.

Sunshine turned to chocolate under his hands, and when he tested her mouth with his tongue he found the waters very welcoming. Her hand clutched his shoulder tightly, and her leg winding back around his and her hips turning his way was all the permission he needed.

Her hand slid from his shoulder to stroke at his abdomen, and she must have liked the feel of it. She crowded in closer to him, rising up on one arm to kiss him while he stayed splayed out on his back. He cradled her head in his hands, tasting the sweetness of her lips and tongue with his. The smell of chocolate was so strong he would've sworn she'd just eaten a whole pound of the stuff. It made her absolutely delicious.

Claudia's hand grazed his erection slightly, and as she froze momentarily he pulled back to look at her face. She was debating, and he didn't bother touching on her thoughts. It was obvious where her confusion was coming from.

"Don't worry," he said, taking her hand in his and bringing it back to his chest. "What we did last night is more than enough for me. As long as I can please you, you don't have to do anything else."

Her eyes were locked on his lips, her own were swollen from the kissing already. She took a shuddering breath, taking his bottom lip in hers, biting at it, then opening her mouth fully against his, forcefully, demandingly. His hips kicked of their own accord, nothing to do with him.

Her hand moved south again, taking him fully in her grip, slowly moving along his length, exploring it. That's when he realized she'd never handled one of these things before, and at the realization his mind characteristically tuned into hers. She was worried she was doing it wrong. That she might hurt him. But she still wanted to touch him.

As long as the want was there ...

His hand closed over hers, and he used his thumb to move hers to his head, running it along the ridge. Her hand was so delicate and careful, despite the fact that he'd personally seen it nearly break a guys' nose ... twice. The contradiction had him ready to release.

This was a different kind of arousal. He wasn't using hers, was he? This was entirely him.

"Show me," she whispered, breaking the kiss long enough for those two words. He took her hand to his base, then tightened her grip, pulling it upwards. She pulled away again to watch his face. On the second pass he had to gasp and hold his breath, keeping his eyes closed.

He felt her confidence swell, the scent of orange mixing with chocolate. She gave another slow pull, and he let go of her hand, bunching up the sheets with his own. His other hand wrapped around her back, holding her against him.

He knew she was watching him, could feel her gaze. So he picked up her frequency and got the live feed of what she thought. That could always run the risk of completely fizzling out any excitement, but he took the chance anyway.

She was fixated on his face, the way his neck tensed so tightly the tendons stood out in stark relief. Even his chest muscles were bunched up like he was lifting a ton of weight. She liked to see him breathing through his mouth, out of control. That's what he'd done to her the night before, now she had him in the exact same place.

Without changing pace she wiggled down along him, and when he felt her mouth close over the end of him his neck jerked, thrusting his head back into his pillow.

How long had it been since someone had gone down on him? God, who knew? This was what you got off on when someone wasn't willing to "go all the way," wasn't it? With him, they were always willing. And he'd never been with anyone long enough to get this intimate otherwise.

Her hand kept rhythm but as her mouth sucked at him and her gorgeous, full lips were drawn back and forth, he gave himself over, cut off her thoughts from his, and just let himself feel it. Which lasted all of ten seconds.

Right as he reached the feeling of impending joy, he pinched off the duct to keep from ejaculating right in her mouth. The sensation intensified until he saw stars and he barked out a curse word, which may or may have not been "Fuck," and then he just let it wash through him until all that was left was his own panting.

When he could focus his eyes again, he looked down at her, and she was staring back at him with rapt intensity. A smile touched her lips as they made eye contact.

"Was it ... was it good?"

He barked out a laugh, aware his dick was still in her hands as well as his. And the little fucker was starting to stir again. "My dear Claudia, there are no words."

She smiled, arched herself back along his side again and stayed there, her hand drawing circles on his chest.

"If I go and clean this up ... will you be here when I get back?" He asked.

Her grin widened. "I think I can stay here a while longer."

"Good."

He wasn't fooling himself as he walked naked down the hall to the washroom. This wasn't sexual preference re-education he was doing to her. She was just curious and he – this was the funny part – was the most non-intimidating man she'd known. That was the only way she could explain to herself why she was attracted to him in the first place.

Once again, he was honored that he was the only man that really knew a woman this way.

Chapter Sixteen

He was on his way to work, rushing to his car because he was late. He got in the driver's seat, fiddled with his keys before he finally got the right one, and was just sliding it in the ignition when the voice came from right beside him.

"Do you have any idea what's happening to you right now?"

He shrieked, flattening against the side window of his car and staring at the man in his passenger seat, a guy that had definitely not been there before.

The man terrified him, he knew that right off. His gray eyes were incredibly cold, his mouth was a thin, cruel line in his face, and all his features were so hard ... he wondered if this stranger had just been released from prison.

"No, I wasn't in prison."

Now he was terrified and completely confused. "How did you ... I'm sorry, do I know you?" He tried to figure the stranger out. He was nicely dressed, in a black suit with a black shirt. Black was perfect for him ... he seemed to exude menace.

"Not yet, but you will. I can help you get everything you want, but we do it entirely on my terms."

"What are you talking about?"

"Shut up and listen."

"I'm late for work here, I have to - " He couldn't explain it. One moment he was talking, and the next it felt as though someone had grabbed the tip of his tongue and was pressing it to the bottom of his mouth while pinching his lips shut. He was incapable of speech.

"You know the things you're doing with your mind lately? Those special talents you never had before?"

He raised his eyebrows but couldn't ask *How did you know?*

"Just pay attention. You have no idea what you are capable of, just with the power of your mind. You can use it towards any means you desire. Women, money ... and really, isn't that all that we want?" He leaned over. "Let me teach you and I will show you the meaning of power. It's intoxicating, it's almost ... sinful.

"You're sent these gifts with a purpose. You don't necessarily know what it is yet ... and it's possible you won't even know what that is until your last moment on earth. But when it comes ..." he leaned forward and grinned a terrible grin. "You will be a fucking God."

"Why would you do that?" He asked, almost out of nowhere, but he was glad to have use of his voice again, as wimpy as it might have sounded in comparison to the man in his passenger seat. "I mean ... why help me at all?"

"Because in a little while I too will be a fucking God. But I need your help first."

Essum stared at the transitioning human, waiting. The man's eyes were moving back and forth, he was in the midst of making a decision. His brain transmitted like a PA system.

He was thinking about the men he'd killed the night before. The woman he'd had in his bed later that same night. And he was tempted. As he thought about the promise of power his cock even got hard.

So Essum waited. He knew he had the guy hooked. And he had a lot of time to wait. Within reason, of course. He was known for being impatient.

He kept staring at this man, wondering how the hell this guy was going to take out his old friend, Voro. The man was still a mess, only a day into his change, unable to control his impulses and scared of what he might be able to do, terrified of overestimating what his powers were. And he was scared of Essum, too. Which showed he was smart, as well as a *decipio*. He was, after all, sent by the side of good. And that was not the team Essum was playing for. He should be pissing himself in fear.

Truth was; Essum had a theory. And he was ninety-nine-point-nine percent sure his plan would work, and it was just so perfect that Voro was the one slated for a little R&R. Voro was very powerful, which came with more time spent among humans. And if Essum played his cards right, he could jump right into the level of power that Voro had. Literally into the flesh form that Voro inhabited at this moment. And it wouldn't take Essum six hundred-odd years to get to that level of power, either.

Again, impatient.

All he had to do was get the *frustro* to kill this *decipio*, then Essum could consume the sin, let the *frustro* become a new Sin Eater, end her mortal life, maybe have a little fun with her first, then kill Voro outright and take over the body as he died, not only killing Voro but his *frustro* in the process, since their lives were linked once she killed the *decipio*. Not unlike how a Sin Eater could grab on to the marionette strings outright if he tried hard enough and had enough energy. Easy-peasey. It would speed up the whole next-in-rotation thing, too.

Plus, the body that Voro had been granted was preferable to the one that Essum usually assumed. His was tall but thin. His face seemed to glower more than Voro's. And women had a distrust of him, and Sin Eaters could only influence people to a certain extent without causing irreparable damage. Like mood-altering substances, people never really performed a task or action that they weren't wanting to complete on some level. Unless, of course, they were completely taken over. And again, that was very difficult and exhausting and never ended well for the human.

At the thought of taking Voro's form and power while the heart was still beating he almost felt his own phantom member harden.

On the other hand ... if this didn't work, Essum was so fucked.

Iola was trying to decide between chicken or beef for supper that night, when something bumped the grocery basket she was carrying with her. She jumped, then looked to see who was rudely impeding on her personal space ...

... and then she smiled, feeling her heart speed up just a bit.

"Vinnie, what are you doing here?" Stupid stupid question.

"Getting groceries. Same as you." His smile deepened his dimples and his teeth were ridiculously perfect. He was wearing jeans and a deep blue T-shirt with sandals, pretty casual.

"Thank you," her voice gave out on her and she tried again with an apologetic smile. "Thank you for the African Violet."

His forehead smoothed when he smiled even broader. "You got it ... that's good."

Then they just stared at each other, mutually mute before they both laughed.

"Are you working today?" She asked as a polite inquiry.

"Yeah, I'm on break right now. So I'm picking up a few things since this place is close to work. And you're off today, right?" He colored slightly. "I mean, I notice that you're never on air Monday or Tuesday nights."

Iola wasn't creeped out by that at all. She thought he was absolutely adorable when embarrassed. "Yeah. I go back to work tomorrow night."

"Well, I'm off at six. I'm on call but ... could I come by and see you?" Vinnie wasn't even trying to mask the hopefulness in his eyes. He was always so sincere and caring. He's probably so attentive in all ways ...

She felt her heart speed up a bit more. "Yeah," she said without hesitation, then cursing in her head because she sounded ridiculously excited.

"Great. I'll come by right after work."

"I'll make supper," she offered, then held a hand out to the meat case. "Chicken or beef?"

"I have no preference. Whatever you like."

"I prefer chicken."

He nodded that it sounded good. "I'll bring wine."

"Okay," she said, aware her voice was getting higher like a school girl. "I'll see you after you're done work."

"If it's later than 6:30 I'll call."

She nodded and was surprised when he gave her an affectionate kiss on the cheek. He stayed close, gazed down at her for just another moment, his eyes going over her face, her lips. "I'll see you then."

She just kept nodding, watching him walk away with his own grocery basket. She didn't fail to notice how his back shifted under his shirt, and how good those jeans looked on his butt. He was every kind of perfect, wasn't he?

She shook herself back to being sensible and went off in search of vegetables, then remembered she hadn't picked up the chicken. So she went back the ten or so steps to get it, giving herself heck the whole time for being so easily flustered, hoping no one noticed what a mess she was.

Whatever. She didn't care. She and her handsome doctor had another date. Iola may as well have skipped over to the produce section.

"I want you in me," Claudia gasped.

Damien lifted his head from kissing her stomach, on his way back to her mouth having just given her a good twenty minutes of lip and tongue heaven. "What?" His voice was hoarse.

"I want you in me."

"Claudia, are you ... are you sure?"

Claudia nodded, swallowing. She was as nervous as a virgin, but then again, every time she had been with a man it had either been while intoxicated or while she was being forced. So ... this was her first time in a way. And she was terrified he would say no, find her unworthy somehow ...

"I would be honored," he said, kissing her stomach just above her belly button, alternating lips and tongue up between her breasts to her neck.

Again his voice had her aching in a low, dark place. She brought her legs up to his hips as he met her mouth with his fantastic lips, his kiss holding her completely hostage. Not that she wanted to get away from it. She cleaved to him with the full length of her body, feeling his erection hot against her stomach.

"I have to go get something first, from my jacket in the living room," he said against her skin, and she nodded. When he pulled away from her, however, she gave a moan of disappointment which made him laugh slowly. "I will be back ... believe me." And the way his eyes flared as he looked down at her, naked in the twisted sheets they'd been making a mess of, made her believe him beyond a shadow of a doubt.

She nodded her understanding, rolling over on to her stomach to watch him leave. That big, heavy body of his was such a pleasure to look at; the thickness of his back, broadness of his shoulders. She'd never been able to appreciate the male anatomy. But with him, it was like she was born anew.

It seemed he knew her history and preferences, and yet she hadn't told him. And he certainly hadn't asked the whys or hows. He simply accepted that ... she wanted him.

Or maybe this whole night and half a day had been a dream. A very vivid, long, explosive dream. Not bloody likely, she thought, touching her eye socket and the side of her nose. The fight had certainly been real.

When Damien returned she smiled up at him, and he stopped for a moment in the doorway, just looking at her. She looked away from him and dipped her head down into the pillow she'd been hugging since she rolled over to wait for him.

"What?" She asked, her voice muffled by down feathers and Egyptian cotton.

"The view this way is ... exquisite." He came forward and sat next to her, leaning over to kiss a trail down her spine that made her close her eyes with a sigh and shiver. He stopped at the small of her back, climbed on to the bed next to her, and ran his hands along the length of her upper body, raising gooseflesh on her back, increasing the ache between her legs.

She made a move to roll over but he grunted that he wanted her to wait, and she hid a smile as he kissed her back again, his hand caressing her butt in a slightly more aggressive way that she didn't mind in the least. Especially as one finger dipped down between her legs to the place that was aching for contact with him.

She gasped as he stroked her from this different angle, parting her legs and arching her back to allow him full access.

Just as she thought she was going to climax again, he rolled her on to her back. His mouth latched on to one breast, and she moaned at how rough he was as he put his hand back to work. Before long she was pulling at his hair and crying out loudly while he got into position to enter her.

She put a hand to his chest, her orgasm just starting to fade. "Wait," she whispered. "I need to be on top."

He stared at her for a moment, then smiled. "That would be … wonderful."

He carefully laid next to her, and she threw one leg over his hips and straddled him. She felt his eyes on her body, her breasts, and she could feel how excited he was.

"I have to go slow," she reminded him, and he nodded.

"We can stop whenever you want," he responded, and that's all the information she needed. She reached down to that part she'd usually been scared of, stood it up, and slid all the way down its length, watching his face as he watched hers. She gasped at how perfectly he fit. How he filled her entirely. And at how her insides seemed to quiver at the mere presence of him.

He grunted, but he kept his eyes on hers, like he was gauging for any sign she was freaking out. But she wasn't. She rolled her hips forward slightly, feeling the friction and then taking him in again.

"Oh Claudia," he groaned, his breath starting to sound incredibly ragged. "You are … sublime."

"Is this right? Tell me what to do," she knew it sounded like begging. Again.

He took firm hold on her hips, raising her weight off of him, then he pushed upwards while lowering her down. The sensation made her breath come out almost like a sob. Then he did it again, correcting the angle this time. As he hit the mark she cried out, holding his hands where they were and trying to get him to speed up. But he resisted her.

Claudia felt frustration but it vanished as soon as he reached that same spot again. She closed her eyes, feeling him inside her, but also becoming aware of how she was letting him in. How she allowed him to fit.

Another thrust and he grunted, and she opened her eyes to notice with satisfaction that he was on the verge of coming himself, the same tightness in his face that he'd had when she'd gone down on him earlier. She rocked her hips against him and he moaned, opening his eyes and smiling at her.

"You think you're ready to be in charge now?"

She nodded, licking her lips. When he growled and let go of her hips, she began moving on her own, throwing her head back and letting herself find the pace that felt ... *good*. And right. He didn't say anything or make a sound, she may as well have been on her own exploring her own body. And that made her affection for him swell even more.

Her pace increased almost like she had nothing to do with it, and she braced herself by putting her hands on his strong chest, his hips meeting hers at the same pace. Now she'd lost some of that control, but that was ... that was why she came.

Her nails dug in as he bellowed with her, her legs tensing, her head going back on its own as she called out his name.

She rocked over him throughout her orgasm, and when she felt the last of the shudders he pulled her down against him, rolling over on to her.

"Are you okay?" He asked sincerely.

"That was ... amazing," she said honestly, the ability to breathe just barely returning.

"Are you sore?"

"No."

He pushed his hips upward and she realized he was still hard. "Oh," she said in surprise, freezing him.

"Something wrong?"

She smiled, putting her hand to the side of his face. "No, not at all. I thought ... I thought you finished."

He smiled almost wickedly, rocking back and forth into her again. The push and drag made her bite her lip, and she was amazed her body was back on board for another go already. But then again, he seemed to know all the right buttons to push with her.

"My dear Claudia," he said slowly, drawing out a kiss while thrusting a few more times until she was panting again. "You will definitely know when I finish."

This had been Essum's next stop, and he'd arrived at a great time. The lesbian woman was really broadening her horizons.

He didn't take form and materialize right in the room with them, but he stayed to watch. God, he really missed the fucking. And this woman's tits were fantastic. He would've given up eternity at that point to switch places with Voro, the lucky asshole. And the prick seemed to have gotten quite good at this. The woman was in total rapture as she climaxed, completely unable to control her body, and the heat of her arousal was like a freaking sun flare against his senses.

And the smell of chocolate ... god, he'd forgotten how good they smelled during sex.

Now she was underneath his old friend, both of them shameless and lost in lust, his friend's back bare to him, his ass the piston of what was pumping into and out of the woman under him, the sounds coming out of her telling him everything he needed to know. And his friend's thoughts were clear to him; fuck yeah, she felt as good as she looked.

Well, there was certainly this to look forward to. He would inherit all of Voro's tricks and knowledge. And once he'd had some fun with Voro's *frustro*, he was coming after this dyke next.

Chapter Seventeen

Iola put the rice in the oven to keep it warm, and was just about to start her stir fry when she heard Claudia's apartment door creak open. She almost had control of her curiosity, but then of course that control totally withered and she ran back to her apartment door to watch out the peep hole.

Five o'clock at night and they were finally out of bed. But Claudia was only in her nightshirt, her long, thick hair tousled at her back of her head, up on her tiptoes as Damien Talon was kissing her good bye. He had his suit coat over one arm, and her wrapped up in the other one. It was one of those hot, sexy and steamy kisses that could only come after really, really good and sweaty sex. The kiss that promised more of the same.

She watched her friend writhe against him, her hips against his, one leg raised up behind her, and he was holding himself right against her, grinding into her.

Iola put a hand to her throat. The sight of him, no matter what he was doing, had heat flooding into her cheeks. And Claudia looked so incredibly ... gorgeous. Even bed-headed and underdressed as she was, Iola had never seen her so ... glowy. God ... he must be fabulous.

When Damien raised his head, smiling down at Claudia, then dropping one more kiss to her pouty but smiling lips, Iola looked away. She couldn't stand herself for spying like that, and she tiptoed back to her kitchen to continue making supper. For the date she had. *Remember Vinnie?*

She put the chicken in the pan to cook, then finished chopping up the peppers. When she heard Claudia's door close, that's when she felt her back finally relax. He was leaving the building. She wouldn't hear them, echoing out of her bedroom, filling her apartment with the sounds of how fantastic they were in bed together. Oh thank God ... it was quiet.

While it had been going on she put on her earplugs and listened to her iPod for a while, but she always found herself turning it down to eavesdrop. She told herself it was to see if they were done yet, but the truth was she was a bit sick in the head. Because she was listening for Damien's voice. And sort of getting turned on by it.

She was such a degenerate.

She chopped faster, stirred the chicken around, and went to her room to change. She wanted to look good, just in case Vinnie got there early, although, of course, that was highly unlikely.

She put on a mid-length black skirt and a red top she liked to wear because it made her feel skinny, and she thought it gave the illusion of breasts as well. The front had a plunging cowl neck to it, and the rest of it sat nicely along her hips and waist. The back was open, too.

Then she hurried back to move the chicken to a bowl and put it in the oven to keep warm. She would wait a while before doing the vegetables, just so they wouldn't get limp.

She set the table next, even laying out a tablecloth she'd forgotten she had. She found one beeswax candle in a drawer and put it in a holder in the center of the table, next to the tulips Vinnie had brought the night before. The closer it got to 6:30, the more excited she became. When there was a knock at the door, she flew there quickly, opening it wide without looking to see who it was, and thoroughly frightened Claudia.

"Oh ... oh, sorry. Hi Claudia."

"Hey Iola. What's up?" Her friend looked her up and down, and Iola found it strange considering Claudia had spent much of the day loudly convincing her she was totally straight.

Well, that was bitchy. Where'd that come from?

Iola smiled. "What's up?"

"I'm just heading to work. Are you ... are you going on another date?"

Iola shrugged, unable to read Claudia's voice. Her friend gave off an air of being totally blissed out, her afterglow was almost unbearable, and yet it sounded like she might be ... jealous?

"Vinnie's coming over for supper. I saw him today at the supermarket."

Claudia smiled, genuinely pleased. "Well, good. I hope he's good to you. I just was just letting you know that I ... work tonight."

Iola nodded, and as Claudia was heading off she had to stop her. "Claudia?"

"Yeah?"

"Was that ... was that Damien I was hearing?"

Her tough-as-nails neighbor actually blushed. "Oh shit. Could you ... could you hear that?" Iola felt a strange emotion she couldn't place to see the flush of pleasure sweep across Claudia's gorgeous face. A look that had been caused by someone else.

Iola felt embarrassed now, too. "Ummm ... yeah."

"Like ... every word?"

She hadn't heard words. She'd heard moans and grunts and cries of delight and squeaking springs and banging headboards. "Well, not every word but ... what's going on?"

Claudia laughed, covering her face. "I don't know. I think I ... fell off the wagon."

"Like, the Lesbian Wagon?"

"Yeah, that's the one."

"Wow."

"Yeah ... it was pretty 'wow.' But I'm sure you could tell."

Iola gave a naughty little smile. "You owe me. I couldn't sleep last night."

"Shit, I'm sorry."

"Don't sweat it. I hope to be returning the favor soon."

Claudia just waved a hand at her. "Have fun tonight, Iola."

"Thanks. You too. Be safe."

"I will."

She watched Claudia down the hall and then shut her door. Damn, she couldn't decide if she was jealous of Claudia ... or Damien.

When he'd watched Claudia shut her apartment door, he'd turned away to head back down the hall to the stairwell. He hadn't expected to smell her in the hall.

Voro stopped outside Iola's door, inhaling deeply. Jasmine and vanilla, unmistakably her. She'd been on the other side of this door ... and had she watched them? The faint trace of chocolate gave him hope that she had. And that the kiss he'd shared with Claudia had excited her.

Then Essum's warning had come back, and he quickened his pace down the hall and the stairs to the fresh air outside. Iola's function was to bring him right into the hands of someone that would kill his mortal body, sending him back to darkness for eternity. Shouldn't that be warning enough? Did he not have the ability to be with whoever he wanted? Was there really anything that could be better than the ease with which he could satiate every hunger he had?

Did he need to be anywhere near Iola?

Of course he did, for one reason only; because he couldn't have her.

The nature of a Sin Eater. Everything came easy to them, if something presented a challenge, they were worse than a dog with a bone.

He should really get some work done anyway. There were sins that had to be released. But first, he had to change.

He drove his Beamer back to his hotel, made his way up to the room Portia was nice enough to pay for, and let himself in with a key card. It was dark, the blinds were closed.

As soon as he stepped inside he could smell cayenne pepper, and without looking up or turning on a light in the room he just said, "Hello, Portia."

The scent of pepper intensified as she flew across the room at him, hitting him from behind into the table next to the door. Her fists pounded his back almost enough to knock the wind out of him.

"You bastard ... you fucking bastard. Where have you been?"

He turned to catch her hands, and she stopped swinging. He turned on a light overhead, just in time to see that she was crying ... and incredibly drunk. And she really smelled like his three thousand dollar cognac.

"Portia, what is it?"

"I came here last night and I waited for you. And you never came back, this is the first time you've been here. Housekeeping didn't even have to come back today, I checked. Where the fuck were you?"

"Portia, what's happened? What's wrong?" He was trying to get into her head but she was so furious her mind was swirling uncontrollably and she was drunk besides, so any train of thought he did pick up on suddenly changed course halfway through. Something about her bitch of a sister, the younger, prettier one. The one that had been a cheerleader.

"Chrissy," she wept. "That little shit sister of mine. She's getting fucking married."

"Isn't that good?" Fuck, he was really working without his net here. As soon as he said it her entire vision turned red with anger.

"How can that be good?" She spat, stalking away. "She's eight years younger than I am."

Shit. If she hadn't been drunk he could have seen this coming. This was in the realm of a "relationship" conversation, and he was really not interested.

"Getting married at twenty-four. She must be fucking retarded." Portia went back to the armchair where she'd apparently been self-medicating. For a while now.

"Did you leave me any?" He asked wryly, tossing his coat on a hook in the entryway. Then he had to duck because she threw a glass at him. "Fuck, Portia," he stammered, putting a hand to his chest like an old lady. The glass rained on to the thick-pile carpet at his feet and he stepped over it.

"Relax, it was empty." She flopped into her chair, and he came into the sitting area, flipping on a light switch that worked the floor lamp behind her. She cringed, but before she could bitch at him he was already talking.

"You can't really be jealous that she's getting married, moving to a suburb and popping out kids while her husband nails his secretary?" He unbuttoned the top few buttons of his shirt. The presence of insanity usually raised the temperature of a room, especially when the blinds were closed. Voro would have killed her to get a window open.

"He's a Boy Scout for Pete's sake. He's madly in love with her. If anything, he should be suspect of his parentage for any of their children."

"So what is this then?" His voice was calming her down, and he was getting the impression that she'd really been needled by her mother more than her sister.

"Mother called," she drawled out, tossing back some more cognac. He winced. She was drinking it like a Pepsi. "She says it's nice to have a daughter that isn't going to let the bloodline down."

"What does that mean?"

"My sister's going to give her grandbabies to carry on our idiotic lineage. That's what she's so pleased about. Nothing else I could have done would have topped that."

"You're running a Fortune 500 company."

"I know."

"You make more income than your parents ever could."

"Trust me, I know."

"So your mother can just go … fuck herself." He stood in front of her now, undoing the cuffs of his shirt. He felt her emit a blast of heat. Now he was talking her language.

"What did you just say?"

The scent of chocolate made him smile down at her. "Your mother can go fuck herself."

She grabbed his belt buckle, leaned forward and pulled him to her. "Say that again."

"She can go *fuck* herself."

Then she fisted him right in the crotch and he doubled over, tripping as his shoes got caught up on the carpet and landed on his ass on the ground at her feet.

"Who the hell is that?'

"Who?" He gasped, cupping himself and bowling over sideways. He thought he was going to throw up.

"Who is it that I'm smelling all over you? It's Alfred Sung. I know; I used to wear it. Who is she?" She was clenching and unclenching her fists. He was going to have to work harder to anticipate her mood.

"Fuck Portia. I think you broke it."

"Good. Now tell me where you were or I will cut you off."

He clenched his hand tighter on his manhood. She scoffed and rolled her eyes. "I meant money, asshole. God, that piece of flesh is really the most important thing to you men, isn't it?"

He eased himself back up to a sitting position carefully. "Isn't it the only reason you want me?"

He had her there, but there was no victory in it. Not if she cut off his money flow. Of course, given his talents he could always get money. But this way was ... okay, he liked their arrangement, too. He'd admit it.

But never to her.

She was wearing a navy blue blouse and a light grey skirt, office attire that he liked very much on her. He reached out and pulled off her heels, tossing them towards the door, then got up on his knees in front of her. He took her glass, poured a serving of cognac out for her, took a swallow himself, then handed the glass to her. She watched him the whole, time, breathing through parted lips.

He was feeling how she hated him and wanted him at the same time. That she knew he was using her, but that she was also using him, so that cancelled out any wrongdoing. And she wanted him to take off that shirt because it smelled like some other bitch he'd been with and she couldn't stand it.

He undid the rest of the buttons on his shirt and took it off. She rubbed her legs together as she eased them to one side, pointedly trying to ignore him and doing a horrible job. She took another drink, rolling her eyes as far away from him as she could.

He put a hand on her leg, pushing it between her knees and leaving it right there. He leaned forward to kiss her neck. She tried to pull back but that was also a lame showing.

"Portia," he whispered, sliding his other hand to the back of her neck. "Why did you wait here for me?"

"So I could rip your balls off with my bare hands."

The scent of her arousal proved that to be a total lie. He pushed his hand further up her thigh, and she closed her eyes, clenching her jaw tight.

"I think you're lying."

"I ... I just wanted to see you."

"Why?"

"To talk."

"Another lie. I think you wanted me to make you feel better." He grabbed her by one knee and roughly turned her to face him, forcing her legs apart and pushing his way between them. She made a sound of slight protest, but she was already breathing heavily. "I'm sorry," he kept going. "You're right. I should have been here. Right when and where you wanted me to be. Doing what you tell me to."

She nodded, dropping her empty glass to the heavy carpet. "Yeah, you should have."

"Punish me however you like."

"I'm not going to punish you."

"Why not?"

"Because you want me to. And I'm not in the mood to give you what you want."

He smiled. "Fair enough."

She kissed him forcefully and he leaned back, pulling her off the chair on to his lap. She may have been drunk but it was completely clear what she wanted. And of course, since she was emitting the scent of chocolate his body was prepared and willing to give her that very thing.

She backed off, grabbing his hair tightly and pulling him back. "What was her name?"

He shook his head. "Why would I tell you that?"

"Tell me."

"Her name is Claudia."

"You mean, her name *was* Claudia."

"It still is."

"No, she's as good as dead to you. You're not seeing her again."

"And why's that," he asked as he kissed his way down her neck, pushing as far against the buttons of her shirt as he could, trying to latch on to a nipple without the aid of his hands.

"Because you spent the night there. And we don't spend the night together. Ever."

"You don't even want me at your house, remember? You tell me that if I'm in town, you want me staying here. And then you always leave right after I've fucked you."

She hated that he used that word to describe what they did. The smell of cayenne pepper flared up again, but he ripped a button from its thread and got a lock on her breast, which made her forget how angry she was.

He carried her to the bed, dropping her in roughly and stripping while she undressed herself. This part of the suite was mostly dark, but that didn't matter. He'd seen Portia climax many times already; he knew very well what it looked like. She was a sad person, he knew that, and he knew he was just making it worse. But he was what he was, just like Popeye, and at the moment he was just a walking fuck toy.

He let his weight fall on her, and she allowed him between her legs without any more foreplay. He thrust in, maybe a bit before she was completely ready, but she moaned against his mouth anyway, repositioning her hips so he could dip deeper.

Her level of intoxication made his experience with her orgasm pretty trippy. He was feeling high as she climaxed once, twice, then on the third one it was like he had absolutely no control and he was screaming along with her. When he let go of her mind the room was spinning.

Portia got up to go to the washroom, and as she passed the hallway next to the door she cried out, and he saw the blood rise on her skin through her eyes as she looked down at the bottom of her foot. She'd cut herself on the glass she'd thrown at him.

"That'll teach you," he said smugly before she even said a word.

Chapter Eighteen

That chrome-domed scary fucker led the way down the hallway at the police department, and as he followed Essum he was feeling incredibly nervous. Under Essum's instruction he just kept thinking over and over, *"I belong here, I belong here. You don't even see me. I belong here."*

And so far, no one had said a word. Not even when they passed through a heavy, metal door that read, "No Admittance Without Permission." And the next thing he knew, Essum was skipping past jail cells, coming to stop in front of one saying, *"Wake up, shithead."*

He tried not to look in the cells. It stunk down here ... holy Christ it stunk like rotten eggs and garbage. He avoided eye contact with the sad sacks that were incarcerated, and when he looked up, Essum was eyeing him with curiosity.

"You can smell them, can't you?" His strange instructor wondered out loud.

He nodded, covering his nose with a hand. "God, what is that?"

Essum just laughed, then jerked his head towards the cell that had got his attention. "Meet Charlie."

He stepped in front of the zoo cage that held a very small man, who was just sitting up on his bed. At the sight of him, Charlie froze.

"Who – who are you?"

Essum spoke first. Or ... he didn't speak. He could hear Essum's voice in his head, but the guy's mouth didn't move. He heard Essum's voice say, *This is the man that's going to make us Gods, Charlie.* It was like THX stereo in his head. Was he ... was he speaking telepathically?

Essum nodded at him. "Yes, yes I am. See, Charlie can't actually see me like you can."

"Holy shit," he muttered, staring at Essum in wonder.

The man in the cell jerked. "Who are you?" He demanded again. "Who are ... who are you talking to?"

He realized he'd turned his head to Essum, and apparently Charlie was getting freaked right out that he was talking to someone that wasn't there.

He's talking to me, shit head. Essum rolled his eyes for his benefit. "We need one with a weaker mind," he said in a confiding manner. "Charlie is really going to come in handy." Then he turned his attentions back to Charlie. *Now, we're going to get this cell open and you're getting out of jail free, again. Aren't you a lucky fucker?*

Charlie was nodding and smiling in a completely insane way. "I am grateful, I am so grateful."

Then get over here and let's blow this joint.

When Essum turned his eyes to his student, he gulped. "What?" He asked.

"Try it," Essum suggested, pointing to the lock.

"What?"

"Just try unlocking it."

What was this, a joke? "How?"

"With your brain, what I've been telling you to use for the last twelve hours. Just think the lock open."

He moved over in front of it, staring at the weird key hole. With his brain, he imagined putting a key in it, turning it, and hearing the tumblers giving way. To his shock, the sound was real, and the door swung towards them slightly. He took the door in his hand, as though he couldn't believe he'd done it.

Essum clapped a few times, slow and sarcastic. "Good job. You're renewing my faith in your purpose."

Charlie came forward with a hang-dog look on his face, and he embraced him. "Thank you," he said. "Thank you."

"Poor Charlie," Essum said, looking at the small man forlornly. "He really is lost."

"What's ..." he felt bad saying it in front of the guy. "What's wrong with him?"

"Nothing," Charlie said to him, pulling back and widening his eyes. "The Master is divine."

Essum rolled his eyes again and shut the cell door loudly. It made Charlie wince, but the guy never wondered why doors opened and closed without keys or hands to operate them. "He hears voices. So adding one more to the mix master in Charlie's gray matter really isn't going to hurt the guy."

He nodded, then looked back to Charlie, who had been following his gaze to where Essum stood. But of course ... he didn't see him. He only saw an empty corridor.

"You ... you can see him?" Charlie whispered with great reverence.

He just nodded, really not liking the crazed devotion he was seeing in those eyes.

"You must be ... you must be a God."

Told you Charlie, Essum chimed in, in hi-fi stereo. *We will all be Gods when this is done. And he is going to be the one to take out Voro for us.*

His head snapped up to latch on to Essum's eyes. "Who's Voro?"

Essum smile again, coldly. "The man whose body and purpose I am going to steal. Charlie will help us, because he and Charlie have already had a couple of disagreements. But more to the point, Voro is ... Voro's the man I need you to kill."

"This was delicious," Vinnie said, wiping his mouth with his napkin then setting it on his empty plate. "Thank you so much."

Iola shrugged, taking the plate and stacking it on hers. "I'm glad you liked it. There are only so many things I know how to make." She took the dishes to the sink as he poured them both another glass of the Penfolds Chardonnay he'd brought. The bottle was only half gone; they were both prudently limiting their alcohol intake. Him because he was on call, her because she didn't want to do anything stupid.

She sat down across from him again, and he reached a hand out across the tabletop to her. She took it, and he smiled at her comfortably. "It is so ... easy, being with you."

"I hope you mean you're comfortable," she guessed.

"I am. That's exactly what it is."

"Good," his thumb was tracing circles on the back of her hand, but his eyes were solely on hers. She met his gaze, not feeling over-scrutinized in the least. Actually, she liked how his eyes felt on her. It made her feel ... pretty.

He stood, keeping hold of her hand, came towards her, then pulled her to her feet in front of him. Only waiting long enough to take a breath, he pulled her in close and kissed her nice and slow, his lips soft but demanding.

She sighed against them, then put her arms around the back of his neck. His hands on her hips were warm, and they made her feel small and dainty.

He pulled back slightly to rest his forehead on hers, smiling down at her. She returned the smile, her hands getting a grip on the front of his shirt. "Wine tastes really good on your lips," he said softly, which made her laugh.

"Well, thanks - " he cut her off with another kiss, deeper this time, lifting her off her feet so she was completely mashed against him and at his mercy.

Just as his tongue was making her quiver in his grasp, there was an odd, alien sound that sounded like the whistle a camp counselor or kindergarten teacher would give to get the attention of a large group.

He put her down, parting from her mouth with a muttered, "You gotta be kidding me."

Her heart was racing, and she felt frustration somewhere a lot lower than that as she gave her best guess. "Work?"

"Yeah, that's the sound for texts from work." He reached across the table to get his Blackberry, flicking it on and staring down at that damn screen. "Shit. I have to go. Car accident."

Iola wanted to stomp her foot, but at the same time ... he was being summoned to save lives. So how could you fault a guy like that?

She shrugged instead. "I understand," she said, not without a touch of poutiness in her voice. "It's not like I won't see you again ... right?"

He smiled at her warmly, stepping against her again and capturing her chin in one hand. "Next time I make you supper, and if I get called to work I'm taking your shoes with me so I know you'll be there when I get back."

"You're going to hold me hostage?"

"Yep," he confirmed before planting a controlled kiss on her lips then turned for the door. She followed, holding the door open as he shrugged on his jacket and stepped into his shoes.

"Well, be careful," she offered lamely. He stepped back into her apartment, pulling the door away from her and then pulling her close for another curl-your-toes, melt-your-liquid-foundation kiss.

"I will miss you," he said after a moment, his voice a bit hoarse.

"I'll miss you," she said back, then he pulled the door open and was gone.

Iola returned to her kitchen, her shoulder sagging and her libido giving her a hell of a dressing down. Her body was actually annoyed with her.

Well, at least she could do the dishes to calm herself down. And lucky her, there was still an entire half bottle of wine left over from supper ...

Something is not right here ... Portia froze in the door way of her home. Her key fob had disarmed her alarm system, but usually she heard the beep as she was opening the interior door of her house.

She didn't hear it. Or had she, and just not paid any attention? She turned back to the curb beyond the lush, well-manicured lawn, but the cab had already pulled away. So she was on her own.

She pulled out her cell phone anyway, flipping it open so she could easily call for help if needed. She toed the door open, wishing for the first time that she hadn't been so hell-bent on completely consuming Damien's supply of cognac. She would have loved to have better control here. The more she tried to focus on sounds and images in the dark of the house, the more overactive her imagination got.

She stepped into her foyer, hand reaching out instinctively for the light switch. She turned it on, but nothing happened. Illogically, she flicked it up and down a few more times, but still nothing happened. The power was out, that's why the alarm didn't beep when she came in.

Then she looked back outside. The exterior lights on the front of the house were blazing, as were the street lights up and down her block. What the –

There wasn't time to finish the thought. She was grasped from behind, and as she watched the front door of her home was closed before she could even shout for help.

She landed on her stomach, her keys and cell phone flying out of her hands and sliding across the hardwood from her. She tried to get up on all fours and crawl towards them, her eyes cutting through the dark to see what else she could defend herself with, when impossibly strong hands flipped her on to her back. She did shriek then, her nails clawing outwards, catching the softness of someone's skin on their flight path. There was a male scream of pain, and she brought one knee up between the legs that were spread over her. The male voice then stopped yelping and moaned. She got out from under him and got to her feet, flying though the entry into her living room. She grabbed a fire poker from the set next to the fireplace, and she held it at the ready while her other hand reached for the cordless phone. She turned it on without looking at it, and brought it to her ear.

There was no sound. Because the power was out and cordless phones don't work without electricity.

Shit. Fuck. Shit-fuck.

There was a laugh, and she wheeled wildly to her right, a man coming into the glow coming through the front picture windows. He was medium-skinned with impossibly pale eyes. She didn't recognize him but as soon as she saw him she was frightened.

Portia didn't know how eyes could inspire that kind of terror. Because his handsome face was smiling at her, non-threatening, yet she knew he meant to hurt her.

"Who are you? What do you want?" She knew it was all standard horror-movie dialogue, but what else could she say? She had to fight her own terror just to get enough air into her lungs.

"Portia Torregrossa. Funny, I thought you'd be taller. Or at least bigger."

She shook the poker. "Who are you?"

"Don't you get it? Your last name means 'Big Tower.' Surely you know the translation of your last name?"

"Get the fuck out of here."

Another form came through the doorway, a small man that was nursing his groin with one hand and holding a knife in the other. He looked understandably pissed off, and his look was no friendlier than this other fucker. But for some reason she was still more scared of the talker.

"This is my friend, Charlie." The talker held a hand out to Charlie, who was just standing there, staring at her. And ... rubbing himself. What the –

Again, thought cut off. The man didn't move, didn't say anything, but she was back looking at steel-eyes without him even telling her to. He took another step towards her. "It's time for you to serve a greater purpose. And if you behave, you might even like it."

"Fuck you."

The man laughed, and it pained her heart to the very core to hear it. It also scared the shit out of her. Even Charlie looked agitated, and he'd been staring at her so intently he was basically ignoring the other man.

"Get out of my house. Just take what you want, and get out of here." To her own horror she began weeping when Charlie took a step towards her. "Please ... please just get out of here."

"We will," the talker said, but all she could see was Charlie's face as he came towards her. Then she got an image ... a picture in her mind of what he was going to do to her, and that's when she started screaming.

Voro was stepping out of the shower when he just felt ... something ... very strange. He put a hand to the center of his chest, and his vision swam for a moment. Then he caught a smell and one word came to mind ... *Portia.*

He swayed against the bathroom counter, then squeezed his eyes shut to steady his vision. Oh God ... she was in trouble, wasn't she? She was hurt. She needed him.

This was strange. He never got neural transmissions from people that weren't with him at that moment. Especially if he wasn't reaching out to them. And Portia ... Portia must have reached her house by now. But ... he was still partially linked to her because of the fucking, right?

That had to be it. But ... what the hell was happening to her?

He tried to sort through the torrential emotion raging through him. She was scared, she was absolutely fucking terrified ... she was mad. She was ... in great pain.

He was dressing as he sorted through this. He'd seen the terrible things people to do to each other, but to have the victim's point of view being forced into his brain ... he couldn't deal with this. As he headed for the door, keys in hand, the room titled and moved on its own, and he put a hand out to the wall to orient himself again. Then he rushed back to the washroom to throw up.

He had to help her. He had to get to her and help her immediately.

He made it down to the elevator, through the lobby and out into the parkade. He had a moment where he couldn't remember where he'd parked, so he flashed the lights using the fob on his key chain. His BMW flashed its lights in response, as if saying *"Over here, dumb ass."*

He more stumbled to the car than walked to it. To anyone else he would have looked too drunk to drive, but luckily no one was around. He sank into the seat and drew a few calming breaths. It was no good for him to go rushing off worked up. Portia was a good twenty minute drive away. He was going to have to speed to get there.

But he had to. She needed him. She really did.

Chapter Nineteen

He sat on the stairs, listening to the screaming in the front living room. No matter how tightly he covered his ears, he was hearing everything clear as day. Not only because there were no sound-proof doors between him and what was doing in the other room.

He could hear her. As tightly as he tried to batten down his hatches, he couldn't block her out. She was absolutely suffering right now. And just behind her utter torment, he was picking up on Charlie's crazed passion as he raped her.

He covered his head with his hands. *I don't want this,* he repeated, nearly unable to hear his own thoughts. *I changed my mind. I don't want any part of this insanity.* Now if he could just gather his stones enough to go in there and help her.

A hand was placed on his shoulder.

"Oh son, you can't help her now," came that calm, cold voice he was beginning to hate. "Trust me, by this point, she'd just as soon die as live."

He tightened his arm tighter around his own neck. Fuck, he could feel it. She wanted to die. She was giving up the fight. He felt the choking grip that Charlie had on her, he felt the way the lights were diming out. And he could still feel the pain of the rape.

"She is going to the good side, though. She'll be happier there. She wasn't terribly happy here, you can sense that, right?"

Shut up. Shut up – stop trying to make this okay.

"As you wish. You're such a tender thing, considering the power you're going to have when this is all done."

He raised his head to look at Essum. "I can't take this. She's in my head and this is wrong and ... I can't." His tears started to run, and he covered his head on his knees again.

"Take this as a training exercise. Try blocking it."

"I can't!" He snapped, sitting upright and sending spittle flying. "She's in my head, I'm trying to pull her out but she's dug in with all ten fingernails. The more I pull the more she rips out of me.

And that fucking degenerate of yours ... I can feel him. I can feel how she hates it and he likes it and it's fucking me up."

"You can ... you can hear Charlie clearly?"

"Yeah. He's a fucking mess ... I can't stand having him in my head."

"You understand him? The mentally ill are harder to read. They lack focus and - "

He groaned and clutched his stomach. The woman had passed out but she wasn't dead, and Charlie was losing his erection so he was pissed off and cutting her ... cutting off her left breast. He was going to throw up.

"He's focused alright," he answered Essum weakly. "He's pretty fucking lucid."

"Poor Charlie. He's incapable of orgasm it seems," Essum chimed in thoughtfully after a pause, almost like he checked in on him as well. "You could really make his day by sending one right to his brain."

"What?"

"All you have to do is think the sensation right at him, and he'll be totally convinced that he just came. Oh, that would really make his day."

He stared at Essum as though he couldn't figure out what the asshole was even saying. "Are you insane?"

"Get in there and give him one. Please. He's been so loyal. He really needs this." The please was said as though Essum knew he really didn't have to add it.

Still, he opened his mouth. "Fuck that - " then he froze, hands going to his throat. Something had hold of him, and though Essum hadn't moved, he knew Essum had taken over the puppet strings and was giving a good hard yank.

"Get in there, and get Charlie off already. You can have a go when he's done, if you like. That shit you pump out won't even show any DNA. You're above CSI now, son!"

He was being frog-marched by invisible hands down the stairs and to the entry to the living room. Thank God the lights were mostly off; the only light came from the street lights through the living room window.

As soon as he saw the scene he wanted to start screaming, but Essum had a hold of his tongue so it seemed.

That's why she got quieter, he thought absently. Charlie had cut off her tongue and put it back in her mouth the other way around. There was blood everywhere, and Charlie's knife work was spraying red all over the cream-colored silk furniture.

He thought he was going to pass out. The scent of sulfur in the room was repellent. It even covered the smell of all her blood. Charlie looked up with him with eyes that were red from crying. "Why can't I finish? What do they do to me that makes me like this?"

Yep, he was going to pass out. Pass out and think this was all some fucking ridiculous dream, and he won't be able to sleep for a month because of it.

Oh god, that sounded good. Just to have it all been a dream ...

Charlie, he's going to help you with that. Just relax.

"No," Charlie said. "I don't like men, I like women - "

Shut up. I know that. But he can do it just by using his mind.

He felt Charlie's dick harden. Saw it on the way Charlie was looking up at him. And ... he felt his own erection swell as well.

What the fuck –

"Just send it to him."

He closed his eyes as Essum's voice ... it was like a soft, warm touch, right on his ...

Oh Jesus. Oh Christ.

His neck stiffened and his head went back, making his jaw crack along the way. He saw white light, and then felt his dick twitch in his pants as it did its messy business.

Charlie grunted, cried out on the floor in front of him, jerking and going stiff over the woman's dying body.

He wanted to cry. He wanted a shower. He really wanted to throw up.

"Very good," Essum declared, clapping his hands. Then he sent a thought to Charlie. *Time to clean up, Charlie.*

Charlie was still panting, his eyes still closed where he rested his head on the woman's carved up chest. He had an ecstatic smile on his face. "Okay," he said blissfully. "Thank you ... thank you masters."

"Put your hand on his head," Essum commanded.

"Fuck no." He didn't want to touch him. He needed out of this room, this house ...

Of course, there was no disobeying Essum. His hand found its way to Charlie, sitting flat on his greasy hair as his body continued to twitch with delight. He felt bile rise up the back of his throat, but as Essum forced his hand into Charlie's hair he stopped worrying about the rape and murder.

Fuck ... what is this?

"It's Sin Eating," Essum explained in a low and reverent voice. "This is what I will soon be back to doing. You find the shameful, dark and buried memories of all the terrible things people have done to others for their own enjoyment."

As Essum was saying it, he was seeing all the women Charlie had killed this way. He saw them like translucent images on a huge screen in front of his eyes. He felt Charlie's excitement, frustration, blinding hatred. He saw and felt all of it.

"Now that you've found his sins, bundle them up, like moving them all to a file folder. And then just hit delete."

It just ... happened. Exactly how Essum said. The sins blipped away ... and then he felt them. He carried them. It seemed as though they became his memories. And instead of feeling like he was going to throw up he felt stronger. He stopped fucking crying, that's for sure.

"What is this?" He repeated with a more confident voice. "Don't they go away?" He put a hand to his chest, but it wasn't hurting.

Essum tilted his head thoughtfully. "I don't know. You're not a Sin Eater. I have no idea what's going to happen to you."

Voro was at a stop light when he felt the tension and fear in his chest stop and melt away. Instead of feeling relief, he covered his mouth and closed his eyes, leaning against the steering wheel. He got his breathing in check.

Then ... she's dead. It's not that she wasn't transmitting because she wasn't hurting anymore ... it's because she died.

It really shouldn't hurt like this, he reminded himself. *You're not human. You don't mourn the deaths of other humans. You have never cried.*

But he felt pressure squeezing his chest, like something was trying to wring it out of him. And when he touched his cheeks, they came back wet. Shit. He was crying.

Most of the deaths he'd witnessed had been evil doers passing into the abyss, and he couldn't mourn them. He didn't know them. And he didn't fraternize with humans enough to miss them when they died.

Except lately, he reminded himself. You attached yourself to Portia, telling yourself it was for money. And now ... now you want to do the same to Claudia just to be near Iola.

Maybe it was time to take a break. Essum was right – six hundred plus years was a long time to keep this shit up. He was turning human, wasn't he?

Okay, that thought terrified him.

Horns were honking around him. The light had turned green.

He drove through the intersection and pulled over in a parking space to decide what he should do. Then his blood ran cold as another, slightly less sinister and more self-serving set of implications made themselves aware.

Shit. Her car was parked at the hotel. His room was in her name. Her ... oh shit, her blood was on the carpet, wasn't it? She cut her foot on that glass ... he couldn't be found at that room. Couldn't been considered as part of her life at all.

A new panic flared. He couldn't go back there. And this car ... in her name, registration and all. Fuck him. He was screwed.

What was he going to do for money? He couldn't use a dead woman's credit card. Shit. Shit shit shit.

How much cash did he even have? He took out his money clip and counted out three hundred dollars. Not much. He could check into a flea bag motel for a while. But just the thought of downgrading his accommodations made him itch.

He could mentally influence people to give him whatever he wanted, of course. He could walk up to a jewelry counter, select any watch and get the employee to just give him the watch. He could check into another hotel and let them book a room to John

Smith, and then they just wouldn't ask him for money when he checks out. It's not hard, and by the time people start wondering what went wrong he's long gone.

But this was just less time consuming, and buying stuff, even if it wasn't with his money ... well, it made him more ... human.

Fuck. He was done, wasn't he? If he got kicked back to the Other Side now ... could he even assimilate?

Voro forced himself to focus on more pressing concerns. He didn't want to get caught in Portia's car. Sure he could convince the cop that he or she saw it wrong. Or that they didn't even see him; he was just a figment of their imagination. But these days there were in-dash cameras and the cops sometimes ran the plate with their dispatch before they even approached the car ... the thought of all the work gave him a headache. He turned the engine off, left the keys in the ignition, and walked away from the BMW ... as much as it made him want to cry. It was a gorgeous car ...

Voro emptied the change from the tray so he could take the subway somewhere, and left the fine example of German engineering unlocked at the curb with its four-ways blinking, keys in ignition. Someone else could explain why they were driving a dead woman's car.

"Dispatch to Car 67."

"Go ahead, Dispatch."

"Just got a call about a lot of screaming coming from a house on Southerland Crescent. Number 815. They said the noise stopped about fifteen minutes ago."

Claudia raised an eyebrow. "What a concerned citizen."

"Want back-up, Car 67?"

"Yes please. Don't want to walk into a domestic by myself."

Claudia switched on lights and sirens, pulled a U-turn and then headed back the way she'd just come, accelerating to a decent speed, relieved when cars were actually pulling over to get out of the way. Then again, this was an affluent part of town. People had respect for law enforcement here ... in theory anyway.

The house at 815 sat beyond a wide yard that was almost as long as a football field. It was a huge stucco monstrosity in an odd peach color with white trim. The lights were all on full inside, the front door stood open.

Claudia frowned as she eased partway up the circular driveway at a cautious speed. This was odd ... her instincts were setting off all kinds of bells. And she usually didn't ignore them.

She parked a few yards from the door, undid her seatbelt and climbed out. She killed the sirens but left the lights on, and that's when she heard the approaching sirens of her back-up. Her eyes were narrowed on that open door. It wasn't just open a crack, it was standing wide open. It was giving her the scratch.

The snap on her holster was unbelievably loud as she released it. Her hand hovered right over the sidearm as she climbed the three concrete steps up to the door then stepped through. The feeling of something big and bad inside intensified. She pulled the Beretta from the holster as a second thought. She wanted it in her hand when she went in.

Next she noticed the smell. It was copper, and it was coming through a doorway to her right. She stepped over keys and a cell phone on her way there, the latter of which began to vibrate and play the theme music from MASH. It made her jump; she almost put a 40-calibre round through the thing, actually.

She came through the white-trimmed and columned entryway, looking upwards into a large, high-ceilinged room with gorgeous white silk wallpaper and furniture with an odd red-brown pattern emanating upwards.

"Oh fuck," she said, taking a step back. That was no pattern. Yep, that was all blood.

The woman was lying on the floor, her neck uncomfortably propped up against a stone hearth. Not that her neck position should be a concern. A fireplace poker through her abdomen was holding her in place like a mounted butterfly, her clothes were shredded and without looking too closely Claudia could see both her breasts had been removed. They were possibly the gore that had been discarded on the floor next to the body. Claudia couldn't be sure. Her skirt was shoved up around her hips, and there was an awful lot of blood down there, too. The woman's legs were open, splayed out like a dropped doll. Her mouth was open, something was jutting out and running blood down her chin.

Claudia covered her mouth with her free hand. The woman just stared back at her, and the silence was almost too much ... too private. She moved her eyes from the woman's own grey ones and that's when she noticed the bruises on the neck. Just like the woman they'd found the day before in that dumpster. Strangled. Although it was hard to tell what in all this gore had killed her.

Claudia felt tears welling up in her eyes. God, of all the stupid things she'd done in her past, this could have been her on so many occasions. So many times she was not in control of her facilities, surrounded by strangers that could have easily done worse to her. But no, she was alive and this tall, possibly distinguished woman who lived in this amazing mansion ... was not. She was hurt and tortured in her own beautiful home.

Claudia was making a lot of assumptions with that whole theory, but it was that same dependable instinct telling her these details, too. This woman lived here alone, someone had known that, and someone had gotten in here, laid in wait, and brutally, sadistically attacked her, then left her to be found in this horrific and disgusting manner. At least try to hide what you've done. At least show that after the rage you realized how wrong it was. But no ... left like trash.

She heard footsteps pounding up the steps and coming into the foyer behind her, felt hands take her by the shoulders and lead her out the front doors. She must have been pale, because someone was telling her to just breathe deep, but it sounded like a voice coming from underwater. Claudia did as told, the night air feeling very cold. It eased her stomach without her even knowing she'd been nauseous.

She heard her fellow officers calling for an ambulance. She knew that they would start taking pictures soon, cataloguing evidence.

Claudia shook her shoulders, trying to clear out her head. She'd seen this shit before ... why was she spending so much worry on this one?

Even more worrisome, why did she feel linked to this woman somehow?

Chapter Twenty

When he was finally by himself, after dropping Charlie off at a hotel with Essum, kind of, he had to come back to her apartment.

The lights were on in her living room, and while he watched from the shadows, she came to the window with a bottle and poured something into the plants that were on her windowsill. He smiled when he realized she was singing to herself. Did she always do that when she was alone? He had no idea.

Then he had a moment of complete dread. What if Essum found him here, looking at her like this? What if he decided he could get him to do his bidding just by threatening to harm her?

He had to block Iola from his mind. He had to keep her totally hidden at all times, especially when Essum was around. If Essum so much as harmed one hair on her head ...

At the very thought of letting that fucking monster Charlie anywhere near her he felt such exquisite anger he wondered if he wasn't glowing. He'd kill the both of them if he had to. Or he'd try his best, anyway. Charlie definitely. Essum he wasn't so sure about. But he'd sure give it the old college try.

He tried not to remember the murder, tried not to see it with Charlie's eyes, tried not to see it from that woman's point of view. But fuck ... He rubbed his forehead and began walking away from the apartment building at a rapid pace. He felt sick. He couldn't deal without seeing it from Charlie's vantage point, and that's the one that really bothered him now. He didn't want to "understand" where the psycho was coming from.

How could anyone like that? How could anyone crave the feeling of terror and violent rage ... but dammit, even as he tried to push it away he felt himself harden again.

No, no no no no ... he was not turning into that sick fuck. Please, let him not be turning into that fucking freak.

And what had Essum made him do? When he'd seen all those things Charlie had done, he ... calmed down. He accepted them as his own almost righteous actions. Now his head was rebelling from the idea but at the time they had all been justified, even as the woman died right in front of them. It was for the greater good, she was going to be fine and taken care of now. Not their problem.

Sin Eating, Essum had said. That did not sound good. He was not interested in trying any more of that. Fuck that. Fuck Essum.

He had to work the next day, late in the morning. He had to get home and get away from this anxious, tight feeling in his guts, and the ridiculous need he had to fuck something right then and there.

Outside his apartment building he had to avoid groups of people cheering the victory of some hockey team, at one time he would have recognized the colors. But at that moment he had other things on his mind.

The woman was standing next to the doors, strung right out. He could almost read her mind. She really needed fifty bucks to get one more hit to see her through the night.

He closed his eyes as he put his key in the front door. She wasn't wearing underwear, she'd had a few customers already that night, and he could smell the filth from other men all over her. His erection twitched. It was craving how nasty she was.

"Fifty bucks?" His voice was coarse. Had he really asked that? He nearly cried when she nodded with great excitement. Usually she only got twenty ...

He nodded to the door sideways as he unlocked it and held it for her. She passed in front of him, going to the elevator banks.

"No," he said with great panic. He didn't want to get caught in there by one of his neighbors. "The stairs." He pointed out the doorway, and she changed course without any concern.

Christ, he could just kill her. And who would ever find out?

His dick twitched again as she shoved the push bar on the door and stepped into the stairwell. There was a dark corner on the far side, underneath the first half-flight of steps. She went there by instinct.

"You wanna wear a condom or not?" She asked while smacking her gum loudly.

He didn't answer her, not really. He shoved her against the bricks, scraping her cheek on the cinderblock. He shoved up the back of her skirt, unzipped his fly, and pulled out his erection in one quick move.

"Mmm," she said, rubbing herself against him. "Quick moves, big guy."

His hand shoved her face against the wall harder, and she gave a noise of protest. As she did he shoved his erection in deep, reared back and shoved in again. He was imagining that he could do worse to her. And wondering why the hell that thought made him pound into her harder.

"Let go of me, fucker." She actually sounded panicked, which was odd for a pro.

"Shut the fuck up," he growled in a voice he didn't even recognize. Then he shot a vision at her where he was slicing her neck open with a knife he wasn't even carrying.

She froze. She whimpered after a split second. "Please, don't hurt me - "

"Shut up," he snarled, pounding into her again. She wasn't playing along anymore. She was trying to get away, but his hands had her totally immobilized, one leg between hers so she couldn't move away to either side.

"Please, please don't - "

He closed his eyes, loving the sound of her pleading. She wasn't playing along, but she was giving him exactly what he wanted without knowing it. He kept thrusting madly, her cries getting softer until she was sobbing quietly, resigned to what was happening.

When he came, it was explosive. He saw white lights and stars and gave a bark of pleasure that made her cry out a bit louder. Then he backed away, tucking himself away with one hand while pulling his wallet with the other. He left a fifty dollar bill on the floor as she sunk down to her knees, crying and hugging herself. He took the stairs up to his apartment, the sound of her weeping following him the entire five floors up.

Iola was singing to her plants, but whatever. No one else on her entire floor was even home. No one could complain.

She'd finished off the wine from supper, and was now resolving to just drink water. She didn't want a headache tomorrow. Her CD player was on, and her plants were her only company.

Iola's neck tingled suddenly, and she brought her head up, just in time to see a shadow duck into the alley across the street. She'd had a vision of how she'd looked from down there ... almost like a vision of loveliness, something to be revered and protected. It was a nice way to be seen, even if it was by some Peeping Tom on the street.

She shook her head. Holy shit, that was too much wine.

The person was gone, and she couldn't be sure he had even been real. When her phone rang she almost dropped the glass iced tea bottle she used as a watering can for her plants. She ran for the hand set, muting the stereo as she answered.

"Hello?"

"Hey Iola."

"Oh, Claudia." She put the glass bottle back under her sink.

Claudia took a deep breath. "How ... how you doing?"

Iola froze, half-way between crouching and standing. Her neck was tingling again. "Claudia, what's wrong?"

Her friend gave a sigh that some would think was a sign of being tired, but Iola knew better. Claudia was trying not to cry.

"I found a dead body, Iola. A woman, in her house, killed all by herself. Alone." Claudia's voice choked on the last word.

Iola sat on the kitchen floor, leaning against her cupboard doors, legs stretched straight out in front of her. "Oh babe, I am so sorry. It must have been bad." For something to bother Claudia this much, it must have been beyond brutal.

"It was beyond disgusting, Iola. How they cut her up and just left her ... oh God, I'll see that when I'm trying to sleep, I know it."

Iola picked at a fiber pill on her flannel cropped pajama pants. She had no words to say that would make it okay, so she was going to let Claudia say what she needed to get out.

"And she was raped, Iola. They think something was used on her first, and then ... well, there was semen. But she'd been violated by something that may or may not have been a poker from a fireplace set."

Iola's breath caught and she covered her eyes. "Oh my God, Claudia."

"I shouldn't have told you that."

"Well, you know you can tell me anything."

"Maybe not that kind of thing. But it's just ..." her breath was a deep and shuddering one. "With all the bad stuff that I went through, this makes me feel ... fortunate. Isn't that ... isn't that fucked up?"

Iola shrugged, even though she was on the phone. "I don't know. Maybe you're feeling guilty that you're alive and she's not."

"That's what I'm thinking, too." Claudia cleared her throat. "Tell me something nice, Iola. Take my mind off this for a second. How was dinner?"

Iola smiled in spite of what Claudia had just told her. "It was ... great. Until Vinnie got called back to the hospital."

"Well that sucks."

"He had to tear himself away from me to go save the life of someone injured in a car accident. Actually, the thought kinda turns me on."

"Hmmm. When you put it that way ... that does sound pretty hot."

Iola's smile faded. It felt so wrong to be talking like this. "So ... you'll likely be really late getting home tonight, hey?"

"Yeah. We've got to process this crime scene for homicide. It's ... it's a nasty one, Iola. God, I'd rather be anywhere than here."

"What about Afghanistan?"

There was a pause and Claudia actually chuckled. It sounded forced but it made Iola feel better. "Maybe not Afghanistan."

"An alligator-infested swamp."

"Not there, either."

"Well ... there's some perspective."

Claudia laughed again and Iola could see her shaking her head. "You're messed up, Iola."

"Just wanted to hear you laugh a bit, Sergeant Bauer. You'll do right by this woman, I know it."

"Portia." Claudia said.

"What?"

"Her name was Portia Torregrossa."

"That sounds pretty."

"It does. Well, I'll talk to you later, okay? Don't bother waiting up. Who knows how long this mess will take."

"Okay. Be safe, Claudia."

"I will. You too."

"I will."

"G'night."

"Bye." Iola pressed "talk" to end her call, then stared at the phone. A woman, killed in her home. Alone.

Iola got to her feet and re-checked that her locks were all thrown on her door. They were. She wrapped her arms around her stomach, hating how solitary she felt just because of one phone call.

The shower had felt nice. He really hated the smell of the blood all over him, but that was one of the hazards of working for the Master.

What really had him humming, though, was the other fellow, the Master's new friend. Not because of the orgasm, either. But because of after that. It made the orgasm seem like nothing.

He felt ... okay, for maybe the first time ever. He wasn't scared. He wasn't nervous at all. So he dressed in the new guy's borrowed jeans and a T-shirt. He put the twenty-dollar bill from the new guy in his pocket and took the elevator to the hotel lobby. As he crossed the floor, he didn't feel like everyone was staring at him.

It was such a relief.

The waitress that gave him his glass of water smiled at him pleasantly, handed him a menu, and told him that the hot roast beef sandwich was the special that night for just $8.99. That sounded good. He ordered it on the spot. He wasn't confused about what he should be ordering, what would seem normal. He just *ordered*.

His hand was steady as he sipped from the water glass. He looked around the diner. It was later, but this place was open 24 hours. There was a man with a newspaper having a cup of coffee.

Charlie thought he must be a shift worker, because who had coffee this late at night? There were two women sitting at another table, also drinking coffee. They were definitely working. They had hard lines on their faces, and their eyes were stony as they only looked at each other, didn't say a word, and drank their hot beverages. He frowned at the feeling he got looking at them. They made him feel sad.

People could be cruel to each other. Charlie knew that very well. He'd had people be very cruel to him, too. But just buying someone for ... well, that.

His heart started racing. The images came back in a flood of red and flesh and hate. He remembered that woman and her nice house. He remembered raping her. How much he'd hated doing it, but even that he couldn't get right. He couldn't finish. He never did. And how mad that made him. To the point where he ...

He swallowed hard, putting the water glass down with a bang. Only the man with the newspaper looked up, then went right back to reading with no reaction at all.

He had to calm his breathing before he started freaking everyone out around him. He wiped his forehead, but he actually wasn't sweating. It was just his heart was racing. He tried to tell it to mellow out.

"Here you go, honey," a plate of food appeared before him. The sight of the sandwich with gravy on a plate with fries made his stomach roll.

Keep it together, Charlie. That was his own voice. He had his own voice in his head for the first time in ... who knew? He couldn't remember the last time he heard his own voice.

He smiled up at the waitress. "Thank you," he said, maybe sounding a trifle strained. The waitress just smiled back. He must have pulled off the "normal" act after all. She walked away, and he looked back down at his dinner.

It smells good. Just eat it. Enjoy. Who knows how long this will last?

His own voice. As he picked up his knife and fork he almost wept.

Claudia escorted the coroner's van to the hospital, then watched as the body was checked into the morgue. She kept an eye on the process of paperwork being signed over, and she was diligent about following procedure with this case. The chain of custody for any evidence, especially a body, had to be set in stone with no margin for error.

But maybe she wasn't the best choice to do it. Her head wasn't in it, she couldn't concentrate. She just wanted to go home. Of all the nights to have a fling, last night – and that morning, come to think of it - was one example of where she should have gotten a good twelve hours' sleep.

God, it seemed like ages ago already that Damien had left her doorway. But in reality, only about ... seven? Eight hours had passed?

She rubbed her eyes and took a seat on a hallway bench. She was going to leave in a moment ... she seriously was. But first ... she had to sit. The hospital was so quiet right then. Soft beeping could be heard down the hallways. Everyone's shoes were quiet. People whispered here at night.

Yep, maybe she should just stretch out and take a nap. It would almost be a public service if she was a bit better-rested before heading back out.

"Claudia, right?"

She sat up straight and wanted to groan at the intrusion into her privacy, then realized it was Iola's doctor sinking down to sit next to her. He offered her a piece of gum wordlessly.

"No thanks," she said, trying to be nice.

"So you brought in the body, hey?"

She frowned. "You've already heard about that?"

He nodded as he started off on a new piece of Dentyne. It was the tooth-whitening kind. "Word gets around. Were you the one that found her?"

Claudia just nodded, not trusting her voice.

"Oh man. I'm so sorry. I can't imagine what you must see in your line of work."

That struck her a bit funny, coming from a doctor. Because she sure wouldn't want to see the fat guy that sprung a hernia or deliver babies or do anything that reminded her how gross the human body was. She just dealt with how gross the human mind could be.

"You clean up a lot of what we see," she reminded him, and he smiled.

"Yeah, I guess we do."

Claudia watched him flip through a chart on the clipboard he held, his eyes shrewd as he read all the doctor-speak that was undoubtedly scrawled on it. She could tell he was smart. Iola was right. Sometimes you can tell just by looking.

"So ... you like my neighbor then?" She said casually, getting his attention again.

He smiled at her, like a damn cherub. "I do, very much. She's something special."

Claudia nodded to show her approval. "Yeah, she is. I've known her a long time. She's one of the kindest people I've met."

"I can sense that from her."

"It's real. And I can also tell you like her plenty. And ... I can tell that it's genuine. I know it's only a couple of dates, but ... well, if you hurt her ... I'll make your life a living hell."

He didn't laugh. She wondered if she might have spooked him, then he said in all seriousness, "Hurting Iola is the last thing I would ever want to do."

Claudia nodded and offered her hand. "That's the right answer."

Chapter Twenty-One

Voro got to Claudia's apartment door and rapped on it lightly. There were no sounds coming from inside, so he had to assume she wasn't home from work yet.

He felt like such an ass, showing up here to beg a nights' accommodation. But he didn't want to be alone, as ridiculous as it sounded. He leaned against the wall of the hallway, and wondered, possibly for the first time in a century, what the hell his purpose really was.

He recalled back in the day when people had actually believed in sin eating. When they would pay a homeless beggar to eat a piece of bread off a dead man's chest and carry his sins off with him to the next town.

Voro had seen it done many times. Hell, he'd even done it himself as an easier way to get a little money. But he'd only taken the money of the wealthy, and odds were always good that at the wealthiest of funerals he'd run into a few people that were just as authentically cursed as he was.

He remembered one particular time when he'd ridden into town on a huge, black beast of a horse, taken the best room at the inn, and set up shop on the porch of the inn with a sign that read "Sins Eaten for Tuppence."

He laughed at the memory of his own damn arrogance. But they had come. He'd taken them all to the privacy of his room, removed their sins and within three hours he'd paid for his one-week stay at the inn. He'd actually even managed to consume some real sins in that town, too. Mothers had brought their sons that they caught touching themselves ... or other boys. Fathers brought daughters that had found themselves in the family way without being married. Adulterers, barroom brawlers, they'd all been desperate to be saved.

And some of the women had just been desperate to be alone with him. He'd had to accommodate, of course.

One man had also come along, achingly poor; if he'd been penniless it would have been an improvement. And he was terrified. Voro could see the madness in his eyes, he was scared of things that he knew couldn't be real, and yet they were real to him. He told Voro pitifully that he'd been sin eating for years; taking the money and the free meal offered and standing in as the vessel to carry off the sins of the dearly departed. But now that he'd done it for so long he was scared he was actually becoming one of the sinners.

Voro had frowned at the phrasing. At that time, everyone believed that they were unclean by their very existence. But the way the man talked of the sinners ... he saw them as Voro did, but Voro could tell this man was not one of the same ilk as he was. The longer they talked the more Voro realized the man was more than human.

Sure, he was crazy. His mental illness made it hard for Voro to get a lock on whether or not the accounts he remembered had happened to him, someone else, or even if they'd happened at all. But when Voro touched him it was like getting a bolt of evil lightning, shot right into his heart. No one specific act or memory, just darkness and evil and malice.

The man was sopping up evil like he was cheesecloth. He was finding real sinners and taking their sins, and who knew how he was doing it but he was. He likely wasn't even aware of it; after all, how many times did beggars pull on your arm or take your hand to get your attention?

Essum's little care-and-share earlier that day came back to him. That old man could have easily been a *frustro* at one time, who killed a Sin Eater's *decipio* and was cursed to carry out the task for the Sin Eater as long as the Sin Eater was mortal.

I give easement and rest to thee, dear man. Come not down the lanes or in our meadows. And for thy peace I pawn my own soul. Amen.

He smiled as he recalled the old incantation that the false sin eaters had used. Good Lord, the thing sounded like someone had just made it up from a desperate need to eat. But people were so dreadfully superstitious when it came to death, even after the church started throwing people in jail for posing as sin eaters. Not because it was sacrilegious, but because it took away the power of salvation from the church itself. Only the church decided who could get into heaven and who couldn't. Like a building of brick and mortar and men dressed in cloaks could sway the powers that controlled good and evil.

Voro sighed and rubbed his temples. He'd been doing this for a very long time. He was starting to feel like maybe some human filth was sticking to his insides after all.

The door across the hall opened, and he straightened up, knowing he probably looked guilty as hell, creeping around outside the apartment of a single woman. But the second those green eyes fell on him, he was spellbound.

"Damien?" Iola asked, yawning. "I thought maybe Claudia was coming home. What ... what are you doing out here?"

He looked down at his hands, not trusting himself to look her in the eye again. "I am quite embarrassed, actually. I feel terrible about this. And I hate to ask Claudia for this, but ... I need a place to stay tonight. I had nowhere else to go." When he looked back at her, her eyes were harsh as she assessed whether or not he was telling the truth. At least, that's what he had assumed she was thinking. Not knowing for sure was really throwing him for a loop.

"She should be back within the hour. I guess ... I guess you could wait with me if you want. I never go to sleep until she's home anyway."

"I would hate to intrude."

"Please," she said, pushing her door open further and motioning him in with the other hand. "Share a cup of tea with me."

His heart sped up three-fold, but he smiled in what he hoped was a friendly, non-threatening manner. "I would love a cup of tea."

Iola's heart jumped up to her throat. The way his accent made the word *love* sound was ridiculously sexy. His voice caressed that word. Made it shine like silver. Would it be weird if she asked him to just say it a few more times?

She turned from the door and held it for him. He allowed it to shut on its own accord behind him. Voro followed her into her small kitchen at a proper distance, and she felt naked as he examined her things. When Vinnie had done that the night of their first date she'd been proud to have him look at her furnishings. With Damien she didn't know what he was thinking of her. Her stuff, that is. Not knowing was sort of ... exciting.

She poured water into her kettle then put it on an element, flicking it on. Damien stood in the center of the kitchen, a vantage point where one could see all corners of her private little world. Other than the bedroom, of course.

"Your home is lovely," he said easily, his unusual eyes returning to hers eventually.

"Thank you," she responded properly, wondering why he spoke so formally.

"How long have you lived here?"

"Two years, a bit longer."

"And Claudia lived here already at that time?"

"Yeah, I think she'd been here about four months when I moved in."

"She has such great affection for you."

Iola frowned. "Well, I count her as a true friend. Probably the only real friend I have." She stepped forward, turning on a light switch that made the table lamp next to the sofa come to life. "Please, have a seat. I was just reading, not really doing anything important." She covered up a paperback with a newspaper, tossing them both on to the coffee table. God, she hoped he hadn't seen the cover of the book, with the six-pack underwear model carrying a woman in a long blue gown up a ridiculous staircase.

"So you always wait up for Claudia when she works nights?"

"Usually. I just ... I feel safer knowing she's across the hall. She's tough as nails, and she's armed usually, too. So ... yeah, I can't really get to sleep unless I know she's over there."

"I think she's happy to have such an alert neighbor as well," he said thoughtfully, his eyes skipping over her bookcase where her stereo sat. "Claudia mentioned you work at a radio station?"

"Yeah, I work a late night shift at KLCD, it's Late Night with Iola Day. Kind of a play on words, what with my last name and all." God, Iola ... shut up.

He nodded, a small smile on those tasty lips. They were unusually full for a man. She can't say she'd ever noticed before if a man had really substantial, sensual lips. When she realized she was staring she looked elsewhere, feeling her cheeks color.

The pause was remarkably uncomfortable, so she continued to stammer on. "I'd usually be at work right now, actually. Mondays and Tuesdays are my nights off. I work weekends. Claudia's schedule is more scattered than mine. And tonight ... well, she might be a bit later than usual." Damien raised his jet-black eyebrows in curiosity. "She called me earlier, she's having a bad night. They uh, found a woman murdered in her home. Well, Claudia found her herself. So ... she was really upset when she called."

Damien's face lost its smile. "That's terrible news. How unfortunate."

"Kind of gets to me to hear about a woman living alone, being killed in her own house. I mean, that's how I live, right? Claudia, too. Could have been either one of us."

Damien's face had completely changed in countenance. He looked uncomfortable, even worried. She was about to ask what was wrong when the kettle started whistling.

She sprang to her feet to take the kettle off the burner and popped a couple tea bags in a pot before filling it with steaming water. When she turned to the cupboard she gave a small yelp because Damien was already standing there. He'd followed her silently and she hadn't even noticed him move.

"I'm sorry, Iola," he said, handing her two cups from the cupboard he had open. "I didn't mean to startle you."

She took the cups with hands that shook like she was palsied. And it wasn't because he had surprised her. It was because he was close to her, a massive male shape, looming. He should be scary; he should look really out of place in her cheerful little kitchen. But he didn't. He looked at home here, he looked comfortable. Mostly, he just looked really *good*. And he smelled even better. What the hell was it that he wore?

"Thanks," she said, delayed and distracted. She put the cups on the counter and then leaned back, arms crossed over her chest. "So ... are you dating Claudia, then?"

Yeah, that helped calm down her hormones; the thought of her good friend that was inexplicably having feelings for this hunk of man meat in her kitchen. Okay, maybe that thought wasn't exactly inexplicable. Maybe it was ... surprising. That's the word.

Damien was studying her face, and Iola wondered how much of her thought process she was giving away with her expression. "Claudia is ... a wonderful woman. I think she's confused by her own feelings. But I won't define what we are. I will rather leave that for her to do. I don't think she'd appreciate being herded into one category of relationship."

Iola was shocked by the honest answer. And yet ... it showed that maybe he understood Claudia quite well. And it was an understanding he'd achieved in an incredibly short period of time, no less.

"Fair enough," she said, nodding. "I think you're ... dead-on about Claudia. So don't hurt her, okay? Don't lie, don't be false with anything you tell her. She's tough but ... she's not made of stone."

Damien nodded. "I care for your friend, Iola. I mean her no harm."

"Good."

They stood eyeing each other up for another moment. Suddenly Iola didn't want him in her kitchen, didn't want him this close to her. She didn't want to see him, didn't want his incredible smell in her nose anymore. Didn't want to feel how warm his gaze made her feel. She wanted her pulse to return to normal, and she wanted the temperature of the room to go back to what she had the thermostat set at.

He took a deep breath, took another step towards her. She didn't back away, she didn't shrink from him at all. She stopped breathing, that was it.

He put a hand out, capturing some of her hair in between his fingers.

Okaaay ... this is weird. This is very not okay. This is ...

He bent his head down to smell the lock of hair he was running over his hand, and when he did all she could see was this thick, strong neck, the way it was connected to his wide shoulders and his thick chest ... and that damn smell again.

Her eyes closed as she listened to him breathe in. She was completely terrified, not because she didn't trust him. She didn't trust herself.

A squeaking floorboard in the hallway made her expel her breath, and her eyes flicked up to his as she blurted out, "That's Claudia. Claudia's home." She ducked away from him, nearly running for her door and pulling it open just as Claudia was fitting her key into her deadbolt.

"You're home," Iola said happily.

Claudia smiled at Iola, then her eyes shifted to the side and her smile faltered just slightly as she set her eyes on Damien, standing behind Iola.

Shit, was the only thought Iola had.

Claudia had jumped as Iola's door was ripped open behind her, but when she'd seen Damien standing behind Iola, she'd felt an odd ... disappointment. Because Iola looked radiant, gorgeous, and totally flushed like she'd been ... well, getting worked over good by a talented lover. Like the one standing behind her.

Like the one Claudia had just had the pleasure of enjoying the night before. But he didn't look guilty, he looked happy to see her, too.

"Hi, guys. What's ... what's up?"

"I heard Damien out here waiting for you, so I invited him in for tea. But I'm glad you're home." Iola sounded like she really meant it, so Claudia assumed maybe her imagination was getting the edge on her.

Damien stepped around Iola and crossed the hall to her, taking her hand. "I heard you had a rough night."

Seeing her hand in his giant paw made her want to start crying, but she didn't, she just nodded.

"I was going to ask if I could stay here tonight. That's why I was waiting. But if you're upset, I think it's better if I go."

She gripped his hand in both of hers when it seemed like he was going to pull away. "No, please. Please stay here. I need ... I need someone to stay here tonight."

Claudia was dimly aware that Iola was closing her door, not wanting to intrude on them. But she kept her eyes locked on Damien's face.

He just nodded. "If you want me here, honestly, I will stay."

"I do. Please, come in."

He followed her through the door, turning on the lights for them. "Do you want to talk about it?" He asked in a very gentle way.

"No. Yes. I have no idea."

Damien took her in his arms, pressing her to his chest. "If you need to sleep, we'll sleep. If you want to talk, I'll listen."

"They were lying in wait for her in her own damn house," Claudia bit out each word. "Whoever it was, they raped her and strangled her and just left her there, bleeding. Oh God, you wouldn't believe what they did to her."

His arms tightened around her. "Let's go to bed. I think you're exhausted."

"I am." He let go of her, turned off the living room light and led her by the hand to her bedroom. Once there he turned on the bedside lamp, and began to undress her.

Claudia didn't fight any part of the process. She watched him carefully put her clothes on the armchair in the corner, go to her dresser and pull out a huge T-shirt, pull it on over her head, then pulled back the bedcovers and steered her to the bedside.

As she settled in between cool sheets and found her comfortable spot on the pillow, he stripped down to his boxer shorts and climbed in next to her. Even in the surreal state she was in mentally, she appreciated the view of his back as he sat on the side of the bed and then turned to shove his legs into the pile of blankets. Her body was aware of him immediately, like a space heater set on "tropics."

As he pulled her against him, she couldn't believe she was turned on. After what she'd seen, what she'd already gone though, here she was, hoping she hadn't sapped out so much that he was basically castrated by her girliness.

She pressed her lips to the warm strength of his chest, waited, then placed another kiss higher up. He shifted around, rolling on to one side to look down at her.

"Claudia, surely you're tired. And upset."

"Anger has a way of numbing me out totally. Can you just ... take away the numbness?"

He captured one hand, turning the palm inwards and kissing it. She closed her eyes, surprised to find that the palm of her hand was an erogenous zone.

"Stop me when you want," he said. That was fast becoming one of her favorite phrases. Then he came in for a kiss that had her heart pounding and her legs opening for him in no time at all.

When he'd stripped them of their clothing, he'd begun to stoke her fire with his hand while keeping his mouth on hers. She matched the movement with her hips, then all but pushed him on top of her. When he continued to touch her, she parted her lips from his to say, "No, now. Just ... do it. I'm ready."

God bless him, he always did as he was told. With him on top, she was totally trapped in the cage of his body, and when he entered her she felt completely full, not against her will just ... out of her element again. Claudia was starting to think that was what she liked about Damien.

While his movements were aggressive and passionate, his attention to the rest of her body was sentimental and non-intimidating. His kisses were slightly more languid, lazy but completely engaged. His dry, hot hands caressed her skin like it was breakable. In those hands Claudia felt softer than she thought possible.

Her orgasm was a gentle one which took a bit longer to pass, definitely no less pleasurable, but she'd been well aware of its approach and she'd buried her hands in his hair, pulling his face down to her shoulder so she could muffle a cry into the slick skin of his neck. His skin was salty with sweat, and as the shudders were fading she found she was now crying.

He froze immediately, pulling free of her body and easing on to his side, a hand on her cheek. "Claudia ... look at me. It's okay."

"I'm sorry," she sputtered, aware now she was shaking as well.

"Don't apologize. You saw something ... traumatic."

"I'm here, and she's not," Claudia sobbed nonsensically. "I get to be here with someone who touches me like this and ... the last person to have his hands on her was a complete monster."

She was held against his chest as she cried loudly. He didn't say a word, just silently comforted her and stroked her back until she fell asleep.

Chapter Twenty-Two

Charlie awoke to the sound of a cart being pushed down the hotel hallway. But he only realized what the noise was when he first remembered where he was.

The sheets were so clean, his underwear was brand new, and he couldn't remember how he'd gotten to a hotel. The last thing he remembered was ending up in jail.

He was here. The new guy had brought him here. He'd had a nice meal just last night. Remember?

He rubbed his face, then pulled his hands away and inspected his arms. They were marked with deep gashes from someone's fingernails. That woman had fought hard.

As Charlie's memories came back again, with the buffer zone of a good night's sleep, he wanted to weep. Or throw up. What made him get so hateful? Why did he have to do all those horrific, monstrous things? That woman's wide pale eyes; she'd been so terrified of him. And whoever else she was seeing in the room. Had she ... could she see the Master like that other man had? He hated that he had to think of that voice as Master, but he didn't have any other name for him.

He got out of bed and headed for the washroom. The wet towels he'd used the night before were still on the ground. He felt bad, picked them up and put them on the hanger. There'd been a lot of blood to wash off of him. Blood everywhere.

Charlie had been so vicious to that woman. Well, another, darker part of Charlie had done it. Not the here-and-now Charlie. Once the Master got hold of him, there was nothing too depraved or disgusting for him. All to please the Master.

Charlie had felt the disgust of that other man. He'd felt it even as his body had been doing awful things and he wanted to stop, that man had been horrified by him. Charlie should have been ashamed but ... again, the darker side had hold of him then.

Charlie frowned. Now that the shock was thinning out, he had to wonder who he was. Charlie had never seen him around before. And why could the new guy see the Master but Charlie couldn't? Was that fair? Charlie had been with the Master for months now. He was disliking the new guy ... then he remembered the fact that he'd actually finished in that woman, hadn't he?

When Charlie turned the shower head on, he became aware of his penis in his shorts, it was stiff and the fabric of his underwear was chafing like crazy. He'd never woken up with an erection ... or had he? He only got them when he was hurting someone, or scaring someone until they screamed. He took off his boxers and stared down at himself, surprised. And when he touched it he groaned out loud. Oh, that was good. He moved back and forth a couple times. It felt like it used to, it felt normal. Charlie got in the shower, and as he continued to stroke himself he remembered the other parts of last night.

The Master had made the new guy give Charlie an orgasm. Not like that, not by touching at all. The Master said after that the man had thought it for him. But the best part had come after that. When the man put his hand on his head. Just remembering, Charlie could feel that warmth again, like he was being washed of what he had just done, it was taken from him.

Charlie felt he'd been forgiven. The man took it all away and forgave him for what he did. That ... that had felt better than the orgasm.

Again, like the night before, Charlie felt ... almost normal. And here he was, touching himself in the shower, just like many other men were likely doing that morning, too. And when the orgasm came Charlie even made a little sound of pleasure. He couldn't be sure he'd ever made that noise before. It felt fantastic.

As he washed his hands of the fluid that came out of him, Charlie felt a laugh bubble up. He was forgiven, if he dropped dead today he would ... he'd go to heaven.

Again, normal. Nothing to feel bad for. Even after remembering what he'd done he felt saved.

Then Charlie covered his eyes as he wept. *Thank you Master,* he was thinking, or maybe even saying out loud. *Thank you.*

He dressed as usual for work, whistling as he knotted his tie, thinking to himself that he looked pretty damn good for once. He felt ... well, he felt great.

God help anyone that fucked with him today.

As he got on the elevator to go downstairs, he recognized a woman he'd seen in this very spot a few weeks before. He'd thought at the time she was gorgeous. Hadn't even bothered trying to talk to her.

Now as the doors slid shut he knew she was looking at him, even though she was behind him. She thought he had nice shoulders, nice clothes, nice hair, and a great ass.

He smiled at the elevator door. This mind-reading thing could be awfully handy. He turned back to her slowly, saying in a friendly tone, "Supposed to be nice out there today."

He'd caught her looking at his backside and she blushed, stammering out, "Oh, uh, yeah. That's what they said on the radio this morning."

"Which station do you listen to?"

"KLCD."

"What's your name, by the way?"

"Tabitha, but everyone calls me Tammy." Of course they did. She was bleached-blonde, injected lips, tan darker than the Williams sisters. Part of the attraction to this kind of woman would have been finding out what parts of her were factory installed and which were after-market.

"Nice to meet you, Tammy."

"It's ..." she lost her breath as he sent her a picture. With his mind. He was imagining her against the wall, legs wrapped around his hips, skirt up around her waist as he pounded into her, her nails scoring his back as she screamed nonsensical words. She blinked and her head dipped forward, and he could feel her temperature increase. And he could swear he could smell her arousal.

"Tammy, I'm off work tonight at about nine. I'm in 8-D. You should ... you should come by. It'll be fun." He didn't let the image go; he kept it going, flowing right into her cerebral cortex. Poor Tammy was having trouble staying upright. She wasn't even trying to figure out what was happening to her anymore.

"I'll be there," she pretty much moaned.

"Good." He took a step towards her just as the doors opened behind him. She met him breasts first, panting wantonly. "And today, I want you to keep listening to KLCD. I'm on all day. I do the news."

"You do?" Her pupils were huge, he could tell now that they were close.

"That's right. You might know the name. Jasper McKay."

Voro watched Claudia get up and leave the bed, headed for the washroom. Morning sunlight was coming around the black-out blinds, and he could make out every luscious inch of her olive-toned skin. She walked slowly, probably knowing he was watching, but not embarrassed to be seen.

She was really starting to impress him. He rolled on to his back again, feeling incredibly relaxed considering she'd woken up ready for more of him, and for the last hour he'd been ridden better and more completely than any other time in his recent memory. She was fucking away pain, he could tell that, of course. But what would he do? Complain?

Then he felt the tingle of despair. While she'd slept she'd had nightmares of what she'd seen, and he'd been unable to avoid sharing it with her. The living room, the blood, the body ... his Portia. Broken beyond comprehension.

His chest ached again, right at its center. He pushed away his chain until the pendant fell under his arm, and he rubbed the dip in his sternum, frowning in concern. He knew she'd suffered plenty. He could still almost feel and taste it. Something very evil had done all that to her. Something that he had to ease out of someone.

God, he didn't want to do it, but now he had to. Or maybe he could just ... hell no, he couldn't do that. He couldn't find the guy that did it and kill him without freeing that demon, could he?

Voro wanted to. He wanted to rid this place of that particular person and what had moved them to such brutality. For Portia.

That would not go over well with the Boss, though.

Whatever. The Boss was out to get him, too. May as well stick it to The Man before he fired your ass.

He yawned loudly, his jaw cracking, but he kept a hand to the center of his chest.

"Heartburn?" Claudia guessed, climbing in beside him. He hadn't even noticed she'd entered the room. That thought had him worried, but as she pressed up along his side and put her head to his chest he forgot about how he'd started to let his guard down around women now. Ironic, wasn't it? A woman was being sent to trap him, and here he was, all warm and fuzzy with one.

"No, not heartburn. Exhaustion."

She laughed, and her chest tickled his side.

"That's too bad. I apologize."

"Mmmm. No need. Any time." He tilted his head so he could see some of her face. "You were much more ... quiet. Just now. Don't get me wrong, I don't need you screaming from a mountaintop or anything."

Claudia laughed again, and her nipples against his skin were driving him mad, not that he would have moved if the bed had been on fire. "Ummm ... the other night we were a little loud. Iola heard us and we ... we kept her up. She said."

Voro smiled, letting himself chuckle. "Oh no. No wonder she couldn't look me in the eye last night."

"Yeah, about that. What were you two talking about while you were waiting for me?"

"We talked about you, actually. She told me she'd tear me limb from limb if I did wrong by you. And then I told her about how you liked to be on top most, and that you preferred a counter-clockwise twist on the left nipple but a clockwise twist on the right - "

She gave him a jab to the ribs, and he made a sound like she'd actually hurt him. "I'll show you a nipple twist," she growled, straddling him and pushing his shoulders into the mattress.

He was smiling up at her as she seemed to pause, her mind going elsewhere. She was thinking about Iola. How she was pretty sure that after him she wouldn't want any other men, she'd be strictly women, but could she even be with Iola?

Voro's cock stirred. He couldn't help it. The thought of this gorgeous women so much as kissing the sweet Iola made him want to fuck anything with a hole. He made a low growl in the back of his throat, and she looked down at him, surprised.

He didn't want her to stop that train of thought. He rolled her on to her back, mounting her again, to which she responded with a hot, heavy lip-lock. She was wishing she could be him, just once, to see what it would be like to please Iola like this. Because Iola was straight, Iola wanted men.

Voro's brain was firing like a rat bastard. He could do that. He could totally manipulate Claudia's brain. He could cross wire her into his brain, so she would feel what he was feeling. And if he imagined she was Iola ...it was pretty damn close to the real thing.

Should he even do that?

Yeah, because doing the right thing at this stage of the game was going to win him brownie points with anyone.

Essum had Voro's *frustro* in sight as she boarded the subway, oblivious to him, even though he'd been following her for two blocks. But then, he had some blockers up. Most humans wouldn't see him, even if they stepped right through him. There was one crazy homeless man that had run from him screaming, but ... well, people were used to seeing that from time to time. No one noticed.

But a *frustro* wasn't entirely normal. He had to be careful around her.

She stood holding an overhead rail, reading a folded newspaper. She was oblivious to everyone around her, come to think of it. She barely noticed when, during a sudden surge of movement, the man standing behind her overreacted to the train's momentum shift and basically threw himself against her, totally getting a handful of her butt. He apologized in a way that indicated he knew he was wrong and she just smiled, looking back to her paper. But he was glowing like a frigging Jack O'Lantern.

Essum just shook his head, saddened that that little physical assault had actually been enough to make a guy's day. Was no one aware of what they could accomplish if they had real power?

He was twitchy. Impatient, but that was nothing new. He needed Jasper to get up to speed quick. He didn't want to give Voro any more time to figure out the holes in Essum's *laqeous* or trap explanation. He'd left a few things out, of course. As much as he and Voro might have been friends at one time ... it was a very long time ago.

He wish he'd known as much as Voro knew back when he'd met Daphne. He would have done things so differently, like head for the hills on the fastest horse he could acquire. But that's easy to say now, when the object of his insane infatuation was long dead, even her delicate bones likely faded to dust.

She'd been so lovely, the daughter of a wealthy land owner. Her neck had been long and elegant, her hair jet black, always arranged in curls. She'd moved with the grace only the truly wealthy can pull off.

He'd met her at her grandfather's funeral. He'd been hired to consume the sins of the old fart. He didn't appear a beggar, but because of his dark skin, sharp nose and shaved head the people of England had labeled him as a Moor. Even though his coloring was closer to the desert people of Arabia. But it didn't matter, not white was not right, to use a modern phrase. And people stayed well the fuck away from him, which suited his purposes just fine.

They'd had the wake for the old man in the living room of his grand country house. Flowers sat on every flat piece of furniture the room held, their fragrance covering the smell of the corpse, jasmine the most pronounced one since that had been the old man's favorite. They had it brought in special for the wake. The body's odor wasn't too rank when Essum arrived. The sins had to be consumed quickly, they believed. If only they knew how truly late they were ...

He'd been paid his fee ahead of time, and Daphne herself had placed the square of bread on her father's chest and set a tumbler of ale on the table next to his head. They waited an appropriate amount of time. Of course it was all bullshit, so he used his sixth sense to determine when the people in the room with him were good and uncomfortable ... and then he'd wait another five minutes. Then he would say, with all the dramatic flair he could manage, "*I give easement and rest to thee, dear man. Come not down the lanes or in our meadows. And for thy peace I pawn my own soul. Amen.*"

His voice had always been deep, the effect unsettling because his frame was thin. When he reached for the bread, took it in his mouth, and then drank the ale, any women in the room would always shrink away, further into the corners to get away from him.

For her grandfather's sin-eating, Daphne had stood alone right next to him, and she crossed herself as he finished, kissing the crucifix that hung around her neck over her black dress. She wasn't scared of Essum in the least.

He was astounded by her, so of course he tried to read her thoughts. When he first met the blank wall that was her mind he had no idea what to do. He was staring at her like she was a lock he hadn't a key for when she'd met his gaze, her green eyes flashing.

"Sin Eater," she said in her proper accent, dropping her eyes from his stare. "Thank you for your service. You may go."

Her voice ... it had hit him like the warmest summer breeze he'd ever known. The tones were crystal and pure. The way her lips formed each word was like watching a master conduct his opus. It had speared him through the heart and held him before her, locked in place, even as she was dismissing him from her presence.

Unable to help his nature, he'd let his dark eyes trail down her elegant form, stopping at her feet and then climbing up her long limbs again. She saw him do this, and the hot spice of her anger had piqued his interest.

She was human, but he couldn't read her. What the hell was she? Of course, he had to know everything about her.

As his eyes trailed up the low-scooped neckline of her mourning clothes, not even trying to be a gentleman, he saw a flush come to her cheeks, even as she became more offended.

"You may leave the premises, and do not presume you are welcome to return," she said, but the words were as agreeable as a love poem to him. That voice held him completely enthralled, and her graceful beauty could not to be overlooked.

He had bowed to her at the waist and made for the door. The fact that he couldn't read her mind had him in quite a flustered mess, but it was nothing compared to the moment she stopped him on the front stoop by grabbing his wrist.

Her skin on his was a jolt of lightning. They both jumped and pulled away from each other. As Essum turned, her lips parted and she was staring at him with a new interest.

The scent of chocolate filled his nostrils, and he ventured a smile at her.

She returned it, which had his body aching with need. Somehow he knew he couldn't have her, and that only made it worse.

Daphne held out her hand, and he cupped his under it. Without touching him she dropped more coins into his hand.

"For my family's rudeness," she said in whispered tones. "I am quite embarrassed they were too scared to be in the room with you. And my brother was in the cupboard with a rifle in case you attacked me."

Essum's smile broadened and he felt a proper fool, but looking at her his heart was singing and he was totally enamored.

Now, surrounded by these barely-clothed modern humans going about their silly, spoiled existence, he longed for that lost era. There was so much mystery to a woman then. And Daphne ... well, even though he was little more than ether at the moment his chest ached right where his heart should have been.

For she was dead now, wasn't she? And Essum had gotten stuck to the fly paper and killed by the built-in poison. He'd languished in more than one kind of hell ever since.

Iola was bounding off the subway, and he hurried to keep up, making himself visible on the platform. Even from a safe following distance he could smell the vanilla-jasmine perfume she carried on her skin, and the ache in his chest grew more pronounced.

Jasmine would always remind him of Daphne.

Chapter Twenty-Three

Iola had checked in on Missus Dean, but she was napping. So she made her way further down the hospital corridor, saying hi to the nurses she recognized, reluctant to stop one and ask if Doctor Aubericus was on the floor.

She somehow knew he was. But just showing up here looking for him ... it was making her feel very silly. Then she spotted him, and at that exact moment he looked up and saw her.

His face cracked into a grin that was probably as goofy as hers was.

He raised a hand to her, then finished talking to another doctor before making his way to her. He was tucking a pen in his coat pocket and still grinning. When he reached her he warmly said her name in greeting, then planted a kiss on her lips. Well, that sure didn't wipe the smile off her face.

"Vinnie," she replied. "I was wondering if you'd still be here."

"Yeah, I was back on shift this morning. Almost done here, though. What are you doing here?"

"I was going to say hi to Missus Dean, but she's having her nap."

"Mmm. Yeah, she's been tired." He lowered his tone, making sure they weren't overheard. "She's stable but ... I think she's shutting down."

Iola wanted to cry. Vinnie put an arm around her and started walking with her down the hall. "Let me finish my rounds, then I'll take you out for an early supper. How's that?"

"Ummm ... sure."

"When are you due at work?"

"About six."

"Crap. We've got a weird, three-hour window here."

"Yeah, I know."

"Don't take this the wrong way, but I really wish my phone hadn't rung last night."

Iola blushed, right to the roots of her hair. "Me too," she admitted.

"But maybe ... maybe this was a good thing. I like being a bit starved of your company."

She smiled at him like a total sap. "Okay. Should I wait for you downstairs or ...?"

"Yeah. I'll be down there in about fifteen minutes. If anything comes up I'll get you paged."

"I've never been hospital-paged before."

"Well, this will be quite a treat, won't it?"

He pressed a soft kiss to her lips before putting her in the elevator headed downstairs. As Iola re-entered the lobby she found an empty bench to sit on and took out her newspaper to read while she waited. After a few minutes the hair on the back of her neck prickled, and she raised her head to look around.

A man was sitting across the lobby from her, on a bench exactly opposite from where she sat. She didn't recognize him ... but he seemed familiar. Iola should definitely remember seeing him. He was tall, thin, with darker skin and a glossed, shaved head. His eyes seemed to be devoid of any color whatsoever, but that wasn't possible, was it? Maybe they were very pale grey. Or maybe he was blind. But he couldn't be blind; he was meeting her eyes head-on. Then, very suddenly, he winked at her.

Usually she'd be embarrassed and just go back to reading her paper, hoping to appear like she hadn't really been looking at all. But that wink jolted her, startled her, even. She jumped, and felt like someone had just goosed her brain.

She looked around the lobby, wondering if anyone else was taking note of this guy, because he should have stood out to anyone. He was terribly handsome, but no one seemed to be looking at him. Couldn't they feel him?

You are beautiful, something was buzzing in her head. Like a radio not quite tuned in properly. So she wasn't even sure if she was hearing it.

Iola frowned.

Do you want to know how I'm doing this? How I can tell your thoughts? How I know the cut of your pretty pink underwear?

She closed her eyes, the paper dropping to the floor. She rubbed her temples, the buzzing in her head making her feel like she had a migraine.

In a few days, Iola. You'll know more than you wanted in just a few days.

A hand fell on her shoulder and she cried out, jumping to her feet. She spun on whoever was behind her, hand closed in a fist. Vinnie bellowed out in surprise, raising an arm to block the punch she might or might not throw at him.

"Iola," he said in a calm voice. "Are you okay?"

Claudia awoke with a gasp, then turned to see if she'd woken Damien. No, he was quiet next to her, completely silent, breathing deep, eyes closed.

She turned her eyes ceiling-ward again, trying to collect herself. When she closed her eyes, all she could feel was ... who knew what that was? She'd been out of her own body, almost.

She'd never had such a vivid dream in her entire life. What had it been? Why was she breathless?

She'd made love to Iola. In her head. As a man.

Iola had been shy at first, letting Claudia do all the work. Claudia had kissed every conceivable inch of pale, silky skin, she'd pleased her with her hands and tongue, and then she'd entered Iola's body with a part she didn't even possess.

She covered her face then rolled to her side to look at the gorgeous man in her bed that was soundly sleeping next to her. She was sure she'd dreamed that she was him. The things she'd done to Iola were the exact things he'd done to her a few times over now. And she'd liked being the one that did it. She swore she could still taste Iola's skin on her lips, feel her small, slight body moving below her, writhing against her with want and desire. And this body that wasn't hers had brought out such exquisite delight in Iola that Claudia reached orgasm at the same time ...which was why she had just woken up.

The images and sensations she was still basking in had all the characteristics of a dream: layered over each other, a certain sight or taste or sound that stood out, other details a little hazier, but a dream. A very vivid, hot, delightful, and real dream. Her afterglow was not lessened by the fact she'd awoken while climaxing. For real. She could feel her body's final twitches of pleasure as she lay here, her breathing slowing.

Good God. No wonder Damien was happy to please her without worry about his own enjoyment. That had been ... absolute perfection.

Claudia's hands were shaking and her heart raced to the point of exhaustion. If Damien knew what she'd been dreaming of ... the thought almost embarrassed her. Almost.

The truth was she was too happy to really care. At some point he was leaving, her experiment done. This proved it; she was only interested in women. Who knew the why and how of Damien, but this was proof positive.

She wanted women in her bed, and she wanted to please their bodies as they pleased her. Probably not Iola, very likely not Iola, but ... women nonetheless.

Claudia pressed grateful lips to Damien's shoulder, and he stirred in his sleep, but it was a shallow disturbance, not one that would wake him. She climbed out of bed on the far side and strolled to the washroom to take a shower, feeling for the first time ever that she knew what she wanted. And it wasn't because of what had happened to her. It was what she wanted.

Essum wanted to burst out laughing at how Voro's petite, dear *frustro* had nearly clocked her suitor. She was a feisty one, all right. And strong ... she'd fought his mind with surprising determination. But then again, until he had a solid body he was only operating on about twenty-five percent power.

He'd never felt power like that before. If Daphne had this kind of strength he'd never know, she was a tightly closed book. But seeing it like this ... the *frustro* truly was something to be reckoned with. Maybe even more than the *decipio* was.

The doctor was saying soothing things as he picked up her newspaper and purse, asking her if she needed any Aspirin. She was saying no, and he released her from his mental transmission. He knew the moment the buzzing stopped because she sighed in relief. He dematerialized back into ether so no one else would notice him.

She looked for him, but he was long gone. Essum misted closer to catch another whiff of that jasmine scent. But as he did so, he could have sworn the doctor looked right at him anyway, his jaw set in a stern challenge, daring him to try something else.

Essum frowned ... emotionally, anyway. *What the fuck?*

Iola let herself be led to the doors, and Essum followed, now truly confused.

A new challenge was presenting itself. What the hell was Doctor Veneratio Aubericus?

The shower kicked into action, the water pipes momentarily making a hell of a ruckus in the walls of the apartment building. It made Voro jump and wonder what they hell happened, what he'd missed.

Holy shit, he'd fallen asleep. True, it had been some time since he'd had a respite of any kind, it was likely overdue. And imposing his imaginary experience into the mind of a human was taxing to say the least. It usually left him completely wiped, and then, of course, sex itself took a lot of energy. If his tank was already running low then yeah ... that little bit of mental juxtaposition likely put him right into Sleepytime Village. Population: one stupid Sin Eater.

Mmmm ... that had been good, though. Very, very good.

His eyes closed again as his hand rested in the center of his chest, his heart no longer aching. Then again, naps had a great way of putting everything back into perspective.

"You had better get back in the fucking game, moron."

He jumped a good three feet off the mattress, his heart hammering away like a jackrabbit being chased by an entire pride of lions, if that could even happen in nature. Either way, he scrambled up against the headboard, pulling a sheet halfway up his chest. At least he didn't shriek.

Sitting on top of Claudia's chest of drawers - which looked more than impossible, since the man was so large of build that he should have toppled the entire thing over with the way his weight was concentrated on one edge – was a man that was so goddamn male-beautiful even the most heterosexual bastard on earth, say James Bond, would be excused for imagining what it might be like to be gay for just a little while.

And why he didn't topple that dresser on its spindly Chippendale legs was no mystery to Voro. Angels were kind of beyond the laws of physics.

Yep. Angels. Why not?

"Raphael? What the hell are you doing here?" Voro breathed in misplaced relief. Because of what he was, angels should not be a relief. But then again, seeing his old colleague hadn't really worked out for him, either. So maybe this would be better.

"Well, Voro, old buddy, old pal. I know this looks bad. And it's not so much that we want to help you ... but here it is." Raphael was so twitchy at having to be there it was making Voro smile. Then the words tumbled out and Voro stopped smiling. "Essum is seeking to double-cross you with this whole *decipio* we've set up for you. If it works, he will be ... he will be beyond reproach. From either side."

Voro understood the words, just not the order they were being said in. "What?" Yeah, that was a brilliant response.

"Essum's got your *decipio* under his thumb. As soon as the man started to transition, Essum found him. We don't know how. And no one knows how he knew you were the one being set up to go back. But if the *decipio* manages to mortally wound you, and if he then is killed by the girl, Essum can ... take your form. He can just take over your body, force you right out of this flesh. And if he consumes the *decipio*'s sin of having killed you, then ... ah, it's really fucked up. Essum has your body and the sin of having killed you. It's like a paradox, right? How can he have the sin of the murder of a body he is in possession of?"

Voro suddenly had a splitting headache.

"But if he's in your body, we can't stop him. He'll kill the *frustro*, and we can't make another matched to a Sin Eater that we already targeted. That match is made just for your flesh. It's done, blueprint destroyed, so to speak. And as for you guys ... well, the rotation stops. He's next, he's already there in your form. His form is gone, your soul is ... well, if you have a soul, that is. But it won't be in that immortal body. It's one hell of a hiccup. Or one of those burps you get that really hurts, right in the middle of your throat. You know, right here?" Raphael pointed to his Adams' apple.

Voro ran a hand over his hair. "What happens to me? When Essum kicks me out of my own ass?"

"There will have to be another vessel in the room. A human, weak-minded. You will have no choice but to hop right in, since you're ... well, whatever you are. You can't pass on to either side. You'll stick to the first thing available and live its mortal life."

He was alarmingly business-like the more Raphael spoke. "What about Iola? Does she become a Sin Eater in my place?"

Raphael tilted his head. "Hard to say, since technically Essum stays a Sin Eater in a Sin Eater's immortal flesh. But she ... she could stay a Sin Eater as long as your former body lives. Which, if it's Essum, could be another six hundred years. But it won't matter. He'll likely have to kill her, just in case she's still capable of taking him out. You know how pragmatic Essum is."

The pain in Voro's chest was back. He dimly became aware that the water in the bathroom had shut off.

Raphael leaned forward, jerking his thumb over his shoulder at the wall behind him. "Lesbian, hey? Nice."

"Fuck off."

"Hey, I haven't been in a body ever, my friend. She's beautiful, man."

Voro studied Raphael for a moment. "Are you in a flesh-and-blood body right now?" It wasn't as stupid as it sounded. Like Essum, Raphael could just be an apparition, the result of an existential being concentrating hard enough to be seen.

"Sure am! Michael finally stepped off for a bit. So here I am, and I was asked to warn you. You gotta get your strength up to deal with Essum and your *decipio*, man. And the only way you're getting strong is to get back to fucking work."

"Is it making your skin crawl telling me to head off your boss's right and privilege before he gets a crack at these people?"

Raphael shrugged, hopping off the dresser and crossing the carpeted floor without the slightest sound. He leaned over to Voro, his long blonde hair falling forward and touching Voro's face. Fresh bread. They always smelled like fresh-baked bread.

"Truth is, Voro, we don't want to have to figure out how to fix this after the fact. We've got a few tricks, don't get me wrong. I mean, there's always a back-up *laqeous* plan. In case the first one falls through. And there's a new prototype in play, but I'm not even sure what it is ... just be careful."

"Can you at least tell me who the damn *decipio* is? That would be a great help."

Raphael rocked forward on his feet, and Voro had the insane thought the guy was going to kiss him. But he stood up instead, laughing. "I can't do that. What if Essum fucks up and the chance is there to bench a Sin Eater that's been on rotation for over six hundred years?"

"Yeah, that wouldn't be fair, would it?"

"Sorry, man. This is as much as I can tell you."

"Are you leaving anything out?" Voro narrowed his eyes at the beach-blonde model standing in the middle of Claudia's bedroom. He was raw male sexual attraction, in looks only because an angel's pureness of heart usually quelled any hot-and-sweaty passion that any human might get out of one. Still, Raphael was as mellow as could be. Voro knew angels couldn't out and out lie to him, but they sure as hell could leave out important information. Just to fuck with him.

"Nah, man. It's all I know. And I told you what I'm leaving out, and why I'm leaving it out. So no ball-busting, okay?"

"I'm going to fight for this life, okay? I'm not going to just roll over and let you stop Essum from doing what he wants, then take my place at the back of the line. I'm going to stop him. It will be messy and it might get grim."

"I know that. You don't think we get our hands dirty from time to time?" Raphael made a *tsk* sound in the back of his throat.

"I know you get your hands dirty, too."

Raphael sat on the edge of the bed, and Voro sat up straighter, eyes on the guy's back as he pushed his hair back out of his face. "You know why we exist, right? You're aware of how ridiculous this whole thing is?"

Voro nodded, but of course Raphael didn't have eyes in the back of his head. "Yeah, I know."

"We work for two kids on a school ground fighting over fucking marbles."

"It's a dick-measuring contest."

"The guy with the most cash wins."

"And these cattle are actually picking sides." Voro knew Claudia was almost done drying off, and he moved to poke Raphael in the back with his foot. "She's coming out soon, get going. I appreciate it, really. But I don't have a reason to explain why you're here."

"Just plant something in her head. Maybe I want to stay."

Voro kicked him, not as nicely. "Get!"

The angel got up, left the room and walked past the bathroom door just as Claudia was leaving the bathroom. Voro blocked her mind from seeing him, but since she was naked, Raphael's head swiveled like a barn owl to track her movement, stopping in his tracks so he could watch her walk back to the bed. Voro wanted to shoot him a *"get the fuck out of here"* look, but he was already blocking her from sensing him and he didn't have the energy to just put her right out so he could kick Raphael's ass.

Raphael stayed where he was anyway, and as she climbed on to the bed next to him Voro noted with satisfaction that the angel was displaying a nasty trait that he wasn't supposed to exhibit: envy.

Claudia smiled down at him, stretching out over his upper body with hers, unabashedly naked and pink from her shower. The ends of her hair were damp and curling on her shoulders. She smelled and looked delicious.

Of course, he got hard immediately.

"You would not believe the dream I just had," she mumbled happily, her lips on his and her chest pressing into him so that he had to rearrange himself to prevent injury. She played with the pendant on his necklace, flicking it through her fingers, totally disinterested in it.

"What kind of dream?" He asked, even though he knew damn well what she was talking about. He must have done one hell of a number on her mind.

She dropped the pendant, pulled the sheets back and took him in her hand, stroking very gently. "I can't even tell you. But it was ... amazing. It's making me feel like ... I owe you something."

"Dear Claudia," he said, smiling broadly, "you owe me nothing."

She lowered her head to his lap, and his eyes rolled up in his head. He looked to the hallway where Raphael still stood, his eyes huge. For theatrics Raphael curled his hand into a fist and bit it as though he couldn't take the sight of her naked body and the act she was currently performing.

Voro smiled at him, then extended his middle finger before a moan brought him back to Claudia and he closed his eyes to let her repay him.

Yeah, he was back.

Chapter Twenty-Four

Damn, damn, damn, Iola thought, stealing a glance over at Vinnie as he drove her through the streets to work. This truly sucked. She couldn't stand the fact that she was going to work. She really wanted to stay with him.

They had a nice lunch, went for a walk by the river, then had ice cream. Now he was taking her to work and that would be it for her Vinnie fix today.

A time would come eventually where she'd have him all to herself for a good twelve hours, she was sure of it. But she might go insane waiting for it to come around.

"Take this alley; I always go in the back door. It's closest to the subway," she instructed, and he turned where she told him to. When he stopped by the metal door with the key-swipe lock he put the car in park and turned to her, smiling.

"I'm going to miss you," he said.

That thought warmed her. "I'm going to miss you. I hate that I have to be at work for the next eight hours instead of with you."

Vinnie leaned across the shifter to kiss her, likely meaning for it to be a nice but still sexy peck on the lips, but Iola flicked her tongue into his mouth, and he didn't even hesitate to meet it with his, and soon enough they were in a full-on lip lock, and Iola remembered the good-night kisses in high school after a date, trying not to look like they're making out when they were, of course, making out in the car.

The kiss did nothing to make her happier about going into work, but he was still the one to end the kiss, putting a hand to her lips and giving an awfully sexy smile. "Iola, I'm sorry. I shouldn't have done that."

She smiled back. "You should always do that. As much as possible."

"Have fun at work. Call me tomorrow."

"I will." She was out the passenger door immediately, shutting it and waving at him through the glass. Then she ran for the door and let herself in before she gave crawling into bed with Doctor Aubericus another thought.

Once she got into her control room she started going through her playlists, getting ready to go on air in half an hour. The door opened behind her very quietly, and she looked up, then felt the itchy sensation of awkwardness walk into the room as her guest did.

"Okay, so I had this dream the other night," Jasper opened with, holding his hands out in a questioning manner. "I had this dream that I called the radio station when I was technically too drunk to be trusted to brush my own damn teeth, and I said some incredibly stupid things to this really nice woman I work with. Tell me this was some kind of nightmare."

Iola laughed. "Jasper, I've never judged people by what they did while intoxicated."

"Oh, thank God. But seriously," he sat on a stool across the console from her, pushing a guest microphone out of the way. "I am so incredibly sorry. For that. It was out of line."

Iola shrugged. "Really, don't sweat it. Like I said, alcohol makes people do some stupid shit."

Jasper got to his feet and circled the console to stand closer to her, and she swiveled to face him. Then she frowned.

He looked ... different today. He seemed taller. His jaw appeared *more* square. Handsome, even. And his dark hair was quite glossy now. Or maybe she'd never really looked at him like this before. Which raised the question of why she was looking at him that way now.

She stood, because he was making her uncomfortable. Or ... *why* was she standing? She frowned, putting a hand to her temple. Usually when she was tired her thoughts were slow, but right now they were downright foggy. Like her brain was firing but the electricity had to go through oatmeal to register.

When she closed her eyes, her breath stopped. It just caught in her throat.

Iola became aware that she was naked, which was wrong since she was at work. She should definitely be wearing her clothes here. She looked down at herself. Nope, naked as the day she was born.

Maybe this was a dream, like going to school in your underwear.

Someone had her in his arms, and she looked up into Jasper's midnight blue eyes. His eyes were locked on her lips, and she became aware of a heat in between their bodies ... which were right against each other. Her bare breasts pressed into his bare chest, his hands hot on her back, holding her in place.

She closed her eyes as he shifted his hips against hers, and she gasped as she felt his arousal. His mouth sucked at her neck, hot and demanding, and her hands shot into that dark hair, grabbing it in clumps. His hand stroked her breast, and as she moaned he pulled softly on her nipple.

Iola's head fell back, and Jasper kept her upright, lowering his lips on to hers. She responded like a wanton harlot, sealing her lips against his and forcing her tongue into his mouth. He backed her up against the counter in front of the computer, then cupped her bare ass and hefted her up on to the work space by it. Her legs wound around his waist, and Iola became aware then that she wanted him desperately, she needed him inside her. Her body was hot and wet with necessity.

"Oh, Iola," he muttered against the skin of her lips.

She couldn't answer. His hand was sliding down her stomach, stopping just above the part of her that wanted his touch the most.

"Iola?"

She opened her eyes, her breath coming with difficulty, and she blinked rapidly. She was standing against the computer counter, and Jasper was across the room, eyeing her with concern. "Iola," he repeated. "Are you okay?"

She put a hand to her lips, then nodded. "Sorry, yeah. I was ... I was lost in my thoughts I guess."

"Well, I just wanted to apologize. But I better go. There was another escape from the jail, I gotta get to the press conference."

She nodded. "Okay. I'll see you." Or maybe she said something like that. Who the hell knew? It was like coming out of a coma of something.

What. The. Fuck?

"Can you ... can you repeat that?" Claudia knew her voice might be running the risk of sounding hysterical, but too bad. She thought she must be losing her mind, that's the only thing that could explain what Constable Vance was telling her.

"Charles Goodwin is not in his cell." Vance sounded like he'd rather be singing show tunes than uttering these words. She knew it wasn't his fault. But still ... *dammit.*

"You gotta be kidding."

"We're going through security tapes but there's one point last night where everything just ... fuzzes out like an electrical storm or something. I've got patrol going by your building at least twice every hour but ... you might want to check into a hotel or something. Just to be safe. You're on days off anyway, right?"

Vance already knew the answer to that. "Yeah," Claudia confirmed it anyway. "I'm off the next three days."

"Stay with someone else or check into a safe hotel, okay? The guy's gotten in that place once already. I'd ... I'd feel better if you were somewhere else."

Me too, she thought, then cleared her throat. "Yeah, I'll do that. I'll have my cell in case you hear anything, but I'll ... I'll head somewhere safe."

"Good. But don't tell me or anyone else where you go. I hate to get suspicious of our pals here, but ... this guy's gotten free twice now."

Claudia's mind would have taken twice as long as Vance's to get to that conclusion, but he shocked it to her early. One of her own co-workers?

"So get out of there and call my cell when you're hidden. Please ... just get going."

"Okay. And thanks, Vance."

"Don't mention it, Sergeant. Just be safe."

She hung up the cordless phone with a slow-moving and numb hand which of course Damien noticed.

"Trouble at work?" He guessed with that calm, easy voice of his.

"Charles Goodwin is free again. He escaped from jail ... for the second time." Yeah, Claudia was thinking she must be losing her mind. Because this was so inexplicably ridiculous.

"So ... where are you going?"

Damien's voice brought her back to earth this time. She stood, then shrugged. "I gotta find a hotel. Check in for a while. They're sending patrols by, but ... the guy that just called thinks I should head somewhere and not tell anyone where I am."

Damien nodded. "That sounds like a good plan."

"Yeah, I guess." She pulled a suitcase out of her front closet, then walked down the hall to the bedroom with it and flung it open on her bed.

"Let me stay here," Damien suggested. "The lights will be on, someone's moving around. Maybe ... maybe he'll try getting at what he thinks is you."

Claudia frowned at him in her doorway, frozen in front of her dresser. "What? No, no. I can't let you do that. You don't need to get involved in this."

Damien cracked his knuckles, jaw set. "I'd love to get that shit in my hands again."

Claudia studied this stranger she'd had in her bed for about 24 hours in total now, wearing only his dress pants at the moment, his bare skin giving way to flexing muscle as he worked his knuckles against each palm. As much as her lesbian identity might have been renewed she was still fascinated by him. And this man threatening violence against someone else shouldn't have been attractive. It *really* shouldn't have been. Not at all.

She wanted to jump him again.

She blinked and carried a handful of T-shirts from the dresser to the suitcase.

"And you'd be doing me a favor. I need somewhere to stay, too, and as much as I'd love to come along with you and sequester the both of us in some hotel suite somewhere ..."

Claudia straightened as he stepped up against her backside, hands on her hips as he pulled her against him. She had to laugh deep in her throat, heat flaring up again at his touch.

"... I still think you might be more comfortable on your own in this situation. And if I'm here ... I can rip the guy limb from limb. For you."

His hands crossed her stomach and his lips kissed her neck and shoulder. "If this is how you talk people into things, I am always going to disagree with you," she laughed, stepping away. Then she shook her head. "I can't believe I'm saying this, but yeah ... feel free to stay here. Just ... promise not to rob me blind?"

"Rob a cop? Do I look stupid?" He flopped on to her bed behind her suitcase, smiling up at her with a twinkle in his eye.

She put a few pairs of jeans in the suitcase, mulling over what she wanted to ask him next. And true to his amazing intuition he asked, "What is it? You have a question, I can tell."

She put the jeans away, then put her hand to her heart. "If you're here, please watch out for Iola. I can tell you know how to handle yourself, I saw that the other day. But just ... watch over her, if you could?"

He nodded. "I swear to you, she will not be harmed."

Claudia blinked, then sat on the edge of the bed pushing the case away. "And please don't sleep with her."

Damien blinked and sat up. "What?" He asked around a laugh.

"Look, she's beautiful. And when you two are around each other ... there's a connection. I can see it. I can feel it. Hell, I can smell it. It's okay, I'm not jealous. But ... this guy she's seeing now? She has a chance for real happiness with him. I don't want sex – granted, amazing, toe-curling brain-numbing sex – but still, it's just sex, and it shouldn't wreck that potential."

Damien blinked a few times, his jaw tight. Claudia was worried she'd upset him.

"I won't touch her, I swear it."

She expelled her breath. "Don't think I'm a jealous wing-nut, please - "

He took her hands while he laughed. The sound was deep and came from somewhere very low in his thick chest. "I know you're not jealous. You're protecting your friend. She's lucky to have you."

Claudia pulled her hands back and got up to get underwear from her dresser. "I don't know about lucky."

"I think she is," he said, leaning back to watch her.

Claudia just shook her head. "If you knew some of the thoughts I had about her … you wouldn't say that."

Jasper left the station out the back door, unable to hide the smug smile on his face.

Holy shit, he'd gotten into Iola's brain. And she hadn't the foggiest idea what he'd done to her.

He climbed behind the wheel of the station's news cruiser, and he had to pause and take a deep breath. He closed his eyes, remembering the moment he'd jumped in her brain, telling her she was naked, then getting an eyeful of what that had looked like.

It was even better than what he'd been imagining all this time he'd been panting after her. So much better. *Thank you God,* he thought as he started up the vehicle and pulled the shifter into reverse.

He arrived at the police station about fifteen minutes later, his euphoria fading pretty quickly. After all, he'd just walked out the door of this place with a homicidal maniac less than twenty-four hours ago. He felt like a cat in a room full of rocking chairs, but the only cops that greeted him were the ones that already knew him from past news stories he'd done. His panic started to fade with each minute that passed.

He was shown into a conference room, and he nodded to his colleagues from another radio station and the local newspaper. He set up his microphone, got his equipment running, and then sat to wait like the rest of them. His fingers were drumming on the table top. Okay, maybe a bit of the nerves were still hanging around after all.

That's just to keep you sharp, buddy.

He jumped, but thankfully the door opened to admit a video journalist from the television station. She was cute with long legs plugged into a short skirt, blonde, and she gave everyone a neon-white smile as she went around setting up her gear. Jasper was wondering when she'd started at the station when the voice came back.

Forget her for just a moment, please. And pay attention.

He looked around at the others in the room, but they weren't hearing Essum's voice bouncing around in his head. And Jasper couldn't see that bastard either, so obviously Essum was pulling a "voice in my head" act on him.

Very good, you're a clever one. That's why you were hand-selected. Now once you're done here, meet Charlie and me at 44692, 24th Avenue North. Come around the back. We'll be waiting.

Jasper frowned and opened his mouth to respond.

In your head, moron. Just think your answer back at me.

Jasper furrowed up his brow and gave it his best shot. *I'm at work here. If I don't go back and file this story people are going to be looking for me.*

He could hear Essum's disappointment in his head. *File the story and meet us after that, then. I'm not going to wait all fucking night.*

That's a 20-minute drive for fuck's sake – Jasper stopped, realizing Essum was gone, like someone had switched off the radio.

Constable Trevor Vance entered the room right at that moment, and they all sat up straighter. There was a crescendo of whining and whirring equipment as everyone got their electronic devices up and running as Vance took a seat in front of all the microphones on the table. He flipped open a folder, cleared his throat and began to read.

"I'd like to thank you all for coming, and as always, we appreciate the media's help in finding missing persons, persons of interest, or in this case, escaped suspects. At approximately 10:15 last evening Charles Goodwin escaped from his holding cell here in the basement of the 12th Precinct ..."

Jasper's panic flared up again, knowing that a picture of Charles was going to be dispersed to everyone in the room. He also knew there might be video surveillance. Surely Essum realized that, maybe he had some kind of voodoo trick up his sleeve to prevent the video from being seen. That would be pretty fucking handy.

"Video surveillance tapes seem to have been tampered with as well, as at the approximate time of the escape the cameras seem to have encountered electric interference. All we have is a photograph of Charles Goodwin, a mug shot taken the second time we took him into custody. It will be made available to all media outlets that request it. I will now answer a few questions."

The newspaper guy was the first one to pipe up. "Can you give us any details on how this guy has escaped from custody twice now?"

"Internal investigations are ongoing, and because of that I can offer no further comment on how it was able to happen. Yes?" He pointed to the new cutie pie from the television station, who had her hand politely raised.

"Is it true Charles Goodwin was able to get into a female police officer's apartment and attack her the last time he was arrested?"

Jasper was surprised at the question. He hadn't heard about that.

"Following the previous arrest the additional charges he faced were assaulting a police officer and breaking and entering, yes. That's all I will disclose on that subject."

Jasper put up his hand, and Constable Vance acknowledged it with a nod. "Constable Vance, is Charles Goodwin to be considered dangerous?"

"He is certainly dangerous, we have DNA proof that he has killed two women at this point. We are going back through unsolved cases and looking for DNA evidence to connect him to those. These are violent crimes, so yes, he is dangerous. But we do not consider him to be armed. Still, people are urged not to contact him, but to call the police instead."

Unarmed, Jasper thought with a laugh. *Having the fucking left-hand of Satan taking care of you should count as being "armed."*

Chapter Twenty-Five

Voro followed a tall man in a mighty fine Tom Ford suit out to a strip mall parking lot, pleased as punch when the guy put his briefcase on the roof of his car to get his keys out. Voro passed behind the man, his elbow briefly making contact with the man's back through his jacket. And there it was; not a big sin. Not layer upon layer of evil. Just a drop in the bucket, really.

The man had raped his roommate's girlfriend in college. He'd been slightly drunk at the time, and so had she, no charges had been laid, the girlfriend hadn't even told his roommate about it. But that girl hadn't been right after that. She'd tried to kill herself the next semester as a matter of fact.

The guy didn't feel bad about it, thought she'd been asking for it, even though he'd hit her in the face a few times to get her to quiet down. He hadn't done anything like that since, but Voro also saw that deep down under the layers of old-school macho bullshit the guy knew it had been wrong, and the only thing keeping him from doing it again was the paralyzing fear of getting caught.

He'd liked it plenty, and still thought about it when he jerked off.

With Essum's touch that sin was gone, replaced with a warm sensation of well-being. The guy didn't even question it. He found his car key, got in the car with his briefcase, smiling like an ass the whole time. He didn't even look to see who had run into him.

Voro felt a surge of strength come back. Raphael had been right. Slacking off on work had been sapping the strength out of him. And he'd need much more than just this if he was going to nip Essum's plan in the bud.

He continued his walk down Stark Street, people hurrying past him, on the hunt for a weeknight meal somewhere other than at home. Most of them were assholes, but not real sinners.

He continued his stroll, knowing it was just a matter of time before he found someone really worth relieving of their mortal wrongdoings. And sure enough, the world tilted back to its natural order.

There was a whore on a corner three blocks from the man in the parking lot. She was smoking a cigarette, boldly working the street with all the aplomb of a time-tested pro that didn't give a shit if she spent the night on her knees or in a cell in lock-up. Getting arrested was preferable to her, she was tired today. She had a scrape on her cheek, and she was acting as though she was a bit scared to be out working, too. Man, she really wanted to get picked up by the fuzz tonight.

Plus her blood and body were polluted with many different narcotics, heroin being the most obvious one that he could smell. The only other smell coming from her was rotten eggs.

Sulfur. Bingo.

He closed his eyes as he passed behind her and caught the hidden memories of her initiation into the trade she was currently employed in. Her first pimp had found her at sixteen. Gotten her into meth right off the bat. It was easy manipulation beyond that. She would do anything to get that high, and as long as she was high, anything could be happening to her. She couldn't give half a shit who she was under.

And she'd helped this pimp in many ways because she thought he loved her. But that was the surface excuse. The Sin Eater in him knew that she was attracted to his cruelty. She'd helped him rape and kill the other girls when they skimmed cash from his cut, or if they'd stolen from his stash. She'd lured them places, held them down while he attacked them cruelly, helped him hide the bodies, and then had sex with him after because the whole time the act had turned her on. The fact that she would turn on her own "sisters" was a testament to the evil that had grabbed on deep to her.

She was one hell of a degenerate. She'd be like seven triple-espressos and a hell of a lot of ephedrine in his gas tank. Perfect.

He made her turn around with just a nudge from his brain, and when she did, he held out a one hundred dollar bill to her. Her eyes widened and her coconut turned into a frightfully good calculator as she was measuring how much H that bill would get her. Good at math and yet here she stood, waiting for a dick to suck.

Her hand snatched the cash, and yet she didn't run away with it. Her eyes were going over his suit and his body, and she was willing to perform the job even though the cash was now in hand.

It's not really a curse to be this desired, Voro thought. But what he said was, "Where?"

"Well, this hotel rents by the hour. Are you paying or me?"

"I'll pay it," he offered, and she sauntered by him with hips shifting and legs strutting. Didn't she know that whores didn't have to really sell the goods? As long as the guy knows you're a sure thing, there's no further advertising needed. You've got him.

She led him through the "lobby" to the desk. He rented a room for two hours, the whole time feeling her eyes running over him like he was not only a meal ticket but also a walking vibrator. She actually wanted him.

He could almost gag, but he told himself that's what happens when he slacks off. He was no longer used to the stench.

The elevator didn't work, so she took the stairs up ahead of him, doing the hip-shake thing the entire way. Her skirt was short and her underwear was missing, so he got the whole eyeful. Thankfully, he had no physical reaction to it. Getting an erection because of this would have embarrassed him.

She leaned on his arm as he worked the key into the lock, fighting to get it open. The heroin in her system was very pure, she barely knew what was going on around her. She also had diseases. She needed an entire pharmacy and priest to deliver last rites, not another hit of H.

Okay, the last bit was a bit blasphemous on his part. But whatever. He knew that once he got in her disease and drug-addled mind, she likely wouldn't recover from what he was there to really do to her.

In the room she flicked the lights on, went to the bed, hiked up her skirt and bent over, hands planted on the mattress. He shut the door, feeling his skin crawl. She was positively putrid compared to where he'd spent the last few nights. But then he cleared Claudia from his mind, not wanting to get any of this filth splashed on his memory of her.

He walked up behind her, putting a hand on her lower back where he was still technically protected by her skirt. But it didn't matter, this was enough contact to do what he had to.

She tried to back up into him, and he kept good three steps between them. This was a nice suit after all, and without Portia's cash it was going to be pretty labor-intensive to get another one like it.

"Hey," the woman whined around her gum, already wearing on his nerves. "Get to it, honey. I want my full two hours' worth." Then she tried to grind into him again.

That was supposed to make him amorous?

He wanted to tell her to put her skirt back down, but he wanted out of this room more. So he went right to it, pushing his way into her frontal lobes as deep as he could, meeting absolutely no resistance whatsoever.

The smell was awful. Her mind was worse.

She'd beaten up her sister as a kid. Okay, that wasn't a sin. But drowning her sister in the paddling pool was. This woman had been raped by her father when she was young, and when he'd started in on her sister she'd gone into a jealous fit she was entirely too young to understand. And she'd drowned her. That was one down.

It had been ruled an accident. Overwhelming joy at having gotten away with it. Then running away when her mother found out about the sexual abuse. She'd been trying to put her daughter in therapy, and that's why she had bolted.

First night on the street she'd been beaten up by two other whores, then raped by their pimp. She got hers back though, once the pimp decided she would work for him. She had helped him kill the two bullies and dispose of the bodies. She'd had sex with the pimp, on the floor next to their corpses first.

She liked that shit. She lived for it.

Two more sins down. She was beyond filthy; there was a lot more to come.

He heard her whimper, because she was also seeing what she had done, without her own emotions tied in. She was seeing it from his point of view, seeing it as wrong for the first time. Her knees gave out and she sunk to the floor, breaking contact.

It was too late. He was in, and he flipped through her nasty little dossier like he could be considering her for a job. Her brain was misfiring like crazy, all the drugs doing nothing to help her recover from being gone over like this. The damage done was irreparable, and when he left this room she would likely die. Last rites indeed.

More murders, more bodies dumped. More turning on her own kind for the lust she had for a monster. Voro would have loved to have found this pimp. He would have been one hell of a sin supply. But he was getting the feeling the guy might be dead. This woman was saddened by the thought of him ...

Hello. Oh, so she'd killed him. In the end she had taken him out. Interesting, and very enterprising of her. She'd spiked his heroin. Nice. Again, that nasty jealousy of hers.

Voro was glad to note he felt no pity for her, or remorse for what she was remembering. And when he got to an episode just the night before where she'd been taken violently by force, he felt no compassion. Even with the money exchanging hands.

Until there was a weird *hiccup* in the video feed. Like a poorly-placed splice that had her faceless john cutting her throat. It wasn't happening, but she saw it and it made her freeze in terror, then and now. Once the guy was gone the image was gone, and she hadn't remembered it.

She did now. She was crying.

He frowned and tried to flip back but the tunnel he'd burrowed was a mess of dislodged prayers she was thinking to herself and weird memories of playing with puppies and her mother making birthday cakes. She was fried.

But those scenes were still at least part of her. That image she'd had of a knife coming away from her neck, covered in blood. That hadn't been real. Someone crudely put it there.

It was a lot like what Sin Eaters did, actually.

As he mentally let go of her, she slumped right over on to the floor. He left her to her whimpering and sobbing. She was trying to piece together happier memories from the good stuff she'd seen. There wasn't a lot and it was on a continuous loop.

Voro wished like hell she'd seen who she'd been with, but she hadn't even checked out his face. She had apparently only held on to the promise of that fifty bucks. Everything else had been periphery.

He turned and left the room, locking the door behind him. He could feel her dying and had to get away, just in case someone came to collect her while looking for him at the same time. Collect her as in her soul, of course. Not the body. That would be there for at least another hour and a half.

The further he got from that room the better he felt, and not just because of the smell. His batteries were almost entirely charged, she'd done him a world of good. At just a hundred bucks she was a bargain.

He left the hotel, noting that the clerk didn't even look up. Yeah, that guy had been working here for a while. He had one hell of a porn fetish, and had a few rooms wired up with cameras to sell a few videos online of his own making. He quality-controlled which girls went to those rooms, though. The one Voro had taken upstairs never would have made that cut.

Despicable: yes. Sinner: no.

He was back on Stark and walking east. A few more like that and he might just be ready to take out Essum and that damn *decipio*, if he ever found out who it was.

Claudia checked the room before letting the motel desk clerk leave. Under the bed: clear. Bathroom: clear and clean. No noticeable tampering with any of the vents, mirrors, light fixtures, This wasn't a complete dive she was checking into, but you can never be sure. She nodded her agreement and the clerk shut the door for her. She didn't care if he thought she was nuts.

It had to be a motel; she needed a window and a door that opened to the outside. She couldn't explain why that was, it just felt safer to her. The motel door also had a security chain, which she would take over an electronic key card any day.

She put her suitcase on the rack, not opening it, and moved to the windows to shut the blinds. She could see the entire parking lot from up here on the third level, and the room was in a corner of the building so she could see both corridors leading up to her door.

It was also furthest from the damn ice machine.

She picked up her cell phone and called Vance. She got his voicemail right away, so she said briefly, "It's me. I'm checked in and safe. Call me if you need anything." Then she hung up and tossed the phone back on the bed.

Okay, she was in a safe place where no one she knew could find her. That should be reassuring, but it wasn't.

Well, as long as the cell was working she was reachable. Speaking of which, she should really plug it into the charger.

Claudia went through her suitcase to find the charger, got it plugged in, then remembered Damien watching her place. They'd discussed Iola, and that's when Claudia realized she should really warn her friend.

Knowing that Iola would be at work, she dialed the number anyway and left Iola a message as well, saying "Hey, it's Claudia. Call me when you get in, no matter what time it is. I need to tell you something, call my cell." She did her best not to sound scared.

If just one other person could know where she was. But that was pretty risky if that maniac was out on the streets. Plus, as small as he was, Claudia was still plenty scared of him.

She flopped on to the bed and flicked on the TV, decided she was uncomfortable, and got up to put on flannel pants in lieu of her jeans. Man, she was twitchy. Maybe being in pajamas would mellow her out.

She pulled a pair out of her suitcase and something hit the carpet at her feet. She frowned, picked it up, a smile touching her lips just slightly. She opened the square of paper as something slid out, landing on the foot of the bed.

It was a piece of her notepaper from home, a quick note scrawled out. "I'm taking care of your place. And your plants. And your neighbor. Are you sure you want me to sleep with her though?" It wasn't signed and didn't need to be. Claudia almost laughed.

She picked up the chain from the foot of the bed, turning the pendant over in her hand. It was Damien's necklace, not that she'd looked at it terribly closely before. She recognized it nevertheless. The pendant was silver, a relief of what look like a goat's head. The chain was similar to what the armed forces' dog tags were hung on. She could swear it was still warm.

She held it in her palm, and feeling ridiculous, she put it on, dropping it under the neck of her T-shirt. The second it hit her skin the rest of her felt as warm as it was. She shook herself back to reality and went to the bathroom to change into PJs.

Chapter Twenty-Six

Iola had to get it together. She was having a hell of a time concentrating, and the show was one of the shittiest she'd even put to air, without a doubt. So she cut down on her chatter and just played more songs.

She had the shakes like she'd missed a meal or something. And she couldn't concentrate. Everything just felt so wrong.

She felt wretched. Gross. Incredibly dirty. Like she'd done something very inappropriate. And it had all started after Jasper left the control room.

She shook herself back to the here and now to introduce the next song. "And now folks, the kind of song you just need to hear, late at night, maybe driving home from somewhere you shouldn't have been in the first place. Here's *Bobcaygeon* by The Tragically Hip on KLCD Late Night."

She rubbed her forehead. She was trying to squish that terrible image out of her head through her ears. She did not see Jasper that way, not at all.

When he'd come back from the press conference he'd been all business, pre-recorded his newscast and then took off again. By now she knew his shift was definitely over, thank God. The less he was here the better.

She noticed that her cell phone screen lit up, so she picked it up and read the text message she'd just received.

U sound off. I'll pick U up @ 2. V.

She smiled down at the phone. Somehow knowing that Vinnie was listening made her feel better instantly. She sent him a message back. *Sounds gr8. See U then.*

Crap. Which song was next? She checked the screen and realized the news was next, and it was already loaded up and ready for her to hit "play." She checked her phone again, no new messages, set it down, then just listened to the dying chords of the song. When the time came she spoke over the end of the song. "Now it's time for the news with Jasper McKay, but I'll be right back after that. You're listening to Late Night with Iola Day."

The news music started, and she hit play on the computer. Jasper's news cast came on, starting with a sound up on a suspect wanted in connection with two violent murders. A suspect that escaped police custody for the second time in as many days. Most recently the man, named Charles Goodwin, had been arrested for assaulting a police officer.

Iola frowned. He'd escaped again? Did Claudia know? Stupid, of course she knew.

She picked up her cell and dialed Claudia's phone at home. When there was no answer, Iola tried her cell. Claudia answered after a couple of rings. "Hello? Iola?"

"Claudia – what's going on? Are you okay?"

Her friend laughed, and Iola could just see her pushing her hair behind one ear as she did it. She was probably shaking her head, too. "That's my line, Day."

"I just heard about this Charles Goodwin. What the hell?"

"Yeah, I just found out tonight, too. So I'm in hiding right now."

"In hiding?"

"I've checked into a motel, and it's being kept on the down-low, you know, in case there's someone in the department leaking information. I'm supposed to be off for the next few days anyway."

"Oh, thank God you're taking this seriously. But nothing happened?"

"No no. They just don't know where he is, and no one knows how he got away again. It's starting to look fishy, so I'm sequestered."

"Man. Now I don't want to go home."

"Don't worry."

"Don't worry? I have to worry."

"No, I mean, I asked Damien to stay at my place. So there will be someone across the hall in case something happens."

Iola was silent, wrestling with her internal monologue. She didn't want Damien there. So close. Without Claudia around. Again, she didn't trust herself.

"Iola?"

"Sorry, what was that?"

"I said not to worry. He's not going to be putting any moves on you. He promised me."

It's not him I'm worried about. "Well, I guess that makes me feel better?" She let the phrase end weakly, which made Claudia laugh again.

"Hell, Iola. If you want, have at him. But I would be very disappointed in you. After all, Vinnie is ... Vinnie is perfect for you."

Iola smiled, noting that the newscast would be ending in about a minute and fifteen seconds. "Yeah, I think he is, too. But I gotta go, news is almost done."

"Oh hey – Jasper's back at work, hey?"

"Yeah."

"Was he sheepish about that dumbass phone call he made?"

"Yeah, he was really embarrassed. And he apologized profusely." *And then I imagined I was about to have sex with him.*

"Good. The dumb ass."

"I really gotta go."

"Okay, call me if you need anything."

"Ditto."

Iola hung up the phone just in time to catch the news music as it faded out. "That was your twelve-thirty news break. This is KLCD Late Night with Iola Day, and now let's pick it up just a little bit. How about a little Tom Petty and the Heartbreakers? This is *Learning to Fly.*"

Jasper was in the corner again, facing dirty concrete walls, trying his best not to listen to what was going on. This time didn't seem as bad. Charlie wasn't so fucking insane, even though he was strangling a woman with his belt.

Her lights were fading, and he could smell the death that was coming for her. When she saw nothing, he knew somehow that there was still another ten minutes before she was actually dead. He could save her, maybe. Some CPR, mouth-to-mouth, he might be able to bring her back.

But then what would Essum do to him?

Jasper was beginning to suspect that Essum was a lot more than he made himself out to be. He was showing Jasper how to use his own mental abilities to control what other people did with their thoughts and bodies. Like this woman? Essum showed him how to completely paralyze her so Charlie could have his way with her.

Always with the rape. Why did he need to rape them? Christ, at least this time he came on his own. Jasper so did not want another assist on a Charlie orgasm. But Jasper was starting to understand where this was going.

The more sins he took away, he stronger his abilities would get. Essum basically confirmed it. If they kept Charlie like a little sin-gathering lap dog, they'd have a never-ending supply of evil depravity to harvest. And with Charlie, they knew very damn well he was never going to try and run away. He was in like Flynn, all the way.

Charlie let the woman's body drop, and when Jasper could only hear the sound of Charlie's rasping breath, he turned around. She was dead on the dirty concrete floor of an abandoned building, and Charlie was looking at him with expectant, hopeful eyes while doing up his pants.

He wants me to do this, this is his new contact high, Jasper realized, just as Essum's voice echoed through the room and right into Charlie's head.

Take it from him, Jasper. Just like I showed you.

Charlie stepped forward, wiping his hands on his pants and smiling. This was the new *why* for Charlie. He didn't make a big mess this time. He didn't get blood all over the place. Wasn't he a good boy?

Jasper put a hand out, and Charlie ducked his head under it, breathing in deeply. Jasper found the fresh sin that Charlie had just committed, focused on it, and plucked it from his brain like a dandelion. Charlie sighed and leaned back from his hand, eyes closed and face breaking into a wide grin.

"Thank you," he whispered, almost tearful.

Jasper swallowed painfully, just nodded.

Okay Charlie, you're free to go. Take the rest of the night off ... but go only to your hotel room. Don't go anywhere else.

"Yes, Master." Charlie said, nodded and wrapping his arms around himself and he left the building out the front way.

Jasper waited for Essum to take shape, which he did, standing on the other side of the woman's body. He was looking at her thoughtfully. "This one was actually quite pretty, wasn't she?"

Jasper just shrugged.

"I think I smell a little sin on you, too." Essum said, stepping over the body and coming closer. Jasper didn't dare step back from him.

"Me?"

"What did you get up to last night, my dear boy?"

"What?" He knew it was pointless to play dumb, but he couldn't help it. Part of him hoped there were still things Essum couldn't see.

"That girl in the stairwell. I watched you take her. And good job with that little mental jab."

Jasper felt his armor crack. He thought, to his horror, he might be about to cry. "I don't know what's wrong with me. I've never done anything like that before - "

"There's nothing wrong with you. You are going to be beyond humans very soon. They are just the tools we use to do our jobs."

Jasper took a breath and nodded, knowing instinctively to not argue with Essum. The guy knew how to give someone a brain hemorrhage just by looking at them. Jasper was not signing up to be on his shit list.

"Just be careful. Having to constantly break you two out of jail will waste a lot of time. You are getting stronger by the day, and when the time is right I want us to be able to act without hesitation. If one of you is locked up, that's all this hard work right out the fucking window."

Jasper nodded, then asked weakly, "Is there anything else we need to do?"

Essum smiled, and the sight was so cold Jasper wished he had gloves. "No, we're done for tonight. I want to give Charlie some time to recuperate after the previous killing. He was quite explosively violent on that one."

"Yeah, you could say that."

Essum shot him a look. "Don't get judgmental. Think about what that episode made you do last night. All on your own, with no one making you do it." Essum stepped so close Jasper would have felt his breath if he'd actually been using air. "At least Charlie only does what he does because I compel him to. What's your excuse?"

Jasper met his gaze, but of course he looked away first, nodding. "Point taken."

"Good. Now go home. That blonde from the elevator is waiting for you outside your apartment door. And she's not wearing any underwear."

Voro felt he needed a shower as the fat man in front of him that reeked of BO fell to the ground in front of him, covering his head and weeping at the visions that Voro was stirring up.

This guy liked to kill little old ladies. He just strangled them with his bare hands and left their frail bodies to be found by home-care workers or family members. There was no reason that Voro could find, no sad sob story to provide background. But for some reason the man thought these killings increased his desirability to the opposite sex.

Voro watched him sob on the ground, wondering how anyone would find the guy attractive. But as the golden, warm cleansing feeling came over him, the fat man flopped over on to his back and looked up at Voro with grateful eyes.

"I'm so sorry," the man whispered.

Voro shook his head. "Apologizing to the wrong team, son. I don't do forgiveness."

The man was thoroughly confused but didn't ask any questions as Voro left the fat man's used bookstore, the bell ringing as the door closed behind him.

That was an awful lot of sin-eating for one night. He was *gorged*, actually. Not that he carried any of the burdens, but his head was tired of the degradation and he was sick of the begging. And tonight he likely caused the deaths of two people by relieving them of their darkest secrets. Three if fatty in the bookstore had a heart attack in the next few minutes.

This took him back, though. Trying to best the number of sins he'd consumed the night before. This was his damn purpose, not getting all simpering soft over a human woman.

Which reminded him, he had to go back to Claudia's to make sure Iola was okay.

Right. How long did it take a lesbian to pussy-whip a Sin Eater? Apparently two nights of sex should just about do it.

But that wasn't it, and he knew it. Iola held him enraptured, and at least he had the *frustro/decipio* aspect to blame that on.

His wandering had brought him full-circle to the block where Claudia and Iola lived. After checking his watch he realized it was one-thirty. Iola was off work at two, usually getting home around two-thirty. His head was pounding and he felt dirty all over, so it was maybe a good idea to call it a night well spent and head upstairs to a shower and sheets that smelled like chocolate and Claudia. Plus a common wall between him and someone that smelled overwhelmingly of jasmine and vanilla.

He used Claudia's keys to get into her apartment, taking the stairs slowly, his head pounding with each step. When he passed Iola's door, however, the headache eased. He wondered for a moment if she was home, but there was no light coming out from under her door. So he let himself into Claudia's abode and flicked the lights on. When they didn't work he frowned and flipped the switch a few more times, then let out a girl-like shriek and covered his chest with one hand as a bright light came out of the darkness right at him, like a train in a tunnel. Then the room lights came on.

Raphael collapsed into laughter, actually doubling up on the sofa, rolling off and hitting the floor in a ball.

"Fucking hilarious," Voro growled, kicking the door shut. "What do you want now?"

"Hey, nothing. Honestly." He paused to collect himself. Angels also thought that surprising people was absolutely hilarious. And the glow-bug routine was pretty standard. "I just wanted to check on how you were doing. And I can see you've been back to work. You reek."

"And you smell like you've been rising in the oven for about the last four hours."

"Don't be jealous, just 'cause you're carrying around the stank of a thousand ages." Raphael got comfortable again on Claudia's sofa. "You feel better?"

"More like myself. But I really need to shower."

"Please do. I brought you something, too."

"What?"

"It's on the bed."

Voro stalked down the hall, his funny bone definitely not tickled in the least, and turned the lights on in the bedroom. There were shopping bags all over the thing, and a few weeks of clothes were inside upon further inspection.

"Holy shit," Voro breathed, then turned back to the door. Of course, Raphael was there, hoping to make him shit himself apparently. But Voro was expecting him this time. "That's sweet, Raphael. You didn't have to do that." He was being over-appreciative.

Raphael made a face. "Whatever. You've been wearing that thing for two days straight. And it ain't the sins alone making you smell bad. I'm not even going to ask about underwear."

"I happen to not be wearing any."

"Like I said, I don't care. Just wanted to help you out. But what are you doing here? Don't tell me you and this broad are getting married."

"You must be retarded."

"Don't get cranky."

"She's got someone after her, she's in hiding. I've got nowhere to stay and she said I could crash here. Plus, she's worried about her neighbor across the hall. She lives alone."

Raphael gave a knowing look. "That's your *frustro*, isn't it?"

"And if it was?" Voro turned his back to Raphael as he shrugged his jacket off and began unbuttoning his shirt.

"You can't be with her, man. You know that, right?"

"So Essum told me. I know that."

Raphael was quiet, and Voro had half a hope the guy had left. But then he spoke again, so no luck there. "I know we make them irresistible, but ... *really*?"

Voro paused in the process of undoing his pants, his head sagging down on to his chest. "You have no idea."

"Wow. That's really ... cruel of us."

Voro shook himself as the angel started laughing again, dropping his pants.

"Hey – what the hell?"

"I told you I wasn't wearing underwear."

Raphael pretty much ran to get out of his way as Voro walked naked into the bathroom.

"Oh God," Raphael was muttering, covering his eyes and immediately stumbling over a foot stool. "I have to gouge my eyes out now."

"Now who's jealous?" Voro waited until Raphael opened his eyes to check if he was in the bathroom yet before cupping himself and waving the handful in the angel's direction.

"Christ, Voro." He turned his back, shuddering.

"Watch your mouth, Night Light."

Chapter Twenty-Seven

Essum had first called on Daphne one evening after dinner but well before dark. He'd asked her to go for a walk with him around the grounds of her family's manor, and she'd agreed, likely because he'd completely caught her off guard. She had been shy, meeting his gaze under lowered eye lids, and asking him the polite questions that people always ask when they first meet. What did his father do? How long had he been in Lincolnshire? What did he do with his time?

Of course Essum already had back-up stories for all her courteous inquires, having used them many times over already when meeting new people. The lies came easily, but they left a bitter taste in his mouth as he said them. He hadn't wanted to lie to her at all. He had wanted to tell the truth, boast that he was a divine being, even if it was from a place most humans worked their lives to avoid.

The more time he basked under her gaze, the more he needed her to believe he was human. He needed Daphne to crave his company.

The walk was over far too quickly, but of course she was an unmarried female and he was The Moor. As it was the groundskeepers froze in the middle of their tasks to gawk, only returning to work when Daphne met their stares pointedly.

She stopped in front of her back steps, and he paused alongside her, thanking her for her time. He touched her hand, meaning to just kiss the back of it.

As his hand made contact, again there was a jolt, but this time he held her hand anyway, and when he pressed his lips to the milky pale skin on her hand, the same jolt hit his mouth and he straightened suddenly, looking up into her exquisite forest-green eyes.

She was surprised too, her rose bud lips were parted as she gasped, and her eyes widened so he could see the white all around them.

"What ... what are you?" she breathed, her chest heaving.

He just shook his head, not knowing what to make of his physical reaction to her. He dropped her hand, hating to let it go but at the same time, he just had to. It was making him ache.

"Will you come and see me again?" She asked, composing herself and adjusting the back of her upswept hair with one hand.

"If you wish."

She nodded, then added, "I would like that."

"It would be my pleasure."

Then, as they'd stood staring at each other, memorizing the details of each other's faces, the door had been flung open and a large man with ruddy skin burst out of the house, yelling at him foully to get off the property.

Daphne had pleaded with him to stop, telling him this anger was unnecessary, that Essum was on the grounds as her guest. It made no difference; the brute pushed at his chest and called him ugly words, telling him he wasn't welcome.

Daphne had grabbed the man's arm – it was her brother, he was able to pull that from the brute's brain – but then he yanked free of her hands, toppling her over so she landed awkwardly on the stone steps. If she had hit her head -

Essum had growled in anger, he'd faced the brute and unleashed all the nasty reasons you don't fuck with a Sin Eater into the man's brain at the same time. Daphne's brother was struck all at once with every fear he'd ever felt and left unresolved, every moment he'd felt small and alone, every moment he'd known he was in trouble all came on him full force, and he fell to his knees, cradling his head on the ground as he wept. It was swift and sudden, an uppercut to the psyche that would take any giant to his knees.

Daphne was staring at her brother, then looked up at Essum in horror. "What have you done?" Her voice was rasping she was so shocked, and she trembled in fear. And anger. He could smell peppers. It was mostly anger.

"I am sorry - " he stammered, his heart breaking at the way she was glaring at him.

"Get out of here," she whispered, then repeated with much more force. "Get out of here!"

He had turned and left immediately, realizing his hands shook and his stomach was turning. At first he thought his human body was having a reaction to something he'd eaten, but he knew that wasn't it. It was because he'd scared her, and she'd turned him out of her life.

And because he'd touched her. The inside of his palm was blistering slightly as he looked at it, white bubbles rising on the thick skin. He'd frowned, then touched his lips. The same thing, painful bumps mostly on his bottom lip.

Of course they healed as he continued to stare at his hand in shock, his lips losing their numbness within minutes. And his stomach felt better as soon as the marks faded.

She'd asked him what he was, and now he had to wonder what she was.

Of course, now he knew she'd been his *frustro*, and the reaction he had to that brief contact should have sent him running. But once the mind is piqued with extreme curiosity, you just had to know everything.

There were no manuals or handbooks for Sin Eaters. Both sides could deal out all kinds of nasty shit that could either help a guy out or send him right back to his maker. And more often than not, you will not see it coming for you.

That's why Essum had such a hard-on to get Voro's *decipio* fully operational and uncharacteristically strong. He couldn't believe the guy could consume and hold on to sins, but then again he was a heavenly vessel. Any sin he carried would eventually be forgiven by the guys upstairs. It was a get-out-jail-free card, this whole *decipio* business.

Essum was perched in the corner of an operating room with his musings, having pushed the room noise out of his mind. But now he was paying attention again as Veneratio Aubericus was wrapping up a straight hour operating on the femoral artery of a guy that had fallen through a plate glass window. He was just finishing up the stitches, and the entire process was giving Essum a headache.

The guy wasn't human, Essum was sure of it, and the operating room had just proved it. At his very touch the bleeding man had calmed, almost as though the pain was gone. And

Essum had noticed a decrease in the patient's anxiety level at that time, too. Anxiety smelled like cordite, and it was eased bit by bit the longer the doctor's hands were on the man's body.

He was able to read this doctor's thoughts, and it was a mess of medical school crap that he echoed to the staff attending him. There was nothing else going on there, but he wasn't likely to be thinking, *"Well, you see, I am a leprechaun ..."* And he didn't appear to know Essum was there, since Essum wasn't making himself visible at the time.

The logical assumption would be the guy was just a simple healer. There were some humans that had a healing touch, and it had nothing to do with either side, they were what they were. But had the doctor seen Essum vanish? Essum was careful about human eyes being on him when he did that. Perhaps the guy could sense him; plenty of humans got a whiff of malevolence when he was around.

Veneratio Aubericus made Essum very nervous. And it was a twitch that wouldn't leave him until he knew with certainty what side the bastard was on.

Voro appreciated that Raphael had gotten him clothing, he really did. But their styles were definitely not the same.

Angels loved to be comfortable above all else. So the bags were full of jeans and T-shirts. Voro's tastes ran towards ... Well, expensive suits and dress shoes that cost what some people's cars were worth. Was that evil? Who knew, it was what he'd come to prefer for himself.

He still had to admit the stuff was easy to walk around in, and less restrictive of movement. The jeans felt almost natural, and the royal blue T-shirt was made with distressed fabric that was like a soft touch. Voro couldn't remember a time when he'd been this comfy, other than naked in bed, of course. When he left the bedroom fully dressed, Raphael was watching the local news on TV.

"That color looks good on you," Raphael noted, then turned his baby blues back to the tube. "Tell me about this guy," he added, pointing with a remote control.

Voro had already noticed the mug shot on the screen. It was the guy that he'd followed off the subway the night he first saw Iola, the guy that had broken into Claudia's apartment. The guy that had killed Portia. Charles Goodwin, and he was back at large.

Of course, Voro knew this already, and he was glad the guy's face was getting splashed around, it would make it harder for him to move around the city. Voro also knew that only about five percent of the population would actually phone the police if they saw a person that was wanted for a crime, violent or not. People, as a whole, were really only interested in anything outside of their daily lives to a certain extent.

And since the guy was completely nuts, he would be totally willing to just walk around anyway, at large or not.

Voro sat on the sofa, rubbing his chin as the anchorwoman droned on about not approaching the man and calling the police immediately.

"So ... this guy is in it somehow with Essum," he said out loud, and Raphael looked surprised.

"How do you know that?"

"He killed Portia, and that is just far too random for me to ignore. He had to have known I knew Portia, and he killed her as a declaration of war against me. Because everyone else this guy killed is from the bottom of the dregs of the city. All of a sudden he bags a millionaire in her own home?"

Raphael was nodding, watching the reporter move from news to the lighter side of the days' events. Apparently the humane society opened a new kennel.

"Should we find out if it was Essum? I mean, we get to the house and we'll know within minutes." Raphael was working the remote around in his hand like a baton as puppies rolled on the grass in Technicolor in front of him.

Voro was nodding and feeling totally exhausted at the same time. "We could do that. I would like to know for sure. We'll have to find a car - "

"No problem." Raphael switched off the TV and rose to his full six-feet-six-inches, stretching his arms above his head so his fingers hit the roof. He gave a loud groan then dropped the remote where he'd been sitting. "I've got one outside."

"Dare I ask what kind of car?" Again, angels were more about comfort and necessity than style.

"Oh, I'm sorry. It's a Focus, all right? We don't have the funds that the unscrupulous can manage to acquire for themselves." He shrugged. "The Sync system's pretty nice."

"Let's just go before I change my mind."

"Voro, you should wear jeans more often," Raphael suggested as he responsibly turned off the lights in the room on the way out of Claudia's apartment. "They make your ass look pretty good."

"Fucking angels."

"I'm just being honest."

"Keep it to yourself." Heaven help him from this idiot. No, really; heaven help him.

Please?

Charlie knew he should do as Master told him, but he was feeling so good and so much better, even better than after the first time Jasper had touched him ... He just *had* to go back to where this feeling good had started. Plus, he really liked that woman's house. It was so nice, and all her stuff had been so clean and tidy ...

He took a subway as close to her suburb as he could. He still had to walk about five blocks, but he didn't mind. The streets were quiet and empty; it gave him time to think.

Obviously he would soon be all better. That had to be the reward that was waiting for him. And the past day had been the first time he felt like a normal person. The new Master was here to help him, Charlie had to believe that. And that's why the old Master had placed them together.

He came up on the house suddenly, realizing he'd been walking longer than he originally thought. The lights on the outside of the house were on, and there was yellow police tape across the door. He looked around, but only green lawns and darkened houses presented themselves. So he walked up the curving driveway, plucked the tape from the door frame, and pushed the door open. It swung inward in front of him, and he was totally shocked that it wasn't locked. There was no sound inside, so he stepped on to the tiles in the foyer and re-attached the police tape behind him before closing the door.

Charlie wasn't dumb enough to turn on any lights, so he used the exterior light spilling in through the windows to make his way to the staircase.

He didn't look in the living room. He could smell the blood still; he didn't want to see what else was left. That was the past; he was going to get better now.

Charlie went up the carpeted stairs to a walkway that crossed over the foyer and living room with doors along one side. He picked one at random, found it to be a bathroom. The next one was a bedroom.

He entered that room, taking a deep breath. He could smell a faint perfume here, and with the amount of extra clutter he knew this must have been her room, not a guest room. There was an armchair by a window, so he crossed to that and sat down. The perfume got stronger as the air was pushed out of the chair's padding, and he closed his eyes. It was a nice smell.

Her eyes. Her blood. Her hands clawing at his arms while the screams were strangled out of a throat he was collapsing with his bare hands.

He shook his head at the fast tide of images that cascaded through his brain. He kept his eyes closed but he covered the scratches. This was the first time he'd been in the home of someone he'd killed, although it would have been the second time if that cop bitch hadn't brought home that man; the one with those weird eyes and strange way about him.

Charlie frowned and opened his eyes. Come to think of it, that man kinda had a lot in common with the old Master, didn't he? He made Charlie's skin prickle to the point of goose bumps, his voice held Charlie's attention like a string in front of a cat.

Charlie shook his head. No, there could only be one God, and Charlie's old Master was it. He just needed help getting people to realize it.

Charlie pulled his feet up on to the chair, curling up in a ball with his chin resting on his knees. When that day of reckoning came, Charlie was going to be saved completely, and he bet the

Master would ask him to be someone important ... maybe even an apostle of some kind. He couldn't wait.

Iola checked the text message she'd received a moment ago from Vinnie. *B there in 10.*

That had been eleven minutes ago. Not that she was incredibly neurotic, it was just that the last train that ran every half hour was due in ten minutes. After that the trains only ran every hour, which meant a long wait for the next one if Vinnie was caught late at work.

Which is where he wasn't supposed to be, but they'd needed him.

She admitted the fact that he was a doctor was incredibly sexy, but man. Did he *ever* go anywhere other than the hospital? The second she thought it she felt like a bitch.

There was a small window next to the station's back door. She used it to check up and down the alley every minute or so. Still no Vinnie.

There were still people milling about, even this late at night. She didn't want anyone to notice her, so her little alley checks were kept discreet. All she needed was to step out the door and get hit over the head for her purse by someone that noticed she was waiting for a ride. It did happen from time to time.

A couple of whores walked by, followed by a man in a long dark jacket. It seemed hot for a windbreaker, never mind a knee-length wool coat, and Iola frowned. Maybe he was from somewhere very tropical and found even their warmest evenings just a touch too chilly. He did have a shaved head, and dark, almost golden-brown skin ...

He turned to look right at her, and she backed away from the window, putting her back to the solid metal door, out of sight from the window.

The guy from the hospital. The one that she thought she was hearing in her head.

How'd he find me?

It wasn't self-involved to wonder that. It was far too random to be seeing him again, down here, at her place of work.

Iola tried to keep herself from panicking, leaning her head back on the door and concentrating on her breathing. He would pass, he'd just keep walking, he didn't even really notice her in the window …

Iola …

She wanted to make a childish noise of frustration, beat her hand on the door. Shit.

Iola … come on out here and see me.

Yeah right. Just ignore the safety of a locked door between her and a total stranger.

Please, I want to see you.

A stranger that could beam his voice right into her head. To hell with not panicking. She was ready to run upstairs and hide under her desk. But her legs wouldn't move, and she couldn't open her eyes, either.

You're not going to do anything except open this door.

Fuck. That.

Come on now, that kind of language isn't very becoming.

And read her mind. This stranger could hear what she was thinking.

That's why there's no point fighting with me. Open the door.

Her heart was racing, she bet she could see her ribcage shaking if she were to look down at that moment. But all she was able to manage was opening her eyes.

She had her hand on the handle suddenly. It moved without her involvement. It was like watching someone else having complete use of her arm, except she felt the metal in her hand … and the wind rushing in as the door pulled open.

Shit.

The man was right in front of her, not letting her speak, not letting her blink. He was just eyeing her up with innocent curiosity, like she was a lab experiment. His head was tilted to one side, and those arresting eyes were locked on her, the only thing she could see.

So beautiful … he was thinking, but his face didn't lose its impersonal expression. *You almost remind me of someone.*

She blinked. That's all she could do on her own volition.

You smell of jasmine, did you know that? Jasmine and something sweeter ... vanilla. It makes you quite irresistible.

She knew he took her hand off the handle only because the door banged shut a moment later. It startled her, but she couldn't even wince or jump. She was frozen to the spot she stood on.

He glided closer, and Iola wanted to run. She would have done anything to have the use of her legs back. This man was all wrong, everything about this was bad. He shouldn't be here, he didn't belong here.

"Shhh ..." he said using his mouth, standing immediately before her. He smelled ... he smelled wonderful. But even that felt wrong. She shouldn't like how he smelled. She should be much farther away from him than this, to be honest. "I wonder if I could touch you."

No, but of course her mouth wouldn't work to say it. *Don't touch me. Please, oh God, don't touch me don't touch me don't touch me ...*

His hand was on her cheek. Again the urge to avoid it was so strong her gag reflex had her wanting to cough, but she couldn't. Her skin was burning all over her body, and not in a good way, like she needed to get out of the fire she was standing too close to.

"You can feel that, can you? I bet you can't feel it from him, though."

She didn't even care who he was talking about. She felt one tear slide down her cheek, and the reaction with her skin at that moment made it feel like battery acid. He caught the drop with his thumb, rubbing it off, spreading the burning sensation across her face.

"I wonder ..." he continued, putting both hands to the sides of her head.

Please ... just let me go.

His lips came to hers, and her entire being was screaming *Get away! Get away from me!*

He backed off, a smile on his face for the first time. "Oh, Iola. You taste like ... heaven." For some reason he found that hilarious, and he collapsed into laughter. As he did, the spell was lifted.

She caught herself from collapsing to the ground, and then she took a moment to make sure it wasn't a trick. When she was sure she grabbed the door handle and yanked it open, rushing right into Vinnie.

"Iola ... Iola, what's wrong?" His voice was like cold water, and arms wrapped her up as she cleaved close to him, realizing right then she was shaking and sobbing.

"Get me out of here, please - "

Vinnie pushed her behind him and caught the door before it eased all the way closed, and Iola tried to hold him back.

"Don't, Vinnie. Please don't go in there."

He turned back to her, confusion in his furrowed brows. "There's nothing there. What did you see?"

"There was a man ... I'd seen him at the hospital earlier today. And he ... I don't know, he just ..." How the hell was she going to explain it? He was likely to put her in a home for the deranged.

"Did he scare you? What did he say?"

"He just ... he wouldn't let me go."

Vinnie uttered a surprising cuss word, and took out his phone. "I'm calling the police."

She covered his hands. "No, no. You know what? Maybe I overreacted."

He looked at her incredulously. "You should see yourself right now, Iola. You are completely terrified."

She wrapped her arms around herself. "Just take me home, get me out of here. Okay?"

"Are you sure? Did he ... did he touch you or anything?"

She shook her head. "No. No. I just couldn't ... get out."

"I wish you'd let me call the cops."

"No. Like I said, just ... take me home."

He didn't want to, but he nodded and put the phone away. He led her to his car with his arm across her shoulders.

Iola was back at her building before the shaking stopped.

Chapter Twenty-Eight

Voro would have never guessed that Raphael was a KISS fan, but that was the CD he was playing in this hatchback Ford Focus as they pulled up the drive to Portia's house. A neighbor came to a window to check and see what was happening, but Voro shot the urgent need to go to the bathroom in the man's head and he quickly veered right past his kitchen window and out of sight.

Raphael had felt him do it, and he shook his head. "That is so cool."

"You could do it, too."

"Nah. Free will, man."

"I didn't mess with his free will. His bladder was full. He just didn't realize it until I pointed it out."

Raphael shook his head again as they headed for the steps. "Tell yourself whatever you like, Sin Eater."

Voro froze with one foot on the bottom step, and Raphael stopped at the door before touching the police tape. "What?"

"You can't smell that?"

"Is it Essum?"

Voro closed his eyes to concentrate. "Essum was definitely here, not anymore though. But ... oh dammit. You really can't smell that?"

It was horrid. Rotten meat and sulfur and *landfill.* It was making his stomach churn.

"I got nothing. You want to go in?"

No. Voro nodded and Raphael pushed on the door. It swung open.

"Are you breaking and entering?" Voro asked dryly as Raphael ducked under the police tape, which was hard considering his height.

"It was unlocked."

Voro frowned. That shouldn't be ... but whatever. He followed the angel then shut the door behind them. The living room was calling to him, the scent of death and violence appealing to his darkness. He fought against it, looking around this cavernous foyer he'd been in only a handful of times.

"So ... you say Essum's been here?"

Voro nodded again. "Definitely. I can sense him."

"So ... it's not smell with you guys? It's just a feeling?"

"Yep."

"Do you smell anything?"

"You don't want to know what it smells like to me in here."

"I'll buy that. But what do those smells mean?"

Voro paced past the living room and made his way back to the kitchen, the dining room. Raphael followed closely.

"I can smell hatred ... rage ... fear ... shame ... evil."

"So, that's all from someone that was here?"

They returned back to the foyer quickly. "Yeah, all that was here, and it was all in one person. It has to be that guy ... Charles Goodwin."

Now it was Raphael's turn to freeze, his head swiveling to the stairs. "Someone's here," he said quietly, calmly. "Upstairs."

Voro sent out his mental feelers, and he found the brain of a living human upstairs. In Portia's room.

Voro felt a growl build up in his throat as he flew up the stairs two at a time.

"Voro," he heard Raphael warn him, but he was too far gone to be influenced.

He basically threw the bedroom door open, making the form in the chair nearly jump right out of his skin. Voro could tell that he'd been sleeping; his brain waves were slow and logy.

Voro grabbed him by his thin arms and shook him so hard the guy's teeth clattered. "You fucking little worm."

Raphael's voice came from the doorway. "Voro. Don't."

Voro held Charles Goodwin's stare as he got ready to unload a lot of mind fuck on the guy at once when Raphael said very softly but with great authority, "Voro. Scan him."

Voro held back, and then did a little flip-though the guy's life. The memories of wicked, disgusting acts were there, polluted with the guy's own psychosis so they didn't really make sense, but they were orderly, neat, and - more surprisingly – clean. Gone. As in ...

"You've been forgiven," Voro breathed, letting Charles go and stepping back.

"A Sin Eater's already gotten to him?"

Voro shook his head. "No, I'd still be able to feel it elsewhere if that had happened. It would be like a trail of scent left in someone's wake. I'd know where it was, even. But he's ... he's completely forgiven."

The man was staring at Voro intently, and with Voro's words he collapsed to the peach carpet in huge, body-shaking sobs. "Thank you," he said pathetically as he touched Voro's shoe, circling his ankle with his hand. "Thank you, God."

Voro looked to Raphael, who was gazing down at Charles with divine pity, making his handsome face completely angelic.

"Can ... can you do something like that?"

Raphael looked back to Voro, surprised. "No, not me. It would have to be someone ... different than me. Someone like ... maybe a *decipio*?"

Voro shook his head. "But the *decipio*'s out to kill me. This guy ... he's nothing."

"He's not nothing. He's part of this whole process, too."

"How?"

Raphael shrugged. "How the hell should I know?"

Once Iola had flown out the door into the arms of her beloved doctor, Essum had released his physical form. Once he was ether again he let himself gather his breath and try to settle himself.

He'd felt her. He'd touched her. And she had felt it.

He wasn't even in his true physical form yet. And she was so warm, even as terrified as she'd been. He'd felt her lips ...

He hadn't kissed anyone since he'd tried to kiss Daphne, and that had nearly killed him since a *frustro* was akin to poison when it came to their matched Sin Eater. It only went one way, though. That was the grossly unfair part.

Essum let his unsolid form wander, out through the roof of the building where he took form again to study the city from six floors up. So many people and yet no one seemed to know anyone. It never used to be like that. Then again, he hadn't been in the human world for ... Two hundred years?

Yeah, two hundred years.

He closed his eyes and tried to conjure up that woman, the love of his existence so far. It wasn't difficult, she was always right there, waiting to return with the slightest reference.

After her brother had man-handled him and she had hissed at him to be gone for good, that very evening as she was going to sleep, she had been sitting at a dressing table in her room, looking down at a small plate where a small cake sat.

A burial cake. Made for funerals, given to everyone that attended with the understanding they ate it to keep the memory of the deceased with them. Ancient and archaic, but Daphne's mother had always thought they were romantic.

Daphne hadn't eaten hers. She'd kept it.

"If you don't eat it, he can't pass over," Essum had said from her doorway.

She jumped to her feet, pulling her dressing gown tighter around her neck. She was instantly furious, and as she opened her mouth to shout at him or raise the alarm, he held out a hand beseechingly.

"Please," he said softly, not wanting to frighten her. "I have to explain."

She didn't shout. Instead she asked, "You dare to come here?"

"I thought your brother had hurt you. I am sorry. But I don't see blood relation as a reason to excuse violence. He honors you not."

Her eyes dropped to the burial cake in front of her. "Is that true?" She asked, gesturing to the small cake, more of a sugary canapé than anything else. She was referring to what he had first said that had startled her.

No, he thought. "It's what I've been told," he said instead. "It's to keep a part of them with you, so they don't have to hover here and make sure you are well."

She looked at him sharply. "Am I well? Or am I in danger?" It was said in the manner of a multiple choice question.

"You are well, I swear it. I mean you no ill."

She sat back down, her eyes back on the cake. "It seems so primitive. Evil. It's like ..."

"Cannibalism?" Essum offered, and she nodded immediately, shuddering. "It is to honor them, that is all. Are you scared that if you eat it you will have nothing left of him?"

She nodded then instantly broke into sobs. Essum was uncomfortable with crying, but coming from her the smell of her sorrow was like strong rain on foliage. It hurt him.

"He is with you whether you eat that or not. So you may as well eat it before the bugs come looking for it. Once they're here you'll never be rid of them."

She looked at him in wonder, then laughed, even as tears were still falling down her alabaster cheeks. He ached to touch her again, but when he thought of how his skin had handled their last contact he held back.

He watched Daphne pick up the cake with delicate fingers and pop it into her mouth all at once, chewing and swallowing like a child eating their vegetables. She had stopped crying but had yet to wipe her tears. Her eyes pointed upwards like she was thinking of other things just to get through this chore.

Essum produced a handkerchief from his pocket and knelt before her to dry her eyes. She let him do this as she swallowed the cake, and he cherished the touch, even with the piece of silk between them. No burning, no jolt of heat, just *warmth*.

As she finished, she looked down at him, on his knee before her, leaning more into the palm of his hand. "I am sorry for how my brother spoke to you and treated you. And I am sorry for what I said as well."

"You need never apologize to me," he said softly. "You may always say and do what you wish with me."

Her hands came to his shoulders, and with his clothes keeping her skin from his all he could feel was the heat from her touch.

"You have never told me your name," she said very softly, watching his face closely.

"Essum," his voice was hoarse, since he'd never told a human his real name. Or maybe it was from something else.

"Essum. What is that?"

"Latin. *Edo Edi Essum*. It means ... devour."

Her brow had furrowed, and the break in her perfectly smooth skin made her even more lovely. "That's an odd name."

"It is," he agreed, since he had nothing to add to that.

"Devour," she repeated to herself, her eyes half-open as they traced across his lips, his jaw, down his neck.

"I should go," he said without much conviction, without movement to suggest he really meant it.

"Wait," she said strongly, tightening her hands on the lapel of his greatcoat.

"For what?" Her eyes returned to his lips and she eased forward slightly, lips parted. "What am I waiting for, Daphne?" He knew his voice had the power to seduce, and damn him if he wasn't using it on her like any other woman he'd ever used it on.

The skin on her lips were soft as wind on water as she brushed them against his, and though he could have moaned at the limited time she gave him to feel them, the second she made contact more forcefully he had to back away and get as far from her as he could.

"Daphne," he said weakly, getting to his feet and making for her door.

"Essum, what is it?" His name was suddenly obscene coming from her mouth.

"I should not be here," he covered his panic. "It isn't proper. I have to go."

He hadn't looked back as he left, willing everyone he passed in the household that they weren't really seeing him. But he'd felt her eyes on his back the whole way down the hallway.

If he'd had his physical form now, he would have wept. Because though he'd meant to stay as far as he could from her, that night had only sealed his fate.

Vinnie handed her a generous glass of wine from her fridge, and she smiled in appreciation. When she did, she realized he was still studying her with grave concern. She set the wine on the coffee table.

"I'm fine, it's ... well, it wasn't nothing. But I don't want to waste the police's time with some guy that just ... scared me. Really ... I'm fine." The more she said it the more true it became.

He sat next to her on the sofa, hand on her knee in a completely concerned manner. "You should have seen your face, Iola."

She put the wine down after taking a healthy swallow, turning to him, putting her hands on his. "I'm sorry. I overreacted. Please, don't worry. Please, let it go."

He mulled that over somewhat reluctantly. "Okay. But - "

"No 'buts.' I finally have you all to myself and your phone is off and I don't want to talk about it anymore."

He burst out laughing unexpectedly, and it made her smile.

"I'm serious," she insisted through a laugh of her own.

"Okay, this is me dropping it."

"No, I'm serious about having you all to myself." She kissed him before he was ready for it, and his surprise gave her enough time to lean in to him, pushing him back into her couch slightly.

After a surprised pause, his hands came to her upper arms, then worked across her back, pushing back against her to sit her up. He pulled away for a moment. "Iola, you don't have to do this."

She put a hand along his neck, slowly working it up to the back of his head, playing with his hair. "I don't have to ... but I really want to. If you do, that is."

Something changed in his face as he closed his eyes, her fingers pulling at the hair on the back of his head then winding deeper. Without opening his eyes to find his way he pulled her to him forcefully, his mouth finding hers easily, his hand pressing her back towards him, one of them going to her hip to turn her more sideways so he could ease her on to her back on the sofa.

She quickly scooted down to accommodate him, biting his lips and sucking on his mouth enthusiastically, so glad his phone was off. She'd made him turn it off in front of her.

Vinnie's hand left her hip to search for bare skin, finding some just above the waist of her jeans, his thumb running back and forth in a frustratingly concentrated area. It tickled her somewhere other than where he was touching. When his hand then ventured to the front of her jeans, she jacked her hips downward to give him room.

He used both hands to get the fly undone, and then suddenly he was off her, pulling his shirt off with one quick motion. A few buttons might have been ripped open, she wasn't sure.

Iola bit her lip to contain herself. His skin was perfectly smooth, tight across his slight musculature. Under her hands it was soft and smooth, but then he got up off the couch and she was worried he'd changed his mind. Or decided he respected her too much for this.

Vinnie moved to the opposite wall, pulling down the roller blinds she had on the two picture windows. As he walked back to her, she pulled off her T-shirt, and he stopped in the middle of the floor, hand on chest. "Iola, you look ... you're just too much."

She held out an arm and he rushed back at her, pressing her upper body into his warm chest, running his hands over her. Iola straddled his lap, leaving herself open to his strong hands caressing her back, her hips, her arms, her stomach ...

And lower. Iola reared her head back and gasped as he stroked at her through her panties. She'd thought he'd take so much longer to get to the point than this but she was ready for it completely.

When he moaned low against her skin, Iola pulled back and forced him to look up at her. She wanted to see his face, and the sight of it was so beautiful she shuddered. Although, that might have been due to his hand, which wasn't still in the least.

"Vinnie," she breathed, then had to stop before saying what she wanted to. All she saw was white light, and she closed her eyes as the orgasm hit her, making her give the oddest squeak before breaking through her every nerve that had the ability to feel pleasure: basically all of them.

"What were you going to say?" He asked after a moment, running his lips along her collarbone while she caught her breath.

She shook her head. "I can't remember."

He smiled up at her, his eyelids low in a very alluring manner. "I want you in a bed. Immediately."

She just nodded and said something incredibly stupid like, "I have one of those."

Chapter Twenty-Nine

Voro and Raphael left Charlie in Portia's house, neither of them having any hope that he'd actually be caught by the cops and held for longer than two hours. Truth was Charlie was just a sad sack that was going to be used until it killed him.

Pity: another feeling Voro was going to have to start getting rid of if he was going to kick Essum's ass.

"Let's get something to eat," Raphael said as he opened the driver's door of the Focus. "I really want McDonald's. I haven't had a Big Mac in ... oh man, too long."

Fast food was another weakness for angels. It was as close to sin as they ever got.

Voro just shrugged. "You're the driver."

"So let's go over this again. The *decipio* is absorbing the sins that Charlie acquires. I didn't even think it was possible."

"I don't get it, because it's likely making the *decipio* stronger. And for Essum's plan to work, Iola has to be able to kill him. Making him stronger is not going to help that. But if Essum can get in the *decipio*'s body, he'd be almost as powerful as I am. Could that be, like, Plan B?" Voro's head was spinning. How had Essum even thought of all this shit? But then again, he had nothing but time on the other side.

Raphael was nodding as though he was following the train of thought. "That could be it. But it'll still make it a lot harder to kill the *decipio*, and Iola has to be the one to do it."

"She won't," Voro added quietly. "She doesn't have it in her."

Raphael shrugged. "You never know. If she feels she's in danger or someone she cares about ... she might surprise you. You never know what a *frustro* is capable of."

Voro knew his belief that dear, fragile Iola could never harm anyone was coming from some crazy, medieval conviction that someone so lovely was weak and delicate, completely incapable of violence. He should know from the last, oh, six hundred years that he was most likely wrong, but his heart was telling him he wasn't.

What the hell … his *heart*?

Raphael pulled into the parking lot of a McDonald's, and as they pushed through the doors the young woman that was walking to the doors made a face of frustration.

They were about to close, Voro realized, but Raphael was smiling at the woman brightly, and she stopped in her sneakers to study him. Appreciatively.

"I know you're probably about to lock up, but I've been out of the country for a long time and I really *really* would appreciate a Big Mac and fries. We won't stay, we'll get it to go, but … it's been such a long time since I've had anything so good."

The woman's nostrils flared. Not in an angry way. She was sizing Raphael up like she was measuring her leg length against the width of his waist.

Voro rolled his eyes. That was a terrible waste of effort on her part, but she was shrugging and motioning them back to the counter.

Raphael smiled at him happily, smacking him across the stomach. "Big Mac!" He bellowed with excitement.

Yeah, angels were like great big children, really.

She gave the order to the kitchen and there was much moaning and complaining, but this woman had "manager" on her name tag so they still did as they were told.

Voro leaned over to Raphael. "You owe me, because the guy in the back was totally going to spit in your burger. I just convinced him not to."

Raphael jogged him on the shoulder with a fist. "You're a good guy, Voro."

The woman leaned across the counter to them, and Voro backed up to cross his arms across his chest. This was a no-go zone for him suddenly. The woman was ready to take them both to a private office in the back, he was lifting that from her mind directly, but he was just … too exhausted at the moment. And getting an angel a burger and fries wasn't a reason to get naked.

Raphael returned her coy lean, looking at her nametag. "Thank you so much for helping me out, Christine."

She was enthralled by him, and her face was a mask of rapture as she just basked in his gaze. Surely she had to know he wasn't all human ... but the effect their kind had was unavoidable. "No problem. It's my pleasure."

"How much do I owe?"

"This one's on me. Twyla's already cashing out the tills."

"I can't do that."

"Yeah, you can. I really don't mind."

Voro wanted to tell Raphael he'd go wait in the car. But this wasn't going anywhere anyway. It was just a question of how long before Twyla realized Raphael wasn't interested in working her out good and hard on a press-board desk, but he was actually falling in love with her.

"Christine, do you wear perfume?"

"No."

"Do you have any idea how good you smell?"

Voro had to admit she did smell nice, even over the odor of greasy food. Like lilacs, almost.

"I smell good?" Christine was tickled pink.

"Like lilacs. A field of lilac trees on a sunny spring day." Raphael closed his eyes and inhaled silently. "It's amazing."

She was over the fucking moon, and when Raphael took a lock of her hair, pulled it towards him and smelled it she actually stopped breathing.

Voro remembered doing that to Iola. He knew he couldn't touch her skin, but her hair had not burned him. Not technically. It was the closeness of her, the smell of her deep in his head that had him ready to collapse at that point.

"Ummm ... I am off work in about half an hour, if you, you know, want to hang out later." McCandy Pants was saying, totally lost in the blue eyes of the angel.

Voro started to pace, and a few people in the kitchen started bellowing "Order!" because the burger and fries had been sitting a minute, and the counter on the computer by the staging area was counting how long it was taking them to fill each request.

Christine shook herself and bagged Raphael's heart attack order. Raphael was gazing at her in wonder. Voro had to lean over and mumble, "Human women do not fall in love with you, remember?"

Raphael just shook his head. "This one could be different."

Christine came back stuffing napkins in the bag marked with golden arches, and she smiled brightly at Raphael, letting her eyes crawling all over him as he smiled down at her.

"Thank you so much, Christine. Hey, can I ask you something?" Raphael asked, capturing her hand.

"Sure. The answer is yes, but they come off easily."

Raphael frowned. "What?"

She smiled a secretive light smile, leaning towards him, pretending to be shy. "I thought you were going to ask me if I was wearing underwear."

Voro started for the door to hide his laughter, and after a moment Raphael followed, blushing bright pink and not meeting Voro's gaze.

"Is she going to marry you?" Voro asked, following Raphael to the Focus.

"Shut up."

"Did she like the ring? Did she let you have it back?"

He did feel bad about how incredibly embarrassed Raphael was by a sexed-up fry pusher. But man, this was going to be a source of entertainment for a few more months at least.

Providing he had that long, he reminded himself.

Bob Dylan was playing softly in the corner, there were a few pillar candles lit on the dresser and night stand. But Iola was not aware of any of it, she was riding the crest of pleasure that was radiating between her legs, up her back and through her neck, exploding at the back of her skull as she gave a quiet groan. Vinnie didn't stop the tongue action there, though, he made sure she was all the way through it before kissing a trail up her stomach, keeping his body pressed between her legs. His touch was still electric on her skin even though she was limp by this point. His hands ran all along her sides as though he was memorizing her lines and edges.

Vinnie sucked on one nipple through the lace of her bra, and she couldn't believe she was still partially dressed, not to mention the fact that he still hadn't taken off his jeans.

"Oh my God," she whispered just as he was kissing her lips again, his own swollen from all the hard work they'd just done. "That was ... amazing."

Vinnie smiled as he kissed her again. "You are amazing."

She had to laugh. "I don't know if I'm as amazing."

Iola was totally shocked by her doctor, stunned beyond belief. For all his good-boy, going for sainthood appearance, he turned out to be a complete rock-star bad-ass when it came to sex. He hadn't wasted any time once they were in her room, assuring her he wanted to please her as much as he was able. And then he'd gone down on her, and *that* had been twenty-four minutes ago.

Now, without so much as a breather, Vinnie's deft and dedicated hands undid her bra clasp smoothly, and he pulled the straps down off her arms. When his mouth parted to breathe harder and his eyes got wider she felt incredibly beautiful. His hands touched her skin so carefully she arched against him, hoping he would be just the slightest bit rougher. She'd never been well endowed in the chest department, but he seemed to really like what he was seeing. Really like it.

"If you don't want me to keep going, just say so," he mumbled, closing his lips around one nipple, his tongue doing very bad good things. Like that was going to happen.

"I would let you know," she whispered, losing her hands in his hair to keep him there.

Vinnie eventually got up off the mattress, sweeping his jeans down off his legs and turning to sit on the edge of the bed as he reached for the condom package she'd already set out on the night stand. He eased his boxers down, and as Iola caught an eyeful of that she had to squeeze her eyelids shut and take a steadying inhale.

Oh Jesus ... was her only thought. That won't fit him. Should have got the Magnum condoms. But what woman would buy those? Someone looking to embarrass and humiliate a guy, that's who. But Vinnie ... *Jesus Christ. Will* I *fit him?* Iola was suddenly as nervous as she was before her first time.

She felt the mattress shift as he lay next to her, pulling the sheets up to cover them. "Hey ... are you all right?"

"I'm fine ..." she opened her eyes, smiling at him.

"What's wrong?"

"Nothing." That was a bit too eager. "No, nothing. Believe me. I'm just … weak in the knees right now."

His hand slid across her stomach, making circles around her bellybutton. "Well, that's a good thing." His lips on her collarbone were utterly divine, too.

"I agree."

"We'll go slow," he whispered, biting playfully at her neck.

Slow was good. "Okay," she answered, and his hand left her stomach to touch her in a spot that was already swollen from wanting more contact with him. He circled across her sweet spot, which was incredibly tender by this point, then widened his palm between her legs to ease them open as he rolled on top of her.

Vinnie kissed her with painstaking gentleness, tasting her with his tongue while his hand worked one nipple. She forgot her nerves with the way his kisses was making other parts of her body tingle, all the other places that tongue had already been. Of their own volition her legs came up to his hips, positioning herself for utter Veneratio Invasion. This was likely going to hurt.

She should have known better. While Vinnie had her on a simmer, he eased in so slowly she wasn't sure he was moving. That was until she became aware that she was stretched completely to oblige him. She was fluid and slick around him, he was hot and hard by contrast, and as her body accommodated his size she was stunned at how completely full it all felt. And how very right it felt.

Once he'd pushed all the way in, his withdrawal was so slight she couldn't be sure she was really feeling it. Then he pushed back in again.

Iola actually hissed at how good it felt. Every part of him had contact with every part of her, *every part*. With a slight upward shift of her hips on his next small thrust, he made proper contact where she needed it and she was beyond anything even remotely resembling pain. She made a small noise, but she was fighting anything that might distract herself from the feeling.

His movements were so small and careful, and executed so slowly she felt like screaming in frustration, but after a few more presses she was ready for climax and it was just a matter of which movement was going to make it happen. She was aware that there was a bloom of sweat on her skin, and his as well, so she let her fingers bite into his shoulders so that nothing changed; not her position, not his. It was just too perfect.

Vinnie made lovely sounds against her throat, moaning as though he was unable to control himself at this slow but steady pace. But he did, even though with every move those noises became more and more plaintive, yet softer at the same time.

That's when the orgasm came with stunning sharpness; arching her back and making her toes curl up. She gasped, whimpered though a closed jaw as the wave of exquisite pleasure ran though each part of her. She felt her inner muscles tighten, but with no extra space the shudders kept going and going until she was panting and weak and close to tears.

Vinnie had stilled while she was enjoying this spectacular moment in time, and as he rose up on his forearms, gazing down at her with such affection, he was smiling in a lazy, knowing way.

"Was that good?"

Iola groaned quietly, turning her head to the side while catching her breath. "Oh my God ... you have no idea."

"Tell me what you would like next."

She swallowed and took a few more breaths, then looked up at him again. "More like that, please."

He laughed, his entire body shaking from the sound, giving her a very interesting tickle directly south of her bellybutton, where he was still fully engaged with her.

"How would you like me to do that?"

"That was so good, but this time ..." she licked her lips and dropped the smile so he'd know she was serious. "Faster. And harder."

Voro unlocked Claudia's apartment door, trying to ignore the smell of chocolate in the hallway, and let himself and Raphael into the living room. Raphael had eaten all his fries on the drive over, and he immediately sat down at the small two-person table to polish off the Big Mac. He hadn't said a word, and Voro could've almost felt sorry for him.

Almost.

"There's beer in the fridge," he offered, and when Raphael didn't reply, he looked at the guy, wondering what he was picking up on. But Raphael's attention was on the door, and he had stopped mid-chew, thoughtful. "What's up?" It was like having Lassie in the room.

"You know what's going on over there?"

Voro felt his neck and shoulders tighten. "I don't care."

Raphael's head tilted, like he was picking up a new transmission. "I think you do," he said, but it was obvious he had a direct line to the apartment across the hall and that was what his main focus was on.

"I don't. Stop spying on them. That doctor is a nice guy, and she's ... she's basically one of you."

Raphael smiled at him suddenly. "Man, not only is he a nice guy ... he's hung like a Clydesdale."

"Shut up."

"They're just getting started with the good stuff. Just jump in his head. You don't have to make him do anything," Raphael's voice got very quiet and gentle because he was totally serious. "But that way you might ... you know. Know what she's like."

Voro shook his head. "Not even I would do that. And I mean it, stop spying."

"Fine, fine."

"I'm going to sleep."

"I bet you are."

"I am. Good night."

"Don't forget to say your prayers, Voro."

He kept the nasty reply to himself, making his way down the hall to Claudia's bedroom. He didn't technically need to sleep at all, but the angel was grating on him and it was definitely putting him in need of some alone time.

And he didn't need the guy suggesting that he plant himself in the doctor's mind to see what balling Iola would be like. Because Voro was already there.

He rubbed his temples, feeling like a world-class shit. But he had to know, and the inability to find out himself was going to leave him strung out like a junkie in the middle of the desert. Not only are you dying, but you're addicted to something you want and dying. If dying slowly could get any worse that would be it.

He sat on the edge of the bed, but in his mind he was in the bedroom on the other side of the wall next to him, cringing at his own invasion of privacy. But then he forgot about it all, slipping in voyeuristically to Veneratio Aubericus's brain and …

He sucked in his breath. Iola was just climaxing, her small body twitching under the weight of her lover, her soft lips open as she made very quiet sounds. She was soft and lovely in the peak of her passion. The internal reality of what was happening to her was wrapped around the doctor's world-class cock, stretching her out so tightly the muscle spasms were no more than flutterings.

Voro could have kicked himself. The doctor *was* built like a horse. And the thought he was using that damn thing on Iola was making Voro see red. No one should be allowed to touch her in any way unless *he* was the one doing it. Not that he had any problems with the size of his own equipment, and God knew no one had ever gone away unsatisfied, but he wanted to be the one delivering the goods, so to speak.

Then he gave himself a few moments of mental-self-lashing. What was he thinking? This was so inappropriate. But then again, he was a Sin Eater, and lack of morality was an actual job requirement. He barely paid attention as the couple went through their cute back-and-forthing, and then when Vinnie asked how Iola would like him to please her again, Voro's ears perked up as those gorgeous eyes returned to Vinnie's face, and Voro imagined himself in the lucky bastard's place as she made her request.

"Faster. And harder."

The poor doc almost blew his load right then and there, and Voro had to admit that if his weapon had been loaded he might have fired off a round, too. He had to laugh though; the doctor was totally at a loss and caught by surprise. And more than excited. The sweet, precious, and delicate Iola liked it a bit naughty.

Voro was now totally lost in love.

Chapter Thirty

Jasper watched Tabitha pull her clothes back on while he threw back a finger of whiskey, not finding her so attractive now that he knew what every inch of her looked like. Christ, there wasn't a single original piece to her, which really made him feel about as proud as he would have felt after fucking a blow-up doll.

Yeah, nothing to brag to your friends about.

She seemed to have enjoyed herself, though. She stumbled as though drunk, and her face had a small, very satisfied smile he recognized from the woman he'd done in the bar bathroom and the other girl from down the hall. He'd liked it well enough, but really it *wasn't* enough. He wanted something **more** wrong.

He'd only come when he remembered the whore from the night before. The one he'd raped? *Was* it rape? He'd paid her. She'd been willing. And yet he didn't release until he had her good and terrified.

He was back to thinking there was something very unethical about him, to say the least.

"Hey baby ... can I see you again?" Tammy was fully dressed and waiting by the bedroom door, like he might walk her out of his place or something.

He shrugged. "I don't know. Maybe."

"I like those odds. See you, Stud." She kissed her fingers and sashayed out his door, and he just shuddered. She was a fucking idiot.

When the door shut he was infinitely happier that he'd given her the mental boot out of his place. He made it seem like it was her own idea. Jasper got up from his bed, naked, and headed for the shower. He had to wash her off of him. He hadn't gone bareback on her, of course, but the smell of her perfume was really bothering him suddenly. It had to go.

He pulled back the curtain, and let out a yelp, jumping back. Essum was in his shower, arms crossed, leaning on the wall, one ankle over the other. Like he was waiting for him.

"I wanted to tell you to rest up for tomorrow, but you were … busy when I first got here."

Great. Now he had audiences he couldn't see. "Did you watch us?"

Essum shrugged. "Of course. It's one of the things I can't do until I'm in a physical body. Doesn't mean I'm not jonesing for it."

"If you kept it off your mind it might help." Jasper reached past him to turn the shower on, knowing the water wouldn't disturb a single hair on Essum's head.

"If I'm out of my head I'm in other people's heads, and guess what they're all thinking of."

Jasper shrugged as he tossed a towel on the counter next to the shower. "Fucking?" he ventured a guess.

"Exactly. You can do it, I can't. You wouldn't understand."

"Hey, until this nasty little make-over you put me through I was hardly out there Hugh Heffing it up."

Essum frowned. "Who?"

Jasper just shook his head. "Nothing. Now get out of my shower so I can clean up."

"Scared to be in here with a ghost?"

Jasper sighed in exhaustion. "Are you gay?"

Now it was Essum's turn to be surprised. "What?"

"You watch me have sex, you want to watch me shower … I mean, what the fuck?"

Essum vanished but his voice punched into Jasper's brain like a migraine on steroids. *Not gay, but I can still fuck you, so watch it.*

Vinnie was staring down at her so intently, Iola had the crazy thought she'd totally put him off. What was she thinking? Telling a guy how to do it better. What an idiot.

"I'm sorry - " she began.

"If you're sure …" he replied at the same time.

Then she smiled. "I thought I … shocked you for a moment."

His lips were lazy as he kissed her again, then he smiled back. "Not shocked. Just … surprised. Delightfully surprised." She locked her ankles behind his back, and his smile broadened as she was opened slightly wider for him. “Oh, Iola ... are you sure?”

“Stop asking me that.” She pushed her hips forward, feeling herself sliding down that length just the slightest bit more. Vinnie growled and latched his mouth on her hers, drew his knees up close to her hips, and thrust deep.

She cried out louder than she meant to, breaking contact with his mouth, but this was what she had asked for, wasn’t it? It wasn’t just a physical invasion; it was a complete over-throwing of her senses and her ability to think straight. She met each thrust with a push of her own against his powerful hips, and the push and drag was all the more amplified by his size. There was no extra room; every movement had her completely inundated.

And yet she was incredibly aware of everything that was happening. She was aware that as he moved his mouth across her jaw and down her neck his bottom lip dragged slightly on her skin, like he needed to maintain contact with her in between kisses. A few hours’ worth of stubble also scratched against her, feeling very male and very, very pleasant. His long, tapered hands may have been pretty but as they gripped her hips they were very strong and able.

When he raised his upper body up on to those hands he was breathing hard through his mouth. She kept her legs locked around his waist, his body rocking against hers with more and more urgency. Iola was aware of the heat building in her belly but unable to concentrate on just that, there was so much more to enjoy and experience.

His eyes may have been hooded by eyelids that were lowered in pleasure, but she could tell how bright they were as they trailed over her. His skin was slick under her hands, and she loved watching the muscles in his arms, his shoulders and his chest as he churned his body against hers. The noises he made were notching up her level of arousal as well. Every push had him growling and moaning and saying her name in a nonsensical rambling kind of way, she wasn’t even sure if he was aware he was doing it.

And the smell of him was perfect. She could smell his soap, his after shave, and the manly smell of a good, clean sweat. She took it all in, as much as she could.

As the orgasm punched the air out of her lungs and sent stars flying through her mind, Iola was pretty sure her body would never be the same. The sensation was like fire under her skin, deliciously hot and ruthless, not wanting to let her go. And he still hadn't finished.

Vinnie didn't even wait, he kept the pace up, riding right through her contractions, making her next orgasm take all of about twenty seconds to achieve. Her body was being rocked back and forth on the mattress and she put one hand to the wall to keep them from hitting it as her third burst had her closing her eyes and crying out pitifully.

Then he came, going completely tense as his mouth fell open and a bellow sounded loud and low, something that was a combination of *"Iola"* and *"oh God."* His erection twitched inside her, and she hung on to him as he went through his own episode of ecstasy.

He collapsed on to her, and she ran her hands over his back, unable to lose the smile on her face. Her eyes closed in complete relaxation, and as she stroked his damp skin his breathing became more and more even. When she realized he was sleeping, she gave a soft laugh and gave him a tickle in the ribs. He awoke with a grunt, then rubbed a hand over his face.

"Sorry," he said, laughing along with her and rolling away. "Oh Iola ... my God."

She rolled on to her side next to him, watching his relaxed expression in the candlelight. He wrapped an arm under her head, running a finger down her arm in a very light touch that made her shiver in spite of the warmth she felt to her very marrow.

"You are ... something," he said wearily, his eyes closed and his smile was so genuine she couldn't stop grinning like a twit.

"Mmmm ..." she pressed her lips to his slick chest, tasting the salt on him. "I think that was all you."

He shook his head in disagreement. "If you had any idea how good you feel, look, taste ... my God."

As Vinnie trembled again, Iola was inspired by a streak of naughtiness, rising up on one arm to look down on him. She loved the feeling of her nipples brushing against his damp, slippery skin as she did so. "What do I feel like?" she asked with a small smile as she teased one of his nipples with a finger.

He gave a groan as she did so, his face breaking into a huge grin. "Iola ..."

"What do I feel like?" She didn't stop.

"Like ... perfection."

"And what do I look like?" She flicked the other nipple with her tongue and he groaned loudly again.

"Like perfection," he gasped.

"You already used that one. What do I look like?" She gave the nipple a slight nip with her teeth this time. He barked out a sound that made her reassess how tired she actually was.

"You look like ... an underwear model?"

She raised her eyebrows, impressed. "I like that. So what was next?"

"Iola ..."

"Was it taste? What do I taste like?"

He still hadn't looked at her, he was keeping his eyes closed as she was toying with him, his mouth open and panting, easing into a wider smile with what she was doing to him.

"I can't ... say."

She pushed the sheets out of the way and sat astride him, making his eyes pop open in surprise. But he kept the smile.

"What do I taste like?" she repeated, her voice surprisingly firm in spite of her wicked little grin.

"Iola ..."

She reached down between her legs, touching herself. She knew he was watching because his eyes got really wide. When she brought her fingers back to his lips, he latched on to them immediately, licking and sucking. "What do I taste like?"

His eyes closed as he let go of her fingers, and she felt his erection return against her inner thigh. His voice was very primal and guttural as he answered, "Like honey, Iola. You're like honey."

"I want to do it again."

"Absolutely."

Essum was waiting for Jasper when he got out of the shower, sitting on his sofa, legs crossed, staring into space. Immediately he jumped to his feet, slapping his hands together. "Get your keys. There's something I want to try."

"What?"

"I just need to find something out. I need to see ..." Essum's eyes shone. "I need to see what you can do."

Jasper had a terrible feeling, but he got his jacket on and headed down to the garage, noting with annoyance that it was three in the morning and he had to be at work at 10. Maybe this wouldn't take long?

Essum directed him to drive to some dive of a dance club in a part of town that he never visited. Ever. The music was loud, the crowd was mostly ready to head out, and Essum told him to wait by the car while he went inside.

Jasper shoved his hands deep in his pockets, leaning against the driver's side door, aware that his body was exhausted and his mind was reeling. What he really wanted was to just sleep.

"Wake up." Essum made him jump about five feet in the air by kicking his feet. Jasper must have dozed off while standing up. It wouldn't be the first time that had happened to him. He'd always been able to sleep wherever he ended up for the night.

Essum was standing in front of a man, large, tattooed, dressed in black leather with a shaved head. Jasper had to gulp and stand up straighter.

Trying to appear calm, he ducked his head in greeting to the stranger, then said in a shaky voice, "What's going on?"

"Can you sense it?" Essum asked, excitement in his voice and his eyes, making them shimmer.

Jasper frowned, looking up at the pile of meat behind Essum. "Sense what?" he whispered, wondering if the Hell's Angel bouncer was supposed to be aware of what they were discussing.

"From him? Can you sense it?"

Something was expected of him here, it was a test he was being thrown into without getting the study notes first. He hated feeling stupid; in front of Essum stupid was a weakness and the guy made a point of cutting you down to size if you showed any of that. So all he could do was shrug.

Essum's shoulder's sagged in disappointment. "He doesn't seem strange? He doesn't smell peculiar?"

"No offense," Jasper met the guy's eyes, "but I don't want to smell him. What is this? What is going on?"

Essum was right ticked off. "Dammit. Dammit. Dammit."

"I'm sorry," Jasper stammered, feeling like he was failing Essum somehow. "What am I supposed to be smelling?"

"His sins," Essum snarled. "It reeks of fire and brimstone and sulfur and everything else that belches up from the earth's core. It's the stink of hell and he is covered in it."

Jasper frowned and waited for the guy to pound Essum into the concrete like a plastic bolt in a Fisher Price workbench set. But the guy was not paying attention to them in the least. His gaze was vacant and his eyes were not focused on anything specific. Essum must have had him under a little brainwashing spell.

"I'm sorry I can't smell his sins." That's something he never thought he'd say. "But why ... why would I?"

"Never mind. Just give me your hand." That was figurative of course, Essum never touched him. Jasper just put his hand out and Essum used some kind of telepathy to maneuver the stoned giant under Jasper's touch. Jasper had to stretch to put his hand on the guy's head, but he did it nonetheless.

"Now," Essum directed. "Find his sins."

Jasper was already in before Essum said another word. The guy's head opened up like a laptop, divided into daily activities like showering, brushing his teeth and walking his dog, but the other half of his life was what they were obviously after.

This was murder. So much blood, shotguns splattering brain matter all over walls, people screaming for their lives as he cut out their tongues and gouged out their eyes for snitching.

Jasper had to close his eyes, then realized that just made it worse. With his eyes closed his here-and-now senses totally shut down and he could actually feel the warm blood running down his arm as hands that weren't his held a man by the neck up against the wall, his neck cut and letting that deep red fluid run all down his front. Jasper could smell the blood and taste the anger and feel the power welling up in him, the power it took to take someone's life.

Now release it, Essum's voice came from nowhere, and Jasper imagined a chalk brush wiping it all away, each thumbnail of every memory this guy kept hidden to one side of his brain. His dark side.

Jasper was shaking as he brought his hand down, but not from the horror of it or because the guy scared the living crap out of him. He was shaking with this man's strength.

The man, on the other hand, crumpled to the ground weeping suddenly, Essum's spell broken and his mind in shambles. Jasper became aware of what he was thinking, how he felt relieved that someone had taken away all the awful things he'd done. He felt better. He knew he was saved.

Jasper studied his hand as Essum watched in approval.

"Well," the mentor said with a half-smile. "You may not be able to find them on your own, but you can take their sins. I don't know how you're doing it, but you are."

"What is this going to do to me?" Jasper asked, tightening his hand into a fist, feeling a tingle as he released it.

Essum shrugged. "Like I said, I have no idea. But it's sure making you stronger."

Jasper had to shrug in acceptance. Strong was good; he could definitely handle being strong.

Chapter Thirty-One

Charlie had woken in the murdered woman's bedroom, hand wrapped around the leg of the armchair he'd slept in before those two other men had come in a few hours ago.

He made his way sleepily down the grand staircase of the house, rubbing his eyes as he realized the sun was coming up. He really shouldn't be here, and the closer to daytime it got the more trouble he could be in.

He still felt wonderfully calm, however. Before his mind had been like a bug zapper; constantly humming and distracting him from those things that normal, everyday people do and have and enjoy and spend their time on. He'd always been distracted from that, like a guy in the dark waiting for someone to punch him

The golden light that he'd felt from the new master, that must be what people felt when they were not like him. To imagine that people could walk around like that all the time ... It was almost too much. He felt like weeping again.

You've been forgiven ...

Relief wasn't a big enough word. Able to breathe didn't really encapsulate everything he was experiencing. This was a new day for Charles Goodwin.

He moved through the woman's kitchen, opening her fridge. Nothing was inside. He had to wonder who would come and empty the fridge of everything except a bottle of mustard and a jar of pickles. Or maybe she wasn't home much and never ate here.

That seemed like a real shame. The house was very beautiful, with high vaulted ceilings that were now lit with sunshine. The stainless steel appliances glinted in showroom perfection.

He moved across a built-in desk between the kitchen and living room where ... all the bad had happened. But his memory of the event itself felt fuzzy. Like it had to have been someone else; as though he had never been capable of such hatred.

A photo on a desk caught his eye. It was the woman, her hair just a bit longer than it had been. She was next to a blonde girl who looked a bit younger than her. The frame was wooden and someone had carved in the top "Sisters and" then in the bottom, "best friends." The letters were cute, like a child's scrawled penmanship. Charlie had to assume this young blonde had given this to the woman who lived here. It matched nothing and had none of the sophistication that the rest of the house had. In the photo the blonde smiled wider, and had that look that let you know she was fun-loving and free spirited. The dark-haired woman's smile looked like it pained her.

Charlie decided she hadn't been a very happy person. Maybe she never felt good enough, like she was sorry for not being better at something.

He shook his head and put the picture back. Here he was, analyzing a photo like a shrink or something. It was a picture shared between sisters. Sisters and best friends.

Charlie wondered if this pretty blonde girl was going to be the one that had to come to this house, go through the dead woman's things and keep what was important to their family.

That's when Charlie felt bad. It wasn't just the dead he'd hurt, was it? He had a whole network of victims he'd never even laid a hand on.

"I'm sorry," he whispered to the photo. The blonde woman smiled. If God could forgive, maybe she would, too. That was a happy thought.

Charlie opened the front door, trying to be sneaky as he ducked under the police tape and pulled the door shut behind him. But just then tires pulled up to a stop in the driveway, and as he was blinking in surprise two men in dark uniforms were grabbing him, slamming him face-down on the hood of a police car. It was all so fast he barely was aware of what had happened.

"About time we got you, fucker."

"You are going to jail for a long time this time, buddy."

Just words, none of it meant anything as the men continued snarling things at him, mean and hateful things, but his brain was still fuzzy from sleep, and the feeling of euphoria he'd achieved earlier that morning.

You've been forgiven. That man may have gotten him arrested twice, but those simple words made Charlie want to hug him. *You've been forgiven.*

Charlie wanted to weep just at the mere memory of the words. Even as these unfriendly hands pushed him roughly into the back of a police car, he felt like this was right. He could do his time, he could die in jail, But he was forgiven.

The last two times he'd been arrested the Master had come to get him out, but of course that was work. He used Charlie to do terrible things, right?

Charlie didn't want the Master to come for him this time. He would rather just stay forgiven. This was better.

Claudia had responded to multiple calls throughout the night. Dead bodies everywhere, most of them Iola. A busy night.

And until her cell phone rang next to the hotel bed she thought she was forever trapped in a cycle of waking nightmares. She sat up to answer it, rested from approximately thirty minutes' total sleep the night before. It was work.

"Hello?"

"It's Trevor."

She nodded, not wanting to prevent him from saying what he was calling for.

"Patrol just got a call saying they saw someone got into Portia Torregrossa's place, and when patrol went by they caught Charles Goodwin exiting the house. So ... we've got him, and I asked them to take him into the ninth precinct just to be safe. So ... we got him."

She expelled her breath, still nodding. "Good. And thanks, Vance. I know that was probably a hard thing for you to request."

"Actually, not at all. Everyone here's totally creeped out by the guy. They took him over there happily."

"So I'm not being set up by a co-worker?"

"I don't think so. But I still wanted to be safe."

"So ... can I go home today?"

"Give it another day to be sure, but if you go over there, make sure you're not alone when you leave, okay?"

"I know, I know. I'll be fine."

She ended the call and pushed herself out of bed. Then she sat a moment, running her hands through her hair, yawning and stretching.

She wasn't likely to fall asleep now, despite the slightly comforting news.

At least her hands had stopped shaking, that was good. A miracle, really, considering those shallow, wake-you-with-a-start dreams she'd been having all night weren't really known for keeping a person mellow.

She'd woken more than once with tears on her face. She'd thought many times her best friend was dead, and then jumped as Iola's corpse had come to life and reached for her. She'd shouted herself awake each time.

She didn't sleep at all until she'd dreamt of Damien. All she'd needed was to curl up in bed, close her eyes, wrap one hand around that weird pendant of his and imagine it was him holding her, not hotel sheets and pillows. That had been dreamless. And not nearly long enough.

But she sure wasn't getting back to sleep now that the room was lit-up like midday. Claudia figured she might as well shower. She grabbed the toiletry case she'd quickly thrown together on her way out of the apartment, then went back to her phone. One more call, just to make herself feel better.

Voro was staring at the ceiling, rubbing the center of his chest absently. At least the two on the other side of the wall were sleeping now, and he could concentrate again.

Still hurt, though.

The smell of chocolate had permeated into Claudia's apartment, along with nutmeg. He was trying to ignore another smell that had him ready to punch a hole in the wall. The smell of summer wind on grass after a spring shower. The smell of love.

It was usually a wonderful smell. But at the moment he thought he might be about to cry like a little bitch.

When the cordless phone next to him rang, he let it go on and on. Apparently Claudia didn't have a message manager or an answering machine, because it wouldn't stop. So eventually he reached out and answered it. "Hello?"

"Is everything okay? Why'd you take so long to answer?"

He had to smile at the worry in Claudia's voice. She'd been concerned, but only that he'd had someone else in her bed. He could hear it clearly in her tone. "This isn't my phone, I was going to let the machine get it."

"I don't have one."

"I realized that eventually. Are you okay?"

"They caught him. They've got him in custody in a different station. So we'll see if it stays that way."

"That's good." He let his voice drop low. "Does that mean you're able to come home?"

She gave a laugh at that and he was willing to bet she was blushing. "They said to wait a day, but ... if I've got a body guard it should be okay to come home today."

"You've got a body guard all right. I'll be on you like - "

"Damien!"

He felt a laugh in his chest, and it surprised him. But he let it out anyway. "I'll wait here, then. Should I shower or do you plan on making a mess of me again?"

"Mmm. Maybe stay dirty for now."

"Consider that done."

She hung up after a bit more dirty-talking then Voro got up to go check the living room. Raphael was nowhere to be seen, so he felt better about that. He got the coffee maker going, then decided to have a shower anyway. He had nothing else to do, and everything seemed to be quiet in the building with the sleep patterns of the lovers next door like warm sunshine on his brain.

After giving Jasper his assignment for the morning, Essum decided to head back over to the apartment where Voro was keeping his harem of women. He could sense his old friend under the roof, and as he spirited himself through the outer walls and up into the hallway in the top floor, he tried to decide where he should go to make the biggest impact for the next part of his plan.

Voro was in the lesbian woman's apartment. Essum made sure to shield his brain patterns from him, then picked up on the *frustro* in her apartment and the sleeping male next to her. It was that doctor, the one that Essum couldn't quite figure out.

Essum was a brat. He was immature. And he couldn't help himself.

He moved through the walls into the *frustro*'s bedroom, the smell of chocolate and nutmeg quite strong here. The couple were wound around each other in spent passion and exhaustion, their sleep patterns indicating that it would be a few hours before they woke on their own. The woman's leg was latched over the male's, the sheets tossed around and barely covering them. In fact, he could clearly see the breast that wasn't pressed up against the man's side.

He closed his eyes, figuratively, of course. He had no eyes. But to concentrate, he got rid of the image before him and let his mind go, tunneling through her deep sleep and nonsense dreams into her psyche.

He knew the moment she became aware of him, because her heartbeat increased slightly, in a bad way. He frightened her, the story of his life. Her breaths became deeper too. She was distressed by his very essence.

Very interesting.

He took his mental trowel and made a hole in her here-and-now, planting in a different kind of thought. A very raw, nasty, dirty thought. He had her imagining she stood before him, bent over to put her hands on her mattress while he drove into her from behind. And he did nothing to suggest she liked it.

Because it came from nowhere, with no fantasy leading up to it, she kicked a leg slightly, making a noise of consternation. Her brow furrowed, too.

He would have smiled if he'd been in solid form. He let her body warm to it now, giving her the impression that he was getting close to the spot inside where she wanted him, and she was now liking his hands on her sides, enjoying the force of each thrust and pull.

He smelled the chocolate for real, and he wished he could jump on her right then with his solid form. But it wasn't that solid, was it? As far as actual physical matter, he needed Viagra worse than a centenarian.

He risked a look at her, and her mouth had fallen open, her brow relaxed and she rolled away from the doctor on to her back. Both breasts were now open to him, and he caught his breath. Her legs scissored under the sheet, pulling it down her hip slightly.

Holy. Shit. It was really working.

He knelt next to the bed, watching her face as the porn movie kept going in her mind. In real life he probably wouldn't last this long, he realized, looking over her body and studying the way she rode each sensation that would inevitably lead to an honest-to-God orgasm.

If he let it.

He leaned forward, able to smell the spent sweat that was already on her skin, just starting to dampen again with the heat of her dream. She licked her lips and turned her face his way, panting now. There may have also been a whimper.

She couldn't see him in her dream. For all she knew it was the doctor.

Or Voro.

Struck by inspiration, he leaned forward, licking his lips as he came closer to her skin. He could feel its warmth, even in his ether form. Essum took one nipple in his mouth …

And he was actually able to feel it and taste it as he sucked at it, her skin puckering and responding in his mouth. The woman moaned, arching her back, and he had to stumble backwards.

If he'd been solid he would have planted right on his ass.

What the hell … he was just a ghost here … wasn't he?

Essum turned his attention back to the sleeping woman, just in time to see her open her eyes. And look right at him.

He vanished right out of there, popping back into the hallway, trying to set his head right. That couldn't happen. That just didn't happen … but she was a *frustro*, wasn't she? And not his *frustro*. Was she more tuned in?

Well no shit. He'd told Voro as much when he told him she could influence other humans somewhat, pick up on things that most humans didn't. She could … she could feel him? She must have felt the kiss before ... he'd assumed he'd just scared her into thinking he'd actually touched her in some way.

Essum thought about paying Voro another visit, but he had to settle down first. Not a great idea to face off with a Sin Eater when you were frazzled.

Iola rubbed her eyes, rolling back on to her side and smiling as Vinnie came into focus. What with the raunchy dream she'd just had ...

She frowned. It hadn't been Vinnie, though. It had been that guy form the hospital that had vanished from plain sight, kinda like he just did.

She rubbed her eyes harder. What was with her? Seeing things, getting herself all freaked out ... or horny, as it turned out.

She settled back against Vinnie, who mumbled something as she came back in contact with him. It must have been the fact that she finally got fantastically laid, making all these weird things fire in her brain. Drawing strange conclusions and outcomes that didn't make sense.

But as she closed her eyes, that feeling came back, the sight of him staring down at her in complete shock with those unnerving eyes, and the feeling that he was working her hard from behind. She moaned as the feeling came back, her eyes flying open to make it stop.

The sound woke Vinnie, making him crack one eyelid open as he smiled and gathered her up in a tight squeeze.

"I was hoping it wasn't just a dream," he muttered sleepily, letting his eyes close again.

Iola blinked a few times to straighten herself out, glad to have Vinnie in her grasp, warm and real and understandable.

"Not a dream," she said, trying to match his tone. "Very real."

"Tell me about it. I'm still exhausted."

"Well we can keep sleeping."

He kissed the top of her head and nodded off again, but Iola was still scared to close her eyes.

Jasper recognized the black Challenger parked at the motel, and his mind told him which room she was staying in.

His hands were sweating, and he was fighting the urge to turn and run. But another part of him had steely resolve, making his back straighter as he climbed the stairs to the upper corridor that ran across the front of the motel. He was headed for the room at the very end, and with each step, he was making up his mind.

He was going to do what Essum asked, simple as that. The guy would make sure nothing bad would come of it, just like he kept helping Charlie escape jail. In return, Essum would become some kind of fucking all-powerful ghost or some shit, and Jasper would be rewarded. He couldn't think anything other than that would happen. He was in too deep now.

At the motel door he paused, reaching inside without the aid of his ears. He picked up on Claudia's brain, she was shaving her legs in anticipation of sex. It was in her mind, and the fact that it was with a guy gave him pause. But just for a moment. He was more scared of Essum than he was curious about her sexual preferences.

He put his hand on the door knob, concentrating on the tumblers inside, willing them to line up and allow him to turn the hunk of brass in his hand. He was rewarded with a click, and he shoved the door inward.

The bathroom door was wide open, and he sent out the message that she was not to notice the breeze that came in the door, and when she registered what sounded like a door closing, he convinced her that it was just her imagination.

He'd never really liked Claudia anyway.

Chapter Thirty-Two

Claudia wrapped herself in a towel and stepped out of the shower, wrapping a second towel around her hair and opening the bathroom door to allow some of the humidity from the small room to escape. She wiped more condensation off the mirror with the hand towel, then brushed her teeth. She was meticulous about teeth.

Once that was done she moved out to the bedroom to get dressed, pulling underwear on under the towel. Just as she was about to drop the hillbilly housecoat there was a creak behind her, and she spun around, tightening her hold on the terry-cloth wrapping.

Her brain was trying to keep up, but her body was reacting first. Her brain was still on *What the hell is Jasper doing here?* as her arm deflected the punch he was sending her.

Then her brain went to *No way I'm getting another broken nose, asshole* as she returned the attempted jab with a shot to his solar plexus. He lost his breath, and she used the opportunity to give him another gut shot. When he doubled over, she drove an elbow into the back of his neck.

Jasper was tougher than she'd pegged him for, though. He tackled her by the waist, taking them both to the carpet. Claudia threw elbows and fists and kicks at him, knowing they were hitting their target by how he grunted a couple of times.

Jasper managed to get one good shot into her jaw, right in a spot that was already bruised and sore. She renewed her subscription to stars and yellow haze and felt her strength flag for one moment, and that's when he grabbed her arms, pinning them over her head. That's also when Claudia knew the towel had come down, it was barely wrapped around her. She was totally naked from the waist up.

Jasper froze, looking down at her with wide eyes, breathing heavy from the fight.

She should have been asking what he was doing but his eyes; they were freaking her out. The black was widening, knocking out the hazel color completely. He looked almost reptilian.

"Your eyes ..." she muttered illogically, since now his eyes had moved down to her naked flesh. He licked his lips.

Claudia knew the moment his motivation turned away from getting her under his control. It wasn't hard to see. His breathing changed from physical exertion to excitement, and his expression went from rage to *want.*

Hell no. She tried to free her arms from his grip, but his position and strength had her at a disadvantage. His weight was resting right over her hips, erection against her stomach, and try as she might to buck him off he wasn't moving. He was staring at her chest with rage and lust. She needed to get out from under him immediately.

"What the hell are you doing here, Jasper?" She was trying to get his attention off her body. But it was too late.

He switched his grip so that her hands were pinned under one arm and he pressed the other across her neck. Her windpipe was still bruised from when Charlie had tried the choking route, and it didn't take long for her to lose air and start to fade.

His mouth was on her breasts, biting at her, but she couldn't worry about that. With just one hand holding her in place his strength was compromised. She could use this lust against him.

Luckily she was still somewhat damp from the shower, and the fight she'd already put up had her sweaty as well. She yanked one hand free, grabbed on to the back of his head by his hair and yanked hard. Clumps of his curly black locks came free, and he yowled, releasing his mouth from her skin. That definitely felt better, on a couple of levels.

Jasper put one hand to the back of his scalp instinctively. That's when she swung her fistful of his hair in a perfect arc, catching him across the nose. Her knuckles weren't in a perfect fist, and it hurt like hell, but mission accomplished anyway. His nose bust open like a dam, blood gushing hot and fast. But the best part was it hurt him good. She didn't even know she had that kind of strength.

She gave him a forceful shove while thrusting up with her hips and rolled him off of her. By then her adrenalin was free-flowing like champagne at a rapper's birthday party. She leapt on him, showering blows into his face and along his jaw. She saw red everywhere, some of it rushing out of his face.

He was trying to grab at her face to push her away, but he couldn't reach between punches. He got hold of Damien's chain around her neck, wrapping it around his fist and trying to use it as a leash to pull her to one side. And then ...

Who knew how to explain it. He had the chain around his palm, and when he closed his mitt around the pendant *something* happened. Claudia was dimly aware of a heat building up in the chain around her neck, like a current running through it. It was enough to make her pause, but not just the temperature change had her about to freak out.

There was a sizzling sound, and then Jasper let out the most god-awful shriek she'd ever heard. There was smoke rising from his fist, and he let go of the pendant like it was coated in acid. Claudia was so sure it would burn her she wanted to yank it off her own neck. But as it swung back and hit the skin between her breasts it was warm. Just like the moment she'd put it on. *What the ...*

He used her surprise to push her back, and she toppled over to one side. But she wasn't worried about him raping her anymore. He was cradling his hand like it had been nearly amputated, which was somewhat comical compared to the damage she'd done to his face. He could barely see out one eye surely, and his lip was split in three places. Not to mention the broken nose.

Jasper was staring at her in shock, and above all else, total confusion. He didn't know what had happened, either.

Claudia stayed where she was, crouched in a ball with her back against the bed, ready to spring right at him if he came at her first. But he didn't, he looked at his hand and bolted out the door, leaving it open.

She fumbled for the towel, wrapping it back around herself with shaking hands. Someone came to the door, asking if she was okay. She just nodded, and when they asked if they should call the police she remembered mumbling something along the lines of, "I am a cop. I'll be fine."

The whole time she'd been talking Damien's pendant was warming her right hand.

Voro was pulling on a pair of jeans and one of his Raphael-inspired T-shirts when he had to pause, completed befuddled by the sensation in his head. Was it possible for a Sin Eater to have a panic attack? 'Cause that's sure what it felt like.

He couldn't breathe. He sat on the edge of Claudia's bed, and suddenly his vision got very sharp, too sharp, even. Details were precise, colors were vivid, but he still couldn't breathe.

Just calm the fuck down, he told himself, closing his eyes and counting the time it took him to inhale and exhale. That's when he had the vision.

Was vision an accurate term? Who the hell knew. All he saw was a man he didn't recognize, looking down at him in hatred, holding him against carpet, he could feel the fibers under his bare skin. But it wasn't him, this wasn't his future. This was someone's *right now*.

Claudia.

His eyes flew open as he connected the dots. He'd given her his pendant. She was wearing it, that was why he could see through her eyes. And she was fighting for her life. But where?

As long as the metal around her neck was in contact with her skin, he could flip back through her memories. He caught the name of a motel on the top of a form she'd filled out when checking in.

Voro knew where it was, but it was about a five minute drive. Come to think of it, he could likely run there in just over that.

And how do you explain that after the fact? If she's okay, how did he explain how he knew where she was? When she called him it was from her cell phone.

Shit.

He closed his eyes again, connecting back to Claudia, and sliding right into her neural pathways. He sent her *strength*, if that made sense. He used his mind to dull her pain receptors, calm her panic, and as soon as she was free of the fog of agony, and the schmuck actually let her go out of concern for his damn hair, Voro saw her toss her attacker off of her so hard he hit his head on the wall.

Claudia fell on him like a street fighter, beating him to a bloody pulp.

Voro smiled. *Atta girl.*

Then the guy's hand grabbed the necklace, and after a moment of delayed reaction, Voro bellowed, clutching his head and falling to the floor off the edge of the bed.

What the fuck is this now?

It was the Sin Eater equivalent of a dog whistle, he was sure. There was a high-pitched ringing in his ears, combined with a nasty burp of microphone feedback with a chaser of fingernails on the blackboard. It was peeling the backs off his eyelids and causing such mental distress he lost the linkup with Claudia completely.

All because that guy had touched the pendant?

The acoustic torture ended very abruptly, Voro had to assume the guy had let go. Now all he needed were about eighty Tylenol-3s and he'd be good as new, fuck you very much.

He shook his head to make sure there weren't any more bats in the bell tower. He seemed to be okay now, so he tried to get the feed connected to Claudia again.

He sighed in relief. She was okay, she was watching the guy run away, and someone was there to help her. A woman.

He should just wait. She would call if she needed him.

"I do not want to go back to work," Vinnie mumbled in between soft kisses on her lips.

"I don't want you to, either," Iola replied, eyes closed against the sweet touches. "Can you just call in sick?"

"Probably not,' he said honestly, landing a few more kisses on her.

"You might be too tired to perform surgery," she observed. "For the sake of anyone needing emergency surgery, you should just go back to bed with me."

"When you put it like that ..." he lifted her off the ground with another kiss, then nuzzled his nose into her neck. "I want the smell of you with me all day."

Iola smiled against the side of his face. "I'm going to miss you."

He held her tight for a few more moments, then put her back down. "Okay," he said, all business. "I really have to go."

She pouted, but he just smiled, took another hungry look at her, and opened her door.

Probably for the best. Another moment in his arms like that and he really wasn't going to be leaving her place during the morning hours whatsoever.

As he swung the door into the hall Claudia's door opened, and Damien stood in the frame, filling it with his large body. Iola was happy to note her heart did not speed up or trip all over itself at the sight of him this time. Then again, a starving person needed time to recover after an entire feast.

"Oh," Damien said, looking like he was encroaching on their property or something. "I'm sorry. Good morning, Iola."

"Good morning Damien."

Vinnie looked from her to Damien, and Iola couldn't read his expression. So she filled the awkward silence. "Damien, this is Vinnie Aubericus. Vinnie, this is Damien. He's staying with Claudia for a while."

Vinnie's look was now leveled on Damien, so she couldn't tell what his expression was conveying. But going by how the larger man squared his shoulders, lifted his chin and stuck out a hand stiffly, Iola had to guess it was not a friendly look.

"Nice to meet you," Damien said in that agonizingly smooth voice of his, and after another few seconds of stand-off Vinnie finally shook his head, and returned the handshake.

"You too, Damien." The he turned back to Iola, wrapping an arm around her waist and kissing her again in a way that had her lifting one foot off the ground.

When he let her go she had to blink a few times, then he was off down the hall, leaving her in her doorway with Damien looking at her, somewhat bemused.

"Possessive?" He said calmly, leaning to one side of the jamb.

She frowned, wishing she wasn't just in a large T-shirt and not another stitch. His eyes were ... studying her, even though they seemed to be right on her face. "Who?"

"Vinnie," he pointed the direction her doctor had just taken. "You should just wear a sign that says 'taken.'"

Iola's frown deepened. "Excuse me?"

"Nothing. Forget I mentioned it. Hey, do you have any coffee? Claudia's out."

She nodded, stepping back. "I'll get some."

He stepped forward, crossing the hall with just a few strides. She was not thrilled that he was coming into her apartment. Not that she was frustrated because he was so forward, just frustrated that as he moved his arms swung, making his chest muscles move under his shirt, the sleeves straining against his biceps.

Look who just digested an entire feast.

He followed her into the kitchen, and Iola handed him the can of coffee grounds she had sitting out on the counter. "Has she called you?" Iola asked, realizing with much guilt that she hadn't thought of Claudia in ... Well, since Vinnie had brought her home last night.

"She called to say they had the guy in custody, and the cops took him to a different precinct, hoping that might make a difference. I think she's coming back today."

Iola knew what he was saying, she could follow it, but he could have been saying anything. That damn voice of his was like sinking into a warm pool.

"That's good," she said quickly when she realized he'd finished speaking and she was just staring at him like a moron.

"So ... what does Vinnie do for a living?"

"Doctor. A surgeon." How nice of him to remind her that she was seeing someone.

"I see. So you had a pleasant night?"

Anyone else would have gotten her cold shoulder and a dismissal. Anyone other than him. In front of him, she just blushed. "Did ... did we uh ... keep you up last night?"

He shrugged, and she noticed the muscles in his shoulders as they fought to get free of the shirt he had on. It made her heart literally skip a beat. "I might have ... heard a few things."

She must have been bright red by now. "I-I'm so sorry," she stammered, looking down at her feet. Shit. Her nipples were hard. No way that was unnoticeable. She crossed her arms, not looking up.

"Why be sorry? Claudia informed me the walls were thin, and she said we might have disturbed your rest a couple of nights ago."

Like she needed to be reminded of that. The sounds that Claudia had been making, her peals of delight mixed with Damien's low, erotic grunts and bellows ...

She needed to get away from him before ... she did something really stupid.

To Iola's surprise, Damien muttered something like "Fuck it," and stepped closer to her. She didn't back away.

Chapter Thirty-Three

Essum had become aware of Jasper's burning agony with sudden alarm. He'd been sitting in a park, watching kids play on swings. There was one little dude he had a certain interest in – the other kids avoided him like cough syrup, keeping a wide buffer zone between themselves and the oddball in the green jumper.

In appearances the kid was totally normal, the same hair-cut as the other kids, freckles on his nose, brown eyes. He was clean, looked after, but the other kids were picking up on what Essum was picking up on. Evil was already with that kid. He'd already chopped up a few woodland creatures for morbid curiosity's sake. He was going to be one hell of a nut job one day.

It was too bad. Sometimes the spirit could just take a kid over, even though technically kids were harder to crack than most adults. Kids didn't have a concept of greed and lust. They didn't question why things were right and wrong. They just knew what was proper and not. And they could always pick up on a weirdo faster than anyone else because they hadn't learned the concept of manners yet. Kids were like drug-sniffing dogs when it came to something being off about another person.

He watched the young Dahlmer-in-training for a while when he had a sudden jolt to his consciousness, an invasion of Jasper's thought patterns. It was like Jasper was on his "friends" list, so every time something happened to the guy Essum received an update.

Jasper was hurt. Not in an obvious way, but something was happening to him. Essum materialized to where Jasper's signal was coming from, finding himself in the hallway to Jasper's apartment building. He'd beat Jasper there, because just as he was turning to Jasper's door the guy came through the fire doors at the end of the hall, his arm cradled against his chest, his face pale and covered in a thin sheen of sweat. He looked like he had the flu to the point of gut-rot.

Now what fun lessons was Jasper going to teach him? Honest to Christ, Essum was starting to think the guy was intentionally fucking with him.

"Not now," Jasper insisted, raising a feeble hand. "I'm sick. I feel like shit. I just want to ... lay down and die."

I can help with that, Essum thought snarkily. Instead he said, "Let's go inside before your neighbors start wondering why you're talking to yourself."

Voro had watched Iola try to stay calm for long enough. The smell of chocolate coming off her was intoxicating, and the way she shifted from foot to foot uncomfortably was causing her chest to brush against the inside of the T-shirt she wore. Her nipples were hard.

There was a growl in the back of his throat, and she looked up at him, somewhat startled. To hell with the stories, there were some kids that didn't know ovens were hot until they got third-degree burns on a stove element. Apparently Voro was one of those kids. "Fuck it," he muttered, and when he moved towards her he noticed her nostrils flare. And she didn't back up. Even when he slammed the coffee tin back down on the counter.

Fuck him. Her chest was heaving, and he couldn't look away from those twin points under that cotton. He was pretty damn sure she had nothing else on.

Another step and her chest and belly were against him. That was all it took for his erection to kick up and make itself known to him. Probably to her, too. But she still didn't back away.

He slid one hand across her lower back, and she melded up against him without any provocation. This was fine. No burning here. Just her breathing quickly. Through parted lips.

What if Essum had just been screwing with him?

God help the wishful thinkers.

"This is a bad idea," she whispered, and he nodded in agreement. Then he brushed one hand down over her left nipple.

She moaned loudly, her head falling back. He brought his hand back to that spot, teasing the tip while she whimpered, eyes closed and face turned up towards him.

The need to get inside her was intense, more than any similar urge he'd ever felt. The scent of her was getting in the fabric of his clothes. It was all he could smell. And she was all he could see.

The hand on her lower back slid lower, almost of its own volition, cupping her small but perfectly-rounded ass. It was his turn to moan. God, it was a fabulous-feeling ass. He kneaded it forcefully, giving himself shit for handling her so roughly but totally unable to help it.

He could smell the reaction her body was having to his touch. More than the chocolate, he was smelling her biological reaction. He wanted it all over his hands and face.

He lowered his hand from her breast, and she opened her eyes, watching him watch her. Her eyes were hot, needing. Her breath was a furnace on his skin.

His hand played with the bottom hem of her shirt, and as she caught the drift of what he wanted to do to her, she turned her back to the counter, leaning against it and dragging him along by the front of his shirt. Her thighs parted ever so slightly, and she raised her chin as though challenging him to do something really, really naughty.

Voro, for the first time in this rotation, had a nagging thought that this really wasn't right. He shouldn't be doing this.

Iola's hands rested on his chest, stroking the muscles under his shirt. He closed his eyes, her caresses and smell making him wonder if he hadn't taken something that impaired his common sense.

She played with his nipples through the shirt, very gently, teasing because she pulled her hands away as soon as he gasped. When he opened his eyes again, his arousal gave another kick and he had no choice. Her eyelids were lowered seductively, and she was panting, staring at his lips and his face and neck and shoulders ...

Voro slid one hand back around her hip to hold her in position by the ass, and his other hand went to the place where she was swollen from the want of him. He could feel the heat of her through the fabric of her shirt.

Voro was scared of her, scared of her skin burning him. But surely this had to be okay.

Iola arched her back over the counter, going up on her toes, her legs tensing with the sensation. Her cries were like a symphony in his ears, the most wonderful thing he'd ever heard, and when she rocked her hips to work against how he was stroking at her, he growled again. He hadn't even kissed her, he realized.

Then the wetness seeped through the shirt fabric on to his fingers. He loved the feel of it ...until he felt the burning. And not the good kind of burning.

"Shit," he said quietly, backing away from her, closing his hand into a fist. It stung like a motherfucker. "I'm ... I'm sorry."

As he broke contact, she seemed to remember herself. She put a hand to her mouth, eyes widening. "Shit," she echoed.

He took the coffee can and went to the door. She didn't follow. When he was safely back on the other side of Claudia's door, he looked at the fingers on his left hand. There were blisters along the insides of the first three digits, literally like he'd grabbed a hot utensil off the barbecue.

It's not just the skin, he realized grimly. Any part of her could kill him.

Claudia was pretty tired of her co-workers having to fill out incident reports about how she'd gotten beaten up. But no one was razzing her about it, especially since she'd been able to tell them who it was and where the fucker worked. Surely the radio station would supply them with his address.

Another Sergeant told Claudia she could just go home, and they would continue with regular patrols past her building until they had Jasper in custody.

She packed her things, threw them in the trunk of her car, and beat feet back to her building. She had to tell Iola about Jasper, she had to warn her. But she didn't want to call her and scare her out of her mind.

It took just five minutes to get back to the building, and she parked in a visitor's stall, daring someone to ticket her. She had bags to carry upstairs, after all.

She shoved her way through the apartment door, dropping her bags where she stood, and let the door fall shut. She threw the dead bolt, then looked down at her things. She really didn't want to unpack all this crap –

Hands wrapped around her hips from behind, and she smiled, immediately recognizing Damien's smell as he nuzzled against her hair and neck. And she recognized the erection he pressed against her as well.

"Welcome home," he muttered, nipping at her earlobe.

"Mmmm. This is a very nice welcome."

"It's just getting started."

He turned her to face him so he could kiss her, and just as she was closing her eyes he suddenly blurted out, "What happened?"

Claudia backed off and put a hand to her face, wondering what he was seeing. Did she reactivate a bruise somewhere? Then she noticed her knuckles, how they'd been pulverized against Jasper's teeth.

"I got jumped," she said weakly.

"What? Who?"

"A guy got into my hotel room. But … I won."

"That's my girl. How'd you do it?"

She shrugged. "I just … lost it on him. I broke his nose, might have knocked some teeth loose."

He put his forehead to hers, a small private smile on those luscious lips of his. "That is so hot." She laughed, and he growled in response. "I mean it."

"Okay, I believe you. Actually," she freed one hand to pull the necklace up from the top of her shirt, the necklace he'd slid into her suitcase. "This thing really seemed to freak him out. I don't know if he's allergic to silver or what, but as soon as he touched it he was shrieking."

"It's not silver," Voro said quietly, dropping it back down the front of her shirt.

"Then what is it?"

"I'm not sure," he said evasively. "But I promise the guy wasn't a werewolf. So ... who was he? Did you know him?"

"Actually, I do." She was alarmed by the look of shock on his face.

"Who is it?"

"A guy Iola works with. I have to tell her, actually. Just to warn her."

"I think she went back to bed. The doctor left early this morning, and they didn't get much sleep last night."

Claudia raised an eyebrow as Damien licked his lips, then bent his mouth to kiss her neck.

"And what did you hear?"

Damien's breath tickled her skin as he chuckled. "I heard enough to make me wish I wasn't alone."

"Did she ... seem to enjoy it?"

Damien pulled back to give her a small, surprised smirk. "Claudia ... why would you ask that?"

"I'm curious is all."

"Should we try to reenact it?"

Claudia felt herself warm down below as his tongue flicked over her bottom lip. "We have to be quiet," she insisted, melting at his touch faster than ice cream at the beach. She shouldn't have been aroused at this point in time. She'd just been attacked, almost raped, she really shouldn't be ...

"I can be quiet," he whispered.

"Take me to bed," was her throaty reply.

"What the hell happened?" Essum snarled once they were inside and Jasper was pacing back and forth in his living room. He was late for work, and he was bleeding like crazy. But most of all, his hand was stinging like he'd shoved it in a vat of boiling fryer grease.

"She kicked the shit out of me," Jasper spat back, studying the burn mark on his hand. It looked like an animal's face, but what?

"How?"

Jasper just shook his head. "How the fuck should I know? She's ... she's really strong."

"She's a woman, and you have the power to crumple giants by using your fucking brain. What happened?"

Jasper took a deep breath. "She socked me right in the nose. Don't you see what she did?"

"Why didn't you get in her brain, just put her to sleep?"

Jasper stilled. He hadn't thought of that. In the heat of the fight his only thought had been to fuck her. He sighed and closed his eyes. "Shit. Shit. *Shit.*"

"What happened?"

"She was naked. I ... I got distracted. I wanted to fuck her."

Essum sighed, rubbing his face. "You moron."

"I know."

"You have the ability to fuck anything you lay your eyes on. All I needed you to do was bring me this one woman in one piece. Put her to sleep, make her catatonic, whatever. You could have even done her then, as long as you ended up bringing her to me."

"I know."

"Do you? Because this logic seems to be giving you some problems."

"I'm ... I'm sorry. Fuck."

Essum was quiet for a moment then he really shocked the shit out of Jasper. "It's okay. We can still get her, it just might be more tricky now. Don't worry." He was calm, not angry. What the hell?

Jasper touched the side of his nose carefully. "Is this going to be okay? I think it's broken."

"It is. Just straighten it out, it'll be fine."

"How do I do that?"

"Thumb on each side of the bridge, pop it back into place."

"Will it hurt?"

"Like a bitch. But you can't let it heal like that."

Jasper went to his bathroom, thankful Essum seemed to be staying put in the living room. Once he'd flicked the light on he studied his reflection with a grimace. His face was virtual hamburger meat. Claudia had beat the living shit out of him. His male ego wasn't hurt as much as his mental health. How had he let that happen? He'd had control, he could have put her under easily.

That other need won out, though. The damn sex. And her breasts ... God, they'd looked so good. They'd felt even better. Damn that bitch to hell.

Jasper moaned as he positioned his thumbs for the nose reconnection. It was starting to swell, and that couldn't be good. When he shoved back to the left he stopped breathing. Stopped everything.

Actually, he fainted.

Following their argument, as Jasper was going to the washroom to realign his nose, Essum had stayed in the living room until he began to get worried. Then he called out to Jasper through the bathroom door, but got no answer.

So Essum materialized through the door and found Jasper sprawled on the tile, dead to the world. Essum gave his brain a good mental goose, but all that did was make Jasper flinch in his sleep. Essum dug right into the subconscious and shook it to wake the bastard. Jasper's eyes eventually opened, and he looked tired. And very, very sick.

"What happened? I felt it when you got hurt." Essum kept his voice soft, because all of Jasper's mental activity was begging him to just leave him alone.

"I don't know. I can't ..."

Essum didn't sound mad, because he was actually worried that Jasper might be useless to him now. "Show me your hand."

Jasper let it flop upwards on the floor next to him. That's when Essum saw the burn on the inside of his palm, wrapping around to the back of his hand. The skin was red, wide open to the elements, and parts were turning black. It was as though he was shedding his epidermis, but there was nothing underneath.

Essum crouched in his physical form next to Jasper, catching the smell of burnt flesh ... and something else. The stink of fire and brimstone. Now *this* smell he knew.

"Was the woman wearing an amulet? Is that what did this to you?"

Jasper just nodded, swallowing a couple of times in quick succession. He obviously felt quite nauseous.

"Fuck." Now Essum was confused. He had no idea how to fix Jasper. He'd always worn the Oryx pendant when he'd been in human form. It was for their own protection against the forces of, well, good. And a *decipio*, no matter how tainted he or she may get, is still on the side of good. So the metal had burned Jasper. Essum knew it could lead to blood poisoning.

"You know her, right?"

Jasper might have been weak but he could follow the line of questioning. He nodded.

"Shit. We have to get you out of here."

"No," the moan was so weak Essum almost missed it.

"I need to get you somewhere where no one can find you. She got away, they'll come for you, and this is your known address. Now let me find us a place. I'll need your help, the longer we wait the weaker you'll be, and if you're in jail you very well may die there."

That got his attention. Jasper licked his lips, sighed, and then opened his eyes to focus on Essum. "There's a hotel, only ten minutes away. Let's get going before I pass out again."

Chapter Thirty-Four

Iola awoke feeling not herself. She had the shakes, and though she had an all-over body sweat she was totally freezing under all her blankets. She woke from fitful dreams that she couldn't recall, and her stomach was churning like she'd had bad seafood.

A look at the clock told her it was one in the afternoon. She'd been asleep for four hours.

She pushed the blankets back and stood, then sat back down on the side of the bed again. Her equilibrium was not on board with standing up that quick.

"What the hell?" She wiped the sweat from her forehead, and fought back the urge to throw up. How had she gotten so sick this quickly?

She waited for the floor to stop tilting and tried the standing thing again, taking it slower. Apart from the constant nausea that attempt worked and she made her way to the bathroom.

She started a hot bath, noting how weird it was to have goose bumps under a marathon-grade coating of sweat. She peeled off the T-shirt she'd fallen asleep in, letting it hit the floor in a damp flopping sound. Iola crawled into the tub before it was full, her body eased by the hot water pooling under her. Her eyes slid closed as the room started to swim again, and the only thing she heard was the water.

There was no one line of thought she could really follow. It seems eons ago that Vinnie had left. And she still couldn't be sure the episode with Damien in her kitchen was real. God, she hoped she'd imagined that.

She used her foot to turn off the taps once the water was sitting over her stomach. That made her feel warmer, but she was still shaking.

Overtop of trying to straighten out what she'd done in the past few hours, she was also wondering if she had any flu medication in the apartment. She would strangle a puppy for some Gravol at this point, as long as it would also knock her unconscious long enough for this to pass.

She got out of the tub while the water was still hot and the room was clouded with steam. The chills had subsided and she wanted it to stay that way. Iola wrapped herself in the terry cloth robe on the back of the bathroom door after drying herself off. She was short of breath by the time she toddled down the hall to her kitchen, and she went right for the cupboard where all her medicines were.

Iola took two Aspirin, two of the Gravol – even though it was expired - and washed the whole cocktail down with water from the tap. She hated the way the water tasted on her tongue ... it left a coating similar to wet dog or something equally gross.

To bed, she told herself. Call in sick to work and go to bed. She almost needed to stop and rest on the way back to the bedroom, but she pushed on, finally collapsing on top of the blankets. She caught her breath before rolling herself in her comforter, still wearing the thick robe. Iola waited impatiently for her exhaustion to get the better of her. Eventually it did, and she fell into a very deep and dark sleep.

Constable Trevor Vance looked up at the apartment building that was the last known address for Jasper McKay and set his jaw. There was already a team headed towards the doorway, wearing full flak jackets and helmets. It wasn't a SWAT operation really, but any guy that tries to attack a cop could be up to anything.

There was also the worry that he'd tried to get Sergeant Bauer in the daytime, when it was obvious to most people it would be easiest to get her in her sleep when she was vulnerable. Or maybe he just came upon her by chance, recognizing her car in the motel parking lot or something.

Vance always thought a cop that drives a flashy car was asking to get noticed when off-duty. He'd tried to get Claudia to trade it in for something that would blend but she refused. Whatever the "how" of the situation was, they had no idea what they were going to be dealing with once they got inside.

He heard through the radio as the door was kicked in, and he started up the stairs to the floor they were on, just in time to hear a constable say over the radio, "He's not here. But it sure fucking smells like death in here."

He was two doors down when he smelled it, and he wondered why the neighbors hadn't been complaining. If this was his building he would have been sure a dead body was next door, unrefrigerated for about three weeks.

He entered the apartment as the two guys with the door ram were leaving, covering his mouth and nose. He found himself immediately in the living room, which looked fine. Then he crossed through the kitchen, also fine, and came to a hallway where the smell intensified.

He dropped his hand long enough to tell a rookie to crack the patio doors open, then followed his nose. The stench was cloying and it wouldn't take much longer before he could taste it.

Remember to burn this uniform after this shift is done, he thought. At the bathroom door he stopped, flicked the light on and looked inside.

Jesus H. Christ ... what the hell?

The stink was worst here, and the room was splattered with a thick, blackish-red muck that was everywhere, mostly in the shower but also on the bathroom mirror, the countertop and floor.

He didn't want to go in. Every nerve in his body was telling him to run from it. So he went to the bedroom.

Same thing. The bed sheets were matted with the same putrid matter, though not as badly as in the bathroom. And it wasn't splattered here, it was like it had seeped out of something.

They weren't going to find a body here, he knew that much. Whatever this stuff was, it wasn't human.

"Okay, I really have to go tell Iola that she has to watch out for Jasper. And I mean it this time. I'm sure I heard the water running." Claudia sat up, but Voro pulled her back to him, cutting off any protests with a kiss, even though his lips felt bruised.

"In a minute," he conceded. He felt bad for it, but as soon as Claudia had gotten home he'd made sure to get her in the mood. The little session with Iola may have literally burned him –

which had healed about three minutes later – but it also left him a bit strung out and randy.

Even though she may not have been initially willing, a little mental coercion was all it took for him to get Claudia bent over the sofa with her legs wide. Once he was done he'd felt like a heel so he took her to her bedroom and had gone down on her for about twenty minutes.

"I'm going, and I'd advise you not to stop me," she said forcefully, which made his dick swell of course, but he let her get up and pull her clothes back on.

"I want to take you somewhere where you can walk around naked all day," he said, running a hand across his pecs as he watched her do up her bra and herd those gorgeous babies into their D-cups.

She shook her head and laughed silently, pulling her T-shirt back on. "Stay here. I will be right back."

"I'm not going anywhere." He pulled the sheet down to show her how willing he was to wait for her.

Claudia's face colored, which he thought was adorable, and she wordlessly left to go warn her neighbor.

Tuned into their orgasms, he thought when he began wondering where all the hearts and flowers were coming from. Whatever. He'd fulfilled the need and was feeling better.

Well, not *better*. He was still wishing he'd turned and walked away from Iola. He couldn't get in her mind to find out what she was thinking of him, either. It had been so incredibly fucking stupid. He was going to get himself killed.

The thought made his skin go cold, but his mind went blissfully calm. "Dead" and "killed" were terms that didn't really register with him of course, but since he'd been doing this for six hundred years it would *feel* like a death. Like Essum said after Daphne had caused his downfall.

That wasn't correct either. Daphne wasn't at fault for Essum. She'd merely been the bait. It was her fiancée that had done him in, all things considered.

Voro had felt no *sympathy* for Essum at the time. Sympathy was not right. He'd felt his own vulnerability. The good guys had created a chink in the armor. It could happen to any of them, and it had been happening for five hundred years. That was when the Boss had stopped the rotation, to regroup and rethink the Sin Eater model.

What if this wasn't Essum's idea? What if the Boss had fooled Essum into coming up with this whole scheme with the belief he was a raving genius?

What a dreamer, he scolded himself. *If the Boss wanted you out, you were just out.*

Voro froze. That was totally true. If the Boss really wanted Voro to report back for reassignment, He sure as hell wasn't going to rely on a mad plan from a jilted minion. He was going to grab Voro by the balls and call him Home.

Voro wasn't due to be retired. Essum just wanted to get through to this side.

Your brain is turning to mush, he was reprimanding himself again. *Took you long enough to figure that out. At least now you might have leverage over that fucking weasel.* Then he had another thought. *Wonder if the Boss is aware of what Essum is cooking up?*

That thought made him smile so wide his cheeks hurt.

Claudia rapped her knuckles three times on Iola's door and listened for the sound of approaching footsteps. The apartment was silent, so she knocked again. She felt bad if she actually was waking up her neighbor, but Iola needed to know about Jasper.

"Who is it?" The voice on the other side of the door was so sad and pitiful sounding, Claudia wondered if she had the right place.

"It's Claudia. Iola, honey, are you okay?"

Now she heard shuffling footsteps, and the door swung inward. At the sight of her usually beautiful neighbor, Claudia gasped. Iola looked terrible. Her skin was pasty, she had gruesome bags under her eyes, and she look like she needed sleep more than anything in the world.

"Iola? What's wrong?"

"I don't know." Iola rubbed her eyes, looking like a child suddenly in her large and fluffy bathrobe. "It's like I went to sleep and woke up with the flu."

"I'm sorry to disturb you, sweetie. But I had to warn you about something."

"Yeah?"

"Jasper attacked me at the motel this morning. I wanted you to know before you ran into him. Did you call work and tell them you were too sick to come in?"

Iola looked confused between the startling information and the question. "Jasper what? He what? No ... I haven't called work yet."

"Here, let me call for you." Just as Claudia was about to open the door more and step inside, Iola's eyes rolled up into her head and she fell forward.

"Holy shit - " Claudia caught her just in time, then strained to pick her up in her arms. She was able to lift her, and she turned back for her own apartment, bellowing Damien's name while catching Iola's door with her foot and kicking it back inward. She carried Iola down the dark hall to her room, where the curtains were drawn and the black-out blinds were blocking out all natural light. She turned the bedside lamp on after laying her friend out on her bed. Iola's skin was slick with cold sweat, and her teeth were chattering even though she appeared to be overheated. In front of Claudia's eyes she was turning pink.

Claudia heard Damien enter the room behind her. "What's wrong with her?" he asked softly and seriously. Claudia turned to him just in time to notice his eyes trailing over Iola's form, concern crowding his eyebrows together.

"I don't know. She fainted when she came to the door. Can you ... can you find her cordless phone and check for Vinnie on her call display, then call him? I don't know what to do here. I don't know if she needs to go to the hospital or not."

Damien nodded, then left the room, his face serious and looking out of place since he was only wearing jeans.

Claudia put her hand on Iola's forehead, and her skin felt very warm, too warm. Her breathing was shallow but being expelled in rapid-fire puffs. As Claudia watched Iola writhed on the bed, making a weird mumbling sound as she threw herself sideways, pulling at her robe and gnashing her teeth.

"What the hell ..." Claudia didn't want to hold her down, but she didn't want the poor thing to hurt herself either. The sounds coming out of Iola were horrible, dark-sounding, nothing Claudia had ever heard before. It could even be another language.

Iola's eyes opened, then fluttered shut again. She pushed her head to the other side of the bed, then gave a loud and low moan again before breaking off into the weird chanting. She arched her back, kicking her legs and thrashing around so her robe opened up.

"Hey, hey." Claudia tried to calm her with her voice, but Iola wasn't hearing anything. She pulled at the terry cloth, rolling in it, before Claudia was able to wrestle her arms out of the sleeves and pull it away from her. Since she was naked as a jaybird underneath, Claudia yanked the sheet up over her just as Damien came back into the room, talking into the phone.

"She appears to have flu symptoms, but it seems awfully severe,' he was saying as he came into the room. Just as he did, Iola let out a keening scream, gripping the edge of the sheet with both hands and pulling at it while her neck strained with the force of her hollering.

"Holy fuck," Claudia muttered, just as Iola threw the sheet back again, winding herself up in it as she continued the whole body-writhing ritual.

Damien was frozen as he watched her, and Claudia couldn't even get mad at him because Iola was naked. Her chanting was insistent and desperate, and she really wasn't herself.

"Let's leave her," Claudia said quietly, turning him out of the room and shutting the door. Damien lowered the phone as they stood in the hall.

"He'll be here in twenty minutes. Longer if there's a lot of traffic." Damien said quietly, and Claudia nodded.

"Thank you."

Claudia's worry for Iola must have been very obvious, because Damien wrapped his thick arms around her tightly, and she turned her face to the side to rest her cheek on his bare skin. His breathing was very steady, she could hear it echo through his thick chest. His pulse was an even thumping in her ear as well.

"Have you ever seen anyone that sick?" She asked, her voice small.

There was a pause as he rubbed circles on her back with his free hand. "No," he finally said. "Never that sick."

Claudia didn't know why, but she felt that if Damien had seen this before it would make her feel better. Which was ridiculous; after all, they had a doctor on the way.

Chapter Thirty-Five

Essum was worried about his protégé. He'd managed to get the guy checked into a hotel by convincing the clerk to charge it all to the credit card of the man that checked in ahead of them, and now Jasper was lying prone on the bed, covered in sweat and convulsing in apparent abdominal agony.

Essum was working without a script, and Jasper did not look good at the moment. All this work, waiting for the right time and the *decipio* was all fucked up.

How did one circumvent the effect of an unknown metal composite made up of unfiltered evil on the skin of a tool from the side of lightness and good? Fucked if he knew. This kind of thing wasn't online, and the Poison Control Centre wouldn't be much help, either.

Use your head, he thought. *What is pure and good ... something to heal a soul of heaven. Something untainted. Something to inspire Jasper to fulfill his ultimate destiny.* Although, he wasn't into the whole "recognizing your full potential" line of work. Essum's time on the planet had consisted of finding the worst dregs of society and cutting them off at the knees before sending them back to meet their makers. Not getting out his pom-poms and shouting "You can do it!"

Jasper started moaning loudly, and it took Essum a moment to pick out that he was moaning words in Latin, chanting an old incantation that took him back a few centuries.

"*Ego tribuo otium quod sileo iam ut tu carus vir. Adveho non eo ire itum vel in nostrum pratus. Quod pro thy pacis Ego pignus meus animus.* Amen."

Voro must have held that amulet back when he would say the words that would earn him a goblet of wine, a piece of bread and maybe even a meal. The Oryx was almost like a hand-held tape recorder crossed with a mind-melding telephone. It held memories the Sin Eater made a point of sending to it, and it could also transmit messages to other Sin Eaters, or just to the person or being that held the thing. Just like it probably helped the Claudia woman get rid of Jasper. Voro must have sent her a little extra Gatorade to get the job done, so to speak. And Jasper still needed to learn more self-control, which is the only reason the damn thing had worked in the first place. Essum had even had to use his once when he was being robbed in his human form ...

How had they gotten the better of him again? Oh yes. He'd just seen Daphne.

He rubbed his eyes. He had to stop thinking of her, but this incident had been the one that caused him he most pain. Not even her death had stung as much as seeing Daphne take the hand of the handsome man that had come to call on her at the request of her father. He was a strapping lad, dressed to the nines, smelling and speaking like the kind of man that should be with a lady as well-bred and perfect as Daphne.

In short, nothing like Essum. So of course, he wanted to kill the guy at first sight.

He was watching from the woods like a criminal, and Daphne took the young man on the same walk she'd had him on through their elegant gardens. But this young man stopped and invited her to sit with him a while on a stone bench. Their body language was welcoming to each other. She liked the looks of this man and he definitely liked the looks of her.

Essum was seething, even before this new lothario put his paw out, and Daphne took off her white glove before allowing her pale palm to touch his, allowing the man to kiss the back of that delicate hand. She watched him with great admiration as he did this, and he kept his lips to her skin for a moment longer than good manners would have allowed. This made her chest heave as she inhaled, and he looked up into those eyes. Those beautiful green eyes that Essum saw in the face of every woman he encountered after meeting her. The eye contact was hot, electric; he could feel the pull of it from where he stood, across the enormous garden.

His hands clenched into fists, he wanted to beat something to a pulp. The stuffy blow-hard in the sharp outfit would have been perfect. Essum was so mad he couldn't even get in the guy's head and make him do or say something so terrible that Daphne would bar him from the premises and her company for good.

But since he couldn't act, struck paralyzed by blinding anger, the couple continued on their walk to the front of the house where Daphne's mother met them and invited their guest in for afternoon tea.

Essum would have never been invited in for tea. Or allowed to call on their daughter. He wasn't good enough for her.

Funny, after all this time the thought still nearly had him in tears. But while distracted by that anger he'd been jumped by a group of four beggars that lived in those very woods where he'd been hiding. They took his pocket watch as they beat him, and it took him a moment to get his bearings. One had grabbed at the Oryx, and that's when his strength came back to him. He sent a jolt of hellfire through the chain, which made the man reel back and hit the ground unconscious. Essum could smell his flesh burning as the other three hit the dirt, writhing and holding their heads as he popped the tops off their internal common sense receptors, rendering them mentally incompetent for the rest of their lives. His damage went deep into gray matter when he was really pissed, and he showed those men no mercy whatsoever.

Now as he looked at Jasper, he thought he might have an answer to what could help him.

"Ego tribuo otium ... quod sileo iam ut tu ... carus vir. Adveho non eo ire itum... vel in nostrum pratus ... Quod pro thy pacis Ego pignus meus animus ... Amen."

Voro had to close his eyes against the mumbling of those words through Iola's bedroom door. It sounded like gibberish to Claudia, but he knew damn well what she was saying. God knows he'd said it plenty, too.

"I give easement and rest to thee, dear man. Come not down the lanes or in our meadows. And for thy peace I pawn my own soul. Amen."

Again, there were no instruction manuals or guides to dealing with this stuff. You were thrown in the water and told to swim, and Voro had no fucking idea what was going on. He knew it wasn't the flu, though, because for the first time, he smelled evil coming from Iola. Not through something she'd done, but it was osmosis, maybe? Something else stained her.

Voro thought back to the guy that had attacked Claudia, and how his skin had burned at contact with Voro's Oryx amulet. It was made with metal not found above ground, or anywhere below it. It came from the same place Voro did, and apparently it stung anyone that wasn't human, or wasn't like Voro.

So if this Jasper guy was the *decipio* he was linked in many ways to Iola, since the *decipio* and *frustro* were paired up, could one of their contacts be a mental link that transferred his pain to her?

Maybe. Even though that seemed awfully unfair. The *decipio* was the bad guy here ...

Voro rubbed his forehead and kept an arm around Claudia as they walked down Iola's hallway to the living room. He was an idiot. The *decipio* wasn't the bad guy, *he* was. He kept forgetting. And if his amulet had caused this, he wouldn't be able to live with himself –

"Hey, are you okay? I hope there's not something really nasty going around this building," Claudia said as he swayed on his feet. She stopped so he could gather himself together.

Claudia worried about him; he read it from her mental blueprint. How strange to have someone actually concerned for him. He hadn't felt this in, well, six hundred years.

She helped him ease down onto Iola's sofa, and as they did so, they were enveloped in the scent of jasmine and vanilla, and Voro had to close his eyes at the heady assault. He was getting that chest ache again, and he knew this one was born from concern for his *frustro*. The being that was created only to destroy him.

Voro pulled Claudia to his chest, dropping an arm across her shoulders. She snuggled into his side without complaint, letting her eyes close as she warmed him. He let his mind slide into Claudia's for just a moment, and her sense of security and happiness and contentment were so comforting. Maybe it would help him think if he could just hop into a happy, balanced mind.

Before long, he realized Claudia had dozed off on his chest, her breathing soft and steady on his skin. He watched her face, slack in its relaxed state, looking a couple years younger without any stress or worry to deepen any lines that might be there. It struck him again how truly beautiful she was. He stroked her dark hair, as much a comfort to him as it might be to her.

That's when he heard a noise in the hall, and he raised his head, his heart thrusting against his chest wall suddenly as he realized he was looking at Iola, naked in the hallway. Her eyes looked lucid but she couldn't be. She was staring at him, unaware she had nothing on. That surely couldn't be normal behavior.

He said nothing. He just stared at her, taking in her thin legs, her flat stomach, her long and delicate arms, her sleek neck. Her small but perky breasts. He wanted to take her. He needed to stand up, walk to her and penetrate her right where she stood. Roughly, animalistic.

He blinked, and she took a step closer. That's when he smelled the chocolate.

She still wasn't talking, and now that he noticed, she hadn't blinked once yet, either. He eased Claudia to the arm of the sofa, not even having to convince her to stay sleeping. She was exhausted.

He stood and walked to Iola, who looked up at him with wide eyes and parted lips, expectant. His brain was screaming at him to stop, this was a trap, this might kill him and then Essum would win. But his cock was also leading the way, and it was much, much louder.

He reached out to put a hand to her shoulder, and waited. Nothing. No burning, no stinging.

Holy hell. Whatever was wrong with her, it was clouding the transmission to protect her from him. He didn't doubt really why he had that figured out so quickly, but another part of him was screaming at him to get inside her.

He put a hand to each side of her face, the skin so tender it made him want to cry. She kept those eyes on him, and even though he knew she had no idea what was happening to her he nearly kissed her.

He wanted to. Satan's Wrath, how he wanted to taste her. This touch alone made him believe he could stroke her tongue with his own, maybe even more. But he dropped his hands from her, leaned back.

Her eyes were vacant. Those beautiful, eerie green eyes looked at him as though he could have been any man and she would have behaved this very same way.

As he broke contact she moaned, trying to push against him again. He held her back by the arms, trying to be tender, even as she was licking her lips and gnashing her teeth at him.

Holy shit. Iola was definitely not home at the moment.

There was a knock on the door, and the animal in him was ready to fly to the portal, confront who was there and take their head off with his bare hands because his body was still dying to appease her. But when he caught a whiff of pure worry and concern wafting from under the door a proverbial bucket of ice was dumped on his back, because it was her doctor on the other side of that door.

Iola grabbed his hair in two fistfuls, trying to put him back to work, but he took her wrists in his hands, then let go, lest the burning start again. When she rose up on tiptoe to try to kiss him he caught her hands again, holding her at a safe distance.

"Go to bed," he said softly, and as he did so, something flickered in her eyes. Like she'd tuned back in. Or just woken up.

He could smell her confusion now. She was likely wondering why he was here. And then she realized she didn't have anything on.

She covered her breasts, and she started to panic. In her confusion she also knew she was aroused, and she didn't know where that had come from, either. But his presence was only making it worse. So she darted back down the hall.

He took a moment to rearrange himself in his jeans. He wasn't wearing a shirt, so that might be interesting to try and explain, but whatever.

Voro opened the door, and when Veneratio looked up at him in confusion and hurt, Voro felt like the biggest asshole ever.

"We met earlier," he reminded Vinnie lamely without further greeting.

Vinnie just nodded, and Damien stepped aside to let him in. As he closed the door he was saying, "She's in her room. We were hoping she'd fall asleep but ..."

He didn't finish, because as soon as the doctor was through the door he was down the hall and closing Iola's bedroom door behind him.

Voro went back to the living room and looked down at Claudia. He couldn't touch her right now. He had Iola all over him, and it felt beyond dirty to put his hands on Claudia. He went to the kitchen sink to wash his hands with dish soap. He couldn't be sure that awful burning wouldn't start again after a few moments.

Claudia murmured in her sleep, and Voro dried his hands and returned to her side. She cuddled up to him immediately, sighing as she fell into place without waking in the least.

Fuck him. He was such an asshole.

Chapter Thirty-Six

The Aztecs used to worship Tlazolteotl, the earth and mother goddess, the mother of child birth. She was also called the "eater of filth," a goddess that appeared to a dying man to cleanse his soul of sins after he confessed to them. The superstitions of the dying were the same no matter what part of the world you came from. And Essum couldn't help but wonder what Tlazolteoltl would have been like. He bet he would have liked her an awful lot.

If his dear Jasper had indeed been injured by the product of Essum's world, Essum thought it stood to reason that he could be healed by the product of his own world. But that didn't mean prayer and holy water and psalms from a collection of short stories. That meant he needed to provide the one thing that only Jasper's Boss could truly find: forgiveness, a releasing of evil that the other, dark half couldn't have.

So in short, Essum needed Charlie back.

As he ghosted his way through the police department, he was also on the lookout for any sinners in that group. There were plenty of "bad guys" on the police force, Essum was well aware of that as soon as he misted through the door. But as far as a true sinner? Not that he could sense. He'd have to keep looking.

Charlie was in a cell on his own, lying on the bottom bunk, facing the wall. He didn't even stir as Essum touched his brain with a gentle, *Charlie ... wakey wakey!*

Not so much as a mental flinch. Essum would have frowned if he'd been fixed in this world.

Charlie ... get up. Master needs you.

Nothing but the equivalent of a telepathic *Fuck off* sighed in response.

Get your ass up. You want to rot in jail?

Charlie sighed, then sat up. "I don't want to go anywhere."

Jasper is sick. He needs your help.

That brought Charlie's head back up. "And he'll make it go away after? Like before?"

That's right. He needs to forgive you, Charlie. That's the only way he can feel better. So we've got some work to do.

Charlie sighed and pushed his hands through his bed-head 'do roughly. "Okay. But no more sex. I don't want to do that anymore."

There was a loud laugh from the cell next door. "Good luck with that, sweet cheeks."

Charlie ignored the other arrestee, and Essum actually felt proud of the guy for a minute. *You just need to clean up some filth, no one ever said you had to fuck anyone, Charlie.*

Charlie pulled himself to his feet. "Okay."

Essum used his mind to unlock the cell door, and Charlie stepped forward when the door slid to the side far enough to let him out.

The loud-mouthed neighbor saw Charlie walk past and was at the bars in an angry instant, mouthing off loudly. "What the hell, man? Whose dick do I have to suck to get out of here whenever I feel like?"

Charlie stopped in the corridor outside the other man's cell, and turned to him slowly. Essum studied his little murderer's face, shocked at the cold calm that was staring out of his grey eyes. Charlie blinked once, twice, and the man backed off, returning to his bunk, keeping a wary eye on the crazy person on the opposite side of the one-and-a-half inch iron bars. Essum could smell the man's relief to have those bars between him and Charlie. Essum decided to let the guy keep the memory of the 90-pound weakling that stared him down. That seemed like a pretty good punishment for being an annoying asshole.

Charlie kept walking, knowing the way out by heart by this point. Essum followed invisibly, feeling something like pride. This must be how parents felt.

Iola's nightmares consisted of fire, flames that licked up as high as she could see. She felt as though she was underground, somewhere dark where no one could find her, and she was so alone. So scared and completely alone. It was making her remember every bad deed she'd ever done. Like cutting off Mary

Futello's braid in the third grade just because she hadn't been invited to Mary's birthday party. Like she deserved this terrible punishment for something so silly.

Or dating her friend Terry Minter's ex-boyfriend. Why had she done that? It was so stupid. Why would she do something so terrible?

Then she saw Damien. And the fire didn't seem to bother him. Actually, he was completely at ease in this terrible place. It stilled her mind, she stopped thinking about pushing her smaller cousin down a couple of steps at her grandparent's house because she'd been jealous of the attention the younger girl was getting. Damien made everything okay.

His eyes on her were like a soft, caressing touch. No, that wasn't accurate. It was like he was mauling her as he was looking at her, his big hands insistent, demanding, and promising. It was like he was making a meal out of the very sight of her.

Her breathing got heavy. Sweat popped out on her skin, and that's when he walked to her. The need to be under him was burning brighter than all the hellfire around them. His large body made the infinite darkness smaller, his eyes bringing hers to him, focusing her attention.

The world got totally silent. And dark. It was her and him, nothing else.

This was just a dream, right? This wasn't real. So she brushed against his bare skin with her own, delighted to see how those beautiful eyes flared with desire.

Just a dream. No consequences. And no one could hold your dreams against you. Could they?

And when he stopped her, she cried out in frustration, trying to keep him with her, focus him back to her.

Someone said her name. Her eyes flew open.

She was in her hallway. She felt sick. She was completely naked, and Damien had hold of her wrists. And she was on fucking fire in more ways than one.

The next thing Iola knew she was covering her head with her blankets, trying to push her thoughts away, hiding from them. Two nasty dreams about the guy in one day was bad enough. But the fact that she couldn't be sure she was dreaming was infinitely more worrisome.

This was the worst fever she'd ever had. Christ, was she dying?

"Iola," a voice came again, and all she could do was moan in response. If she was dying, she wanted to do it alone. Just leave her to pass away, let her fall asleep and not wake up.

But then the dream came back. That wouldn't be passing away peacefully and quietly. Something was very wrong here.

"Iola? Honey, please talk to me. Look at me."

Some part of her turmoil stilled slightly. Now this voice she knew. She was trying to connect this voice to the person. It had to be Vinnie.

The blankets were pulled off her head, and she looked over her shoulder at him. Shit. She was still dreaming, her walls were on fire, the paint peeling back, igniting the drywall, all of it curling in blood-red embers. It was only black underneath. He was going to burn.

She tried to push at him, tried to tell him to get away, but he held her hands away easily. Iola's strength was totally sapped, but she didn't stop trying to shove him away, somewhere safe from her and this God-awful place she was stuck in.

He held her hands down at her sides, pushing her on to her back. Iola was pinned by the arms, his body holding her in place as he leaned sideways over her. Iola tried to focus on his face, but he seemed totally unaware that the room was burning down around them. And once the room was gone, there could only be deep, cold darkness. He didn't seem to get it.

"You have to get out of here," she was panting. "Please, save yourself and get out."

"Iola? Tell me what's happening. I want to help you. What can I do to ease you?"

She squeezed her eyes shut, craning her neck backwards. *What can I do to ease you?*

Damien had been about to ease her a whole hell of a lot, that much she knew. At the very thought a jolt of intense need and pressure shot through her very core, and she became aware that she was still naked, hot, and under a male.

"Iola? What should I do?"

She opened her eyes, focusing now on the face that was in front of her. He was so beautiful. He couldn't possibly be in this place with her. Could he?

"What should I do?"

"Fuck me," she mumbled, and he didn't hear her clearly.

He lowered his head. "What was that?"

"Fuck me," she hissed, latching on to his lips, biting the bottom one when he tried to pull back.

He cried out as she bit him, pulling away. She could taste his blood on her lip.

"Iola, I ... I can't." He was flustered. And something else.

Scared. She was scaring the shit out of him.

When he eased up on his hold, she grabbed his shoulders with sudden, surprising strength, yanking him against her bare skin. She forced her lips to his, not waiting to penetrate his mouth with her tongue. One hand had him by the hair now, and he was trying to pull away again ... but just for a moment he hesitated, even maybe responding to her.

She pushed her hands at his crotch, finding his pants were in the way. She tied to undo them, and he caught her hands again, pushing them away and breaking contact with her lips. She groaned in frustration, trying to turn away from him, but he held her in place.

Iola could sense he wanted her, but he was doing the right thing. Still, his eyes on her were hungry and wanting. Desiring.

"Fuck me," she repeated under her breath, but he shook his head, his eyes moving up from her breasts to her face.

"I need to ... try something. Just please ... be still. Then I'll ... fuck you." He had to swallow before he said it. "I promise. But let me try something."

She stopped pushing at his hold, watching him intently. He let go of one of her hands, bringing his palm to her forehead. She watched his hand as it passed over her face, and when his palm flattened itself on her skin, she sighed. Her eyes slid closed.

His hand was so cool, so gentle. It broke the fever she suffered through instantly. The burning on her skin was fading outwards from his touch. Iola felt the air get thinner, easier to breathe, and her gasping stopped. Her pulse calmed, her muscles stilled, and the demanding ache between her legs ceased. Even her toes relaxed.

"Iola?" The voice was worried and tentative, and she opened her eyes, Vinnie's face coming into focus very slowly.

She exhaled shakily, the sight of him like a glass of water. The world wasn't burning, she wasn't headed for oblivion. Her room was back to normal, her heart no longer raced. Everything was so *calm*.

"Are you okay?"

She nodded, and for some inexplicable reason she started to sob. She shouldn't feel this clean. What could she have possibly done to deserve it?

Vinnie took his hand from her head, and as her bawling became more violent he gathered her up in his arms, hugging her to his chest, stroking her back and her hair, mumbling nonsense designed to make her feel better.

"You're okay. I got you. Nothing to be scared of. I got you."

Charlie was staring into the face of the man whose life was leaving his eyes like receding headlights on a highway. The man's look was pleading with him to not kill him, to let go of his throat, call and ambulance and leave him so he can be saved.

The Master was in Charlie's head, though, overriding any pity that Charlie might have felt. The Master was telling him how this man was a lot like Charlie, how he had to hurt people to feel good. And this guy liked to hurt and then kill very young girls.

But Charlie felt no victory strangling a man who was basically paralyzed. The Master had rendered him incapable of fighting back, and all Charlie had to do was crush his throat, deny air any access to the man's lungs, and in doing so, end this skuzzy, filthy and pathetic life.

All Charlie really cared about was that warm, glowing feeling of relief that the new Master would provide for him. That was the carrot at the end of the stick.

The man's esophagus gave out completely right then, Charlie felt the tube crunch as his thumbs bit into the man's thick neck, like a grape under his opposable digits. *Thrunch.* Gone. Not a tube anymore, just a busted pipeline. He would surely die now unless someone found him in time to get him to a hospital.

But Charlie knew they couldn't leave until the man was definitely dead. He was only ever allowed to leave when the truth of what he had done was hung on him like a shroud, a heavy robe that made his shoulders curve inward and his head hang lower as though it was weighted. He knew that the Master needed the wickedness on him for some reason. And now the need to have the evil stripped off him was a very heavy addition indeed.

Charlie had never felt as though he was inheriting anything other than his own act. But with this man ... The foul essence Charlie felt was seeping into him, too, making his thoughts darker. More putrid than anything Charlie had felt on his own.

This man had done things that no Master was telling him to do. Things he'd just wanted to do all on his own. But unlike Charlie, the man hadn't wanted their fear. He'd only wanted to ruin them. They were clean, pure, and he wanted to be invariably the one that took that all away from them.

Charlie felt sick at the thought of some of the stuff the Master was saying to him about this victim. Because the more he heard, the more he felt like he was taking on responsibility for the short, husky man he held by the throat. Maybe, just maybe, the new Master could take this all away too, shake it off of Charlie and make all the nastiness disappear.

He hoped so. This was evil that even Charlie wanted gone for good.

When the man was no longer breathing, and felt eerily still in his hands, Charlie let the heavy weight fall, and realized he'd started crying. Must have been one of the stories the Master had been telling him about this piece of breathing garbage at his feet. All the little girls that this guy had sought out to taint, and then when he realized what he'd done, he'd made them disappear. For a while, anyway.

Charlie didn't want to know about the terrible things people did to children. It made him remember too many things.

Come now Charlie, I know what will make you feel better.

"The new Master?" His voice broke with all the hope in it.

That's right. Jasper will take it all away. Don't keep him waiting. This will make him feel better, too.

Chapter Thirty-Seven

Claudia sat next to Damien on Iola's sofa, waiting for word from Vinnie. They couldn't really hear what was going on in the bedroom, but as soon as Claudia recognized the sound of sobbing she wanted to jump to her feet and run in there.

Damien took her hand as though she'd telegraphed her intent, and she stayed where she was. He seemed to know that nothing bad was going on in there.

Claudia relaxed back into the cushions, rubbing her eyes. When Damien had woken her up she'd been having the kind of dream that you know is just an unconscious recounting of something that actually happened to her, manifesting itself in a different way. Claudia had images of people in filmy, black cloaks of some kind, trying to grab her. She fought them with everything she had, but every time she hit air she only disturbed the cloudiness of their clothes, which always melded back to together as though she hadn't even touched them.

Creepy as hell.

Damien had woken her by sliding into the sofa next to her, saying he'd just gotten up to answer the door. Then he'd told her the doctor had arrived, and they'd sat wordlessly ever since.

"Should we leave?" she finally asked quietly, feeling worse than useless by this point.

Damien shrugged his shoulders, putting an arm along the back of the sofa behind her. "We should wait for the doctor. He might want you to stay here and make sure she's taken care of."

"Why just me?"

Damien shook his head, smiling as he pushed her hair over her shoulder. "I don't think he wants another male in the apartment."

Claudia frowned. "What did you do?"

"I didn't do anything. He's just protective of her. I mean, I answered the door without a shirt on."

Claudia put her head on his chest, chuckling. "Men are so stupid."

"Yes. Yes they are."

She gave him a jibe in the ribs. "That means you, too."

"You think I'm stupid?" His tone was teasing, which made her smile. "There are many things I may not know about, but I think you are well aware that there is plenty that I do know a lot about." His hands were drawing circles on her back in a lazy, casual way, but as his voice dropped low and suggestive like that the touch suddenly became very ... sensual.

"Damien ... what are you doing?" She said teasingly, and his hand came to her arm, running up and down the bare skin there.

"What makes you think I'm doing anything?"

His voice was rumbling low in his chest, and it was rumbling in a lower part on her body, too. She raised her face to his, meeting lips that were already headed for her. He pulled her higher up on his chest, forcing his tongue into her mouth as she wrapped her arms around his shoulders.

They were interrupted by a throat being cleared in the hallway, and they flew apart like teenagers in their parent's basement.

Poor Doctor Aubericus looked uncomfortable, but he smiled anyway as they stood and straightened out their clothing.

"She should keep resting," he said immediately, and Claudia nodded. "Call her work and excuse her for tonight and tomorrow night. If you wouldn't mind staying here to make sure she doesn't get ... that way again, I'd really appreciate it. I'll come over once my shift is done."

"What was it? What happened? And how'd you make it stop?" Claudia blurted it all out at once.

Vinnie shrugged and sighed. "All I can think of is that she had a severe fever and that it just broke, very suddenly. I don't know where it came from, but ... she seems to be over it. She's asleep."

"Okay. I'll stay here," Claudia offered without hesitation.

Vinnie nodded, adding on, "Just make sure to let her sleep." His eyes flicked over to Damien, and Claudia felt the testosterone flood the room suddenly like she was front row at a cage match. Shit, Vinnie didn't trust Damien around his woman in the least. Even with her here.

"Can she eat?" Claudia was trying to discourage any cock fights before they broke out.

"Definitely. But you know, nothing too complicated. Soup broth, that's about it. As long as she rests. She needs her strength."

Claudia nodded and followed Vinnie to the apartment door. "I'll make sure she stays in bed. Ah, resting, that is."

Vinnie nodded, then looked at his feet as he opened the door. Claudia knew that look. It usually meant someone was going to say something she wasn't going to like. But to give the Doc credit, he said it anyway, not giving a crock if he offended her. "That guy. He ... he gives me a bad feeling. Make sure he doesn't hurt her."

This guy cared more for Iola than Claudia could have imagined. She loved him right then. She loved him because he was perfect for the woman that Claudia cared about most.

"Iola will be fine, I swear it." Her voice was honest and unwavering, and when Vinnie looked her in the eyes, he knew it. He nodded his thanks and left without another word.

When Claudia shut the door she felt a great kinship growing between herself and Vinnie. Neither of them wanted to see Iola hurt.

Jasper was annoyed when he heard the door open, but relieved that Essum didn't turn the light on. The digital numbers on the clock were throwing enough light to make his temples pound. He felt like death-by-dog-shit, overheated in the microwave.

Then he smelled Charlie. The guy stunk like garbage again, which made Jasper's stomach roll. But he sensed something else that pulled at him, made him sit up even though the room tilted like a psychotic ride at the fair.

"Charlie needs you to eat the sin he just committed," Essum said, matter-of-factly, and Jasper reached out to turn the bedside lamp on.

Charlie stood next to his bed, looking at him with eyes that were hopeful. And at peace.

Something was different about Charlie. But it didn't matter. He needed to get rid of whatever was troubling the guy because the smell was going to make him throw up.

Charlie ducked his head down so that Jasper could reach him better, but even that was too much work. After a moment's hesitation, Charlie slid on to the bed with him, stretching out next to Jasper so that he could lie down and touch him.

Okaaay. Even as sick as he was, Jasper was a bit weirded out by a guy crawling into bed with him. But the same pull that made him wake up when Charlie first entered the room made him now roll on to his side and put his hand on Charlie's head. He found the murder easily, since it was the newest file in Charlie's sick repertoire. But there were almost subfolders there, stuff with girls no older than about eight, sick, degenerate shit he could almost taste in his mouth. It made him dry heave.

"What is this?" Jasper gasped, taking it all and erasing it. "This isn't Charlie. Who did this?"

Essum's voice worked through their internal speaker systems. We killed a real sinner today. So Charlie inherited what the man had done. This was like a double sin-eating in one.

Jasper wanted to give Essum shit for not giving him a warning at least, but he stopped because the nausea was now gone. Jasper sat up, and the room didn't shift in front of him. He shook his head, and his equilibrium remained intact.

You're here for salvation, Jasper. That's the only thing that could heal you.

Jasper checked out his hand. The burning had stopped, and the wound looked pink again. Not black and rotten. It was healthy flesh.

Oh, thank fuck.

Thank Charlie, Essum corrected him. *He doesn't seem to enjoy his part in our little deal any more. He didn't want to help at first.*

Well, Jasper had to admit he could understand that. The stuff Essum made the guy do was deplorable, and if Charlie was getting his stones back that could only be a good thing.

Charlie took Jasper's hand and choked on a sob. "Thank you," he said. "I'll do as I'm told, as long as you always … make it go away. I swear I'll do as I'm told."

Jasper patted his hand, nodding, and easing Charlie's grip off of him. "It's okay, Charles. I swear I'll make you better if I can."

Charlie collapsed in relief, his head resting on Jasper's lap.

What the hell?

Essum smiled down at the two of them. "That's so cozy. I think he likes you."

Jasper just shot Essum a look that was meant to convey that he should shut the fuck up.

"I mean, *like* likes you."

Jasper just looked down at Charlie, feeling something like pity in his chest. The poor guy's brain was going to be Swiss cheese soon. A part of him wanted to help Charlie. But *how*?

"I'll leave you two alone for the time being. Let him stay here. After all, he is wanted by the police."

Jasper nodded, knowing Charlie wasn't hearing Essum anyway. Then Essum vanished into thin air, and Jasper was left with a homicidal maniac napping on his lap.

Iola rolled over on to her opposite side, sighing as she realized how comfortable the bed was. She was never going to get up ...

The nightmares came back suddenly, and her eyes flew all the way open, making her gasp as she nearly sat up in shock. Which she would have done, if she hadn't been so weak.

Man, had Vinnie really come to check on her? Had she been that out of it? She'd done something else, too. Something she really shouldn't have done but it was like trying to pick color out of an oil spill on top of water. It was there, just unattainable.

Or it was just part of the nightmares?

She rolled over to the other side, trying out a stretch to see how it affected her. Turns out it was exactly what she needed; it felt wonderful.

Maybe she could try standing after all. She still felt achy like someone had pushed her down the stairs then backed a tank over her. Iola sat up very cautiously, and a headache kicked in immediately, but it wasn't as bad as she was expecting. She realized then she was naked, and the thought that Vinnie had been here when she was nude and out of it made her blush. But she trusted him.

Iola stood on wobbly legs and picked up the terry cloth robe from the floor where she must have dropped it. She wrapped it around herself tightly then became aware of voices in the living room.

Frowning, she eased the bedroom door open and padded quietly down the short hallway to her living room. Damien was sitting on her sofa, tossing a deck of cards back and forth between his hands like a blackjack dealer. He was looking up at Claudia when Iola entered the room, and as those purple-greyish eyes fell on her she had a moment of recollection. Of him looking at her, wanting her. Touching her. But that hadn't happened. Had it? These dreams she'd been having were just too damn vivid.

Then his eyes flashed with something else: utter alarm.

Claudia flipped her phone shut and spun around with a slightly disappointed look on her face. When she saw Iola, the look dissolved into immediate concern.

"Iola? Honey – you okay?" Claudia put a hand to her arm, and Iola just smiled.

"I feel ... much better. What time is it?"

Claudia was looking at her like something just wasn't computing. "Well ... that's good. But you were ... you were incredibly sick. I thought you had brain-fry from a fever. But you're ... okay? Already?"

Iola frowned. "Why? How long was I out for?"

Claudia looked at the watch on her wrist. "Less than an hour."

Damien got to his feet, which of course they both noticed. "If Iola's feeling better, we should let her rest. We'll let the doctor know, and he said he'd be coming by after work anyway."

Claudia frowned up at him, then looked back at Iola. "Well ... okay. I have to check in with work about Jasper anyway."

Now it was Iola's turn to be alarmed. "What about Jasper?"

"Oh, you were out of it when I told you the first time. He came after me. At my motel, although we have no idea how he knew where I was."

"Oh my God, Claudia. Are you okay?" She wrapped her arms around her friend. "Oh my God, I'm so sorry!"

Claudia gave a dry laugh and patted Iola's back in return. "It's okay, I was able to fight him off, and he ran away. Some of the guys were going to check out his apartment but I haven't heard anything. I'm assuming that means he wasn't there."

Iola gave her a final squeeze and backed off. "I had no idea he had it in him."

"He didn't, as it turns out," Damien said from behind them, his voice seeming incredibly low all of a sudden.

Claudia patted Iola's shoulder. "That was your work I was just talking to. They'll find a replacement tonight and tomorrow night, so feel free to take it easy."

Iola yawned and covered her mouth. "I don't know, I feel a bit weak, but I mean ... I'll likely be better tomorrow."

"No pressure, they're not expecting you." Claudia looked at Damien over Iola's head. "Let's leave Iola to get her rest, hey?"

Damien was silent, and Iola turned to see him nodding. When he caught her gaze, he nodded a bit formally to excuse them, but as he did so he licked his lips.

Iola felt the slightest wisp of pleasure slide up between her legs, and her lips parted to exhale in surprise. As he passed her to follow Claudia to the door, it may have been her imagination, but he seemed to wink.

When they were gone and she was standing alone in her apartment, she felt a bloom of warmth all over her skin. Like she'd done something very, very shameful. She was incredibly embarrassed all of a sudden, as though she'd been called to the front of the class to tell everyone she'd been bad.

The only trouble was she had no idea what she'd done.

Chapter Thirty-Eight

When Jasper was toweling off after his shower, he was feeling almost back to his normal self. The burn on his hand looked no worse than if he'd accidentally touched a hot pot on a stove, and it was healing bloody fast. His head was clear, his stomach was staying put for the time being, and he felt fucking fantastic. Invincible, even. Especially since he'd just washed all that stale sweat off his carcass.

He pulled back the shower curtain while wrapping the towel across his hips, and when he saw Charlie standing in front of the sink he jumped, shrieking not unlike a girl and almost falling over the edge of the tub. The fact that Charlie was totally naked took about ten more seconds to register.

"Charlie?" Jasper tightened the towel around his waist unnecessarily; it was still firmly in place.

"You have been very kind to me," Charlie mumbled, head down. Jasper stood stock-still, even when Charlie started to touch himself. "I know people aren't just nice for no reason. If you want me to ... do anything ... you can ask me."

Jasper tore his eyes away from what Charlie was doing to look at himself in the bathroom mirror. Yep, he was shocked and more than a little grossed out. At least that was normal.

"Charlie, please stop that. Don't - "

"I can touch you. Or I can suck on it. I don't care. Sometime people used to want me to just touch myself ... like this. It's just to thank you."

What. The. Fuck?

Jasper shook his head, squeezing his eyes shut. "Charlie, please stop it. Don't ... just put your clothes on, man. Please."

Charlie stopped stroking at himself, thank God, but when he let his dick go it stood out straight, half-erect and all the more pitiful because of the look on Charlie's face. "I'm not unworthy, Jasper."

Jasper closed his eyes again, dragging his hands across his face. He was so going to need another shower. "Charlie ... I don't do anything because I want something from you. Okay? We're both just doing what Ess – the Master says. We just have to trust in him."

"I've been with the master for much longer than you. And I never got rewarded before."

"Charlie, please. I don't want ... that. And it's not because you're unworthy. I just ... I like girls, okay?"

Charlie was nodding when Jasper opened his eyes again, and he leaned down to pull his underwear back on. As he did so, Jasper caught a flash from Charlie's brain, the shame of the memory so intense Jasper couldn't ignore it.

Charlie had been raped as a child, Jasper caught it as surely as if it had been his own reminiscence. It was a family friend that had done it, a man Charlie's parents had known for a long time. Jasper could smell the man's sweat and nearly-expired cologne, and he could feel not only the pain but the fear and shame.

Jasper had to hang his head. The poor guy was so much more screwed up than Jasper had expected. No wonder he heard voices.

That's when Jasper felt honest, true rage towards Essum for the first time. This guy wasn't just a nut, he was a victim. And Essum was taking advantage of the effects of his whole fucked-up situation.

Charlie had tried to tell his mother what had happened, she hadn't believed him. She'd told him he was bad, she's slapped his bare bottom with a wooden spoon to straighten him out. And Charlie thought that even though she denied it, his mom believed him. She knew it had all happened. And she'd chosen to blame Charlie for the whole thing. Charlie was probably right.

Jasper stepped out of the shower, and Charlie sat on the floor in front of the vanity, curled up tightly into an alarmingly small ball. His arms and legs were impossibly thin twigs. He looked so very young right then.

Jasper put a hand on Charlie's shoulder, and the shaking under his hand told him Charlie was trying not to cry and doing a terrible job of it. At the contact, Charlie's remaining sordid life came to him in a fast flood of horrific images. A small teenager on the street, easy prey for thugs, whores with aspirations to be thieves, and the cops. He'd been picked up a few times, beaten, and thrown back to the curb. Men beat him and took what few valuables he might have had on him. And more sadistic bastards that wanted to humiliate and rape him under the guise of friendship.

Yeah, this all made sense now.

Jasper pulled all the memories together, bundled up like the sloppy mess that it was, and just sent Charlie one thought, *None of these things are your fault.*

Charlie sniffed, raising his puffy red eyes to Jasper. "What?"

Jasper nodded as if to show that Charlie knew very damn well what he was talking about. "It's not your fault. And I'm sorry this all happened. But none of it is your fault. Do you believe me?"

Charlie was deathly still, as though the act of breathing was too much exertion for him. The only movement was in his eyes, imploringly searching Jasper's face for a punch line. But there was nothing. Jasper thought it at Charlie again: *It's not your fault.*

Charlie's sob was like a bellow, and it was so explosive it broke Jasper's heart. He found himself wrapped up in the man's small arms, Charlie's thin chest trembling against his own as he wept with thankfulness and misery and shame.

Jasper patted his back, letting him cry. How he was able to feel pity for Charlie was a mystery, but he felt it all the same, even *if* the guy had homicidal tendencies. Which were all the work of Essum, come to think of it.

Charlie without Essum? Well, that was a totally different situation, wasn't it?

Voro went to Claudia's to get fully dressed then immediately begged off, saying he had business to take care of. The truth was he had to get the hell out of that building and back to doing what he was supposed to.

He came across an old lady coming out of the drug store who had slowly poisoned her husband to death only a couple years before. He pulled her into an alley and pulled the stink of that sin out of her failing little mind, and when she left the alley she had the glow of a clear conscious that he could only envy.

No one was taking away what he'd nearly done to Iola.

The next street over brought him to a young man of about twenty, who had been raping his little cousin for the past couple of years. Same thing. Voro ate that sin, set the man's mind free to go and do it again. That one was difficult to let go, but he did. It wasn't up to him to judge. It was up to him to make sure it wasn't forgiven.

Every step on the pavement made his anger rise, made Voro feel the nature that he was sent to this world with, reminded him what he really was.

He'd been here too long. It was time to go back. This place was changing him.

But first he was going to stop Essum. That had to happen. Essum wasn't going to rip open some unknown divide between heaven and hell by trying out his stupid science experiment, and he sure as shit wasn't going to let Essum sic either of his degenerates on Iola.

He'd die to prevent that. Well, "die" in the way a Sin Eater dies. Not eternal, just a bit of fire-and-brimstone-poolside R&R. To recharge. Assimilate. Get his damn programs straight.

It wasn't the fact that he'd done what he'd done. It was the fact that he'd done it and now it was troubling him. Like he had some kind of conscience all of a sudden. He didn't even know a Sin Eater could grow a conscience.

And his second worry was a real head-scratcher. When Iola had come out of the bedroom after the doctor had left she'd been all better. And not just in the fact that she appeared lucid, back to normal, and no longer grinding up against everything in her path like a bitch in heat. The evil was completely gone. In its place was the smell of fresh-baked bread.

So now he had another puzzler to figure out. Who or what was the doctor, and why did he leave Iola smelling like a goddamn angel?

The sinners were out in full force that afternoon. Every ten years or so he noticed a marked increase in their numbers, and in large population centers like this one it wasn't hard for him to find work. He wondered if he wasn't creating his own job security more than anything else. If Voro was the only Sin Eater left at this point in time, then he was wallowing in the filth he'd created all on his own this past six hundred years.

He had to find this Jasper guy, first and foremost. The guy knew Iola and knew where she lived. He was definitely Voro's *decipio*, so the guy had to die. Voro didn't care if he did it himself, even though he knew Iola was supposed to do it. Or maybe ...

Ridiculous. He could protect them all, these two women he was starting to - choke, *gag* - care about. The only way it could end was with Iola killing Jasper.

But then she'd become the Sin Eater, Voro would be mortal, and Iola would have to clean up human kind's filth until Voro died. He could help her. He could show her what to do, explain it all to her after the fact. And then maybe he could even *be* with her.

He stopped in the middle of the sidewalk suddenly, causing the man following him to plow right into him. He didn't budge and the man had to move around him.

"Fucking prick," the guy mumbled, not into his cell phone either.

Voro narrowed his eyes at the back of the guy's head, and delivered a psychosomatic Charlie horse right to the left quadriceps. Cell phone man went down to one knee, dropped the device attached to his ear and lost it under the tires of a passing bus.

That felt better.

The thought Voro had before the asshole had bumped into him made him start walking again, taking long strides that carried him swiftly though the human herd on the sidewalk. Jesus, if he could spend this mortal life with Iola, anything he had to do to get her to kill the *decipio* was worth it.

He needed Raphael, and he was pretty sure where he could find him.

Iola had dozed off on the sofa once Claudia and Damien left, and a knock at the door brought her awake with a decidedly unladylike snort, wiping drool from her chin. The clock said it was four in the afternoon.

She made her way sleepily to the door, eventually realizing the nausea and dizziness were gone, and all that really remained was the need to go back to sleep. A quick peek through the peephole and she wanted to curl up into a ball and disappear through the floor. But instead she opened the door, tucking her hair behind her ears like that was going to make her not look like death warmed over.

Vinnie smiled anxiously as soon as he saw her and she wordlessly stepped aside to let him in. He had a plastic bag slung over one hand, so he used the other hand to wrap his arm around her waist in a sideways hug. "Iola, how are you?"

His concern made her feel warm, and she frowned as another thought hit her. "Aren't you supposed to be at work?"

"I'm taking my lunch and supper break right now. I brought you chicken noodle soup."

She shut the door and followed him down the hall, stopping in the doorway to watch him fuss around her kitchen finding bowls, napkins and spoons.

"You didn't have to do that," Iola said slowly, knowing she was smiling like an idiot anyway. Something about him stepping away from surgery and broken bones to come and tend to her upset stomach made her feel like royalty.

"I was worried. You seemed to have a hell of a fever." He cracked the Styrofoam container of soup open, and as soon as Iola saw the steam rising off the top of the liquid her stomach grumbled.

She put a hand to her tummy in surprise, and he raised an eyebrow at her. "See? It's a good thing I'm here."

She let him steer her to the sofa where he covered her legs with the afghan she'd had slung over the back, fluffing up pillows at her back so she could stretch her legs out across the cushions while remaining sitting upright. The he brought her a bowl of soup and a spoon, sat next to her, pulled her legs over his lap and watched her eat.

She frowned as she swallowed the second spoonful. "You're not eating?"

"I'll eat when you're done," he said absently, smiling at her in the sweetest way.

"That makes me uncomfortable. You're going to watch?"

"Don't make me feed you. Eat it." But Vinnie was smiling so she did as she was told like a good patient.

"Oh," he suddenly remembered, taking the empty bowl from her and uncurling her legs so he could stand. "Missus Dean passed away this morning."

Iola took a moment to think about that and nodded. "That's too bad."

"Yeah. She passed quietly in her sleep, which is the most we can really hope for."

As he was in the kitchen getting his own serving ready Iola mulled that over.

"Vinnie, what do you think happens when we die?"

There was a pause, then he came back into sight with soup and a spoon, taking his place next to her on the sofa again. He shrugged once he was settled. "I don't know. I'd like to think you get to go to a place you'd always wanted to see. Peaceful. No pain. No evil. And everyone you've ever liked will be there, too."

"That sounds nice. I hope that's where she went."

Vinnie smiled down into his soup. "Missus Dean definitely went to the good side."

The thought made Iola smile. "To see her husband."

"And all those dogs they used to have."

Iola laughed, remembering how Missus Dean had been able to remember the name of every dog they'd had on the farm growing up, and that had been about four dogs at any given point in her life.

"You will definitely be going to the good place," Vinnie said around spoonfuls.

"How do you know that?"

His spoon froze halfway to his mouth, and he lowered it back down to the bowl. He shrugged off her question absently. "I just know it."

"Is that where you're headed, too?" She meant it to sound playful.

Vinnie's eyes met hers, his face serious. "Sometimes ... I don't know how I know things, I just do. And I know that once this life is done ... something important will happen to me."

All kinds of thoughts swirled through Iola's mind right then, all along the lines of Oh shit, this is what's wrong with him. He's a religious nut bar.

As though reading her mind, he laughed and set his soup bowl on the table, turning sideways to put his hands on the outsides of her legs, rubbing them gently, absently. "I'm not some Jesus freak, you look absolutely terrified."

She laughed, letting her head fall to the back of the sofa. "I'm sorry."

Vinnie took her hand and kissed it, smiling brilliantly. "Maybe it's you. Maybe you make me feel like I'm headed for bigger things."

She smiled shyly. "That's the nicest thing anyone's ever said to me." Then he kissed her hand again.

"I want you to get used to hearing nice things."

"It's a deal."

"Can I finish my soup now?"

Iola laughed again, rewarded by his dimply smile and a twinkle in his eyes. The he picked up his bowl and Iola dozed off again to the sound of his spoon on the bottom of the bowl and the occasional soft chuckle from the man she was starting to really fall for.

Chapter Thirty-Nine

Essum took shape in the living room of the lesbian woman's apartment. He could hear the shower running in a room down the hall, so he assumed he was alone for the moment.

He'd had enough waiting around. He was going to get his way, and he wasn't waiting another goddamn night. He'd freak out this woman to the point where Voro would sense it, get Jasper and Charlie here ASAP, and then just get this friggin' thing over with. Before that doctor came back to visit the *frustro* next door.

If he'd had solid hands they would be trembling. He had a nervous sensation, a buzzing of bees in his subconscious. He'd be nauseous if he had a stomach. He hadn't been this anxious since ... Hell. The last time he'd seen Daphne.

He forced himself to solidify in Claudia's smallish living room, sinking down on to one of her footstools. He put a hand over the center of his chest. Yeah, it still hurt. After all this time the very thought of her still gutted him.

Thomas Cromwell was the man she was engaged to marry, arranged by her family to consolidate a large amount of fertile, well-producing land. The worst part of it was that she really seemed to like the guy.

Essum had fumed watching them take their walks together. When he saw the man kiss her one afternoon, right on her perfect lips, it took everything he had to prevent himself from lurching towards them, fists curled, making a much uglier picture of the handsome fiancé.

He was as territorial as a guard dog when it came to Daphne. He acted without thinking, and of course that's what killed him. Moving too quickly, not thinking far enough ahead. The night he met his demise was after one such vision, his precious Daphne caught in the arms of her fiancé. The man's arms were tight around her waist, holding her chest to his. His sweetheart made a low moan in her throat, a sound that was as much a welcome under her skirt as an unconscious murmur of approval.

Essum had fought off the urge to peel him off her, beat him within an inch of his life and then spirit her away. Where he could take her he had no idea. But he couldn't, *wouldn't*, have her marrying this man.

They parted ways in the dusky light of a clear sunset, and Essum followed him. It wasn't hard, there was a lot of traffic on the road to town that night, and the man on the horse a few strides ahead of Essum didn't notice another galloping trail behind him.

Thomas stopped at a tavern in town, and Essum saw his chance. He spotted the man as an occasional drinker, and he knew that Cromwell would likely have one helping and then call it a night. And he was right.

A half-hour later Thomas Cromwell left the tavern, approached his stallion, and that's when Essum struck.

He wrapped one arm around the young man's neck, gaining leverage by curling his hand into a fist and holding that fist in his opposite hand. Thomas batted pitifully at the arm that was choking him, robbing him of oxygen. It did nothing, and even if Thomas had more strength it would take a group of ten or more to get him free from Essum's hold.

Or a woman's voice, as it turned out.

"Sin Eater," a voice said sharply behind him, and he turned, keeping his grip on Thomas's neck. It was Daphne.

He felt like the lowest form of dog shit as her sharp eyes took in the scene, and when she saw who he was attacking they reddened and were immediately wet with tears.

"Essum," she added softly, covering her mouth with one gloved hand.

"Daphne ..." he stammered inelegantly. "What ... what are you doing in town this late? Alone?"

She just shook her head, hand in place, still not believing what she was seeing.

Thomas took the opportunity to elbow him in the gut, and as he lost his breath the little bugger twisted in Essum's hold, getting free and giving him a good, hard shot across the jaw.

As Essum lay on the ground, trying to keep up with what had just happened, he looked up at Daphne, and she gasped, moving her hand down to her throat. "Essum ... what's ... what's happening?"

He frowned as he studied the blood he'd wiped from his lip. "What do you speak of?" Then he looked up again.

Now Thomas was staring at him, a startled expression making him look even dumber than he had before. "Your eyes ... what's happened to your eyes?" The other man muttered.

Essum looked back to Daphne, and she stepped away from him. Something was off here. His skin felt like it was on fire. He needed ... He needed to tear it off or he wouldn't be able to breathe.

He stumbled to his feet, pulling at the stiff collar of his fine silk shirt and jacket, his throat closing up like his tonsils were trying to reach out and hug each other. His vision was swirling, blending edges and colors until he was sure he'd been drinking and poisoned all at once.

He tripped over something he couldn't see, sprawling out in the muck and filth in front of him. But he couldn't see it, smell it or taste it. It was like his very senses were melting. Sounds were echoing around him. His olfactory was solely picking up on rotten eggs. Shit, that was him he was smelling. All he could taste was a slow, steady burn on his tongue.

Essum heard a shriek, realized after a delay that it was Daphne. He held her booted ankle in one hand. He couldn't remember how he'd gotten to her, or how he'd been able to find her, but he did. She kicked at him, screaming repeatedly.

He heard the unmistakable sound of metal being drawn from a leather sheaf. He stilled, and thought one word as Daphne whispered in a voice that was not even her own: "You have to cut off his head."

Fuck.

That was all he knew. In the many years afterward he'd pieced it together. The three of them in close quarters like that had initiated the process. It struck him down first, so the other two could kill him.

He to this day had no idea what his eyes were doing at that time. He imagined they were maybe glowing red, that's what they did on the Other Side. Like the three of them in close contact had brought out what he really was. And how she knew to cut off his head. Who knew? Again, maybe when the time came the *frustro* just knew.

At least it hadn't hurt when he'd died. And he really hadn't died. Here he was, back in the saddle and itching for another chance to walk amongst the humans.

That night the two of them had been planning to elope, he learned later on. But then there was the "robbery" by a mad man, and Daphne was so shaken and her family so scandalized that eloping was out of the question. She would be marrying Thomas Cromwell in the proper manner. And that chapter he'd managed to get back for, he caught the sad end almost totally by accident.

Essum suddenly heard the water turn off in the lesbian woman's shower, and he turned to face the hallway and wait for her to enter the living room.

Voro found Raphael at Burger King this time, biting into a Whopper and closing his eyes to savor it as though it was the sound of Gabriel's horn. Voro sat down opposite the angel, who opened his eyes and smiled around his mouthful. He gave Voro the thumbs up and swallowed.

"Man. I really missed the Whopper."

"Listen, I need your help."

Raphael stopped himself from taking another bite, frowning. "With what?"

"The *decipio*."

Raphael set his burger down on the paper it had come wrapped in. "Voro - "

"Don't give me any bullshit about how you can't. I know you want Essum stopped. I help you, you help me."

Raphael thought about it briefly before shaking his head. "I don't know."

"Essum can't win. I promise. I can get rid of him. But if Iola kills the *decipio*, if she's really convinced that Claudia or Vinnie are in danger, she can kill him. She would do it to defend her friends." Okay, so he wasn't entirely convinced but he needed the argument. "If she does it, I'm mortal and she's a Sin Eater, right?"

Raphael nodded, looking around to see if anyone might be listening to the couple of nut bars in the next booth. No one was.

"What if someone divine ... someone pure ... someone like you forgave her? Could you take that away?"

Raphael balled a napkin up in his hands. "I don't know, Voro. Technically she's ours and will be no matter what. But your side is just as powerful, remember? If we take one of yours, you get one of ours. At least for a little while."

Voro rubbed a hand over his forehead. "I'm begging Raphael, see what you can do."

"I'll brainstorm it, that's all I can promise."

"Good. And thanks." He waited until Raphael was swallowing his next bite before asking, "So, which side is that doctor on?"

Raphael frowned and took a sip of his fountain drink. "Who?"

"Iola's boyfriend. That doctor from last night."

"Oh." Raphael shrugged. "I don't know everything Voro."

Voro grit his teeth. They don't lie but they aren't obligated to answer everything either. "I wish I could scramble your brains," he growled, stealing one of Raphael's French fries.

Raphael just laughed. Fucking angels. "Oh Voro," Raphael said, shaking his head as though the Sin Eater was just plain silly. "There's always a way around everything. But trust me ... you won't like it."

Jasper got back in his car, watching Charlie through the windshield. The guy's back was straight with purpose, his resolve was apparent in the set of his jaw. Charlie was still terrified, and it made Jasper feel awful. But where Charlie was going, Jasper couldn't follow.

Well, not yet anyway. Who knew where Jasper's chips would fall when this was all done. He had the feeling that he might wind up dead.

A strange calm came with that thought. Death maybe wasn't so scary. Not as scary as Essum, anyway. It might be a nice break, even if there is nothing.

He rubbed both hands over his face impatiently. His mind seemed cloudy for some reason. No matter what he was thinking, he kept going back to Essum and wanting to kick the guy in his mystical nuts. Jasper was developing an obsessive compulsive disorder.

Jasper watched Charlie walk through the glass doors slowly but with a purpose, and Jasper had to smile. This part had actually been Charlie's idea. He had no reason to feel guilty but still, he felt like the guy was his responsibility.

Jasper put the car in drive and took off, headed in the general direction of Iola's apartment complex. It would take him about two and a half hours to get there, but he just had to. Who knew the why of anything he did lately. Maybe he just wanted to catch one more glimpse of her before he died.

Claudia was toweling off when she heard her cell phone ring in the bathroom. Taking the towel with her, she went to the dresser and picked it up. Trevor Vance was calling.

"Trevor?"

"Claudia, thought we should let you know. We found a third vehicle registered to that Portia Torregrossa."

Claudia's instincts perked up. "Really? Where?"

"It got towed in a few days ago, it's been in the impound lot over at the fourth ever since. Someone finally ran the registration and the name set off a few red flags, as you can imagine."

"Did you find out where it was?"

"Downtown, I'll get the exact address. The towing company said it had just been left there. The four-way flashers were still on when they got there, keys in the ignition."

"What was the car?" Claudia felt some confusion, since there was a Jaguar registered in the Torregrossa woman's name that had been found at a ritzy downtown hotel, and there had been a Lexus SUV still parked in the double garage.

"Nice one, brand new. Only a few days off the lot, a really sharp car. It's a uh ..." there was a shuffle of papers as Vance was apparently checking details. He knew she'd want the exact info, not his best guess. "Ah. It's a 2010 BMW X6-M. Holy crap. How much are those things worth?"

"More than either of us make in a year," Claudia replied absently, a sick feeling in her stomach.

Vance gave a whistle, then there was a pause. She could just see him leaning back in his office chair as he flipped a folder closed. "The guys over at the fourth went to talk to the salesman right away. They say it was sold to a man. Tall, intense-looking. Couldn't remember much more about him. But her co-workers said they thought she had a boyfriend or lover or whatever the kids call them these days. Some guy that she regularly met at that hotel where we found the Jag. I think he might be of interest to us, considering there were no signs of forced entry at her front door ..."

Vance kept talking, but it was all elevator music to the sudden thoughts that she was having. And they all stemmed back to the evening when she had helped Iola prep for her date with Vinnie. Going to the drugstore, picking out make-up, meeting Damien, and coming out of the store to see what she had immediately assumed to be Damien's car, since it went with the clothes he wore. The car he drove her home in one night.

A black BMW X6-M.

"Hey Vance, thanks for filling me in. I'm going to turn in early, okay?"

He sounded a bit surprised, and Claudia then realized she had cut him off mid-sentence. But she couldn't for the life of her remember what he'd been saying, and he just replied, "Oh. Okay. We'll see you day after tomorrow, Sergeant?"

"If not sooner. Thanks." She cut the connection before he could respond and started opening drawers to get dressed.

She had no idea where her mind was going, but eventually it got stuck on the night Portia Torregrossa had died. Claudia hadn't seen Damien that night. She'd been at work, and he'd gone ... where? She'd run into him the next day, and they'd spent most of said day in bed. Where the hell did he live? How did he afford those suits? That car? He'd been at her place almost exclusively the last few days. *Except* for that night. So he seemed to have no job yet had money to toss around like beads at Mardi Gras. And she hadn't seen that car since.

Deep breath. Damien, a killer? Sure he had no markings that indicated he'd been in a fight. But Claudia's instincts were firing off like crazy, and she'd learned to put a lot of trust in them.

Shit. She'd brought him into this building. With Iola right across the hall from her.

She stood up, pulling on jeans, and as she did so the heavy metal amulet brushed against her skin, suddenly feeling very wrong and not comforting in the least. She grabbed it, pulling it off over her head, and put it on the dresser, then as an afterthought she opened the top drawer and tossed it inside, shutting it away from sight. She didn't even want to look at it.

Just as she pushed her head through the neck of a long-sleeve T-shirt she heard a cold voice say from the doorway, "So, starting to wonder about your new lover then, hmm?"

She spun quickly to see who the hell was in her place without her knowing about it. A tall, slight man filled her doorway, his head shaven clean, his eyes a steely light grey that almost didn't register.

"How'd you get in here?" She demanded, not eyeing up her holster on the dresser. Of course she knew exactly where it was and how easy it would be for her to lunge for it.

"Not important."

"It's pretty important to me."

Then the guy stepped closer and all of Claudia's muscles clenched. She went for the gun but ... She just couldn't. Her muscles tightened to the point of pain, and they just wouldn't move for her. It wasn't excruciating, it just hurt the more she struggled against it.

There was the sound of a dark, disturbing chuckle, and the next thing she knew the man's face was inches from hers, his eyes filling her vision and his voice right inside her head.

You will be my own little frustro, the voice said, booming around in her ears. *You will bring him to me so I can take over.*

And then those eyes swallowed her attention, the pupils widening to fill his entire eye socket, and then the blackness was all she knew.

Chapter Forty

Voro left the BK in a decidedly foul mood. Raphael had been characteristically honest: Voro didn't like the solution to saving his dear, sweet Iola from a human lifetime of sin eating. In fact the solution gave him the scratch. His reaction had been to blame Raphael's suggestion on the fact that the well-coiffed angel was still miffed that certain fragments of Christianity didn't count him as an actual archangel. Then Voro felt bad about that, even though trying to tread on an angel's ego was a lost cause. Angels just weren't built the same as Sin Eaters.

Thank you, Captain Obvious. Fantastic insight.

Voro decided to head back to the apartment block to check in on his *frustro*, which was likely becoming more and more a terrible idea with each passing hour, but what else could he do? If this thing was going to happen, if this Jasper dude was going to show up at some point and try to kill him, then kill Iola, Voro had to lay in wait to make sure at least one of those events didn't happen. And if Essum somehow managed to weasel his slimy way into the mix, Voro sure as shit was not going to walk away and let it happen.

Outside the stairwell leading up Voro cast his mind upwards, trying to scan for Claudia's brain waves. There was nothing there, she must have gone out. In the hallway outside Iola's door he caught a whiff of vanilla and jasmine, so he knew Iola was still home.

He knocked on Claudia's door lightly, but didn't hear a response. Not sure why, he tried turning the knob, and was surprised when the door swung inward.

Yeah, a cop that doesn't lock her apartment door when she leaves. That set off alarms.

Voro stepped inside, his instincts immediately firing at top speed. He could smell that Claudia had been here, and he also caught a trace of peppers, like she'd been angry. And something else. Burnt rubber; an acrid, smoky and totally unpleasant odor.

Fear. Utter terror. Claudia had been here, and something had scared her.

Voro stalked down the short hall to her bedroom, and sure enough a few drawers were pulled out, the lamp on the bedside table was knocked over, her watch was broken on the floor in front of the dresser.

His amulet, he just had to focus on it and he could find her ...

As soon as he thought of it, he felt an internal pull to the dresser, and he had a sinking feeling. Sure enough his hand went to the top center drawer, pulled it open, and there it was, staring back at him. The Oryx sitting before him, totally useless now to find Claudia.

Voro slammed the drawer shut. Why would she take it off? Maybe she took it off to shower and someone had intercepted her before she could put it back on. But who would be able to actually kidnap her ...

Suddenly his senses were overloaded with the feeling of total foreboding. He felt malice in the air, which would account for Claudia's fear. The permanent feeling of unease and ... wrongness. He knew one being that left that kind of funk in a room, whether he was vapor or solid-form. It wasn't a smell; it was a signal of his intent.

Essum had been here.

Voro wanted to throw a tantrum and hurt something, but that was incredibly impractical. Essum wouldn't permanently hurt Claudia until he'd gotten what he wanted, so it would be a while before Claudia was in any real danger. Essum was nothing if not resourceful. He knew what his assets were.

That meant he was waiting somewhere for Voro, right? There would be signs, Voro just had to make sure he paid fucking attention at the right moment. Getting worked up and kicking things would likely impair his sense of observation. Which had taken a beating lately, come to think of it.

So there was no need to worry Iola, and no need for him to go looking for a fight. He should stay where he was, and wait for the trouble to find him.

Iola had been slumbering in the peaceful oceans of utter calm, half aware that Vinnie was next to her on her sofa, lazily tracing lines on her leg as he watched TV with the volume very low. As she slipped in and out of a deeper sleep, her heart was full of contentment and her body was totally, blissfully relaxed.

That is, until the nightmare came back.

She felt it grab hold like a bolt catching and holding, the calm coolness quickly being replaced with uncomfortable warmth and a feeling not unlike fear. Anxiety.

Dread.

She wanted out. She needed to open her eyes. But the warmth surrounding her held her body in place exactly as it was, like her joints were made of wax and the warmth had made them ooze out and gum up the entire contraption of muscle, bone and sinew. She was a puddle. And she couldn't see a thing but dark.

Things brushed against her legs, but paralyzed as she was she could only tell herself it was nothing, nothing was going to hurt her here. It was a dream ... just a dream. It had to end soon.

Oh Iola ... it will be ending very soon.

She wanted to weep. This voice in her head was so cold and terrifying ... and she'd heard it before. Somewhere ... where was that?

I have a friend of yours, and I won't kill her, as long as I get what I want. And it's not even you ... I want that stranger that's moved in across the hall. I need you to bring him to me.

If she could have, she would have bit her lip. Because she was feeling something else now, and if she had the ability she would have been begging it to stop.

It's only going to get worse from here on out. But if I don't hurt her, even just a bit, he won't be able to find her and bring you to me.

Shit, oh Christ. It was Claudia. Iola could sense her as plainly as if she was in the room with her at that moment. This prick had Claudia ...

Iola ... don't do it.

Iola sat up straight, gasping. Next to her, Vinnie jumped a foot off his rear end, giving a slight bellow like she'd totally caught him off guard.

Iola blinked a couple times, convincing herself that she actually had woken up, that this wasn't some new level of the dream. Vinnie pressed his hand to her shoulder in comfort, frowning in concern. "Iola … are you okay? What is it?"

Iola pressed her eyes shut, but her stomach was rolling with the feeling of what she'd just experienced. Vinnie waited patiently, and as she was settling her stomach she became aware of a terrible odor, like a gas leak or a septic system backup. Sulfur.

Vinnie smelled it, too. "Man … where's that coming from?"

Iola opened her eyes, meeting his gaze. "We need to find Claudia. She needs me."

Her head was echoing as she stared through Vinnie, wondering how the hell they were going to do this. *Iola … don't do it.* It had been Claudia's voice. And she was in terrible pain.

"Where is she?"

"I don't know. But if anyone has an idea … it'll be Damien."

Claudia's head snapped to the side, and she tasted blood in her mouth. Even her teeth were ringing with the force of the impact from Essum's fist.

She wished she could spit out the blood, but the gag only allowed her to swallow the warm coppery fluid and tell her stomach not to get sick. She had no idea how long this had been going on for, but when the creepoid in front of her had paused between punches, she had no delusions about it being all over. No, he was making a telepathic phone call to Iola. And she'd been on the other line, listening in.

She didn't question her sanity, and she didn't question whether or not it was real. It was definitely real. Her eye swollen closed and the newly loosened molar proved that just fine, thank you very much. And if she was losing her mind maybe it would just be short term.

She didn't recognize this dim apartment she was in, bound in a dining room chair, gag expertly tied in place, her bonds cutting her skin in a perfect amount of looseness that makes you think you can get out, only allowing you enough slack so that as you strain the cord can dig in deeper. The one thing she wished was impaired was her olfactory. The place stunk like days-old refuse, dead vegetation and putrid meat.

Claudia couldn't recall how she got there. She did remember the guy standing in front of her right now, breathing heavy with fury, glaring down at her. He'd been in her apartment; he was the one making hamburger out of her face.

"When I want your input, I'll take that rag out of your mouth. Until then, you keep your thoughts to yourself."

Claudia made no motion or sound of agreement, but he walked away, crossing the one-room kitchen and living area to sit on a recliner. He sat watching the television, and although the volume was low she knew it was Two and a Half Men. The one where Charlie proposes to Chelsea, if memory served her.

Claudia took a few calming breaths. Her entire body ached, and the room was so stuffy. The heavy curtains were drawn across the windows, and the heat from the sun that did manage to get in was trapped in the room with her. Her stomach was not happy. Her jaw was not happy. Her entire face was miserable, come to think of it.

She gave a few more tugs at the twine that held her arms to the chair, painfully twisted behind her. No give. The knots didn't budge.

She sat quietly now. She'd been inside Iola's mind. She didn't know how, but she'd felt a certain recognition coming from somewhere. Likely from Chrome Dome's mental loudspeaker. Iola had heard her. Iola had been worried about her.

Claudia didn't feel better knowing that. And this freak wanted Iola to go to Damien to bring him here in exchange for Claudia. What the hell were these two guys up to?

What were they, period?

Jasper parked his car in the same spot he usually did when he came to watch Iola's window in his less-proud obsessive moments, but this time everything seemed different. He wasn't here to get all moon-faced about her; he was here to help her.

Hopefully, to protect her.

He locked the car doors with the key fob as he crossed the street, and got as close to her building as he ever had: he rang the buzzer for her apartment on the panel next to the security door.

A voice came on, one he immediately recognized and felt all the better for hearing. "Yeah?" It was Iola.

"It's ... it's Jasper."

Pause. "Jasper?"

"Yeah." His heart was pounding so hard the blood was singing through his ears, so he almost missed her cursing under her breath slightly. "Iola, please let me up. I can explain everything about what happened with Claudia. I swear it."

She gave a choked laugh of disbelief, but she didn't cut the intercom, either.

"Please, Iola. You can go get Claudia and we can talk with her, too. There's something I'm mixed up in, and it's not good. But I would ... it would kill me if you got hurt. Please. I need to talk to you."

A long, agonizing pause again. "Okay. You have a lot of explaining to do."

He had the door wrenched open as soon as it buzzed him in and he took the stairs two at a time until her was on Iola's floor. As he came through the fire door at the end of the hall, the door to Iola's apartment swung open. He was about to greet her when a man stepped through the opening, a bit taller than Jasper, with a very young-looking face. But the set of the guy's jaw put aside any suspicions that he was in any way "wimpy." He was selling distrust like it was going out of style.

The stranger pointed to the door across the hall. "Iola's calling Claudia right now to warn her. Knock on the door, and move slowly."

Jasper nodded, admiring the guy's commanding presence. Some guys were lucky enough to just demand a person's respect without much effort.

He raised his hand and rapped on Claudia's apartment door, then stepped back towards the fire door again. He didn't want to crowd the guy that was standing guard in any way.

Actually, as they waited for what must have only been fifteen seconds with just the sound of Claudia's phone ringing through the door, Jasper was starting to feel twitchy. His clothes were suddenly itching him. His skin itself was crawling.

The air wasn't agreeing with him, if that made any sense. And he was pretty sure Prince Valiant was crowding him, even if the guy hadn't made a single move towards him.

He heard a slight shuffle, and looked up to see Iola standing behind her protector. The look on her face as she saw him shamed him more than he would have thought possible, and he immediately ducked his head and began weeping.

Fucking Essum.

He was sniffing to get himself under control, but his gut was rolling and his head hurt and he felt like something stuck to someone's shoe. He couldn't make himself small enough to escape being noticed.

Jasper crumpled to his knees with a sob that was far too loud, rocking back and forth until he came to a stop with his forehead resting on the carpeting.

No one moved. No one said anything. He was sure they were shutting the door, locking him out while his apparent psychosis sorted itself out ...

A hand touched his shoulder, then flattened on his back and slid across to the opposite shoulder. The simple gesture was so divinely comforting it made him ache between the halves of his miserable rib cage, and then there was a slight squeeze.

"Jasper, I don't understand it, but you better come inside and tell me what's going on. Because Claudia's not answering her phone or her cell. I need to know if you can help us find her."

Iola's voice was close to his ear, and her trust made him feel like a real shit heel, but he nodded anyway and got to his feet, rubbing his nose with the back of his hand.

She let him into the apartment, and the man Jasper didn't know pointed to a kitchen chair that was in the middle of the square of linoleum that denoted the difference between the living room and the kitchenette. Jasper sat immediately, and he approved of how this guy made sure to stand between him and Iola.

"Should we call the police?" The guy asked in a low voice, and immediately Jasper shook his head.

"No," Iola answered at the same time. "Let's see what he has to say, then we'll decide what to do."

"The cops can't help," Jasper added. "This is ... this is exorcist bullshit I'm talking about."

The guy straightened his posture at the curse word, but Iola patted his arm and sat on one of the dining room chairs, across the table and the room from him. "Just talk, Jasper."

"If Claudia's missing, I think I know who has her. And we're going to need some kind of ... supernatural help. Because while I'm sure I'm not totally losing my mind ... if I say this out loud it will seem nuts, even to me."

"Just tell us," the new guy said, and without hesitation, Jasper started talking.

He told them about meeting Essum, about how the guy could talk to him in his head, even when Jasper couldn't see him. He told them about the murders he'd seen Charlie commit, confirming with Iola that it was indeed the same guy that kept coming after Claudia. He told them that Essum had wanted him to grab Claudia to trap some guy named Voro, who Jasper never met. And after spewing out a few theories about how he felt like he was healing people as he forgave people's trespasses, he concluded by saying that he had helped Charlie turn himself in earlier that evening. And he also added that if Claudia was missing, it was most likely Essum that had her.

There was an awkward pause, and Jasper raised his eyes for the first time since he'd started talking, expecting the other man in the room to haul off and sock him one. Instead the guy was looking down at Iola, who was peering up at him in confusion.

Finally Iola broke the silence. "Is it weird that I find myself believing him?"

The guy smiled at Iola so sweetly that Jasper had to look away. He felt the sting of tears again.

"If you trust him, I trust him."

Iola leveled those green eyes back on Jasper. "I trust him. But he knows he's done wrong, and he'll have to answer for it when this is done."

The guy rubbed circles on Iola's back, then looked at Jasper himself. The dude had insanely blue eyes, crystal clear, with permanent crinkles in the corners. Jasper even smiled a bit in response at how open and trusting the guy was.

He would do anything to help this guy and make him proud. He'd even follow the guy into battle, down a well, anywhere the guy led.

Where the hell was *that* coming from?

"Jasper, if this guy ... entity ... being ... or whatever ... has Claudia. Where would they be? I mean, did you always hear or see him in the same place?"

Jasper bit his lip, trying to think. If Essum was hoping to draw people to him, with Claudia as the bait, where would he take her? Somewhere that Essum hoped people would assume them to be.

"I don't know. I was staying at a hotel with Charlie for a while, but ... actually, I haven't been to my place in a few days. I wonder ..." Jasper's heart stopped. That's how he knew he was right. "They're at my place. I .... I feel it."

Chapter Forty-One

Voro had been getting to his feet to answer Claudia's phone when it rang, but he never got to the table where the handset was making all that racket.

He dropped to the ground, pulling at the collar of his shirt, feeling like it was shrinking around his neck. But it wasn't, it was perfectly in place.

There was a nasty ringing, buzzing, interference-type sound echoing around in his coconut, and it was causing him a very sharp pain between the eyes.

What the hell was this?

As soon as he heard the voice, he remembered. He knew what this sound, this feeling meant. His physical form was about to be momentarily scrambled, misted away so that someone could talk to him.

Someone awfully important in the great scheme of things.

The misting felt like a tickle, and as soon as it started he was gone on the air, nothing but ether. There was no "here," he was asleep in the dark, listening to a radio with his eyes closed. There was nothing else to steal his attention. The air was neither hot nor cold, windy or still. There really was nothing until ...

Voro, the voice vibrated between his cells. *You have to get rid of Essum.*

He gave no reply, but obviously he was in agreement.

The guy you don't know, the one you can't figure out. He has to do it. He has to wait until Essum is solid, and smite him down. Take off his head. With steel. It should slide through him like butter, no matter how sharp the blade.

Essum waited, but nothing else was added. *Then what?* he tried, hoping for an answer.

Of course, there wasn't one.

He came to on the floor of Claudia's living room, sucking carpet fibers into his mouth at a rapid pace. Holy shit, that was sure hard on the body. The in and out of it was so abrupt, he wouldn't have been sure it had even happened if he didn't feel like he'd been hit by a train.

He rose up on one arm, muscles protesting like they were actually sore from lactic acid buildup or something. He hadn't really been in pain for a long time. He'd gotten used to not feeling anything.

So The Boss was on to Essum after all. And the heads' up about who should be doing the smiting was interesting, to say the least. Usually his kind was left to figure it out on his own.

That must mean Essum's plan was actually feasible. The bugger had an actually functioning hypothesis. So that was what was making The Boss jumpy.

He stared at the carpet for a while longer, waiting for the discombobulated feeling to pass. He had to find Essum now. Claudia needed him now.

Iola was leaving her apartment now.

He hefted himself on to his feet unsteadily, and stumbled to the door. He peeked through the fish-eye in the door, and saw Iola's boyfriend leaving first. The guy was shrugging on a light jacket, nodding to something being said behind him. Next came another guy, pretty gangly, not as tall as the Doc, dark eyes, dark hair that fell kind of limply on his forehead like it needed a wash. Unremarkable in almost every way. Voro let his eyes flick behind this inconsequential man to Iola, then the guy drew his attention back.

This guy he'd seen. In the middle of a nightmare transmission from Claudia, alone in her motel room as she was beating the living shit out of this fellow. This guy, *Jasper*, was staring at the peephole like he must have known Voro was there. He almost irrationally took a step backwards, but instead he frowned and studied the guy closer.

The guy was just *wrong*. And as he continued to stare at Claudia's door, Voro was getting the scratch, big time.

What the fuck was this guy?

Almost in response the guy gave a cold smirk, and Voro would have sworn that just for a minute those brown eyes flashed blood red.

Iola had the strangest sensation that none of what had happened over the last twenty-four hours was actually real. Following Vinnie out of her apartment building with Jasper trailing behind her was one of the most surreal moments of her life.

Of course there's a force of uncompromising evil holding Claudia hostage somewhere. What else could it be? And of course she felt like this was all just conjecture leading up to the lambs being brought to slaughter. But why not go along and see if it's all true?

To say she had a foreboding feeling would have been one hell of an understatement. And yet as Jasper had spoken she couldn't ignore the sense that it was all true. It was all going to be fine.

Her own mind was telling her to trust Jasper, and go along with him. He meant her no harm. He wanted to help.

As long as Vinnie was there, with Jasper, Iola knew nothing bad could happen.

At the curb next to Vinnie's car, Jasper climbed in the back and Iola got in the passenger seat. Jasper sat behind her, and she got the impression he did that so Vinnie could keep an eye on him in the rear view. There was real tension inside that sports car as Vinnie pulled a U-turn and headed towards Jasper's apartment, with Jasper providing the directions in a thin voice from the backseat.

As they pulled into the parking lot of Jasper's apartment complex, Iola's sense of impending evil intensified about three-fold. Jasper pointed out a visitor parking spot that was open, and Iola bit her lip to keep from yelling out that they should just get the hell out of here.

She had to force her legs to get out of the perceived safety of Vinnie's car.

Now they followed Jasper, and he led them to the complex marked "Building D." He unlocked the door and started for the elevators, not looking up, his head slung down as though he didn't want to look at anything. He wanted everything to be over with.

In the elevator everyone was silent again. That was when Iola realized no one had said anything since they'd left her place, other than Jasper's directions to Vinnie.

The elevator doors slid open, and Iola wanted to scream to cut the silence, to do away with the tension. Instead they all stepped on to the burgundy hallway carpet and Jasper led them to the fourth door on the right.

Things were getting more and more wrong by the second. Her skin was crawling, she wanted to turn and run more than she had ever wanted anything in her entire life. The hair on the back of her neck was trying to head the opposite way for Christ's sake. Vinnie touched her arm, as though he knew what she wanted. She felt the strength return to her backbone.

Claudia, she reminded herself. *We need to make sure Claudia is okay.*

Jasper stopped at a door so suddenly Iola nearly plowed him over. He had his keys ready, and with a steadying breath he slid the key home and turned the knob, pausing almost unnoticeably before pushing the door open.

Show time.

The hallway leading into the living room was dark, but Iola immediately knew that Claudia was there. She could hear uneven breathing, slight sobbing, and it was coming from somewhere straight ahead.

The men sandwiched her, with Jasper leading the way and Vinnie right behind her. He walked into the dim living room like it was a demilitarized zone; prone to landmines.

The second she saw Claudia, all logic flew out of Iola's head. Her beautiful friend was drenched in sweat, sitting rigid in a chair as though tied to it. The only movement was the rise and fall of Claudia's chest. Iola ran to her side, dropping to her knees and trying to free Claudia from ropes that didn't exist.

"What ... what's going on? She's not tied up," Iola was mumbling, pulling on Claudia's arm. It didn't move in the slightest, and Claudia's eyes remained closed, her brows drawn in a look of anguish.

"He gets in their heads." Jasper's voice remained hollow. "With the suggestion of his mind you believe you're trapped in whatever he projects. He has her convinced that she's bound. So, she will not move until it's broken."

"How do we break it?"

Silence. Iola turned to Jasper.

"How can we break it?" She repeated, and Jasper finally met her gaze with fresh tears in his eyes.

"He's here," Jasper whispered, his voice catching. "Oh God, Iola, I'm so sorry."

Voro lost no time at all convincing a man on the street to give up keys to his brand new truck, and took off after the good doctor's sports car, staying a safe distance back. He knew well the area of town they headed for: on its outskirts lived some of his best customers.

When the car pulled to a stop outside an apartment building he drove past, circled around and came to a stop behind the doc's Audi. The other three had already disappeared inside, and as he waited in the cab with Willie Nelson croaking from the stereo Voro scanned the building.

Claudia was there, but her brain was clouded; not unlike a coma patient. It was closed off to his influences, like a security alarm had been rigged to her. If he tried to break her free, the person that had overcome her would be alerted.

Fucking Essum.

He turned the truck off, taking the keys with him. An old lady who was exiting the building with reusable grocery bags allowed him to pass behind her into the building through the security door without him having to pull any mental acrobatics, and he followed the signature scent of Iola up to the fourth floor.

The voices came through the thick apartment door all muddled, but all he could get from inside was Claudia's beacon. The doctor was giving off a slightly concerned vibe, but it wasn't that strong. And again the third guy was giving him nothing at all.

Just like Iola.

Voro paused with his hand on the door. The guy was a bank vault to him, so that had to mean he was in the same league as

Iola. This Jasper fucker was definitely his *decipio*, there could be no doubt.

He backed away from the door. Sure, he wanted to help Claudia. And the plan to trump Essum's coup and make off with Iola for himself was tempting, but standing here knowing that the playing field was tilting towards him was … well, that was a whole new reality, wasn't it?

He rested his forehead on the door, listening for voices. He could hear Claudia's cries, muffled like she was gagged. Of course she wasn't, Essum wasn't even in solid form. He couldn't touch things or people, only suggest it through control over all the sensory receptors, like he had apparently done to Claudia.

Voro could have released her easily, but if Essum wasn't here he would show up pretty damn quick when the alarm went off. A tight knot was pressing in Voro's stomach. He couldn't help Claudia. Not yet, anyway. He had to plan his actions first.

The knob turned in his hand, and he was able to get into the apartment without making a sound. As the door snicked shut he placed one silent footfall in front of the last until he stood in the living room.

Claudia was in a chair, all right. Her body was clenched tightly, her muscles constricting painfully against her will, propping her up and holding her arms and legs in place through sheer will. But otherwise the room was empty.

Wait, where'd the doc get to –

The sharp crack on the back of the head was a total surprise, and while it didn't hurt right away Voro knew that when he woke up it was going to ache like a bitch.

Iola covered her mouth as she gave a surprised cry, and Damien's large form crumpled to the carpet. Vinnie stepped out from behind him, holding a frying pan that seemed to still be ringing.

"Holy shit," she added as they both stared down at the man on the floor. He was breathing but definitely down for the count.

Jasper and Iola both stood up from their hiding place behind the sofa, and Vinnie put the frying pan down with distaste. He clearly had something against concussing people.

"What do we do?" Jasper asked after a moment of silence, and Vinnie met his gaze unwaveringly.

"Get some ropes, ties, anything that'll hold him."

Iola was surprised by the tone of Vinnie's voice. It was so matter-of-fact. He noticed the look she gave him and gave her his charming grin.

"Don't be scared. I promise: everything's gonna be fine."

"I don't understand. How do we know he's dangerous?" Iola was thoroughly confused.

"He is," Jasper confirmed, then left to run the errand.

Iola studied the man on the floor, wondering what had brought Damien to them. He had obviously followed them. Jasper said he was dangerous, and she knew she believed that without question. He was terribly dangerous, that must have been part of the draw. She didn't know it until just then.

Iola looked to Vinnie, hoping for answers. Vinnie shrugged weakly. "I've got to go with Jasper on this one. What choice do we have?"

Vinnie and Jasper bound Damien's hands behind his back and tied his feet together using neckties. They left him face-down on the floor once Vinnie assured them he was likely going to have a slight concussion but otherwise he'd be fine. As she stood next to Jasper, with Vinnie double-checking Damien's breathing and pulse, a strange calm came over her. Sure, Claudia was still in some kind of mental prison, but she'd be fine. There was a bald boogie-man out there that they had no idea how to handle, but that would come. She looked up at Jasper, but he was staring down at Damien. He hated the guy, it was obvious. She had a slight thought that if they let him, he would kill the guy in a second. And yet she had the insane impulse to take his hand.

She shook the thought from her head and perched on the edge of an armchair that was draped with an afghan. Her focus shifted back to Claudia, and her poor friend's labored breathing and obvious agony. Claudia was still making sounds of tortuous pain. But again, Iola was sure they could fix it.

"What do we do to help her?" She asked almost calmly as Vinnie knelt before Claudia and opened one eyelid to check her pupils.

"This is so weird. Her involuntary responses are normal, her voluntary mobility is ... shut off." Vinnie was muttering quietly as he pulled on an arm, patted a cheek.

"Have you seen this before?"

"It's like she's in a coma. And her body is trapping her in this position somehow." He tried to lift one arm by the elbow but it wouldn't budge.

"Do what you did to me," Iola suddenly said, and Vinnie's eyes flicked to her. "To break the fever. Do that."

He clearly wasn't sure that it was a good idea, but he also had genuine concern for Claudia. He put one hand on Claudia's quaking shoulder, the other on the side of her face. He furrowed his brow in preparation for intense concentration, and then closed his eyes.

Iola held her breath, and Jasper behind her did the same, because something was definitely happening in the room. It was like someone had turned on an old-fashioned tube TV, there was a sharp electricity running through the air. The hair on her arms stood up. She felt suddenly very awake.

She wanted to cry, because it felt wonderful. She felt alive and energetic and ready to take on anything. It was such a beautiful sensation Iola knew she'd never forget it. When she looked at Jasper, she knew he felt it too. A new crop of tears rushing down his face, and he hung his head, unabashedly sobbing.

He knelt on the floor next to her, and she stroked his hair absently, watching her gorgeous neighbor's face grow slack, the pain sliding away, her body relaxing to its natural, exhausted posture in the dining chair.

And then a beautiful sound. Claudia's voice, weak but aware, stammering out ... "W-w-where's ... where's Iola?"

Chapter Forty-Two

In his meditative state, Essum was able to rejuvenate the old brain-battery, reflecting on what was driving him to usurp an eternal lifetime from his dear old friend. It wasn't a lust for power, or sex, or money, or anything other than revenge.

The system sucked. The system was cruel and it made every player – even the pathetic human pawns – nothing more than notches made in the sand by two kids on the school ground. He could cause such a disruption that it would all grind to a halt for at least a couple millennia.

He could give a shit about Voro personally, and his respective *frustro-decipio* package deal. It wasn't them; they were a means to his end. Even Jasper with all his extra add-on parlor tricks. Essum wasn't sure how it would help the good guys if a *decipio* could eat sins. But then again perhaps there was a reason. And with his luck, Essum would find out at the last fucking minute in the worst possible fucking way.

Better change thought patterns. You need to be sharp and calm. Think of something happy, something soothing. But no.

Daphne. Poor Daphne.

He'd been absolutely powerless to stop her death. The truth was *frustros* never met a good end. It was always violent, painful, and before their time. There had not been a *frustro* in history that died of old age. They were all slaughtered by the *decipio* eventually, who in time inevitably would go mad and off themselves and the world would say, "Well, he was crazy. Remember how he killed that poor woman/man?" Essum knew the facts. He'd done his research since his own sad chapter came to pass. It was how the game worked.

Daphne was no different. She was killed cruelly at the hands of the man she meant to marry, and Essum had watched in the vapor form that trapped him now. Impotent. Useless.

Essum could not physically close his eyes against the images burned into his memory. He tried to shut them down and couldn't.

After his demise at the hands of young Mr. Cromwell, Essum had been serving time re-acclimating in his natural environment. When he'd been able to, he began to watch over Daphne. She was preparing for a wedding, she was excited, but troubled in her sleep by nightmares of the Sin Eater that had accosted her; the one Thomas had killed to defend her from.

Thomas himself was having troubles coming to terms with the taking of that life. Of course, it didn't help that Essum himself was planting nightmares in his mind, immature revenge tactics. So stupid and beneath him. And poor Thomas also took to drink with great enthusiasm: always at night when he was scared to sleep, always when he was alone, and always to the point of blackouts.

The night before their wedding Essum had been watching Daphne prepare her hair for the next day. She had bathed in water infused with rose petals, and the scent would rise with every brush stroke as she sectioned her hair and wound it around rags to give her gorgeous tresses curls when dry. She was thrilled, humming with excitement. She loved her fiancé and was anxious to be his wife. Anxious to be a woman as well. Essum could see her skin flush at certain times when she would get lost in thought, brush stopping mid-stroke as she daydreamed.

He still couldn't read her thoughts, and at that moment he was glad for it.

A *tick-tick* brought her from her vanity to her window which overlooked the courtyard. She pushed aside the panes of wavy glass, squinting into the darkness to see what had caused the noise, her face breaking into a stunning grin as she spotted Thomas on the flagstone below.

When he saw her, he immediately climbed the ivy trellis to her window. It was sturdy enough to hold him, and Daphne showed no concern that he might hurt himself. Essum wished he could push the trellis over. But of course, one needed a body to do that.

Thomas reached the window and rested elbows on the sill to gaze up at her.

"Daphne," he said softly, as though he was seeing the work of God before him. "You are so beautiful."

"What are you doing here? It's late."

"I know. I had ..." he paused awkwardly, and Essum's alarm bells went off as Thomas frowned to get his thoughts back.

He's drunk off his barge, Essum thought, just as Daphne insisted that Thomas climb in lest he fall to his death.

Thomas all but fell to the floor, making Daphne giggle even as she was shushing him to be quiet. Thomas stood uncertainly, took a single glance at Daphne in her dressing gown, and immediately wrapped her up in his arms while pressing his lips to hers aggressively.

Essum's hackles were already raised, but at the sight of that he wanted to kill something. He wanted to knock something off the walls, break a mirror, anything to scare them back to reality. But what could mist do?

Daphne melted against her suitor, thrilling in the way his arms travelled up her slender back before pushing into her damp hair, holding her as close as he could. She gave a moan as she clenched the lapels of his jacket. Thomas scooped her up in his arms and carried her to the bed.

Essum stood in the way to no effect. That this man would rut against the beautiful Daphne like any other whore infuriated him. He should marry her properly, then she could be his.

Daphne was silent the whole time, and yet as he laid her on the bed and crowded her into the mattress with his entire body she broke the kiss, gasping.

"Thomas ... wait. We can't. Not yet."

His lips were greedy on her neck, and as she pushed at his hands Essum's anger went from warm bath to gushing volcano. Forgetting himself, he tried to grab Thomas's coat with invisible hands. No result. He kept trying in a futile effort, merely flapping imaginary limbs.

"No .. Thomas. No." Daphne's voice wasn't impassioned or teasing. It sounded as though she was scared.

Essum came back to himself, realizing Thomas had pulled her gown open, revealing Daphne's form under a thin nightdress. It didn't hide her shape in the least.

Thomas Cromwell made a most ungentlemanly sound as he shoved a hand roughly under the bottom of her gown. Daphne was struggling now, still not wanting to wake the household. She really didn't think he was going to hurt her.

When he opened the fly to his trousers, she drew breath to scream. One of his hands clamped down on her mouth, and that's when she really started to fight.

Essum had never seen such naked anger and aggression. She fought like a tiger, scratching, biting Thomas' hand, trying to get a knee into a good spot. But in his drunken desire Thomas was truly beyond pain, even as his own blood flowed from the hand that she had bitten into. A stream of scarlet traced down her cheek to the pillow.

He knew when the penetration happened. There was a muffled, strangled sound of pain, then Daphne's eyes closed and she just *stopped*. Shut down completely.

Thomas noticed it, too. But it caused him no guilt. He seemed to want a reaction from her. So he let go of her mouth, and wrapped both hands around her snow white neck.

Her eyes flew open again, wet with tears and she stared at him in shock. As he fucked her, he squeezed the life right out of her.

Essum couldn't leave. Couldn't stop it. Couldn't do anything. He watched his *frustro* as she was soiled and strangled. Essum was disgusted. Furious. And powerless.

In that moment his resolve had flooded his nerves like cold steel. He was going to find a way to stop the *frustro-decipio* horse shit. He wanted the playing field leveled.

Thomas at some point realized what he had done, and rose from the bed shaking and screaming like a psychotic in an institution. And when the family arrived, they had the same thought. Daphne's brother threw him down the stairs, and even though his back was broken in the fall he survived, to spend the next ten years in a hospital, refusing to eat until he died. The doctors said his organs shut down, then cannibalized themselves.

Essum had to stop his recollections at that point. It was too painful. Had he any tear ducts he would be blubbering like a babe.

Then everything changed. He heard a buzzing, like the universe had scrambled his brains then turned on a vacuum cleaner. Essum's trap had been sprung.

Claudia's body relaxed gradually, like she'd been vigorously weight lifting for about a week straight. It was obviously painful, and as she stretched her arms she grimaced.

"We should really get out of here," Jasper said, looking more and more twitchy.

Claudia was startled by the voice, and at the sight of Jasper she tried to scramble to her feet. She was even able to form her hands into fists, but her leg muscles weren't tuned in yet and she lurched forward. Iola caught her, stroking her hair.

"He's okay, don't worry. There was something wrong with him, but now he's on our side. We have ... a lot to explain to you."

"But not here. We have to get out of here," Jasper repeated, his head shaking from side to side as though listening to something no one else was hearing.

Iola had the same feeling he did. She was overly anxious to bolt, too. Once the warm glow of Claudia's awakening faded, she felt like fire ants had taken up residence under her clothes. She really wanted out of that apartment.

"What about him?" Vinnie nodded to where Damien was still out cold.

Claudia's face grew cold as she recognized him. "Leave him. Call the police. I think he's a murderer."

Iola was shocked, and gave her friend the appropriate look. "Are you serious? How did you find out?"

"His car belonged to a victim that we found a few days ago. I'm pretty sure he'd been her ... well, lover. Gigolo. Whatever."

Iola looked at the handsome man face-down on the floor. She couldn't believe it. Yes he seemed dangerous, but psychotically homicidal? He was too functional, wasn't he?

"How did he even find you?" Claudia was wondering.

"He must have followed us," Iola concluded. "Maybe he was at our building."

Jasper had silently slipped out of the room. Iola hadn't even realized it until he reentered with a handgun.

"Hey, what the -" Vinnie was cut off as Jasper cocked the pistol and aimed it at Damien, his hand not shaking in the least.

"Jasper? What are you doing?" Iola thought she said it at normal volume, but it was more likely that she had whispered it. Her entire body had frozen in position.

"I'm going to kill him. He has to die." Jasper looked up at her then, and Iola backed away a step, aware that Claudia had stood and pushed her way in front of her.

Jasper's eyes had turned blood red. Not glowing, not shining with the light of a thousand suns. They were red like a fire hydrant, like raspberry juice.

"What the fuck." Claudia muttered.

No one moved. Jasper was still grinning in his macabre way, like every horrifying circus clown you'd ever seen. Vinnie had raised his hands slightly in a non-threatening way and was also glued to the spot.

Iola's twitchiness understandably worsened. How had they forgotten how Jasper had attacked Claudia? No matter how sorry he had seemed back at Iola's apartment, here was a reminder that he was dangerous.

Jasper's right, a thought came to her. It wasn't a voice, it didn't use words, but suddenly she was aware of what had to happen. *This is what has to happen.*

No it's not.

Iola and Jasper both flinched, covering their ears. The cold, familiar voiced boomed through their skulls like a rock concert. Jasper even dropped the pistol, which Vinnie scooped up. Jasper didn't even notice, he now looked terrified.

That's when Iola knew it was Essum talking to her, and she felt the icy realization that Essum had been in her head before, too. But who the fuck was he?

Go ahead and kill him. It's what you're meant to do.

Jasper was shaking his head. "Get out. I can't ... if this is you making me do this ... I won't. I refuse."

I just told you. It's not me. This is what you are supposed to do. Now ... where's Charlie?

At that, Iola knew Jasper had lost his mind. Because he rolled over on to his back, and he ... was he laughing? How the hell could he be laughing?

Jasper's voice was hoarse in its screaming. "I took him far away ... and he's not going to be here to help. You fucking bastard!"

Iola could see that Claudia was speaking to her, concerned. But she was about as clear as someone talking under water.

Jasper, kill him. Kill the fucker, then Iola is all yours. Even though Iola heard it, she knew it wasn't meant for her.

Iola frowned, meeting Jasper's gaze. He was still covering his ears, but his jaw slackened. His eyes were still red, and he was gone. On auto pilot. She saw the moment his logic and personality evaporated; his eyes went vacant and turned to her.

Shit.

Kill Jasper. It's the only way to save Damien. Take the gun from the doc and kill Jasper.

Essum knew this was trouble. He'd been sending this very simple command into the *frustro*'s mind, but she was staring at Jasper in shock, not receiving his signal. Her receptor was turned off.

This had never happened. Well, not since Daphne. He couldn't influence Iola at all. He could "speak" to her, but not command her.

That could cause a problem.

Jasper was eyeing up Voro's *frustro* like a beggar at a wedding feast, and Essum felt his luck change. There was the bait; that was the pot of gold at the end of the rainbow. It was such a beautiful and simple trap. He wished he'd thought of it.

He switched his attentions to Jasper only. *Take the gun back, and kill the man on the floor. Iola will want you, she will see how brave you were protecting her from this monster.*

Jasper's red eyes flicked to the form on the floor who, annoyingly enough, was starting to come around with a grumble and the furrowing of his brows.

It'll be the easiest thing I've asked you to do. This man is evil, he intends evil at all times. His intentions to Iola are not pure.

The doctor jumped as Jasper swung his gaze back his way. Jasper held out a hand, and Vinnie took a step back. Foolishly, he raised the pistol with both hands and leveled it at Jasper's face. "Get in that chair," Vinnie said with a dead-calm tone.

Essum could've giggled. Humans were almost delightfully stupid. He reached into the good doctor's mind, trying to find that spine so he could rip it out by the root, and then he stopped.

The doctor wasn't just booby-trapped like Claudia had been. The doctor was laced with emotional and mental poison. The second Essum felt it he felt everything sliding away. Like his skin had started to shrink but the rest of him couldn't keep up with the change. He was being Hoovered up like cat hair from the sofa. He was being cast away by he didn't know what.

White light took over. Essum could no longer see, didn't know what was going on in the room. It was as though he had been scattered like grit in the wind.

Iola watched the large handgun in Vinnie's grasp. It wasn't even quivering. But Jasper showed no fear, covered the ground between them in three swift strides, and pressed his chest to the barrel of the weapon, a smirk on that terrifying countenance of his.

Jasper's voice sounded alien when he spoke, it wasn't anything like the tones she knew. "You can't and won't do it, Veneratio. You may be her *praesul presul*, but this is not something you should be playing with."

Iola hadn't taken Latin. *Praesul presul* was going to be Googled if she made it through this okay.

Claudia was suddenly next to her, pulling Iola by her arm and swinging her slowly behind her. Claudia's concern touched her, but in a numb way. Whatever panic, disconnect or inability to comprehend what was happening Iola was suffering from had her emotions cut right off.

Iola surprised herself by throwing Claudia off. "It's the only way," she said, not of her own volition. "You have to shoot him in the head. If you can't let him do it." Her eyes now leveled on Jasper. They shared an odd communion. They were supposed to be in this together, right?

Vinnie must not have heard her, because he raised his chin, as if a dare had been laid out. "Get in that chair. Sit and be quiet."

Jasper's fist came so fast Iola didn't even see it; she only saw Vinnie's head swing back, a look of shock on his face as the gun was wrenched from his slack grasp. One hand reflexively went to his nose, which instantly gushed red. The other tried in vain to get hold on the pistol again.

Jasper had the gun, had control, and had a look in his ruby gaze that against all sensibility thrilled Iola to her toes. But then Jasper pointed the gun right at her.

"One more move or threat or fucking word from you, and she is dead." Jasper looked from Vinnie to Iola. "My sweet *tentatio-onis*, it would pain me. But I would do it."

Iola opened her mouth to speak, but her voice suffered a frustrating impotence. Jasper cocked his head sideways, a small smile playing on his lips. He winked at her, and she felt a smirk touch her lips. He couldn't hurt her. He was in love with her, right?

Then Iola noticed Vinnie's expression of horror as he looked at her. Part of her wanted to ask what was up with him, the other half couldn't care. She and Jasper had a job to do.

Claudia half-turned to her, and even Claudia took a step away. She didn't look scared, but her gaze turned wary as she looked from Iola to Jasper and back again.

"They're realizing that we're the same. Better than them," Jasper informed her. "But still ... the same."

"Must be ... jealousy."

Jasper thought that was terribly hilarious and broke into an insane giggle that she found amusing, too.

"Iola, you should see how lovely you are right now. Come," he took her arm and she followed like a good little girl. He stood her before the glass door of the entertainment center. "See? We're on the same side. We want the same things." His breath was brushing her hair against her neck, raising goose flesh.

She barely heard him. All she knew was her reflection. Her light green eyes were gone, replaced with something much darker. And red.

Chapter Forty-Three

Voro's head was pounding out an excruciating rhythm, but he forced his eyes open anyway. The voices around him drifted and bobbed together, he couldn't understand anything that was being said.

First thing he did realize was that his hands were bound behind his back painfully. The second thing he knew was that the room reeked of sulfur. It was the kind of stink that probably only he was aware of. After all; it smelled like home to him. Both details were very bad news.

The fabric that held his arms back was slick. As he tugged his arms apart it slid a certain amount, then stopped altogether. But that didn't matter; he'd made enough room around each wrist to wiggle his hands free. It wasn't as easy as it could have been since his hands were both asleep, but he made do without seeming to draw attention to himself.

He lowered his arms to his sides, feeling the human prickling of blood flowing back into his fingers. He was mildly embarrassed that he had been knocked unconscious. By a human. But he'd been in such a damn rush to get to Iola ...

Iola. She was here, at the very thought of her he picked up on her scent. Like cool water to a man crossing a desert; that scent made him feel totally at ease.

But as his eyes focused he saw Iola across the room from him, being held in front of a glass door by the man with the odd eyes. She was staring at her reflection, and Voro suddenly had a very sinking feeling that only intensified when she turned around and leveled eyes on his that were the color of dried blood.

Holy. Shit.

Panic hit him hard. This was it. This was his *frustro* meeting his *decipio* and the two of them taking him right the fuck out.

That same panic drove him to his feet, even as the cold numbness was still in his limbs. He was upright, towering over the two of them as the strange man stepped in front of Iola. He had a gun in his hand; a semi-automatic from the looks of it. And it was pointed at Voro without hesitation.

Iola looked at him very calmly, and Voro felt a slight twinge of regret. All his plans of getting her to kill this *decipio* scum were dashed. It was the definite tug of the inevitable: not destiny, just all the pieces coming together as they had to. He was not going to be saved, he was not going to make love to Iola the rest of their lives and help her adapt to Sin Eating.

Can't do it, his brain was saying irrationally. Can't do that to her.

It was too late, anyway. The process had begun, and there was no cancel button on this fucker. He could feel his skin prickle, he felt like he'd been doused in battery acid and lit on fire. The burn was on him, and as Iola's eyes then Jasper's fell to him, he knew he was done for.

He looked over to Claudia, where she stood ineffective to stop anything that was happening. She hated not knowing what was going on and how to stop it. She hated the very sight of him as well; he could taste her disdain in the back of his throat. From her brain he picked up the murder scene she had encountered when called to Portia's house. It was tinted red in her rage, and that rage was directed at him. She thought he had done it.

Well-played, Voro though drily, immediately knowing Essum had set that up. Just another little dig to get under his skin. Hurt the people he very nearly cared about.

Don't lie; you care plenty, his own mind was scolding him. He looked back to this other fellow, the one with glowing red eyes that matched Iola's. The bastard that had to kill him, and then as legend had it, he would kill Iola, too.

There was one way to fix the whole thing, the way that Raphael had lowered his station enough to share with him.

Ultimate sacrifice.

The concept didn't fit his skin, but as he saw Iola's eyes and felt the pull of the universe falling into its rightful place, he knew it was his only option.

Claudia was eyeing Damien with hatred, and she did nothing to betray that fact. But in truth, Damien wasn't scaring her at the moment. Jasper and Iola and their fucking Halloween theatrics were getting to her just then. Damien would have to take a goddamn number.

Vinnie was rooted to the spot, bleeding from the nose and no longer trying to stop it from dripping on the carpet. He watched the scene enraptured; his face totally unreadable.

No help there, either.

Okay, so Claudia was going to have to shut down the freak circus on her own. Fine by her. Too bad there was a firearm involved, however.

The gun in Jasper's hand wasn't so much as quivering. It was rock-solid with its bearer's purpose. She was going to have to take it, and it would have to be by surprise. But for the moment Iola was still too close to that pistol, and Claudia wasn't going to jeopardize her friend, even if Iola seemed to have a bad case of the eye-bleeds.

She brought her arms close to her sides, and no one noticed the movement. Damien and Jasper were having a cock-measuring contest in the form of a stare-down, and Vinnie still seemed unable to move. So she shuffled a half-step towards the coffee table and the ugliest brown-glazed bowl she'd ever seen in her life. But it looked heavy ... and it might just do someone some damage.

Jasper's voice echoed through the room and it caused her to freeze.

"Get down on your knees and put your hands behind your head."

Claudia looked up, startled, but saw that Jasper was still concentrating solely on Damien. So she took another half-step sideways as Damien put his large hands on the back of his head and started to lower himself to the ground. As he did so, his eyes flickered her way as though he knew what she was about to do. He even seemed to be smiling as though he approved.

Jasper noticed his attention shift however, and swung the gun around her way. Instinctively she dropped to the ground, but no shot was fired. She looked up to where Jasper was to see that

Damien had grabbed the gun. Jasper was infuriated, and without another word he flew at Damien, wrapping thin-looking hands around his throat. Damien tried to push him off, but Jasper was much stronger than he looked. Or just crazy.

Damien had just tried to save her. What the –

Time to worry about more important things. Claudia lost no time grabbing the ceramic work of horror from the coffee table and smashing it across the back of Jasper's head. He howled as he dropped, his hands covering the impact site. As she watched in utter shock, thick red blood began oozing between his fingers. Blood that was too dark, too slow, and not right.

The smell hit her and she backed away. This wasn't real. That wasn't even blood. And why was there so much of it? Best case scenario: it should have merely scratched him. As she watched it seemed to have nearly shorn his scalp from his skull. He flopped over on the floor, shrieking in apparent agony.

Iola immediately dropped to his side, mewing unintelligible nothings, try to soothe him.

Claudia and Damien exchanged a look, and he nodded to her. He kept the gun trained on Jasper, but she knew he wanted her to get Iola out of the way.

Claudia took Iola by the shoulder, but Iola shrugged her off. As she glared at her, Claudia wanted to weep. Iola didn't know her; didn't even recognize her. And those fucking eyes ...

As Claudia remained distracted by wrenching an immovable object that looked a lot like her good friend and neighbor, there suddenly came an ungodly screech as Vinnie suddenly found his legs and tackled Damien around the waist, line-backer style. Both men went down, most likely because Damien was caught completely by surprise.

Iola was distracted by that as well, so Claudia wrenched her friend to her feet and tried to pull her out of danger's way. Iola was inhumanly strong, and managed to topple Claudia over so her head caught the side of Jasper's iron and glass coffee table in a particularly painful way.

She saw stars, and an inky blackness started to seep into her vision. She tried to get to her feet and shake it off, but all the light in the room collected in the center of her vision, and as she turned her attentions to Iola and Vinnie she blinked rapidly. The light seemed to glow around them, enveloping them in light. And that's when she fainted.

Voro barely knew what was happening. He was aware somewhat that the doctor had knocked him to the floor, both of them actually sliding into the kitchen on the linoleum. He maintained his grip on the gun, and tried to hold the doc at bay without hurting him. God knows why he wanted to avoid seriously injuring Vinnie; he just did.

He blocked a punch, and while Vinnie was trying for another blow he pistol-whipped him across the jaw which made the poor guy go down like a sack of cement. He got to his feet and surveyed the damage.

The doc was bleeding on the floor. Claudia had knocked herself out on the coffee table, and although she would have a slight concussion when she woke she would still be okay, just like the doc. Jasper had a huge flap of skin lifted off his cranium, and he was in considerable agony but still conscious. And still glaring at Voro with those freaky eyes.

Iola stood in the center of the room, looking down at Claudia, totally unconcerned. She seemed to be making sure her friend wasn't going to get up. Then she turned and raised her chin, giving Voro a challenging glare.

Her voice shocked him to the core, and in spite of himself, he physically reacted to her strong tone and the command she sounded. He wanted her as she spoke.

"Sin Eater. Do you desire to ... *epulor*?" Her lips curled in obscene amusement.

The Latin word for "dine" had an unexpected effect on him. The invitation was obvious. He was doing the exact kind of dumbass thing he was supposed to. Lower his guard, give into her, then she'd keep him distracted long enough to allow Jasper to slaughter him.

But he couldn't look away from her as she crossed the floor to him, hips swinging like a cat on the prowl. She may as well have tied him down and strapped blinders on him.

Iola stopped within touch but short of contact. He was staring at her in a totally undignified way, he knew. But that was part of it. There was little he could do but stare down the inevitable. This wasn't about the legend. This was the animal in him that made him not human.

She licked her lips in an agonizingly slow circle, and he was aware that he was holding his breath. She smiled a secret smile and lowered her eyes to run over his chest, his arms, down to where he kept a good grip on the gun.

"Voro," she said in a chiding tone. His real name sounded vile coming from her mouth. "Are you going to shoot me?"

Her hand reached down to toy with the barrel, but of course she didn't touch his skin in any way. She rubbed the metal in a suggestive way, and he had to close his eyes. At her soft chuckle he opened them again to see her looking at him, totally amused by the obvious agony she was causing him.

"Or is there something else you'd rather use on me?"

She crushed against him, and he closed his eyes again, willing himself not to feel her warmth through their clothes, or the softness of her small breasts on him. Her hands were on his chest, running up to his shoulders, and he took calming breaths. He had to do it, he had to ...

There was the slightest scuffle, and his eyes flew open as he instinctively raised the gun behind Iola and fired one shot in Jasper's direction. The bastard had been trying to get up, but the round tearing a hole in the carpet so close to his head made him think twice on his motivation. Finally; some sense.

"What are we going to do about this?" Iola was cooing now. "How in the world can we make this work?"

He looked back down at her, finding his voice. "Make what work?"

She was smiling again. "How can I be with you? In every sense of the word?"

He wasn't sure he was understanding her, but everything south of the belt was assuming it'd not only heard but comprehended clearly.

Her hands traced up and down his arms as she drank in the sight of him, wanting him. This was what he had wanted: Iola to be his, all she had to do was kill Jasper.

"You have to kill the *decipio*," he said, testing how much she really knew of what was happening. In response she tilted her head, trying to understand him. Voro pointed with the .33. "Him. Jasper. You have to kill him."

Iola studied his face, and then lost all playfulness. He almost felt relief; that he had called her bluff and now she would rebuke him, as she should.

Instead she pulled the gun from his hand, turned and calmly pointed it to Jasper, still on the floor, cowering now. "Like this?" she asked.

Voro grabbed it away quickly. The panic he felt had nothing to do with a single iota of concern for Jasper. He couldn't, *wouldn't,* let her be soiled like this.

He knew only one way to end it.

"I'm sorry," he whispered, making sure she was looking at him. Then he put the barrel of the gun in his mouth and pulled the trigger.

Claudia's vision was coming back just as Iola turned the gun on Jasper. No part of her could worry that Jasper would end up dead; she hated him. But she didn't think Iola could handle it ... assuming Iola wasn't already certifiably insane. Killing Jasper would be the final nail in the coffin of her poor friend's psyche.

Claudia closed her eyes, knowing she wouldn't get there in time. She didn't want to have to testify that she'd seen this happen –

The shot rang out loud, and she opened her eyes just as Damien's form fell back and hit the floor with a heavy thud. She was stunned for a moment, waiting to see if she was misinterpreting what had happened. Jasper was alive, Damien was shot?

Iola's hands had flown to her temples as Damien had hit the floor. She slumped to her knees as though her head was about to shake her apart. She was sobbing.

Jasper was still on the floor, but he must have fainted from loss of blood. And from the kitchen she heard a calm, reassuring voice ask, "Is everyone okay?" It was Vinnie.

She got to her knees, the world tilting like a sick carnival ride, making her stomach lurch. It hurt right down to the roots of her teeth, and she was sure she was going to be sick. She crawled to Iola, talking her friend in her arms and cradling her as Iola cried in big, heaving sobs. Vinnie came over the threshold from the kitchen. His eyes were cast down on Damien, and he seemed reassured that the large man wasn't going to be getting up.

Jasper gave a groan, and Vinnie crossed to him, checked his injury, then went back to the kitchen. No one said another word until Claudia could hear Vinnie calling for an ambulance.

Then he returned with a dishtowel, which he pressed against Jasper's head after taking his shaking hands away from the wound. Poor Jasper looked like the walking dead as he stared blankly at the far wall, no longer making a peep. As Vinnie's gaze met Claudia's, they had a moment of shared confusion.

Neither of them had any idea what had happened.

Iola's first recollection was the gun going off, a spray of blood flying out the back of Damien's head, and then him falling. Like a microphone picking up its own signal a screech exploded in her ears, forcing her to drop to her knees. The next thing she knew, Claudia was holding her and she was sobbing so hard her ribs hurt.

She felt anxious, like her adrenaline had been fired without her knowing it, and was now suddenly gone but she couldn't remember it being activated in the first place. Something important was missing. She was forgetting something ...

A calm man was now talking to her, shining light in her eyes. Somehow she'd ended up on the sofa, and he was kneeling in front of her. She had never seen him before and she felt disoriented, until she saw someone she did know. Someone that immediately brought her back to herself.

Vinnie. He was standing behind the EMT, hands folded in front like he was trying to avoid getting involved in her examination.

The second she saw him she was on her feet, basically knocking over the poor paramedic and running into his arms.

Vinnie.

As he hugged her back, everything clicked into place. Not that she remembered anything, of course. But suddenly everything was just going to be okay.

Raphael clapped him on the back, laughing at him the whole time. "I told you; you weren't going to like the solution."

Voro basically sighed, gazing down at his body, spread out on the floor and leaking blood everywhere out the back of its head. "They can't see us?"

"Nope. We're just ether right now."

"But you just hit me."

"Well, I can hit you and you can hit me. We have nothing to do with them right now."

Voro watched the doctor hugging Iola, and he had to admit ... it hurt. Well, emotionally anyway. He was beyond physical pain now. But that sight ... well, that just sucked. He turned his attention back to Raphael.

"So ... when will I be collected?"

Raphael suddenly looked back to his corpse, avoiding his gaze. "Well, umm ..." he cleared his throat. "Actually, that's why I'm here."

Voro nearly laughed. "Come on. I know that's not how it works. I get dragged back below by the hair. When do I go?"

Raphael's angelic eyes were once again pointed his way. "I'm telling you, I'm the one collecting you."

Voro waited for the punch line.

"Voro ... I told you how to save Iola. She will be fine, this Jasper guy will be fine. You've saved them both ... and they are both instruments for the good."

Voro was getting an uneasy feeling suddenly, but Raphael continued without noticing.

"Your last act was self-sacrifice for two innocents. You ... you really think you're going back from whence you came?"

Hell no. "You've got to be fucking joking - "

"You never asked me what would happen to you. You just asked how to save Iola from becoming a Sin Eater, and I told you. Unfortunately that means you've been recruited." Raphael slapped his back again. "Next step: we're gonna size you up for some wings."

"You can't be serious."

"Hey, it ain't bad being an archangel, let me tell you."

They were quiet again. Voro took a breath and asked the obvious, "And Essum?"

Raphael shrugged, all chill. "You can't fuck with the brain of an angel. It's the quickest way to be sent back to wherever it is you came from."

Voro frowned. "Who fucked with an angel? Could Essum see you?"

Raphael shook his head, his hair swaying. "Nah, not me." Then he nodded his head towards Vinnie and Iola. Vinnie was holding Iola tightly, stroking her hair, calming her. There was just something about that guy that really gave Voro a terrible feeling –

"Fuck. Me." Voro whispered.

"Yep. When we captured a Sin Eater, we studied how they became flesh and bone. Very interesting process, incidentally. Some of that hardware went into this *decipio*, but we weren't really sure what we could use it for. Other than heading you guys off at the pass, so to speak. So we decided to take it one step further. Veneratio was born of mortals, will live as a mortal, but really ... he's one of us."

"Does he know what he is?"

Raphael shook his head. "Not a clue. That's the beauty of it. He was born just a regular human. He's not, of course. He has a healing touch, perfect that he saw fit to pursue a career as a doctor."

"He's just placed in the womb of a regular woman?"

Raphael nodded this time. "But they were selected, too. Intellectuals that would teach him right and wrong, not just a base theology but everything."

Voro shook his head. "I still don't like him at all. Is it ... is that Michael?"

Raphael laughed. "You'll fit right in."

"That figures. Did you see the cock he gave himself?"

Raphael made a sound of dissatisfaction. "Voro, you're going to have to clean that shit up if you want to be an angel." Then he all but dissolved into a fit of giggles.

"I told you," Voro growled. "No one wants to be an angel."

But Raphael was already off on another giggling fit, holding his stomach and doubling over. Voro wanted to punch him.

Denouement

Charlie was sleeping in a basement cell of the police precinct when he was awoken by a horrifying yell, a man bellowing in such agony it bounced around the inside of his head, up until the moment he sat up in bed, then it was gone like a lingering nightmare.

Master, was his initial instinct, and he had a horrible inkling that his tormentor and advisor had returned with one final mission for him. But after a moment he realized he could not sense the Master in the slightest. Not just like someone had left the room recently; more like, he couldn't be sure the Master had ever really been with him in the slightest. An erased memory. Lingering déjà vu. The questioning of his own sanity was a sweet consolation; he hadn't experienced that luxury in a while. Charlie smiled in the dark as his feelings of well-being intensified, and as he lay back down and pulled the coarse wool blanket back up to his chin he thought that maybe, just maybe, he was going to be okay.

The Master was gone, and by the sounds of it, he'd been pulled back to Hell kicking and screaming the whole way.

Charlie slept better than he had in months.

Claudia blinked in the mirror, feeling the tug of stitches in her scalp where her head had hit the iron table. It had bled a lot, but it had all been in her hair and she hadn't noticed until the paramedic had been examining her for a concussion. His hand had come away red and she'd agreed to go to the emergency room. It took four stitches to close that gash up, and it was bisecting her hairline on her right temple. Somewhat visible, but the scar would be mostly hidden.

She couldn't make herself understand what had happened in that apartment. As far as she could tell, Damien had taken her, Jasper, Vinnie and Iola prisoner in Jasper's apartment. And somehow Iola had talked him into killing himself. Or something?

The cop instincts she had were screaming at her that none of it added up, yet what else had it been? There had been no reason, no list of demands, no cohesive agreement about a chain of events.

None of them remembered how they got there. That much she knew. And until she could ask everyone else what their recollections were, well, she was stuck with the most unlikely explanation as her only option.

The doctor had cleared her to leave, so after freshening up in the hospital washroom she stepped through the front doors of the emergency ward, out of the stench of chemicals and antiseptic into the refreshingly unscented air of a clear, spring night. The warm wind picked up, tossing her hair, and it sent a shiver down her spine.

Jasper was going to be okay but he was still going to do hard time. He'd be charged with assaulting a police officer and attempted sexual assault. So that satisfied her almost as much as seeing that partially-shaved head of his with its grotesque line of stitches leading across the back in a crooked, nightmarish design. She'd done that, she reminded herself with a smirk. Not sure why she'd done it but she had.

She turned as though hearing her name on the wind, only to find she was completely alone. Claudia felt an infinite sadness suddenly. Iola had Vinnie. And here she was, alone. Again.

She wouldn't think about Damien; she just couldn't. He was dead, and she didn't dare let her mind linger on the ache in her chest that throbbed as she pointedly didn't consider him.

She wrapped her arms around her waist and made for the cab sitting at the curb. The nurse had called for her, and Claudia was surprised that it had only taken a few minutes for the driver to get there. The hospital was quite a way past the city limits.

She climbed in the back, reciting her address and suddenly realizing she didn't have keys anyway. So she gave the address for the police station as a correction after a short apology.

"No problem," the driver said, turning around and offering a polite smile.

Claudia smiled back. It was nice to see a friendly face right then, even if it was a guy. And a skinny guy at that. But she sort of liked his steel-grey eyes. And the shaved head was a bit of a turn on for her, too. After her last experience, she wasn't into long flowing locks on a guy anymore. As a matter of fact, she was surprised to have that reaction from a guy at all.

"Thanks," she said, suddenly shy, and she settled into the seat as the car carried her away.

About C.D. Breadner:

C.D. Breadner is a self-published author. Her first novel, *Sin Eater,* was the beginning of The Sin Eater series and she looks to branch into other genres since there are many kinds of creative juices following through her.

Recently she was christened a contributing author to The Freak Circle; a collective of amazing and supportive writers. She lives in a cozy home in the woods with her wonderful husband and two German Shepherds.

Connect With C.D. Breadner:

Visit C.D. Breadner's Blog: http://cdbreadner.wordpress.com/

Follow on Twitter: https://twitter.com/CDBreadner

C.D. Breadner's Amazon Author Page:
amazon.com/author/cdbreadner

Soul Stealer (Now Available)

It was always biting. The jaw tingled with the need to sink its teeth into meat and tear at it. Chew it. Swallow from necessity then repeat.

Blood would fill his mouth, tangy and coppery, wonderfully warm. Fluid and real; the opposite of what he was at that moment.

The last time he'd held solid form was ages ago, yet he could remember the carnal thrill of taking something smooth and unmarred and ruining it with his own teeth. Souls went down smoother, sure, but that was just energy for the metaphysical batteries. Until he was stable he only had dark dreams and memories of far-away places.

These were moist, green, tropical and lush locations where they sacrificed young women with fair hair and skin to keep him from stealing the souls of the entire community. Virgins volunteered for the honour of dying for the greater good. Rumor was his bite brought orgasmic pleasure at the moment of death.

Not true in the least. It hurt. He felt their pain as he tore into that tender skin, hardly touched by sun. They screamed and it only made him more ravenous. He tore with clenched teeth and the straining of his own neck muscles. The blood would spurt and spray all over their thin white shifts, running hot down his neck and chest. His face was completely wet with it, and the victim would be gasping, eyes pleading for death. When they were mad with the need to pass he would let his mind wander in to theirs, finding that spark inside that drove the whole mechanism of their human bodies. He tore it out by the root, and that's when death occurred.

The dark-skinned tribes of small jungle islands used to give gold and chocolate. In return he'd take their killers and rapists in their sleep. It was punishment for evil-doers, and they kept paying him for it until he would become tired of the climate and move on. In the North they didn't do sacrifices. So instead he was the Arctic boogeyman; a tale to caution people on how dangerous it was to wander away alone in the coldest of the cold and dark months. He couldn't be picky on what he ate there: he took anything he found for months then headed for the equator to thaw his hungering body.

But lately every time he tried to solidify, starting with a few souls taken here and there, growing his power slowly but surely, he lost the will to keep going. He would scatter again to the winds of time, blown away to linger and wait for the urge to hit him again. Months and months of existing off of souls was no way to thrive. It was a difficult hill to crest; he needed blood. He wanted the meat.

Maybe this time. If he held the memory of that food as a goal for going through with all the work of becoming fixed in the world, maybe he could see it through this time.

That first soul had been lovely. So pure, sweet. Completely untainted. How delicious the young ones were ... Their flesh was even better.

Yes, the souls were necessary; they were the vegetables that kept him healthy and going. But next to that he had to have the living, breathing, bleeding and still wriggling meat to make it all worthwhile. He only lived once every few millennia. He had to make it worth the effort.

35837795R00221

Made in the USA
Charleston, SC
19 November 2014